WHERE
THE
ICE
FALLS

The Falls Mysteries

When the Flood Falls
Where the Ice Falls

WHERE THE ICE FALLS

THE FALLS MYSTERIES

J.E. BARNARD

DUNDURN
TORONTO

Cover image: istock.com/ViktorCap
Printer: Webcom, a division of Marquis Book Printing Inc.

Library and Archives Canada Cataloguing in Publication

Title: Where the ice falls / J.E. Barnard.
Names: Barnard, J. E., author.
Series: Barnard, J. E. Falls mysteries.
Description: Series statement: The Falls mysteries ; 2
Identifiers: Canadiana (print) 20190117354 | Canadiana (ebook) 20190117362 | ISBN
    9781459741447 (softcover) | ISBN 9781459741454 (PDF) | ISBN 9781459741461 (EPUB)
Classification: LCC PS8603.A754 W55 2019 | DDC C813/.6—dc23

1 2 3 4 5   23 22 21 20 19

 Conseil des Arts du Canada Canada Council for the Arts   Canadä    ONTARIO ARTS COUNCIL CONSEIL DES ARTS DE L'ONTARIO an Ontario government agency un organisme du gouvernement de l'Ontario

We acknowledge the support of the **Canada Council for the Arts**, which last year invested $153 million to bring the arts to Canadians throughout the country, and the **Ontario Arts Council** for our publishing program. We also acknowledge the financial support of the **Government of Ontario**, through the **Ontario Book Publishing Tax Credit** and **Ontario Creates**, and the **Government of Canada**.

Nous remercions le **Conseil des arts du Canada** de son soutien. L'an dernier, le Conseil a investi 153 millions de dollars pour mettre de l'art dans la vie des Canadiennes et des Canadiens de tout le pays.

VISIT US AT

 dundurn.com | @dundurnpress | dundurnpress | dundurnpress

Dundurn
3 Church Street, Suite 500
Toronto, Ontario, Canada
M5E 1M2

To Geoff, Phyllis, and Loreena

When I began planning this book, I worried that I might not understand what it's like to face death — one's own or that of loved ones — especially with the choice of medically assisted dying. While I was writing the first draft, my father, Geoff W. Barnard, walked the MAID path with courage and dignity to his final breath. My early crime-writing mentor, Phyllis Smallman, healthy when I began this journey, left us too rapidly between the second and third drafts. Yet my friend Loreena Lee, who received a terminal diagnosis early on, still daily lights up the Shadow of Death with her friendship, her artistry, and her zest. She'll hold this book in her hands yet.

You three, you taught me much about living well and dying well.

Thank you.

PROLOGUE

Wind shrieked through the vent screens, sending swirls of snow against the young man's face. His eyes flew open and he raised his head. How long had he been leaning against the wall, half dreaming? He pulled himself upright, stumbled over to the plywood door, and pushed as hard as he could. It wouldn't budge. He stood back and kicked it, over and over, with the same result. He threw his shoulder against it. Still nothing. Finally, he began hammering on it with his gloved fists and yelling for someone, anyone, to let him out. The wind whistled through the drafty shed, mocking him with a howl like his own. He slumped to the floor.

CHAPTER ONE

Just before dawn the blizzard let up, leaving the wilderness shrouded in white, the roads snowdrifted, and the oil derricks iced over. Far out on the shoulders of the Rockies, the scattered chalets at Black Rock Bowl were hidden under the blanket of snow. No sign of life disturbed the stillness, save a lone spire of chimney smoke rising up into the lightening sky. As the sun rose, revealing this new white world, it kissed the roof of the shed, slowly melting the snow, the water dripping down to form ever-lengthening icicles.

Six more days of melting and freezing followed before the plow from Waiparous Village reached the deserted resort. It rumbled around the Black Rock Loop from the northern end, its operator keeping an eye out for a red Toyota Camry reported missing on the first day of the storm.

Day by day and week by week, the sun added more icicles to its artwork, until the front of the shed resembled a waterfall frozen mid-tumble. The diamond clarity of the ice reflected the surrounding snow, sky, and forest. November ended. December began. The icefall thickened.

CHAPTER TWO

"Do you want to find my emaciated body in the next chinook, Mom?" Lizi Gallagher pointed out the back door of the chalet, her glittery nail polish glinting in the sun. "Niagara Falls froze over that woodshed. It'll be Christmas before I get the door open."

Zoe rolled her eyes. "You should be in school, but you insisted on coming along to help. Now go. Two hits at the top with an axe and it'll all come crashing down."

With a loud sigh, Lizi flounced out onto the porch and slammed the door. A line of slender icicles shivered on the eaves. She stomped down the steps and set out across the glade, axe on her shoulder, ostentatiously lifting each leg high before lowering it gingerly into the next drift. The woodshed was barely three car lengths away, well clear of the surrounding forest, but here she was treating it like a death march across the Columbia Icefield.

Teenagers. Ugh.

Zoe started the kettle and leaned against the granite countertop. The warm, rustic cooking space of her memory had been replaced by a sleek, modern kitchen —

slate-grey cupboards, brushed steel appliances, slate-tile backsplash, and a floor that appeared to be coated in concrete. Basically everything was grey apart from two rust-brown throw rugs that matched the stools along the breakfast bar. Nothing about the room said *cozy ski chalet* or *relaxed weekend getaway* — more like *desolate industrial wasteland*. Perhaps a reflection of the owner's second marriage?

The kettle let out a whine, as if it, too, was conscious of its dismal surroundings. Boiling already? She reached for it. But the appliance was cold, not even a hiss coming from its snub nose. The sound rose to a wail. It was coming from outside.

Zoe leaned toward the window and saw Lizi flailing back through the snow, her mouth wide, her pink-gloved hands waving above her head. By the time she opened the door, Lizi was halfway up the steps, gasping and screaming alternately like a broken steam whistle. She lunged inside, grabbed the door, and hurled it shut. The icicles plunged from the eaves and shattered, one after another, onto the porch.

CHAPTER THREE

The yard with the Christmas lights, the first sign of civilization Lacey McCrae had seen in ages, vanished from the rear-view mirror. The forest crowded in again, dark and thick beneath the pale winter sky. "We're lost," she said. "We should turn around and head for the airport. We can eat there."

"We can't be lost." Dee turned the screen of her cellphone toward Lacey. "See? Only one road."

"I'd feel better if you had a data signal placing us on that screen."

Lacey steered the SUV carefully around an ice-rutted bend. Dee's Lexus was a warm, safe bubble travelling through the frozen wilderness. A human out here alone would be a self-propelling hot-meal delivery for the Alberta foothills' apex predators: cougars and grizzlies and wolves. As if answering her thoughts, a deer bounded from a snowmobile trail that intersected the road, barely touching down before vanishing into the next section of trail. She hit the brakes, sending the phone flying. It clunked against Dee's walking cast and dropped into the footwell. Lacey fished it out and handed it back before driving on.

After a few minutes, Dee pointed. "There's the sign: Black Rock Bowl."

The Lexus rumbled over a log bridge with its side rails capped by fresh white powder and emerged from the woods onto a model village square bounded on two sides by Tudoresque buildings decked with green boughs and wreaths. Faux-candle lanterns hung between the metal grilles that shuttered the storefronts. A huge tree sat dead centre on the snowdrifted paving, its massive purple decorations peeping through the snow that covered its branches. Beyond it, the ghostly pylons of a ski lift marched uphill toward the grey-black of the upper mountain.

"Uh …" said Dee.

"Let me guess. The mall wasn't here last time you were up here."

They left the shops behind and followed a plowed single-lane track up the Bowl's north shoulder. The first snow-filled driveway led to a large modern chalet with a high glass front and a wide veranda. The second was similar. In the third, a rustic bi-level squatted near the road, its age-darkened logs almost black against the snow. A half-buried shed slumped against the treeline, and what appeared to be a rusty garbage incinerator poked through a snowdrift.

"That definitely isn't JP's place. Nobody would bother putting keypad entry and security alarms on that hovel." Dee fumbled her phone. The screen glowed. "Yay, I've got a signal again! There must be a cell tower for the ski hill. Hmm … looks like we should have crossed behind the square and gone up the south shoulder instead.

Damn! Oh well, this road loops around the upper Bowl, runs under the ski hill, and goes where we need to be. It'll just take a bit longer. And that's assuming it's plowed all the way."

"It looks like the plow only went through one way," Lacey said, "otherwise it'd be wider." As the land fell away to her left, she kept the SUV centred on the narrow track and hoped they wouldn't meet the plow coming back. They passed a dozen more chalets before reaching the tunnel that ran under the upper ski lift. When they re-emerged into the light, Lacey looked down the long slope at the shops far below. A white truck with a crest on the door sped past the square. She slowed for a better look, but it vanished into the trees on the south shoulder before she could make out whether the insignia was Alberta Sheriffs Branch or RCMP. What trouble had come to this winter playground on a quiet weekday afternoon?

Zoe threw the last split of birch onto the fire and went over to the window. The sap crackled as flames licked up its length, mocking the cold room with its illusion of warmth. She cupped her hands against the frosty glass. "Blue lights. They're almost here."

"Mommy, come back," Lizi whimpered. "What if he comes inside?"

"He isn't going anywhere, honey. I ... checked." Zoe slid onto the couch and wrapped her arms around her daughter, trying to protect her from the chill. Too soon —

and not soon enough — came the sound of heavy boots thudding on the porch. She detangled herself from Lizi's clutches and pushed a pillow into the girl's arms before opening the door to admit a blast of frigid air and a huge Mountie. "Thank God you're here. He's in the woodshed … out back. Do I need to show you? My daughter's in here and I don't want to leave her —"

"Mommy, it's cold."

The Mountie said he'd find it himself, and Zoe hurried back to her daughter, murmuring soothing words as she stared into the flames.

A second, younger policeman entered the room and looked around. "Excuse me, ma'am. I'm Constable Markov. Did my sergeant come through here?"

Zoe pointed to the kitchen, then watched as the snowy trail left by his boots melted on the hardwood floor. That mess wouldn't have mattered in the old cabin, or to the first Mrs. Thompson — Arliss — but Phyl Thompson would probably have a conniption if she saw her beautiful new floor being marred.

Lizi yanked another tissue from the box on the coffee table and blew her nose. "Will they take him away right away? Or will they have to do a whole bunch of investigating here first, like on the cop shows?"

"I don't know, honey. It's not every day you find a body."

The RCMP sergeant reappeared, filling the kitchen archway with his bulk. Zoe lifted her eyes to him. "Do you know who it is? I saw it was a young man, but —"

He took out a small notebook. "Did you recognize him?"

Zoe said nothing.

"You could save us a lot of time, ma'am, if you tell us what you know."

Zoe looked sideways at her daughter and shook her head slightly. If he was a parent, he'd get the message. "I'm going into the kitchen with the sergeant, honey. You stay here by the fire."

Lizi grabbed her hand. "No, Mommy, please don't go."

Zoe looked helplessly at the officer.

Lacey swung the Lexus around a hairpin turn and slammed on the brakes. She stopped with her grille a whisper from that of an RCMP cruiser stopped mid-track. Dee leaned forward. "Oh no, that's JP's driveway. I wonder what's going on."

"I'll go see."

Lacey got out, bracing herself against the raw wind, and hurried to the driver's window. The cruiser was empty. Trudging up the drive, she passed a white RCMP truck and then a blue minivan parked in front of the etched-glass doors of a huge log chalet. She'd raised her hand to knock when an officer appeared around the corner of the porch.

"Markov!" she said, frowning. "Hi. Is this JP Thompson's place? What's going on?"

It took the constable from the Cochrane detachment a second to recognize her. "Oh, hi, McCrae. Yeah, it is. What brings you here?"

"My friend and I, we're supposed to be photographing the property for the owner today."

A deeper voice came from behind her. "Since when are you a photographer?"

Lacey spun around. Her old RCMP training buddy, Bulldog Drummond, stood holding open one of the glass doors.

"Actually, Sergeant, it's Dee, my roommate, who's taking the photos. I'm just the driver. We expected the place to be deserted."

"Missing person found out back," Drummond explained. "Deceased. And we're short-handed. Help me out, McCrae. You finished your Victim Services training, right? Can you sit with a witness until she can give her statement?"

"I can't leave Dee in the car, and she can't walk very well in the snow. She's still in a cast from last summer."

"Markov can bring your vehicle up. Are the keys in it?"

Lacey nodded.

"Okay. You comfort the kid while I take the mother's statement." He hustled her into a spacious living room that overlooked the Bowl. "Lizi, this is Lacey McCrae. She'll stay with you while I talk to your mom."

Boots dripping, still wearing her coat, Lacey lowered herself onto a huge leather couch beside the shivering teen. The girl was clutching a cushion like it was a teddy bear. Streaky black mascara ran down her cheeks, and dyed-blond locks poked out from under a knitted pink toque. She was maybe sixteen, Lacey figured, wearing blue leggings and a hip-length hoodie splashed with neon colours. Pink, fingerless gloves kneaded a crumpled tissue.

"You must be freezing." Lacey tugged a quilt from the back of the sofa and wrapped it around the girl. "Your name's Lizi?"

The girl nodded.

"Is that short for Elizabeth?" Lacey asked, to keep the girl's attention off the voices in the next room.

Lizi sniffled, blew her nose, and tucked her feet up underneath her. "Kinda. It's actually Lizaveta. Russian, like my mom."

"Is your dad Russian, too?"

"No. He's from New Zealand." Gradually, through answering more innocuous questions, Lizi began to relax. Soon Lacey knew she had a cat named Toomie at home and two older half-brothers who lived in New Zealand with their mom but were coming to Alberta for Christmas. "Me and my mom, we're here to get the place ready for the holidays. Her boss is letting us use it, and all the skis and snowmobiles and things. He's in England for the holidays."

"Her boss is JP Thompson?"

Lizi nodded. "It's supposed to be our greatest family holiday ever. Kai and Ari are coming all this way, and now it's ruined." A sob slipped out. "I can't stay here after seeing that dead body. I just can't!"

Lacey wrapped the quilt tighter around the girl and left an arm over her shoulder. The fire settled, its half-eaten logs collapsing in a shower of sparks. Her eyes followed the embers, then the chimney stones up to the varnished railing that crossed the upper level. To get the

Christmas-themed photos Dee wanted, she calculated they'd need a two-storey tree and endless ells of evergreen swag. She slipped her phone from her pocket and snapped a couple of photos surreptitiously, trying to give Dee a sense of what would be needed. Not quite subtly enough to evade Lizi's attention, though. The girl sat up.

"This isn't the crime scene. Shouldn't you be taking pictures of that shed instead?"

"Actually, my friend and I are here to take photos of the chalet for a sales portfolio. My friend's a realtor."

"Mr. Thompson is selling?" Lizi tossed her scrunched-up tissues onto the coffee table. She pulled her own phone from the pocket of her hoodie. "Maybe I should tell my friends what's going on. They'll be wondering why I haven't sent them pics of this place yet."

"Don't say anything about that body until the police give you permission. What if that person's family finds out he's dead from a social media post?"

"Yeah, I guess that wouldn't be cool." Lizi frowned. "I didn't think of that. Too stunned from finding him there." She blew her nose.

"So, you found the body?" Lacey asked. No wonder the kid was a mess.

"Uh-huh. Mom started the fire with the kindling that was left in here and I went out to get more wood. They didn't dig out the shed when they did the driveway and the porch. That's why I'm so cold, really: my legs are soaked. I had to wade through waist-deep snow the whole way, then hack the ice off the door." Lizi shivered. "It was thicker than my hands. I thought I'd need a blowtorch to melt everything off the crossbar. But it all fell off with a few good whacks, and I pried the bar up so I could open the door halfway. I sort of scrunched in sideways. Then the light came over my shoulder and fell, like, right on his f-face."

Lacey tensed for another bout of weeping, but Lizi only breathed heavily and tugged on a loose strand of hair. "It was awful. I screamed and I just kept screaming, I guess, while I ran back here. Mom made me wait here while she went to look. Then she called the police." She scrubbed her streaky face with the backs of her gloves and stared at the smeared wool. A wood splinter was caught in a dangling shred of pink wool on her palm. She tugged it out. "Mom doesn't want to say who it is, but I think I know…. A university student went missing last month in a blizzard. If he fell asleep and got hypothermia, or whatever … that could be him, right?"

"There can't be too many missing persons in this area."

"It isn't so empty on holidays. When we went to get the keys from Mr. Thompson, he bitched the whole time about how the old ski trails were better and how the new stores down there attract people who don't even ski — they just clog up the parking lots and stink up the fresh air with exhaust fumes. Maybe that's why he's selling the place."

Bull Drummond reappeared in the doorway. Behind him, Lizi's mother carried a steaming mug. "Here, honey, I found some hot chocolate. It'll make you feel better." She turned to Lacey. "Thanks for sitting with her."

"She's been very brave." Lacey got up and faded back toward the foyer as Bull moved to the couch. His turf now.

Lizi peered at him over the rim of the mug. "Was it that guy?"

Her mother sat down beside her. "I'm fairly sure it is Eric Anders, although the last time I saw him he was even younger than you. But you can't tell anyone that, honey. Don't text it or tweet it or tell your friends. You don't want his family —"

"I know. She" — Lizi jerked her head at Lacey — "told me already. It's gonna be hard for them, finding out he's dead so close to Christmas." Her voice wavered. "Imagine if it was Kai or Ari? Dad would totally lose it."

"We all would." Zoe tugged the quilt tighter around her daughter's shoulders. "We have to help the sergeant now, so he can go tell that family right away. He needs to take your statement, since you were the one to find Eric."

Lacey managed to catch Bull's eye long enough to twitch her head at the door. *Can I leave?* He shook his head once. *No.* She leaned against the wall, listening to the calm questions and clear answers, Lizi's repetition of the account she'd given Lacey earlier. But something wasn't quite the same. Lizi had told her she'd knocked the ice off, then lifted the bar to open the door. If the bar was the usual kind that fell into a bracket and couldn't be raised from inside, the victim couldn't have lowered it into place from inside, either. It had either fallen shut or someone had barred the door. Lacey tried again to snag Bull's attention, but he was walking Lizi through the sequence a second time, looking for anomalies.

"Your mom tells me you were the first person to go to the woodshed. Is that right?"

Lizi nodded. She set down the mug and picked at another splinter in her glove.

"Can you tell me again, in your own words, what you did, and what you saw?"

She repeated everything pretty much exactly, except she again left out the part about raising the crossbar. Bull repeated it all back to her. "Is that everything?"

"Uh-huh."

Lacey gritted her teeth. *Think, Lizi. Don't make me interrupt or it'll seem like I'm coaching you.* But Lizi only sniffled and reached for her hot chocolate. With a mental sigh, Lacey shifted until she was directly behind the couch and waved her hand until Bull looked at her. She pointed to her palm, mimed pulling the wool. His eyes sharpened.

"How did you snag your pretty glove, Lizi?"

CHAPTER FOUR

Lacey stood outside in the deep-blue dusk, watching Zoe back her minivan past the other vehicles. "So, can you?" she asked Bull as he came around the porch. "Can you move that bar from inside the woodshed?"

"Not a chance. When it's not in the bracket, it hangs straight down. Good catch on the mitten. It seems to match what's snagged on the bar. I'll get a crime scene unit out here." Bull was silent for a minute, then said, "That woman was hiding something, you reckon?"

"She looked over at the kitchen once or twice, almost like she heard something. Could be a guilty conscience. But why on earth would she send her kid out to find the body?"

"Not likely, when you put it that way. She works for the owner of the place, though. Maybe she knows something about him, or suspects it." Bull resettled his hat. "Thanks for standing in. My nearest female constable is on a roll-over with fatality near Morley. She could be hours yet."

"Won't that bounce to Traffic Services to investigate?"

"You still think like a townie, McCrae. Urban practice is to clear the scene fast and restore traffic flow, and so it should be. But Morley is not only rural, it's also a First Nation. If there's a death, we offer the family time for a ritual — smudge or prayers or whatever."

"Hours of it?"

"It takes as long as it takes." He thumbed through his phone. "Drive safe."

As they drove down the chalet's driveway, Dee asked, "What the hell was that all about? You go in to ask the cop to move his car, and the next thing I know, he's getting in and driving me up there. I texted my mom's nurse to say we'd be a bit late. She won't get it until they're off the plane, but at least she'll know we didn't forget."

Lacey concentrated on keeping the Lexus between the snowbanks. "He didn't tell you what happened?"

"You were 'assisting the police,' is all he said. If it's a break-in, I need to tell JP."

"They wouldn't send two vehicles for that. They found a body in the woodshed, frozen, and it looks suspicious. That'll tie up the scene for days. Your photos will have to wait."

Dee's face paled. "But I have to sell that place ASAP. If I don't get a decent commission in the bank by February, I'll have to sell the roof over our heads."

"As bad as that? Shit, Dee. I'm sorry. I'll email Dan when we get home. Maybe he's finally had an offer on our house. Or I can coax him into buying me out."

Dee huffed. "Eight months and he hasn't had a single offer? When the Lower Mainland is the hottest market in the country? Please! Anyway, I won't have you grovelling to that asshole to get me out of a jam. Lord love me, what a disaster. Don't tell my mom, either, eh? She's got enough on her plate."

CHAPTER FIVE

Zoe steered the van with trembling hands. She cast another glance into the rear-view mirror, looking for that black smudge that had been following her ever since she touched the dead boy's cheek. Of course there was nothing there, but the distinct feeling of a presence remained. It was the same feeling she'd had years earlier, that had haunted her day and night until she'd ended up in a psych ward.

The passenger-side mirror grazed an overhanging bough. "Whoa, Mom," said Lizi. "Are you okay?"

Zoe straightened out the car, white-knuckled, as her reassuring-mom mode beat back her terror that she might be having another breakdown. How could she manage the full hour's drive back to Calgary if she started hearing things? And maybe seeing things, like she had back in grade ten? She pulled up at the Y junction, near a sign for Waiparous Village, and opened the window to suck in some cold, crisp air. *Focus, Zoe. Keep it together for Lizi. Yes, Eric's dead, but everyone at TFB knew this was a possibility. If you start hearing voices, you go ask for your old prescription, and you'll be fine. Just get*

Lizi home safe. The wind knifed into the vehicle, clearing her mind. *I have to tell JP. He'll have to make a statement on behalf of the company. He'll get in touch with Eric's parents.* That was the next step: tell JP. She closed the window, cranked up the heat, and held her fingers over the air vent.

"Sorry about that, honey. Just needed some air. Hang on a sec while I call JP."

"We aren't supposed to tell anybody."

"That means on social media." Zoe dug for her phone. "So the family doesn't find out before the police get there. But I have to tell JP what's going on at his place."

"You can't call him now. It's like three in the morning in England."

"Oh damn, you're right." Zoe stowed her phone and put the van into gear. "I'll email him when we get home."

"What are we gonna do about the holidays now?" Lizi picked at her fingernail in the absence of the gloves the RCMP sergeant had bagged. "I won't stay there. I just can't."

"I won't make you go back there. We'll figure out something else."

As they passed a lone street lamp, Zoe glanced over at her daughter. In the yellow glow of the pole lights, Lizi twisted a lock of her shaggy blond hair between two fingers. A sure sign of stress.

"I mean it — you don't ever have to go back, honey. If you're upset, use your words. Talk to me."

Lizi lowered her hands. "If I tell you something really weird, will you promise to be chill about it?"

"I can try."

"Okay, well, ever since I ran out of the woodshed, it's like there's ... like there's something, um, following me.... Or *somebody*."

Zoe's chest squeezed with a new fear. It wasn't only her, then, who felt that creeping presence. Was this curse inherited? Mama would say, "Just pray, Zoe. Trust God to take the demon away." But prayer hadn't worked for Zoe, and it wouldn't work for Lizi, who had hardly ever been to church. And it wasn't a demon, anyway, unless a trick of brain chemistry counted as demonic. What could she say without giving away how freaked out she was? Moms had to seem in control, even when they were hanging on to sanity by their fingertips.

"You've had a horrible scare, honey. It's natural to be creeped out. Once we're home, with some hot food and Toomie to cuddle, the feeling will fade." *Please, let it disappear!*

Zoe forced out a breath and tried to concentrate on driving, searching in the glare of the headlights for anything moving across their path. But each time she looked in the rear-view mirror, she held her breath, terrified she might see a set of cold, dead eyes looking at her from the back seat.

CHAPTER SIX

Lacey wheeled Dee into Calgary International Airport twenty minutes after the flight from Hamilton had landed. Passengers were still trickling out from the Arrivals doors to congregate by the baggage carousels. Last came the wheelchair passengers. Dee's mother was third and clearly the most ill, her sallow skin sagging under her green cap. The backs of her hands were badly bruised from months of IVs and blood draws. Her nurse, who was pushing her chair, wore a puffy winter coat that covered her from ears to knees. Her toque — from which a few sandy curls escaped — was white with pink sparkles, and it matched the mittens that hung from her sleeves on strings. Against that snow-white purity, Loreena looked more corpselike still.

Dee sat in stunned silence, her fingers clutching the arms of her own wheelchair in a death grip. Lacey took a deep breath, stepped forward, and stooped to kiss Loreena's weathered cheek. "Hello, missus."

Loreena's thin lips quivered with the effort of a smile. "Lacey. How nice to see you, dear." Her once-vivid blue eyes squinted in the glare of the overhead lights.

The nurse shoved a sturdy paw toward Lacey. "Hi, I'm Sandy Walsh. You're Lacey? And you must be Dee, then," she said, turning to face Dee. "I've heard so much about you. I hope you've both had your flu shots. Your mother's immune system can't fight off the germs, you know. Speaking of which, can we get her out of here? She's very tired. Plus there are so many people around, coughing and sneezing everywhere. Who knows how many strains of flu were circulating on that plane?"

Dee forced a smile that wavered like her mother's. "Of course. The sooner we're all settled at home, the better we'll all feel. We're parked right out front." She gestured at her wheelchair. "One perk of needing this thing, at least."

Being the last passengers off, their suitcases were already at the roundabout. Once Loreena was bundled up to her chin in a coat and blanket, Lacey led her and Sandy outside with the first two cases, leaving Dee to guard the third. Sandy lifted Loreena into the prewarmed front seat while Lacey opened the back hatch. She had to fold down the dogs' kennel to stand the suitcases along the rear seat and still leave room for both folding wheelchairs. Then she went back for Dee and the last bag.

As Lacey approached, Dee hastily wiped her eyes with the backs of her hands. "God, Lacey, she looks so much worse than I expected. She should be in a hospital."

"It's one thing to be told she's sick, and another to see for yourself. Chin up, now. You're giving her a last good Christmas, remember?"

"Right." Dee sighed and gripped the arms of her wheelchair. "Let's go home, then."

As the vehicle reached the snowy fields on the outskirts of Calgary, the city lights fell behind them. Snow-capped peaks kissed the velvet sky ahead. The wind sent tendrils of snow skirling across the road. Loreena dozed in the passenger seat. In the back, Dee sat chewing her lip, and Sandy looked out into the darkness. "I forgot how bright the stars are here," she murmured.

When they pulled up in front of Dee's house, Lacey and Sandy got Loreena's wheelchair out of the back. Sandy wheeled Loreena to the house while Lacey ferried in the luggage. Dee, she found, had stayed in the vehicle. "Pull into the garage," she said. "I need a minute." She sat, tears streaming, brushing her cheeks with the back of her glove. "Oh, God, Lacey, she's dying. That nurse must be costing her a fortune. How can I even think of asking her for a loan now?"

"I didn't realize you were going to."

"I have no choice. I was counting on that commission to keep us afloat in February. It's pretty hard to re-mortgage a house like this on long-term disability with no idea when I can go back to work. Every project I had has moved on without me. Even if I went back tomorrow, I'd need months to catch up."

Lacey stared bleakly at the rear wall of the garage. She'd coasted since Dee's injury, buying groceries on the part-time work from Wayne, rationalizing her lack of action against Dan with how much energy it took to cope with Dee's medical appointments and shopping and the household chores. Now things were dire, and she was no closer to getting her equity out of the house in Langley. "I can maybe get some work as a mall cop through Christmas."

"I'll need you here, though, Lace. Mom's nurse is going to her son's for Christmas. And look at her. I can't possibly care for her when I can barely take care of myself. Adding an outside job right now is impossible."

There was no counter-argument to that. "Maybe the case at JP's will be closed quickly. We'll get your photos, and that chalet will sell fast once it's all gussied up for the holidays." Lacey gave Dee's hand a squeeze and opened the car door. "It's been a long day for all of us. Let's just get through tonight and worry about the rest tomorrow."

Screams shattered the still night. Torn from a troubled doze, Zoe rolled from her bed as her husband woke. Ignoring his muttered "What the fuck?" she raced to Lizi's room. Putting her hands on the flailing girl's shoulders, she said forcefully, "It's okay, baby, wake up, baby. It's just a nightmare." She repeated it over and over until Lizi came awake, her screams fading to a whimper.

"It was him. Oh, Mommy, it was him. He followed me home."

Zoe groped for the bedside lamp, panic seizing her chest. It had to be just a nightmare. But she couldn't stop herself from peering fearfully into the shadowy corners of the room, searching for ... what? Shivering from a chill more atmospheric than real, she tucked the blankets tighter around Lizi's shoulders and rocked until both their breathing settled. Eventually, Lizi drowsed, and Zoe eased herself off the bed. "I'll leave the light on for you," she whispered, then crept back to her own room.

As she snuggled up to her husband's back, he asked, "What was that all about?"

"She had a nightmare about the dead boy."

"Not surprising." Nik rolled over and wrapped his arms around her. "How are you doing? No nightmares?"

"I haven't been asleep long enough to dream."

"You should try. Tomorrow JP will have a whole bin of new jobs for you. Maybe enough to pay for rebooking a vacation somewhere else. The boys and Lizi are counting on real powder skiing, and last-minute chalets at a decent hill will bite us bad, especially at Christmas."

He was asleep in minutes, his chest warm against her back, his thick arms holding her close, his steady breathing stirring her hair. He was so calm, as if the biggest issue with finding Eric was that the kids might not get to go skiing. Learning that his wife and possibly his daughter were sensing ghostly presences would be a nasty shock. He hadn't known Zoe back in high school, when she'd driven herself into that breakdown trying to escape from the whispers that nobody else could hear.

After trying in vain to fall asleep, Zoe got up, grabbed her fleece hoodie, shoved her phone into the pocket, and headed downstairs. Since they'd probably be having Christmas at home, they'd need decorations. Soon she was pulling out strings of lights, winding garlands around the banisters, and setting out twenty years' worth of Christmas-themed knick-knacks on the mantle and the bookshelves. She sorted through miscellaneous boxes of tree ornaments: store-bought sets that needed hooks, glitter-and-glue creations Lizi had made, Popsicle-stick reindeer and stars that Kai and Ari had mailed to their dad years ago. Eric's mother came to mind. She might be weeping over his childhood decorations this very night. He'd been missing for a month, but she had to have hoped he'd still miraculously come home. How could any mother face the tinfoil stars and hand-painted snow-men of a child she now knew was gone forever? How could she ever celebrate Christmas again?

Lizi came down an hour earlier than usual, her face ghostly white and her eyes smudged thumbprints. She was wearing her warmest fleece pajamas. "Can't sleep either, eh, Mom?"

"I don't know what to do about Christmas," Zoe said, not entirely lying. "Your brothers expect skiing and snowmobiling and snowshoeing, not sitting around the house for two weeks."

"I was, too … looking forward to the skiing, I mean." Lizi slouched into the kitchen. "Tell me we have some of that double-dark hot chocolate."

Zoe watched her go. Lizi hadn't mentioned the night-mare, and maybe that was all it was. A result of shock. But for Zoe, the feeling persisted that someone else was in the house with them. All night, she'd felt like some-thing was just beyond a doorway, or behind her, or leaving a room two steps ahead of her entering it. There hadn't been any sounds she couldn't explain, no strange fluttering of a curtain. Still, every time she passed a mirror or saw her reflection in the window, she'd expected to see the young man standing behind her.

Truthfully, she had no real recollection of what Eric looked like when he was alive. He was JP's old neighbour's son and had hung out with JP's son; they'd probably come into the office together when she worked at TFB, but that was years ago, when the boys were pre-adolescent. When JP had contracted her to start the corporate cleanup process, Eric wasn't one of the staff members she'd met. He had already been missing for two weeks by then. Worrying about hearing the voice of a dead young man she wouldn't even recognize was probably pointless. She wouldn't have been this anxious under normal circumstances. Unfortunately, these weren't normal circumstances. Instead of controlling her own schedule with her handful of small-business clients, she had the daily downtown job's stress, plus her adult stepsons' pending arrivals for a vacation that would be spent crowded in their small house with nothing to do. If she did end up seeing or hearing a ghostly presence in the middle of all this, she might start screaming louder than Lizi.

She pushed herself out of the pile of decoration boxes and followed Lizi into the kitchen, telling herself firmly that the worst was over. They'd found the body, they'd called the police, she'd messaged JP and, sooner or later, presumably she and Lizi would be called in to sign a statement. Otherwise, they were done with the investigation. Food, sleep, routine. That was what she needed. Those would bring her back to herself. And Lizi, too.

When she heard the shower start upstairs, she pushed the button on the coffee maker and got Nik's mug out. Routine.

Her phone rang. It was JP. "Sorry, did I wake you?" His voice was hushed and urgent. "You'll have to be the company's point person with Eric's family. He only drove out there that weekend because he wanted to talk to me. Since I didn't ask him to come, it's a grey area as to whether he was on company business, but his parents could sue me or the company for negligent death. That's a huge problem with the sale looming, so ..." His voice trailed off. "Zoe? Are you there?"

"I'm moving into my office. Take a breath, JP." With the door shut behind her, she went on. "Do you honestly think your neighbours for years, the parents of your children's friends, are going to sue you because their son went out in a blizzard? You didn't ask him to. What is there to sue over?"

"He's their son," he said. "I can't imagine how bad they feel right now. They'll want somebody to blame." A rustling sound came over the phone line, and the sound of a lighter clicking. He was smoking again, then. "I asked Arliss, but she says she has to be their neighbour and friend first. I want you to be available to them instead, for whatever they need. Take my condolences in person. Tell them how he was found." He checked himself. "No, maybe not that. If they ask, assure them it was peaceful. Freezing to death is peaceful, right? Promise them the company will look into whatever needs doing, find out if they need help with the burial expenses. But, you know, phrase that tactfully."

Her hand shook as she pulled the phone from her ear and stared at it. *I found that boy's body,* she wanted to scream at him, *and I'm not feeling very damned peaceful about it. I don't owe you this.* But she didn't say any of that. After all, he had contracted her to ready the company for sale, and biting the hand that signs the paycheques wasn't good policy. During all the years she'd been his firm right arm, she'd managed the "people problems" at the company because he was so damned inept at it. He trusted her to be unflappable and competent, so that was what she would be. She needed the money, and even more than that, she needed the routine, the distraction of work to prove to herself that she wasn't losing control of her own mind.

"I'll say what's fitting depending on how I find them. There's not much more I can do, JP. Not to sound cold, but I have to reorganize my family Christmas, too. The chalet will be surrounded by police for a while yet, and anyway, I can't take my daughter back to a place where she found a dead body."

Typically, JP didn't bother pretending to care about Lizi's possible distress. "Why would the police keep it taped off? He died in the blizzard, didn't he? It's terrible, but it happens."

"The sergeant said yesterday they'd have to figure out why he didn't just go into the chalet where he'd be warm and fed and safe. Or why he didn't stay in his car, wherever that is. It's going to be a while before they finish up out there."

"Shit on a stick." JP's voice dropped further. "Look, Phyl's back from her massage. I have to go. I promised no work on this trip. You deal with whatever and email me every day with updates, okay? Call for anything urgent and leave a message."

Zoe set the phone down on her desk. Her head dropped onto her arms. There she sat, slumped over, exhausted and angry, as the midwinter sun crept over the snowy yard and delineated the window blinds in strips of golden light.

CHAPTER SEVEN

Lacey admitted a slow-merging transport truck to the main lane and glanced sideways at Loreena. Dee's mom was gazing out the passenger side window, smiling. Her skin hadn't entirely lost its yellowish cast, but this was not the corpselike woman they'd picked up from the airport two evenings ago. A couple of days in bed had helped her recover in body and spirit, and now she was looking forward to the Christmas market. Unbelievable.

Dee leaned forward from the back seat, pointing. "Up here you get a good view of Cochrane and the Bow River Valley."

"It's beautiful," said Loreena, "with the blue sky and the golden-brown of the grass sticking up through the snow. Or is it hay? This is big ranching country, right?"

Lacey pointed to a sign. "We're on what's called the Cowboy Trail, which runs through the heart of Alberta ranch country. Bragg Creek is another stop on it."

Dee called her mother's attention to the wide, flat bench of land on the far side of the valley. "All that used to be one ranch, from here almost to Calgary. The owner left it to the province in his will, and now it's protected parkland."

"So there *are* environmentalists in Alberta," said Loreena. "Another myth demolished. Dated any tree-hugging cowboys?"

"No," said Dee. "Cowboys smell like horses, which I understand some women enjoy. If they smelled of dog, now …" She laughed. "Like most Calgary office workers, I own the obligatory cowboy boots to wear during Stampede, and I know to say 'ya-hoo' like a local instead of 'yee-haw' like a tourist."

Thanks to Dee's handicapped placard, they snagged a prime spot near the end of the Old West downtown, almost at the hay-bale barricades. The snow had been piled high around the light standards, leaving the pavement bare, so pushing the wheelchairs around was no problem. Lacey handed Dee the extra lap blanket to cover her legs, and followed Sandy, who was briskly rolling Loreena toward the rows of brightly decorated booths.

Dee pointed. "Look, holiday gifts for dogs."

Sure enough, the second booth advertised all-natural pet treats: hard biscuits in the shapes of bells, candy canes, and stockings, some studded with dry-roasted peanuts and others with jewel-like dried cranberries.

The man behind the display turned out to be Dee's neighbour, Eddie Beal. His faded sheepskin hat covered his shaggy hair, its ear flaps folded down over his cheeks. His straggly beard stuck out over a faded red scarf that didn't match his red plaid coat. He grinned as they approached, exposing stained teeth. "Over here, Miz Dee.

I got treats for them young dogs of yours. All good stuff. Cleans their teeth and their breath. Keeps 'em regular, too. Nice fat shits."

Only Eddie would think that yelling about dog crap was a good sales strategy. But then, responsible dog owners picked up the stuff on every walk, so maybe his pitch wasn't such a stretch.

Dee introduced her mother and Sandy to Eddie. While he extolled the virtues of his homemade rawhide peanut butter rolls and cinnamon pig's ears, Lacey looked up the street to where the sunlight glinted off red and green foil garlands that looped between the shopfronts and lampposts. Plastic candy canes as big as barber poles bracketed the doorways. Giant Christmas balls hung from a huge blue spruce tree. Two Clydesdales stamped, jingling their harnesses, while parents lifted tots up to a straw-filled wagon. A teepee anchored the far end of the block. Nearby, members of a children's choir warmed their hands around a firepit. Their next performance, advertised on a billboard nearby, was in half an hour. The teacher with them looked faintly familiar.

"Hey, Dee, are those the kids who sang at the museum opening last summer?"

Dee looked the group over. "I think so. But my memories from June are pretty shaky. If the teacher comes over, introduce yourself quickly so I can get her name in case I've already met her."

Sandy and Loreena rolled away, lured by warm gingerbread aromas coming from a booth filled with snow-topped gingerbread houses and candy-eyed cookie people. Bidding Eddie goodbye, Lacey pushed Dee after them. Eddie waved. "I'll be over in the mornin' with yer eggs, Miz Dee!"

A woman from the first booth hurried after Dee, calling her name. Lacey turned the chair as the stranger caught up.

"Marcia," Dee said, with a bright smile. She introduced the woman to Lacey as an accountant at TFB Energy, JP Thompson's company.

This woman must have known the dead intern. Lacey mentally catalogued this potential source of information just as she would have done back in her RCMP days. Marcia was a sturdy woman on the north side of fifty, with dark, thick curls that spilled around the edges of her red, white, and blue knitted ski cap. She had what was called a generous mouth, which Lacey had always taken to be a nicer way of saying "large." Firm lips, square jaw, and penetrating brown eyes gave her the look of a taskmaster.

"Are you working here?" Dee asked.

"Yes. Backcountry Safety Association," said Marcia, her voice deep and assertive. "I teach a winter wilderness survival course and lead cross-country ski trekking, too. Everyone needs a life outside the office, right?"

"Especially right now." Dee clucked her tongue. "The death of that TFB intern is just terrible, isn't it? How's everyone over there dealing with it, now that his body's been found?"

Marcia glanced back at her unattended booth. "It's not as if it was unexpected, after he'd been gone so long. To be honest, he wasn't a good fit at the company. No understanding of office manners, these young people. But it's come as an awful shock to JP."

"Oh, I know. On JP's property, too," said Dee. "You know, we were there that day, when they found the body."

Marçia recoiled. "You found the body? I thought —"

"Not us, no. We happened along soon after the police arrived. Lacey's a Victim Services volunteer for the RCMP, so she stayed to help that poor girl who found him." Dee wrinkled her brow. "What was he doing out there anyway? Wasn't it a long weekend? When he went missing, I mean."

"Taking paperwork out to JP, I suppose. If you remember that weekend, they'd announced a blizzard from hell was coming. JP heard it and headed back to town early, but it seems he and Eric missed each other. I spent the whole next week trapped at my cabin across the Bowl. JP asked me to keep an eye out, but there was no sign of Eric or his little red car, and no smoke coming from that chimney, either." Marcia frowned. "Where was he found? Did they say?"

Dee shrugged and raised her eyebrow at Lacey. Unsure how much detail the police had released, Lacey avoided the question by instead asking, "You were snowed in for a whole week? How did you stand it?"

"Oh, I'm used to it. I'm from Ontario." Marcia shifted in place and glanced again at her booth, where a lone person stood poking through the brochures. "In case you've never seen lake-effect snow, it's massive there. Wet and heavy, and way deeper than anything you get out here. Nothing to see out the windows but white. On the farm we survived with stacks of library books and lots of wood for the stove."

Dee tipped her head farther back, keeping Marcia's face in sight. "Will there be an office memorial service? I mean, you all worked with Eric, didn't you? And wasn't he a pet project of JP's? When we first spoke about selling the chalet, he said couldn't relax there anymore because his protege was missing in the area."

Marcia's eyes narrowed. "What? Selling the chalet? It can't be. Phyl would have told me if they were thinking of selling."

Lacey read sudden unease in the way Dee plucked at the blanket on her lap, so she pulled the chair back, putting some distance between them. "We'd better move on, Dee. Your mom and her nurse are halfway around the market already. Nice meeting you, Marcia. Happy holidays."

As soon as they were out of earshot, Dee let out a big breath. "Thanks for getting me out of there. I shouldn't have mentioned the sale, but I didn't think they were keeping it a secret from their friends."

"She's a friend of JP's as well as an employee?"

"She hangs out with his second wife. But it's not my business to overshare about a client. I wish I knew when Sergeant Drummond will be releasing the chalet. It'll be a lot harder to sell it if we're almost into the spring."

"I'll phone him when we get home. Let's see if your mom's ready to bail yet."

As they caught up with the other wheelchair, Loreena greeted them with a yawn. "I got the cutest gingerbread-man puzzle for the little girl next door. And a few ornaments for your tree. When are you planning on putting the decorations up?"

"Soon," said Dee brightly. "Ready to head home?"

"So," said Lacey, when they were alone making supper, "where do you hide the decorations?"

Dee grimaced. "I don't own any. We, um, used to hire a decorator who brought all that stuff with her."

"How were you going to decorate that chalet, then?"

"Borrow from the neighbours, of course! Jan and Terry have reams of holiday tatting from when his mom sold her house, and they told me I could help myself. Actually, I'd better email Jan. There might be some stuff she doesn't want me to mess with."

"I'll do it. You stir that pot."

Closing the office door behind her, Lacey dialed Bulldog Drummond's personal number. He picked up on the third ring.

"Whaddya want, McCrae?"

"Wondering if you'd released the crime scene yet."

"All but the woodshed. What's it to you?"

"My roommate wants to get the place on the market ASAP. When can we go back and take the photos?"

"If she's got the owner's permission, I can't stop her. But stay away from the shed."

There was a pause while Lacey tried to calculate how much she could ask about the investigation. Bull saved her the trouble. "On rechecking the scene, we found a poppy pin in there, down between two logs. Nobody said the victim was wearing one, but he went missing Remembrance Day weekend, so it might be his. I've sent it for fingerprints."

"If it's not his, it might belong to one of the Thompson family. They were there that weekend too, until a few hours before he drove up." Lacey pictured the young man struggling through the blizzard, the gale whipping his face and tugging at his clothing. "He was found wearing a scarf, right? Were the ends loose or tucked in?"

There came the sound of papers being shuffled. "Wool scarf around his coat collar. Outside. Why?"

"If it's his poppy, how did it not get lost during the blizzard? Those things come off every time you shrug. It's unlikely to have stayed on if he'd been struggling through the storm, hunching his shoulders and pulling his scarf up to his face."

"Good question," said Bull. "I'd like to know how far away his car is, too. First, though, I need you as Victim Services contact to follow up with that woman, Zoe, and her daughter."

Sure, if it'll expedite the chalet sale. "What do you want me to do?"

"Ask how they're coping and when they can come in to sign statements."

"Anything I can tell them about the progress of the investigation? They'll be sure to ask."

"The body was formally identified as Eric Anders, and the investigation is proceeding. We thank them for their co-operation. If they've thought of anything they'd like to add to their statements, or if they'd like to amend them in any way …"

During a pause filled with Bull's breathing, Lacey gazed out on the snowy driveway. "What do you mean, amend?"

"If the girl grabbed the woodshed crossbar and slammed it down because she was panicked about finding a body inside, we need to know that."

"You don't believe it was closed when she found it?"

"Gotta know for sure. She might've been closer to the victim than she admitted. Plus, he had a couple of loose sleeping pills in his pocket. His family told me they weren't prescribed. They say he hated swallowing any pills."

Lacey put her feet up on an embroidered footstool, thinking. If Eric hadn't struggled through the blizzard at all, but had instead gone directly from a car to the woodshed, his poppy might well have covered the distance with him. Then someone could have moved his car afterward. Or maybe he left his car somewhere and drove to the house with someone else. So many questions. But did Zoe or Lizi have any answers? She doubted it.

"Do you think the girl is lying, or the mother? Or both?"

"I don't think anything. I want to know what the facts are. The kid was upset. She could have been mistaken. We're doing the tox screen for those pills, but the results could take weeks unless we have a reason to expedite — a reason like someone connected to that kid takes that same brand of sleeping pills."

"So, in addition to finding out how Zoe and her daughter are holding up, giving them a so-called progress report, and inviting them to come in to sign and/or amend their statements, I should question them gently about their drug use? No problem. I can make that sound real casual."

CHAPTER EIGHT

Lacey tried calling the number Bull had given her for Zoe Gallagher, but it went straight to voice mail. She left her cellphone number and a message about setting a time to sign the statements. When they called back, she could ask to meet, to gauge for herself how they were coping. Whatever Bull expected of her, there was no credible way for a civilian volunteer to ask about a stranger's prescriptions over the phone. Next, she checked her email. It was mostly newsletters she couldn't remember subscribing to, but one was a holiday update from an RCMP wife she'd only ever met once, at Langley detachment's annual Christmas party. Overcome by a sudden loneliness, she opened it. A few paragraphs of sanitized brags about adorable children would surely remind her why the life Dan wanted for them would never have satisfied her.

The red poinsettia border promised good cheer, but the first words after "Dear Lacey" shattered the illusion.

> It's not my place to say anything, but you should know you've hurt Dan terribly by going off without a word, and refusing to

speak to him in person or on the phone for all these months. He's really struggling to keep the house in shape and so lonely. He's a good man, Lacey, and you're forcing him out of his home too by insisting he sell it. Our men do a hard job and they sure don't need this kind of grief from their wives.

Lacey's stomach churned. She clicked Delete and the poinsettias vanished.

What had Dan told this woman to get such sympathy? Lies, obviously, because she had talked to him over the summer, by phone and by email, until it was only too clear he was stringing her along, working to sabotage her confidence and her efforts to build a future that didn't include him. If she hadn't had Dee to look after, there was a remote possibility she might have slunk back to Langley and taken a more acceptably feminine job, one that didn't challenge Dan's masculine pride. But she'd chosen Dee's needs instead of Dan's, so here they were, eight months later, with him living in their house at full pay and her scrimping to afford basic groceries out of erratic part-time wages.

That line about struggling with the house … was he sabotaging the realtor's showings? Was that why the place hadn't sold yet? To wipe the foul taste out of her mouth, Lacey rattled off a poinsettia-free email to Jan Brenner. Even while far away on a glamorous Caribbean cruise, Jan would enjoy hearing news from home. And she knew the oil patch and its associated companies and personalities. After passing along Dee's query about the decorations, Lacey switched gears:

You weren't gone two days before we stumbled onto another body, or rather, onto its discovery …

She filled in the bare details, each keystroke punching through her old RCMP habit of not talking to civilians. Surely Jan or her husband could answer her oil patch–outsider questions.

What could an intern possibly discover about an oil company that would give someone a motive to silence him? He's a computer tech, nothing to do with oil drilling. He might have stumbled on a spill cover-up, I guess, since everyone in Alberta seems way more into oil than the environment. If you or Terry can think of any possible motives, or any oil-patch gossip about JP Thompson or his company that I would never hear as a newbie/outsider, let me know …

She included a description of Eddie Beal yelling about dog shit at the Christmas market and signed off just as Dee called out that supper was ready.

The chairlift made its distinctive whirr as it descended from the second floor. Sandy was standing by as it reached the bottom, but this time Loreena moved under her own steam to the dining room table. She smiled at all of them in turn. "I'm finished my wrapping. Is there a post office in the village? I'd like to send some knick-knacks to a few people back home."

Lacey was giving Sandy directions when Dee called from the kitchen, "Lacey, can you get this pot, please?" Sandy carried the side dishes, leaving Dee to hobble in on her walking cast. They had barely gotten the food dished out when Dee said, "Mom, I think you should stay in Alberta with me."

"Why would you say that, dear?"

"Because you don't —" Dee started again. "Because I want to spend time with you, and it's hard for me to travel right now. I have to be here to earn money."

"If you need money, I can give you some." Loreena put down her fork as Dee shook her head. "You'll get it soon enough, dear. It's not like I'll need it forever."

"Don't talk like that."

"You have to face this, honey. I'm going to die."

"I know!" Dee's voice rose. "But why can't you stay here until then?"

"We can discuss that, dear. Nursing homes here should be as good as those in Ontario. Maybe less crowded, too."

Sandy, who'd been eating steadily through her tortellini, raised her head. "Not all nursing homes have good standards for patient care, though. The last thing you need is one that slacks off on virus protection protocols. If all staff and residents don't have their flu shots, never mind the visitors, you could lose your remaining time to pneumonia, stuck on a ventilator and sedated."

Lacey lowered her fork. "You're speaking from experience, Sandy? With nursing homes, I mean."

Loreena nodded. "Sandy worked at the Waterloo nursing home when I ran art sessions for the residents. When I needed someone to drive me to chemo and help me out around the house, I thought of her." She smiled at Sandy. "She'll be with me until the end, won't you, dear?"

"To your last breath," Sandy said. "I've seen inside plenty of seniors' homes, both in Ontario and here. If you decide to stay, I'll check out a few with you." She filled Loreena's fork with pasta and sauce and handed it back to her. "I could stay in Alberta, too — for a while, anyway. I could live with my son and help him out with the finances. He's been off work the past couple of years and things have been a bit tight."

Loreena nodded and changed the subject. Each time Sandy pointed to her fork, she took another bite of something. But when Sandy went upstairs to arrange Loreena's bed, Dee pounced. "If you can't afford an Alberta nursing home, stay here with us." She gave Lacey a pleading look.

Lacey's shoulders sagged. How could they look after a dying woman here for months? She could barely keep up with her part-time work for Wayne, and driving Dee to physiotherapy and doctor's appointments, on top of all the housekeeping, snow shovelling, dog care, and groceries. How could she possibly look after Loreena, too, for months of steadily increasing care needs?

Loreena glanced between them. "It isn't the money, dear. I've enough between my pension and your dad's. But Alberta is a bit, well, backward in some areas. Or at least that's my impression." She pushed her plate away.

Lacey collected it, along with Sandy's, and took them to the kitchen to scrape.

"What areas?" Dee's sharp tone reached Lacey from the other room.

Loreena's answer was quieter. Lacey strained to hear it. "Are you sure you want to do this right now? Wouldn't you rather have a nice Christmas first?"

Sandy, returning to the kitchen for Loreena's night-time pills, frowned and glanced toward the doorway.

Dee's voice rose again. "It's still a week until Christmas. Are we not supposed to talk about your illness? Or the plan for the rest of your life?"

"Since you insist." Loreena's voice was more brittle than Dee's. "I've already discussed with my Ontario doctor the procedures for applying for medical assistance in dying. If I moved to Alberta, I'd have to start over, convincing a doctor I've never met that this is what I truly want —"

Her next words were lost in the sound of Dee's chair scraping over the floor. Then came a clatter that Lacey recognized: Dee's cane hitting the floor. She dropped the pot lid she was holding into the sink and hurried back to the dining room. "Is everyone all right in here?"

Dee was leaning on the heavy dining room table, her face ashen. Lacey picked up the cane and put her hands on Dee's shoulders, urging her gently back to her seat.

Meanwhile, Sandy helped Loreena out of her chair and said to Dee, over her shoulder, "I see you're upset. It would be better to continue this discussion tomorrow." She led Loreena from the room, and a moment later Lacey heard the chairlift start up.

"I'll make tea." Lacey gathered up the last of the dishes from supper and retreated to the kitchen, giving her friend time to regroup.

As Lacey was cleaning up, her phone rang. It was Zoe, who reported that she was managing okay and that her daughter seemed calmer. She asked if Lizi really had to go through the whole experience again for the statement.

"Yes, but it won't be that bad, I promise. The statements are already typed out. You'll simply read each of your statements over and sign them. Any changes you want to make, you can scribble them on the page and they'll print out an amended one."

"Is tomorrow afternoon okay? Lizi has school, but we can be in Cochrane soon after four."

"I'll make the arrangements." Lacey confirmed a meeting place and hung up.

The last can of evaporated milk sat alone on a shelf. She held it up as Dee limped into the room. "If there was ever a time for the ultimate stress reliever, this is it."

Dee pulled a mug toward her. "I can't believe Mom dropped that bombshell on me."

"You did push her."

"I want her to move here, not kill herself." Dee tipped the open can over her mug and watched as a dollop of thickened milk swirled into the amber liquid. "I've been trying to keep my financial situation from her, but she might have guessed. God, she wouldn't kill herself sooner to leave me more money, would she?"

"Lord, no. If she's already talked to her doctor in Ontario, it can't be because of you." She saw Sandy crossing the hall and waved her in. "Tea?"

"I'll take Loreena's up first."

When she returned, Sandy poured a cup for herself and added a generous helping of the canned milk. "Sometimes on a busy shift, the calories in my canned milk were the only lunch I got. That was back in my hospital days — I didn't start working with the seniors until about twenty years ago. I wanted to understand what I'd face. Most old people don't have much family support, or they don't like to ask their families to do the intimate body care, you know. It's easier to ask a nurse, a stranger."

Dee stared into her tea, possibly considering for the first time doing for her mother all the embarrassing personal-hygiene tasks her nurses had done for her during those months in hospital.

"About this assisted dying," Lacey said. "Did you know Loreena was pursuing it? Is it easy to get in Ontario?"

"Yes, I knew. And it depends where you are." Sandy sipped her tea and let out a satisfied sigh. "The public hospitals and secular nursing homes usually have a designated person on staff now to explain things to the patient, and to go through their rights and help them talk to their doctors and their families. Religious hospitals and nursing homes might refuse to provide the counselling, but they have to refer the patient to someone who will. You require two independent medical professionals to be convinced that you're in an incurable decline of health and also mentally competent to make an informed decision. Loreena would qualify right now, but she's worried about being more heavily medicated as her health declines. Too medicated and she won't be considered competent to consent to the procedure."

Dee still said nothing, so Lacey followed up. "What about Alberta is she afraid of?"

"There are a lot of religious people out here," Sandy said. "My son's kids went to a Catholic school for a while, and they were being taught that dying before God takes you is a sin that'll send you to Hell for eternity. And there are all those homeschooling evangelical types, too. Let them get their teeth into anyone's assisted dying application, and it gets ugly fast. Loreena saw a news report about someone signing his dying application in a bus shelter off the hospital grounds, in a rainstorm. She's not strong enough to fight all over again for her rights in Alberta." Sandy raised her mug and then put it down without drinking. "Before you ask her again to move, maybe look into things, Dee. Find out what resistance she could face here."

Dee raised her head. "I'll check it out right away, and if this is really what she wants, I'll support her. But I won't rush her into anything. I want her to be alive as long as she can be. I'm just finding stuff out." She picked up her mug and cane and hobbled off to her office.

When she was out of sight, Sandy said softly, "I didn't want to upset Dee more, but if she intends to stall her mother, please talk her out of it. Loreena is very set on dying before she becomes incapable of providing consent. I don't want her to lose hope. If you take someone's hope away, they may take things into their own hands."

"Suicide, you mean?" The weight doubled on Lacey's shoulders.

Sandy reached for the teapot. "Honestly, I think Loreena would just wait until she was back in Ontario and do it on her own terms, but then she might not tell Dee her plans for fear she'd try to stop her, and they wouldn't get to have a proper goodbye. It's best they work things out while we're here. Now, let's talk about something else. You were a cop, right? And Loreena says you were married to one, too?"

Lacey nodded.

"My husband, Dennis's dad, was a cop, too. Mean bugger at home. Treated the family like suspects, interrogating us instead of having conversations."

Lacey flicked a quick look at the nurse. Until the end, Dan had only used verbal techniques and mind games, usually when Lacey was exhausted after a hard shift, weaseling his way under her skin when she needed wind-down time and sleep, not to have to defend herself against baseless allegations. But he had come at her that last time, a huge escalation into physical attack. She probably should have reported him right then, but who do you call when your abuser's co-workers and shift-mates are the ones who'll respond to an incident report? She looked at Sandy contentedly slurping her tea. It was a comfort to be reminded that not all police wives were sanctimonious poinsettia-posters. Or maybe it was a nurse thing. Tom's wife was a nurse, too, and she hadn't hesitated to back up Lacey when she needed it.

"My friend Marie is married to another RCMP officer, Tom," Lacey said. "I shudder to think what she'd do if he ever tried treating her like a suspect. And she works with mostly women, which makes a difference. I really only came to have friendships with women after I moved in with Dee. Because I was an officer, too, I couldn't seek out support from the other RCMP wives without risking them telling their husbands and having the whole detachment gossiping about our marriage. And I didn't feel any of the male officers would have had my back when it came to going against Dan. Well, except for Tom. He was the closest thing I had to a partner on the Force. Dan used to accuse me of sleeping with him. But most of the male officers, no way. They talked after domestic violence calls like it was more the woman's fault, either for provoking her partner or for not leaving."

Sandy licked her teaspoon. "I understand. Between Den's dad gaslighting me and being a single parent, I didn't have room for female friends either, not until I was nearly forty. Then a woman I worked with, Pat, she moved in down the block from me, and we started carpooling. Before I knew it, I was telling her things I'd never told a soul before, and she didn't bat an eye. Came back with stories of her own screw-ups, and oh, how she would laugh about them. 'You'll laugh, too, soon enough,' she'd say, and eventually I did. She helped me to be stronger during some dark times." She got up and rinsed her mug. "I see that kind of friendship between you and Dee. You treat each other as equals, and you sure don't rub her nose in it that she needs you right now more than you need her."

"I'd say we're about even."

That night Lacey dreamed that Dan was looming over her at their kitchen table in Langley. Fists clenched, he spoke in that low, dangerous voice she'd learned to dread. "You were out with Tom again." She groped for something, anything, to protect herself, and woke with her right hand tangled in the blankets.

As she huddled in the dark, listening to her pounding heart and the warm air hissing through the vents, she thought of Tom and Marie and how they'd given her a no-questions-asked couch to crash on last spring. Marie had lied without blinking when Dan had called there to ask where Lacey was. The police brotherhood protected male officers first, and the wives protected the brotherhood. But Marie had protected her.

CHAPTER NINE

Zoe bumped the van door shut with her hip. "Of course you need a nap. Their plane might be delayed, and you'll end up asleep on a bench at the airport, drooling down your chin for a bunch of tired strangers to see."

"Fine." Lizi flounced into the house.

Zoe sidled through the front door with all her parcels and kicked it closed behind her. For the first time all day, she felt as if she were shutting off that strange gaze whose source she couldn't pin down. She was overtired, that was all. She'd feel better after a proper night's sleep. If not, she'd make a doctor's appointment first thing tomorrow. Her to-do list was too full to wait for a psych referral before medicating.

Nik called from the kitchen, where something sizzled and sent promising aromas through the air. "You're kind of late. A phone call would've been nice."

"Sorry, I had another long list of old contracts to dig up. I'll be so glad when the sale's ready to go forward." And not only because she could finally bill the company for all these hours. With the sale, her old shares of TFB Energy would pay out — and at a premium — rewarding her for all the missed meals and late nights she'd put in when TFB was a brash young start-up taking on the established Alberta oil patch. She hung up her coat and headed to the kitchen to give Nik a kiss.

"Mmm, meat."

"Any luck finding an alternate ski resort?"

"Not so far. Everything is hundreds of bucks a night. Per room."

Nik ran his greasy fingers under the tap. "If I'd known we'd be stuck like this, I wouldn't have invited them for Christmas. We'd get a much better deal on airfare and accommodations in January."

"None of us could've predicted this." Zoe reached for the wine bottle. "And before you say anything, no, we are not spending the holiday at JP's place even if the police clear it. We can't take Lizi back there."

"I know." Nik stirred his concoction. "I hardly get to see my boys, and I promised them a skiing holiday, but I don't see how we can, with the economy so slow. They keep saying it's turning around, but we're only drilling half the wells we did last year."

"Day trips, I guess." Zoe poured two glasses. The red wine swirled, mesmerizing her with its blend of light and dark, like looking into a world just beneath this one, or out a window into the darkness. Out of habit, she looked up at the kitchen window. Her hand jerked, tipping a glass. Nik grabbed it as it fell off the counter. Almost in slow motion, the purplish-red fluid flowed from the glass toward his tan pants. He leaped back and the wine fell to the tiled floor, splashing his pant cuff even as he danced out of the way.

"What the fuck? This was my last work-worthy pair." He gulped the remaining mouthful and set down the glass.

"Sorry." Zoe looked again at the window, her pulse thudding in her ears. There was no face now. No young man out there in the cold, staring in. She was over-tired. She grabbed a dishtowel and dropped it onto the spreading liquid. Even if the stains never came out, replacing one dishtowel was easier than explaining to sensible, grounded Nik that she'd seen a ghost on the deck. She watched the red liquid soak into the yellow towel, turning the cloth a noxious brown, a poison in-side her defences.

Doctor's appointment first thing tomorrow. The nurses kept a slot or two open for emergencies, and this was one of those. She gathered the cloth and wrung it out in the sink, willing away the disruption. "How long until supper? I'll go hunt for discount bookings online."

In the quiet computer room, Zoe first sent her night-ly email to JP, reporting on the progress on his list of files. She didn't mention Eric. Making that first phone call to his family had been too stressful. Each time she'd dialed, she'd been so thoroughly sick with terror that she'd hung up before it rang. What if contact with them pushed her over the edge? Was it even fair for JP to expect her to be liaison when she and Lizi had found the body? Too many jobs, too much responsibility, and now Nik blamed her for ruining his sons' holiday. She liked Kai and Ari just fine, but for all those years of their childhood, she'd worked full-time and more for JP, pay-ing the bills for the Calgary family while Nik's money went back to New Zealand. That was the second wife's burden: her needs and wants came after those of the first family. She could fume about this all night, and had done in the past, but there was no time to work off the anger by cleaning a closet or painting a guest room. They had barely four hours until they had to leave for the airport — time enough to eat, get the beds ready in the downstairs room, and, hopefully, to create an alternative holiday plan.

Lizi wandered into the computer room, her big, fluffy cat overflowing her arms. She kissed it between the ears. "I'm sorry I bitched at you, Mom. You're right, I should have a rest." She leaned on the corner of Zoe's desk. "If ... well, I heard you and Dad, about the money for skiing. I don't want to spoil Kai and Ari's holiday. If you want to take them to the chalet for the week after Christmas, I can stay here."

Zoe leaned over to scratch the cat's neck. "Honey, we'd never leave you here alone, especially at Christmastime. We'll find some way to make this work. Go set the table for Dad, please."

Alone again, she added a final paragraph to her email:

> The police will probably release the chalet soon. I'll know more after I've talked to them tomorrow. Are you sure Arliss can't handle Eric's parents? And should the company have a memorial moment or time off for the funeral, whenever it is?

She hit send and left the room, wondering if she should phone JP's ex-wife directly. They hadn't spoken since Arliss and JP split up, but Arliss might know how her next-door neighbours were handling the loss of their son. Arliss might tell her it was all under control, and she could avoid a meeting that loomed with a weird blend of horror and longing.

After they'd gulped down a quick meal and made up the guest room, Zoe took her own advice and lay down for a nap. But she soon woke again, shivering from a dream in which cold, dead Eric kept opening his eyes and then his mouth, trying to talk to her.

CHAPTER TEN

The sunset above Highway 1 was streaked dirty yellow from diesel exhaust, mirroring Lacey's mood as she sped toward Cochrane. Bull clearly hoped she would convince that fragile teenager to admit she had inadvertently barred the woodshed door herself when she ran from the scene. Well, he'd be disappointed. Pressuring witnesses wasn't Lacey's style, not when she'd been a cop and not now, as a Victim Services volunteer. She could only open the possibility to Lizi of amending her statement. With any luck, she'd also have a chance to sound out Zoe about whether JP Thompson's oil company had any hidden issues — oil spills or whatever — that Eric could have discovered. Anything serious enough to kill him over, that is, though she wouldn't spell out that part for a civilian.

Five minutes later she set her Tims cup on the table across from Lizi. The girl was wearing her pink hat and neon-splashed hoodie again, but her thick black mascara and eyeliner had stayed around her eyes this time instead of running down her cheeks. The dark circles under Zoe's eyes were another story.

"Rough few days?" Lacey asked.

"Nothing unusual for the time of year."

"How about you, Lizi? Things going okay for you?"

Lizi fidgeted with her mug of frothed whatever-it-was. "I might've forgotten to say so, but thanks for hanging out with me out there, after, you know ..."

"No problem." Lacey blew on her coffee. "How are you sleeping?"

"She has nightmares." Zoe took a sip of her black coffee and stared into its depths.

"Just that first night." Lizi gave herself a foamy milk moustache and thoughtfully licked it off. Her phone chirped and she scooped it up.

Lacey tried to get her attention back. "You don't take any medication to help you sleep?"

"Only herbal tea." That was Zoe, again answering for her daughter. "Can you please explain to Lizi what we're doing today?"

Lacey moved her hand on the table, dragging Lizi's eyes away from her phone. "You'll read a typed copy of the statement you gave to the sergeant out at the chalet. If you want to add something you forgot then, or clarify something that you said, you can change it. Don't worry that the police will think you lied. People often overlook things or say them in the wrong order during a stressful time. The staff will type up any changes and print out a new copy for you to sign. That will only take ten minutes or so. Do you have any concerns?"

Lizi's eyes slid to her mother, but Zoe was still staring silently into her coffee as though the secrets of the universe lurked in its shifting darkness. "There's nothing to change," she said. "I broke the ice, lifted the bar, and yanked the door as far as it would come through the snow. I squeezed inside, and when I saw him, I screamed and ran out." She turned her mug around on the table, studying the foam.

"The ice — Zoe, could you see that from the kitchen?"

"The door was covered in it, all gleaming in the sun."

"And the crossbar?"

"It was hanging from its bolt when I got there. I went in. I called to him. I touched him on his cheek to see if he blinked. But he was so cold." Her eyes lifted. "I can't remember if I told the sergeant I touched him. Will it make a difference? Can we go right away and get this over with?"

Half an hour later, reading through her statement at the RCMP detachment, Zoe raised the point again. "So I did tell you about touching him, sergeant. That's a relief. I was pretty shocked then, and worried about Lizi. That's the first dead body she's ever seen."

Sergeant Drummond focused his attention fully on Zoe, putting Lacey in mind of a dog's ears twitching to a sound too high for humans to hear. *Lizi's first*. Lacey's old cop senses had picked up the same phrasing. Was Zoe implying she, herself, had seen dead bodies before?

Of course, neither of them would ask her in front of her daughter.

Lacey pushed back her chair. "Sergeant, did I see the canine unit out front? Can I show Lizi the dog? If he's still here?"

"I'm a cat person," said Lizi, but she followed Lacey outside.

Bull Drummond shifted into the chair Lizi had vacated.

The police dog was a hit — or maybe it was the dog's handler, who was no more than twenty-five, broad-shouldered and bashful. When had that age started to look young to Lacey? People in their thirties were not supposed to be rehabilitating friends and nursing dying mothers. They should be taking adventure vacations and rising through the ranks at work. Lacey's life belonged to someone thirty years older. She watched Lizi watch the handler demonstrate basic commands. What it was to be young and innocent. At Lizi's age, she hadn't yet met Dee or Dan, much less joined the RCMP.

When Zoe emerged from Sergeant Drummond's office, she looked more haggard than before. She thanked Lacey and added, "JP, the chalet's owner, asked me to be his liaison with Eric's family. Is there anything else I can tell them, like when they can make funeral arrangements?"

"Sergeant Drummond didn't say?"

"All he said was that the investigation is ongoing." Zoe put her hand to her forehead and closed her eyes briefly. "I'm not looking forward to seeing that family, but I promised."

This was hardly the time to start grilling the woman about TFB Energy's company secrets. Maybe Dee's acquaintance, Marcia, could help with the business angle. Lacey made a mental note to ask.

When the mother and daughter had left the building, Bull came out of the statement room and gestured for Lacey to join him in his office.

As soon as they were inside, she asked, "Did Zoe say anything about previous dead bodies?"

Bull dropped into his chair, which groaned alarmingly. "She said her comment was a general concern, and she'd never actually touched one before Tuesday." He rubbed a huge hand over his five o'clock shadow. "One strange thing, though. She asked if the police ever take tips from psychics. Think she plans to anonymously phone something in?"

"Damned if I know. I was going to gently probe her for information about the company she works for, but I've got no official standing to ask directly, and I'm out of Victim Services reasons to follow up. She told me she's the oil company's liaison with Eric Anders's family. I'm not their Victim Services contact, but should I check on them, too?"

"They have their own VS, and I hope some relatives have stepped up by now. That mom is a wreck. The search went on for a week once Black Rock's road was plowed, but the kid's Camry probably won't be found 'til spring, if ever. Another scab for the family to rip off just when they might be starting to heal." Bull rubbed his stubble again. "We've reviewed every statement from when he was first reported missing, followed up with everyone by phone or in person. There's no viable motive for killing him. Unless he picked up a hitchhiker who locked him in the shed and stole his car."

Lacey hitched her hip onto the corner of the desk. "An intern heading to his boss's place picks up a hitch-hiker and takes him along for the ride? Unlikely."

"Really long shot, I know." Bull waved at the map behind his desk. "There's a lot of wilderness to hide a vehicle in. We sent up drones, but even a red car won't show through metres of new snow or tree cover. It's mostly evergreens out that way. That one small corner of my turf has more tree-filled gullies and sharp drop-offs than anywhere else in K Division."

Lacey looked over the map. Black Rock was a long way from anything resembling civilization. If Eric hadn't been inside a building, protected from predators, he might have stayed on the missing list in perpetuity. "Two questions: how did he get locked in the woodshed? And was he dead or alive when the bar was dropped?"

"Autopsy established he wasn't moved after he died, and it was hypothermia that killed him. Unless one of our outstanding interviews explains how that door got barred, this file goes to Major Crimes. I'll break the news to the family myself, but I'm hoping it won't come to that. Not before Christmas."

"Who do you have left to speak to?"

"The resort manager is checking his files for which employee cleared that chalet after the storm, and we're waiting on the snow plow contractor to get back from Mexico. He might have noticed the shed door when he first cleared the driveway, and slung the bar over without looking inside."

"Slim chance. But you have to check everything. You'll let me know either way?"

"Can't hurt." He grabbed the next file off his in-tray. She was dismissed.

As she walked back to the Lexus, she thought again about the oil company and Eric's internship. Someone there might have tried to prevent him from seeing the boss. But why? And could she find out in time for Dee to sell the chalet before their joint finances got so dire she had to sell the roof over their own heads instead?

With her sleeves and shirt front coated in archival dust, Zoe backed out of the file racks. A grey-white cloud rose as she dropped the files onto the table. Sneezing, she flipped gingerly through the oldest deals, with her own decade-old handwriting annotating the scrawls of long-departed contractor workers. The number seven with a little crossbar, she recalled, belonged to Gunter, who'd gone home to Bavaria when his mother died, and then there was the Land guy who wrote the four that looked like a nine. Or was it a nine that looked like a four? Pete from Red Deer. Well sites in Jumping Pound, Sundre, Nordegg, Caroline ... all the wells they'd drilled a decade or more ago. Some were still producing, while others had been sold off for stripping. A few had been swapped for blocks of land closer to TFB's higher-producing sites for tie-in. She was sure those good wells into the Cardium Formation had been drilled in 2007 — they'd celebrated for a week when those all came in — but the original contracts did not seem to be down here. If there was a production-cap share clause like the one she vaguely remembered discussing, it would have to be included in the pre-sale report. Someone in Accounting might have the files on their desk right now, to check payment history or follow up with a sub-contractor. But which someone?

Marcia, the acting head of Accounting, stuck her head into the dingy basement room. "How's it going in here? Anything I can help with?"

"Before your time, I'm afraid." Zoe shoved her bangs aside with one dusty hand. "Who in your department would I ask about checking the payment history for our Cardium wells?"

"Cardium?" Marcia frowned. "Is that an oil company? I don't remember seeing any invoices under that name."

Zoe looked down at the files, hiding the incredulity that she was sure showed on her face. After nearly four years working in the oil patch, now as acting head of Accounting, Marcia still didn't know the difference between a world-famous oil-producing geologic formation and the oil-production companies that drilled wells into it? She let out a slow breath. "Cardium," she explained, "is a thousand-kilometre long geologic formation along the eastern side of the Rockies, with thrusts out into the plains, in which a vast reservoir of hydrocarbons is trapped between layers of black mudstone. The biggest, highest-producing oilfields in Alberta sit on top of it. The Pembina field, for example?"

Marcia looked blank.

"Pembina is the super-field of the Alberta oil patch. Dozens of companies, ours included, have blocks of land rights there. 'Our Cardium wells' means the wells this company has drilled into that formation." She paused, trying to think how to avoid underlining Marcia's complete uselessness while still getting the information she needed. "The wells all have individual identification numbers. I can send my request to whoever is the current senior production accountant. They'll know." They might not know right off who had the missing files but they'd recognize the well reference and know who to ask.

Marcia's face cleared. "That's Kim, but she's on mat leave. Send me a note and I'll figure out who's covering her job."

Wonderful. Zoe had noticed things seemed to be drifting in JP's absence, but had HR not bothered to assign a temporary production accountant? The year-end books would be a disaster if someone with serious petroleum accounting experience didn't take the reins very soon. Well, nothing she could do but put that information into her nightly report to JP. Preferably in upper-case, bolded, bright-red font. She pulled up a smile that felt as constrained as Marcia's accounting experience.

"That will help, thanks. While I have you here, about Eric Anders's death ... should there be a company gathering? Coffee and donuts or something? Or should we just say that anyone who wants to attend the funeral can do so?"

"I see no need. He was only here for two months, and to be honest ... JP wouldn't like me to say this, but Eric wasn't working out. He was supposed to be learning Information Technology, but he was always nosing around other departments, disrupting their staff. I talked to JP about terminating his internship, but Eric was his old neighbour's son and could do no wrong in his eyes."

"So, no need for a company-wide event then," said Zoe. A chill crept across her neck. Time to get out of this cold basement. "I'll find out the time and place of the funeral in case anyone wants to go. Someone ought to represent JP."

"Better you than me," said Marcia. "I'm leading winter survival and ski-trekking courses every spare minute."

The accountant was halfway out of the room before Zoe's brain made a connection. "Marcia?"

The bigger woman turned back. "Hmm?"

"Ski trekking, would that be something my family could do over the break? My stepsons are visiting and we were supposed to have a ski week, but it's been cancelled."

"My lessons are single-day and half-day only. Do your stepsons cross-country ski at all?"

"I'm not sure," Zoe confessed. "I know they snowboard."

"If they want to learn cross-country, I can teach them the basics in a couple of hours. But it would have to be after Christmas."

"Thanks. I'll ask at supper and get back to you."

"No problem." Marcia turned away again, then stopped. "You know the ski lift is running weekdays at Black Rock now, right? Started this week for the holidays. You could take them out there to snowboard."

Faced with explaining to this tough wilderness woman why she wasn't up to taking Lizi or herself back to a place where they'd found a body, Zoe smiled weakly. "Good to know. Well, I'd better get back to these files. Thanks for your help."

Alone again, she hauled another dusty stack of folders from the rack. She found original contracts for two more share wells, but not the Cardium ones. Bloody nuisance. She texted the land numbers up to Marcia, then re-shelved everything except the files she'd need to photocopy.

Something clicked behind her. She turned. Was that a person's shadow in the hallway? Any sound of footsteps was lost as a bus rumbled by on Sixth Avenue, setting the window grilles vibrating. Maybe it was a flicker made by someone walking past at sidewalk level outside. But the feeling that she was not alone down here was creeping up her spine. She grabbed the stack of folders, closed and locked the file-room door, and hurried to the elevator. As she waited for it to arrive, she alternated between willing the glowing button to turn green and peering over her shoulder at the empty corridor. When the elevator door began to open, she was almost sure she saw a face peering over her reflected shoulder. She whirled around, but there was nobody in the hallway.

Hallucination. She'd overslept and forgotten to make the doctor's appointment. If she went home and had a good nap this afternoon, would it stop?

Up on the fifth floor, feeling safer and more grounded, she settled into Accounting's dedicated printer room to copy papers that would interest any potential purchasers of TFB Energy. One of the recent employees, a blond in her early twenties whose name Zoe couldn't remember even though she'd been introduced only a few days ago, came in looking for a report that should have been sent in from a field office to one of the printers.

The woman sighed as she looked around the room. "It feels like there's a third person in here." Meeting Zoe's eyes, she added quickly, "Sorry, I know that sounds crazy. But the IT department had an intern, Eric, who was in here a lot unjamming machines, and we used to chat. I guess I still feel like he should be here. I'm very sensitive to people's leftover vibrations. Even more than my auntie who reads tarot cards."

Zoe picked up the next document and pretended to skim it while she digested the implications of the comment. Maybe she was not alone in sensing a presence. Maybe it was Eric's "vibrations." She slid the page into the copier, searching her mind for a pretext to prolong the conversation.

"Eric didn't disturb your work?" she asked.

"Oh no. He was great. Totally into what I was doing. I showed him how the monthly reports get compiled and a lot of other little things about accounting." Blondie smiled. "I think he was crushing on me."

"I heard he wasn't popular with the other workers."

Blondie cast a glance over her shoulder. "He wasn't popular with our acting chief. She distrusts all the younger guys. Maybe they used to egg her house at Halloween or something." She looked around the room again. "It sure feels like Eric is still around somewhere. I'm going to light a candle in my office for him so he feels welcome. Do you know when the funeral will be?"

"Not yet. I'll send out a memo when I find out."

As Blondie departed, muttering about lying liars in field offices, Zoe looked around the small room. So, this had been a regular stop in Eric's day. Could his spirit have followed her from the woodshed, hoping to find a familiar place? What if she wasn't crazy? What if she was, like Blondie, sensing his leftover aura or whatever? When she'd cracked up as a teen, the voice she'd kept hearing was a dead neighbour's, and then only after the new owners of his house knocked down his backyard workshop. There'd been no room for this kind of thinking in her mother's version of the Greek Orthodox religion, however, and after the prayer circle failed to cure her of the "demonic influence," as her mother called it, Zoe had been so terrified of being possessed that she couldn't fall asleep. Sleep deprivation could also cause hallucinations. Maybe the combination of the two had put her in the psych ward. Maybe she'd never been truly psychotic.

As she returned the folders and the photocopies to the appropriate stacks in her temporary office down the hall, Zoe struggled to recall any aunts who'd read tarot cards or done other strange things. She could call Nana, but would Nana talk about this honestly, or would she tell Mama, who would call in her priest for an exorcism? Was it worth the risk of starting another round of *How crazy is Zoe, anyway?*

She drove home through the lunchtime rush, half listening to the noon-hour call-in show on the radio. Today's oddball guest swore his dead mother had told him where to find her lost diamond ring. "My mom hadn't worn makeup in fifteen years, but there was the ring, slipped around her mascara tube. My daughter got engaged three days later wearing it."

He sounded so convinced that his mother had communicated with him. Was it remotely possible Eric's ghost was trying to communicate with her? Maybe if she saw his family, he would transfer to haunting them. Or she could go back to the scene where he was found and see if that would put her own haunted thoughts to rest.

When she reached home, Kai and Ari were eating cereal at the kitchen table. Kai got up. "I made coffee. Want some?"

"Thanks." She accepted a mug and pulled up a stool to the counter. "There's eggs and ham and stuff in the fridge."

"No place to work it off," said Ari. "All we've done since early yesterday is sit around in airports and airplanes, eating junk."

Kai nodded. "Is there someplace we could go to swim or work out?"

Zoe swallowed a sigh. Spend the afternoon hauling her stepsons to rec facilities, or get this ghost issue sorted? Or … maybe there was a way to do both.

"It's short notice, but would you guys like to go snowboarding? That ski chalet has snowboards and lift tickets. I could take you there. As long as you don't mention it to Lizi. She'd be horrified." She watched the grins spread over their almost-matching faces. Kai's was wider, more open, like his nature, and Ari's was a bit more reserved. They both looked very much like their dad.

A quarter hour later, Zoe took a mug of red pepper soup into her office and Googled *psychics*, *ghostly presences*, and a few other terms before realizing she could sit there reading all day without finding a trustworthy answer. She slid her office door shut, opened her address book, and found her grandmother's phone number.

If Nana was surprised to hear from her, it didn't last long. Nor did she laugh when Zoe finally asked outright about ancestors who might have talked to ghosts.

"I wondered if that would turn up again in you or your daughter."

"Inherited psychosis?" Zoe held her breath.

"Hardly psychosis, dear. Just a quirk that shows up in some families from the old country. Usually in teenage girls." Nana's voice sharpened. "Was that your trouble in high school? Your mother skated all around the subject."

"That was it. A neighbour died." Weights rolled off Zoe's shoulders. "So I'm not crazy?"

"Well, probably not. I wish your papa had told me what was going on. It was my cousin Tiana with the ghosts. She came to live with us one summer, haunted by a man in her village who had recently died. The way she told it to me was that he wanted her to tell a woman — not his wife — that he still loved her. Tiana didn't dare pass along the message, but he kept pestering her, even in her bedroom at night, which was quite terrifying for a girl of our generation."

"What did she do in the end?"

"Confessed to the priest." Nana sighed. "Naturally he told her it was the devil tempting her to cause strife. He forbade her to mention it, and she faithfully kept telling the ghost to bugger off, but then people started whispering about her talking to people who weren't there. Her parents sent her to us to get her away from all that."

"And did she? Get away from it, I mean? The ghost didn't follow her?"

"It didn't. But she did see other ghosts after that, later, as an adult."

Zoe tipped back her chair and stared at the window blinds. Sunlight glanced off the edge of every slat, like a jail cell with bars made of light. Would she have the courage to open those blinds and look beyond, to possibly face a dead boy out there looking back at her?

"What did she do about it, Nana? Whenever she saw a ghost after that?"

"She sat quietly and asked what they wanted. When they told her — if they told her — she would either tell them she would try, or she'd say they should talk to somebody else."

"Talk to them? That's it?" Zoe tipped her chair down again. The furnace cut in and the blind slats wavered, showing her a glimpse of the bright outdoors. No ghost.

"That's it. If you or Lizi are being bothered by a ghost, I suggest you ask it what it wants. But not where anybody else can hear you."

A couple of hours later, Zoe turned off the van and looked out at the snow-dusted steps of JP's chalet. There hadn't been much of a lineup at the chairlift on a Thursday afternoon, and Kai and Ari were probably halfway up the mountain already. She guessed she had about three hours to herself before it got too dark for snowboarding. If this was the ghost of Eric, he had better show her a sign, and then she could tell him to buzz off. After that, she could start the inventory of sports equipment and furnishings that JP was sure to decide he needed. He might be ruled by Phyl in where he lived going forward, but he had a lot of good memories bound up in Black Rock Bowl, some of which he might want to keep.

CHAPTER ELEVEN

Lacey cracked the window open to let in the crisp mountain air. Sunlight sparkled on snowy boughs, and small birds flickered in the trees. The yard with the Christmas decorations appeared, its myriad lights pale starbursts of colour against the white background.

Dee smiled at her from the passenger seat. "We'll have lots of days like this. More sun than cloud, as many warm as cold, afternoons ideal for skiing, snowshoeing, and snowmobiling, or simply walking through a glorious winter forest." She looked down at her phone again. "I should have made time to go through those boxes of decorations and pick out the best stuff. Staging 101: a few high-toned holiday touches will make a property seem the perfect Christmas gift for an oil baron's teenage kids or trophy wife, without us having to decorate the whole place. We'll do outdoor and window shots while we have the sun, minimally decorate one tree to try in different corners, and see what other shortcuts are possible."

Lacey steered the SUV over the short log bridge. The creek below cut through the trees, its banks edged with jagged ice. "Where does that creek go, anyway?"

"To Ghost River. It's not far. Look — all the shops are open, and the ski lift is running. I guess the holiday schedule has officially started. You'd never get a ski bus up that road, which is all that keeps the plebs out."

"Oh, right. No hotels, either. I guess they don't sell ski-week packages here."

Dee nodded. "You don't ski here unless you can afford a good four-wheel drive and a million-dollar chalet. That's my target market."

They followed the road up the Bowl's south shoulder. Lacey turned in at JP's chalet, following a set of fresh tire tracks in the snow. Pulling up near the porch, she frowned. "That looks like the same blue van that was here the other day. Zoe Gallagher's."

Dee peered at the bumper. "Yeah, it's got that Dungeons & Dragons bumper sticker I stared at for half an hour while I was waiting for you. Why's she back? Staging the photos will be impossible if the place is filled with family clutter."

"One way to find out." Lacey opened her door and stepped out. "Can you walk that far, or should I ask her to move her van?"

"I'll go ask." Dee swung her legs out. "You stay here and park closer when the van's out of the way." She clambered up the steps and opened the front door.

Lacey sat in the SUV, the sunlight warming her arm right through her coat. The remains of the crime scene tape fluttered from the woodshed. It could be gone by this time tomorrow if only someone would come forward to say they'd accidentally barred the door without checking inside.

A few minutes later, Zoe came out, waved, and moved the van over to the garage. Lacey pulled up as close to the front door as she could get and started unloading the decorations. When she got the first boxes inside, she realized there was no family to work around. Only Zoe was here. She'd come in through the back door to the kitchen and was perched on a stool, chatting to Dee in an atmosphere of strained politeness. Once she'd gotten the box holding Jan's biggest tree inside, Lacey kicked off her boots and joined them. An electric kettle hissed on the countertop, and a teapot sat lidless, waiting for hot water.

Dee filled Lacey in, her voice giving no hint of her thoughts. "Zoe is doing inventory for JP. Contrary to what he told me, she thinks he'll keep some of the furnishings and sporting equipment. I was about to phone him, so I don't mislead potential buyers." She hobbled out to the living room and gazed out the great front windows.

Lacey looked over at Zoe, who still seemed worn out, but not as deathly pale as she had been the day before. "I'd have sworn you'd never want to see this place again."

"I didn't." The kettle clicked, and Zoe warmed the teapot. As she rummaged for teabags, she added, "My daughter panics at the thought."

What are you really doing out here? Lacey was keenly aware she had no standing to ask questions; she wasn't a cop anymore. This wasn't her investigation. She was Victim Services, though, and this mother and daughter were her concern.

"How was Lizi after the statement signing? Has she had any more nightmares?"

Zoe shook her head. "She's tired today, but that's because we made a midnight airport run. Her half brothers arrived late yesterday from New Zealand. Otherwise she seems okay. I think she's moving past it."

"And you? Are you able to move past it?"

Zoe set the teapot down. "I wish I could. I still have to go see Eric's parents."

"I've heard his mother is taking it very hard."

Whatever Zoe might have been about to say was forgotten as Dee hobbled in. "Is that spiced tea I smell?"

"Some exotic blend Phyl bought." Zoe shrugged. "There are lots of gourmet treats here, too. We'll have to dispose of those if the place sells."

Dee opened a few cupboards. "JP says the dishes and kitchen appliances all go with, and the snowmobiles can be thrown in as a sweetener. Did he mention to you that you can take any of the skis and other snow equipment you want?"

Zoe poured tea into three mugs. "Uh-huh. I'll donate any extra stuff to one of the kids' charities TFB supports. There's more sports stuff his kids have outgrown at his Calgary house. If this had happened a few weeks earlier, there'd be Christmas charities lining up for it. It's all high-end and barely used."

Lacey's eyebrows popped. "You have keys to his Calgary house?"

Dee gave her an indecipherable look. "She was JP's confidential assistant for years. I didn't realize that. He trusts you completely, doesn't he, Zoe? He said you'll give access codes to the realtors when he sells it."

Zoe looked up from the tea things. "So, he's going ahead with that, too? Or, more accurately, his wife has convinced him to sell every Canadian asset. He warned me it might happen."

Lacey exchanged a glance with Dee. "What else is he selling? This chalet, his house in Calgary, and?"

"The company. He's got me digging through old files, making sure all the loose ends are tied off, assembling a package for potential buyers to show assets and liabilities and quirky little deals that have yet to play out. All confidential so far, because the vultures will start to circle if they think the company's vulnerable. Phyl, his wife, wants them to live in England, where she comes from. They're house hunting over there as we speak."

While Dee and Zoe sipped their tea and discussed the possible arrangement of Christmas decorations, Lacey clambered through snowbanks shooting the chalet's exterior. After a complete circuit, she stamped and brushed the excess snow off herself on the front porch before bringing the camera into the foyer. She'd tried to follow Dee's instructions: don't shoot into the sun, get some unusual angles, and if you're shooting windows, check what they're reflecting. The windows on the end opposite the drive were all blank, smothered in heavy, dark drapes, a complete waste of her effort traipsing through drifts that were up to her thighs in places. Hopefully Dee didn't want any more photos of those. Did Bull realize the owner of this crime scene was selling every possession that tied him to Canada? If he'd only decided to do so after the death of his intern … well, there could be something there …

The thought nibbled at her concentration through the next hour, while she coped with Jan's mother-in-law's giant white Christmas tree. Under Dee's direction, she looped it with silvery-blue ribbon and moved it between the big front windows and the fireplace ell, adjusting the ribbons according to Dee's directions to better catch sunlight or the camera's flash. While she was outside fighting snowbanks, Zoe had looped garland up the stairs and added clusters of Christmas balls at intervals. Those got close-ups. Dee had arranged a display of figurines over the fireplace and twined lacy white garland around them. She shot those from several angles, too, and then sat down to go through the images while Zoe helped Lacey repack. The whole process took barely two hours. Staging 101, indeed.

As Lacey toted the decorations back to the Lexus, she pondered Zoe's helpfulness. How much of her motivation was loyalty to JP, and how much was a determination to put this place and its connotations behind her? Would she cover for JP if he had accidentally — or on purpose — locked his intern in the woodshed and left him to die?

As the sun slipped down behind Black Rock Mountain, lengthening shadows stalked the SUV down the road. Under the yellowish smudges of parking-lot lights, a few weary snowboarders and skiers trudged toward their vehicles. An Alberta Sheriffs truck made a slow circuit around the town square, a visual warning to the snowboarders against lighting up their pot before they drove. She'd done the same thing times out of mind as a patrol constable in the Lower Mainland —

not around snowboarding sites, but outside skateboard parks, rock concerts, any venue that attracted the young and heedless. Oh, the old days, when she'd had access to the whole Canada-wide RCMP database to check up on people who did something suspicious. Not that she was completely cut off. Besides Bull, there was Tom, who owed his life to her quick action when he was stabbed seven years ago. He now worked Commercial Crimes in Calgary. If there was anything fishy about JP's oil company, Tom or someone he worked with might know about it.

Dee looked over at her as they crossed the log bridge. "That Zoe woman ... when I first caught sight of her, she was sitting cross-legged on the floor by the fireplace, holding a piece of firewood over her head and talking out loud. I thought there must be someone else in there with her, in another room, maybe. But she was alone."

"Her phone?"

"Nope. It was in the kitchen. She turned it on to check messages later."

"A bit weird." Lacey slowed to admire the swaths of coloured lights in a lone, snowy yard. "She seemed generally level-headed over the statement yesterday."

"Yeah. It's like she's two different people: one rational and competent enough to be completely trusted by JP, the other talking to people who aren't there. When I came in, I tapped the snow off my cast and she said, 'If that's really you, tap again.' I said something like 'I beg your pardon,' and she leaped up like a scalded cat." Dee flicked to the next image on her camera. "It was just weird."

They reached home too late to eat with Dee's mother. Loreena had eaten some soup, Sandy reported, and was already upstairs for the night. "She's taken it into her head to go to a Blue Christmas service in Calgary tomorrow. She saw it on the evening news and figures it'll ease you into the grieving process."

Dee shrugged off her coat and slung it over its hook in the mudroom. "I'll go up and see how she's doing. Lacey, can you scrounge us up something for supper?"

"Oh, and I want to run you through her bedtime routine," Sandy added. "Tomorrow night is my first overnight with my grandkids. You can phone me there if you need additional instructions, but I'll feel more comfortable leaving her if we go through it all thoroughly tonight."

Briefly alone in the kitchen, Lacey rested her forehead against the gleaming black fridge. For a decade she had handled dozens of emergencies per shift and bounced back, but now that her life was mundane, she was exhausted by the months of caring for Dee. No gym, no winter running, no outlet for the unending buildup of stress hormones except the regular dog walking, because if she slipped and fell and was out of commission, both she and Dee would be up the creek. Now Sandy was prepping to leave, adding the weight of Loreena's physical and emotional well-being onto Lacey's shoulders. The end of her rope was knotted in her hands and there was nothing else to stop her from falling. If she fell, Dee and Loreena fell with her. The reflection of her tired eyes stared back at her from the glossy black depths of the fridge door.

CHAPTER TWELVE

Kai and Ari were quiet on the drive home, worn out from jet lag and their high-energy afternoon. The silence suited Zoe. Her brain bounced between two distinct personalities: the calm, focused executive assistant who was enjoying the challenges of JP's massive life-and-business transition, and the woman who had just tried to talk to a ghost by tapping on the fireplace grate with a piece of wood.

When they got home, Nik was making supper. "There's a message for you on the house answering machine," he said. "You should take it in the office."

"Only telemarketers use that line. Who's it from?"

"You'll see." He splashed balsamic into a sauce pot. "I'll call you when we're ready to eat."

Zoe ditched her coat, poured a glass of wine for herself, and shut the computer room door behind her, muting the family's voices. She slumped in her office chair and pushed the button on the old answering machine.

"Hello, Zoe? It's Arliss Thompson. I realize it's been a few years since we spoke, but JP finally got around to telling me you're back at work." It was JP's first wife.

She'd been the company's office administrator for its first decade, a blunt general who kept everyone marching in the same direction. Zoe had waffled for days now about shunting responsibility to her for Eric Anders's family. It meant disobeying JP's direct command, but if Arliss wanted to be involved, Zoe could leap off of a particularly unwelcome hook.

Arliss went on, "JP says you're the company's representative to the Anders family. If you haven't spoken to them yet, you might want some background. Call me back if you do. Hell, call me back regardless. I'm still a twenty-five percent shareholder in TFB, after all. I have a right to know what's going on."

Uh-oh. She sounded militant. JP had clearly been his usual tactless self.

"Nik," Zoe yelled over her shoulder. "How long until supper?"

"Twenty minutes, give or take."

"Yell really loud in fifteen, can you, please? If Arliss is on the warpath, I'll need an out." She picked up the landline. Until she knew what mood the older woman was in, no way was she revealing her current cell number.

"I blame you for none of this," were the first words out of Arliss Thompson's mouth.

"Thank you." What else what there to say?

"How long have you known JP's moving to England?"

Her loyalty to JP had never necessitated lying to Arliss. "Less than two weeks."

"And what about the company sale?"

"He first approached me in mid-November. Succession planning, he said then. I didn't find out he actually planned to sell until December." Zoe gulped down a mouthful of wine. "He sprang the rest on me when he offered me the chalet for the holidays. It was a scramble to get Nik's boys here."

"I can imagine." Arliss's voice was grim. "Well, I found out on the fifteenth, when my eldest informed me that they're all going to be spending Christmas not in Calgary or Black Rock, but in a fancy hotel in London. JP is supposed to consult me about any holiday plans. Frannie and Ben are both still minors. He needs my permission to take them out of the country. If not for that fact, I probably still wouldn't know."

"TJ chose to go, too?" Arliss's older boy had been navigating between his parents since he was ten.

"He says he has to fly over with the younger ones." Arliss grudgingly added, "He's got a point. They've never flown unaccompanied before. But we usually split the holidays — one house for Christmas and the other for New Year's. Now JP says the kids will be in England until the school term starts, and he's not coming back at all. I'm supposed to let my kids go jetting off to England for holidays for the rest of their lives and not say boo about it? I can't compete with that. JP's net worth tripled the first year after our divorce. Mine flatlined. Now the kids are aging out of child support and this house is just plain aging. I'm losing ground, Zoe, and he's retiring at fifty-five to live like a bloody English country squire." She ranted away for a bit longer, then veered back on topic. "Anyway, about Eric. Of course I knew he was missing — I still live next door to his family — but now they say he was found at our ski shack. What the hell is going on?"

Zoe's mind snapped back to that bright winter afternoon: Lizi's screams, the police, the cloud that had hung around her ever since. "I'd like to know what the hell is going on, too. Lizi found his body in the woodshed. We called the police. We had to give formal statements. She's had nightmares."

"Oh, god, I'm so sorry." Arliss paused. "I had no idea it was you who found him. Poor Lizi! And here's me dumping all my crap on you. How are you coping?"

Being haunted by your dead neighbour. "I'm not sure. I just get up every day and tackle the to-do list."

Arliss clucked. "And cry later, because that's how us women get through."

"Yeah, pretty much."

"Listen, honey, I'd take this off your plate if I could, but the Anders are my neighbours. If they think I'm being supportive just to keep the company off the hook, it could backfire. Their daughter is Frannie's age, and Eric and TJ were inseparable until they hit puberty and went off to separate schools. Eric's brother and sister — Aidan and Clematis — need a stable adult right now like never before, and I'm all they've got handy."

"What about their parents?"

"God, no. Eric was Leslie's darling. She's been weeping in her room since the day he disappeared. Her husband, Brian, he travels a lot with his well services company. Even when he's home, he's completely checked out. Aidan — he's the eldest — more or less raised his little sister. He has his own apartment, but he's been staying at home a lot lately."

"I don't quite understand what JP expects me to do. 'Keep them from suing,' seems to be his entire game plan."

Arliss sighed. "It's to everyone's benefit for this not to get uglier. I'm sure you and I can cope together. Check back with you in the morning?"

Zoe set down the receiver with new hope in her heart. The load was shared. Arliss knew the family and could help Zoe be supportive with minimal time away from work and her own family. She went to supper smiling and had a truly enjoyable evening playing board games with the gang. No ghostly faces, no work calls, no shadow over the evening — but, still, the looming problem of how to give the kids their skiing getaway without breaking the bank. She went to bed tired and almost happy as the first local evening news report came up on the rec room TV.

The house phone rang when she was on the fuzzy edge of sleep. The bedroom door opened. "Hey," Nik whispered. "You still awake? It's Arliss again. She says it's important."

Zoe reached a hand out from under the duvet and wrapped her fingers around the phone. "Uh-huh?"

"I hoped you'd stayed up for the news. I've got a way for you to do something for Eric's family that will be fairly low stress but still force them out of their bubble."

"Yeah?" Zoe struggled to sit up. "I'm listening."

"You ever heard of a Blue Christmas church service?"

CHAPTER THIRTEEN

As the pipe organ's deep tones swelled, Lacey found herself standing at parade rest in the pew as if she were in the RCMP chapel at Depot. Except for a few weddings in the intervening decade, that was the last time she'd been to church. No sea of red serge here, though. It was a motley congregation — all ages, sizes, and modes of dress. On her left, Dee sang valiantly along to a hymn neither of them had heard since high school. On her right, in a wheelchair slot cut out of the pew, Loreena sat with her eyes closed, trembling lips whispering the words she lacked the energy to sing. Around them, voices lifted and trailed away. Someone's cellphone chimed and was hastily silenced. Lacey's phone was in her jacket, muted, but that text from Bull, received as she was walking into the building, reverberated through her bones. *Plow guy never left his machine.* The chalet was officially a crime scene. The case would go to Major Crimes on Monday. She hadn't told Dee the news yet. Let her have this hour, this evening, to be with her mother and not stress about that chalet sale.

The organ's last note faded and the readings on grieving — some biblical and some secular — began. The readers' faces floated in cones of old-gold light from antique hanging lamps. The glow hardly reached the huddled groups and solo strangers in the pews. How many had come to mark a murder victim? How many domestic violence? Alberta had the highest rate of domestic violence in Canada. According to the ratio of abusive spouses to non-abusers, some in this room had to be abusers themselves. Statistically, more abusers occupied these pews on Sundays, probably unashamed because the church preached the subordination of women to their husbands. To drive the message home, one stained glass window showed women kneeling at the feet of a man. So much domestic violence had its roots in buildings like this one.

Someone in the row behind her stifled a sob. A pew creaked as someone else shifted, murmured comforting words. A few rows up sat a man with one thick arm slung over the shoulders of the boy beside him. The boy was staring down at a handheld gaming device, his dark curls haloed by the blue light from the tiny screen. The same light kissed a tear rolling down the man's cheek. So much sadness gathered into one building. Did this Blue Christmas service really comfort people?

Loreena's hand touched hers. Lacey wrapped her fingers around the frail ones and understood from their twitch that she should take Dee's hand. Around them, other pairs and groups linked up, too. There they all sat during a final melancholy musical performance, and none of the three let go, not even when the reverend offered a blanket invitation to a post-service social down in the church hall. Holding each other together for whatever lay ahead. Next December she would suggest to Dee that they come again, to remember Loreena and this moment. There was comfort in that thought. She squeezed the yellow fingers gently before releasing them.

As people stood and fastened their coats, Dee leaned across. "Mom, do you want to attend that social?"

"No. Can we wait here until most people are gone, though?" Loreena leaned away from the crowded aisle. "I'd like a few peaceful minutes near the altar, if they're going to leave the candles lit. Lacey, you can go get the car if you want. I don't expect you to stay a minute longer here when this all makes you uncomfortable."

"I'll wait and get you up to the front. Dee, can you hobble that far?"

"I'll stay here." Dee stopped short of pulling out her phone, but Lacey had seen her fingers twitch toward her pocket more than once during the service. She was probably dying to get back online and tweak her photo layout to send out to prospective buyers at the earliest possible moment. Lacey would have to kill her hopes once they were home. Promoting a Christmassy chalet the day it was featured in the local news as the site of a suspicious death could seriously damage its prospects for sale.

Lacey parked Loreena's chair close enough that she could see the cross and breathe the spicy scent of the evergreen baskets on their dark wooden pedestals. "How's this?"

"Perfect. Thank you, dear. I really appreciate what you're doing for me, and for Dee. I'm glad you'll be with her when I'm gone."

Lacey summoned a smile that felt as shaky as Loreena's hands. "I'll do my best for both of you, as long as you do your best to stick around until Dee is ready for you to go." That was as close as she could come to saying *Please don't kill yourself*. She left the two in their separate solitudes and slid between clusters of mourners in the foyer. Snippets of conversation floated past as she headed for the door.

"I didn't know you lost someone this year, too."

"My son — I haven't seen him since 2010. I don't even know if he's still alive."

"If you need anything else, you know JP and I will do what we can to help."

The words rebounded into conscious recognition. Lacey turned, scanning the crowd. Past the shoulders of a family group, Zoe's face brightened as their eyes connected.

"There's someone who might know. Lacey? Lacey, can you come over here, please? This is the woman from Victim Services who helped Lizi and I. Lacey, this is Eric Anders's father, Brian, and his mother, Leslie. His older brother, Aidan; his younger sister, Clemmie." She raised a hand toward a shorter man half hidden behind the brother. "And this is Calvin Chan, Eric's best friend."

Lacey uttered her condolences but doubted Eric's family heard them. The mother wept continuously into what looked like a cloth table napkin as the father gazed over her head into space. Clemmie, who looked about the age of Zoe's daughter, peered at Lacey through wary brown eyes. Her dark hair was pulled back in a messy bun, the wisps around her face held back with a black headband. She looked completely washed out. Eric's brother, tall and dark-haired, was the only family member who offered Lacey his hand. She shook it reluctantly. Many murders were committed by family members. Did one of these people lock Eric in that shed to freeze to death?

Aidan started to speak, but Calvin pulled at his sleeve. Aidan clapped him on the shoulder. "Calvin, can you take Clemmie out and bring the car around? I don't want her out there alone."

The girl cast an aggravated look at her brother, but Calvin grabbed the chance. "Yeah, let's go," he said in a quick rush of words. He grabbed Clemmie's coat sleeve and towed her from the room.

Aidan turned aside to speak to Lacey. "So you're from Victim Services?"

"Yes, I'm the volunteer for Zoe and her daughter."

"We haven't heard from our volunteer in a week. Maybe you can help me out. We're trying to plan my brother's funeral. The Medical Examiner told us they're releasing his body on Monday, but nobody has mentioned his personal effects. He always carried his favourite stuff in his backpack, ever since he was a little kid." His lips tightened. "You can see my mom isn't doing so well. If we had his backpack, she could pick out something to display at his funeral, you know, to remember the happier times."

"That's a good thought," Lacey said. "What do you need from me?"

"Can you find out if we can get his backpack?"

"I'll talk to the sergeant at Cochrane in the morning. How can I reach you?"

Aidan pulled a business card from his pocket. "That's my cell. Call me during business hours." He looked beyond her. "Shit. Here's Calvin already. Don't let on that I asked about anything. He's not coping well, either. He's a computer genius but has zero emotional comprehension." He hurried to intercept Calvin. Lacey watched him shake Zoe's hand and steer his weeping mother toward the door. His father followed.

Zoe came straight over. "I'm so glad you showed up. I was at a loss for how to move them along. It's like they're all mired in this little puddle of grief, paddling in smaller and smaller circles until they freeze in place. I'm going nuts enough with all JP's asking me to do."

"You seemed to be managing. How's Lizi?"

"Coping. Her half brothers are a great distraction."

"What about you? Any nightmares?"

"I'd have to fall asleep first. What I wouldn't give for eight hours of real sleep. Even with the odd nightmare." She added wistfully, half-apologetic, "Merry Christmas, by the way."

Zoe's hands were shaking as she tried to unlock the van, and she dropped the key fob in the snow. As she crouched down to retrieve it, running her gloves through the shadowy space under the running board, she realized tears were freezing on her cheeks. *Oh, Mom.*

Oh God, Mom. The voice whispering into the winter air wasn't her own. It throbbed inside her head, not like a migraine, but a floating feeling, almost like she'd been smoking pot, something she hadn't done for twenty years. Brain aneurysm? Tumour? That would explain a lot. She leaned her aching forehead against the van and swept her arm over the icy ruts. Please let her not get stranded here with her sanity leaking out her ears.

At last, her fingers felt the key ring. She brushed off the snow, pushed the button, and climbed into the driver's seat. Her brain pulsed with jumbled feelings and images she didn't recognize, and some she did: Eric's parents in pain, his siblings in their desolate self-reliance. No wonder Arliss put those kids first. Layered over all those visions were shock, dismay, and a desperate feeling of guilt. So much pain! She laid her head on the steering wheel and wept.

After a bit, she sat up and groped in her coat pocket for tissues. Why should she feel guilty? She hadn't caused that family's grief. Eric had been dead long before she found him. She straightened her shoulders, shifted into reverse, checked the rear-view mirror, and said to the young man staring at her from the back seat, "It isn't my fault you died."

The snow began to fall in earnest as she drove. Signalling for the turn onto Elbow Drive, she looked again in the rear-view mirror and registered the empty seat. Speaking to a ghost hadn't worked at the chalet, and yet she had just done it, speaking to him as she would to Kai or Ari. Why had she been able to do so here and now, but not earlier? She needed more information about the process. And about Eric's family, if their presence could bring his ghost forward, where she could communicate with it. The chalet was out of bounds but there were plenty of other places to cross-country ski. She could invite those young people to ski with Kai, Ari, and Lizi.

Her phone buzzed. More trouble?

It was a text from Lizi. *Can u pick up pizza & wings? Movie marathon with bros.* It was so normal, so teenager, that she nearly wept again out of sheer relief. Then she said out loud, in case the ghost was listening, "If you're going to watch movies around my kids, don't scare Lizi."

Zoe walked into the TV room with a stack of takeout boxes. "Hey, *Farscape*."

Lizi stared at her. "You know *Farscape*, Mom?"

As far as Zoe knew, she'd never seen the show before, but the red alien and his tentacled face were familiar, and that purple four-armed thing was, too. How had she known the show's name?

Ari took the boxes. "It's an old fave of Dad's."

Lizi pouted. "He never showed it to me."

"You were too young," said Kai. "You didn't watch ten entire seasons of *Stargate* with him, either."

Zoe headed off to bed while the brothers filled Lizi in on every sci-fi series they'd watched in the last decade as a bridge between them and their faraway father.

Nik was already asleep with his phone on his chest. She crawled in beside him, weary to the bone, grateful for his warmth. Ghosts, grief, guilt … all of it could wait until morning.

Sometime later, Zoe woke shivering.

Nik pulled her against his chest. "Jeez, you're freezing. Are you coming down with something? Should I run you a hot bath?"

"I don't know," she said. "I'm just so cold."

Nik got up and tucked the duvet around her tightly. "Stay right there. I'll get Lizi's electric blanket." He left the room, and she heard him rummaging around. "Lizi, where's your electric blanket? Mom's sick."

But Zoe knew she wasn't sick. Despite the near-paralyzing cold, she felt calm. Peaceful, like she could drift off again any minute. Suddenly, in the back of her mind, someone was screaming, *If you fall asleep you'll die. Get up. Get up. Open the door!* Zoe's eyes flew open. The bedroom door was open. The dream had taken her unawares.

Nik returned with a cup of hot chamomile tea. "Lizi said to put some booze in it, but you're better off with honey until we see what we're dealing with."

"I'll be glad to have something warm inside me." She pulled the duvet up, and warmth gradually returned to her limbs. "Whatever that chill was, it was temporary."

Nik looked at his phone. "Three in the morning. What a time. Like when Lizi had that bad flu. Up all night."

Zoe cradled her mug, breathing in the steam. "You were great with her. Taking your turn getting up with her. Lots of guys don't do that."

Nik made a face. "I wasn't so good with the boys. Too focused on my job, I guess."

"Now you have to make up for it with extra time and attention?"

"Feels like that." He slid under the duvet, careful not to jiggle her and the tea. "If we can't find a way to give everyone a ski holiday, I don't want you stressing. I'll take them on day trips and let you get on with work. If you don't mind us being gone during the holidays."

Zoe's heart thrilled at the prospect of days to herself. A good mom should want to spend time with Lizi and the boys, but there was so much work to get done. And this ghost thing must be sorted out. Maybe Nana would have more ideas. She'd call her in the morning.

CHAPTER FOURTEEN

A lone light came on in the brown-brick split-level. Zoe watched it through the windshield, her hand wrapped around her travel mug. Despite the coffee, she'd dozed off behind the wheel, less an actual sleep than a loop of dazed hallucinations of walking around inside that house: stairs on the left, leading up and down half flights; kitchen straight ahead; living room on the right, a brick fireplace on the far wall. She had no earthly reason to be here, and yet the compulsion to walk up to Eric's house was so strong that twice, she'd found her hand on the van's door handle. She remained in the van even after Aidan got into his car and drove away. She couldn't walk into that house, couldn't take Eric home to his own bedroom, and yet the pull was constant.

Next door was the house JP had owned with Arliss until their divorce. Arliss had remained in the split-level, which was white-sided with blue trim. It looked spacious but not fancy; sturdy, not flamboyant. Like Arliss herself. A couple of years later, JP had fallen for the charms of a sylphlike British redhead. Phyl hadn't by any stretch wrecked his first marriage, but she'd immediately instituted a new regime that saw the children sent to nearby private schools. JP and Phyl had moved into a Mount Royal mansion with marble floors and an elevator, indoor and in-ground pools, and a whole basement level devoted to entertainment for all ages. The children crossed the socio-economic gulf between the two homes on alternate weekends and holidays, gradually losing touch with their best friends from next door. But Arliss remained. Would Eric's ghost — if it really was Eric's ghost — transfer to Arliss if given the chance?

Arliss's kitchen light had gone on half an hour ago, and sitting in the van was getting Zoe exactly nowhere. She pulled out her phone and cued up the number she had lifted from the phone at home.

"Hi, it's Zoe."

"Hey, Zoe. I was just about to call you back. If you're not busy this morning, come over for coffee and tell me how the sale prep is going at TFB."

"How soon?"

"How soon can you be here?"

"Very."

After another scan of the brown-brick house next door, Zoe forced her unwilling feet toward the white house. Inside, it was relatively unchanged: neutral walls and dark furnishings, parquet flooring protected by striped runners. A Christmas tree stood half assembled by the big front window. The layout was the reverse of what she'd imagined — dreamed? — for the house next door.

Arliss led Zoe to the kitchen, where patio doors looked over the snowy backyard. After pouring their coffee, she started straight in about the sale of the company. "I could fight this as a shareholder, you know, and probably get the kids to side with me."

"Will you have enough shares between you?" Zoe asked. JP had assured her the family was fine with him selling now, even though the company would be worth a lot more once oil prices rebounded. Did Arliss want her to stall him until times improved? "Do you have a problem with me working for JP?"

Arliss eyed her thoughtfully. "Not a problem, exactly. I'm just surprised you didn't talk to me. You and I remember more of the early years than anyone." She straightened the napkins and tucked them back into the holder. "Remember when we could write out every gift tag for the families' Christmas party without once referring to the list? It's been a long time since I knew an employee's baby's name. I hardly ever go there anymore."

"Phyl doesn't, either. Imagine if you both showed up, though." Zoe sipped her coffee, thinking hard. Arliss could complicate her job immensely if she decided to fight the sale. Setting down the mug, she asked again, "Do you and the kids have enough shares to halt a sale?"

Arliss sighed. "Not technically. I doubt you remember this, but I got twenty-five percent straight up in my settlement and the kids split twenty percent. Plus there's ten percent in the employee share program. Between us all we have fifty-five percent, but the employees will mostly vote with JP to get their money out, and of my kids, only TJ's twenty-one and old enough to vote his own shares. Frannie and Ben's proxies stayed with JP. I'd have to get them to pressure him, and I really don't want to drag them into this, make them choose between us. I'm just hoping you can tell me he didn't set up some lowball deal with a pal that'll give him back his shares while I lose mine."

Ah, the old fire-sale technique: unload the family assets for cents on the dollar, with a buyback guarantee for only one of the parties. Zoe met Arliss's eyes straight on. "As far as I know, he's looking for an honest evaluation and intends to call in an outside sales team to manage the process. It should be all above board. Will you be all right for money if TFB goes at market value?"

"Better than I am now, with no dividends since 2014." Arliss bared her teeth. "And you're probably right. Phyl likes money far too much to let JP sell for less than top dollar. I bet he can't talk to you when she's around, right?"

"How did you know?"

"The kids tell me she calls the company their 'investment.' She wants her English friends to believe she's into post-work wealth now. The sale will wait until they get the perfect offer, and JP will twiddle his thumbs while the company sputters along without a leader. Such a comedown for the sort of go-getter he used to be."

"That explains the drifting around the office." Zoe grimaced. "Nobody's putting in a hundred percent. I thought it was just holiday distraction at first. So you figure there's no rush?"

"If he fire sales it," said Arliss grimly, "I'll tie him up in court forever to protect my retirement and the kids' trust funds. I hope you'll warn me if anything starts to stink." With that, she seemed to have gotten all the snarkiness out of her system. She topped up their coffees. "You were going to spend Christmas at the ski shack, right? I assume that's off."

"Dragging Lizi back there would be beyond callous. Did you want to use it? Was I stepping on your toes by accepting JP's offer?"

Arliss snorted. "God, no. That place, the way it is now, has nothing to do with me. All industrial chic and Jacuzzi tubs. Huh. The kids are afraid to put a foot wrong. Part of the fun in the old days was crowding in together with no TV, no internet — just us and games and good outdoor fun. It's what made us a family."

"I've never asked, because … well, I never asked. But why did you and JP split up? Did one of you have someone else?"

"Nah. We poured all our energy into building up that business, and once it didn't need me anymore, we had nothing left to talk about." Her brown eyes flicked over Zoe's face, leaving her feeling self-conscious. "You've only been back at work a few weeks, and I can tell by those dark circles under your eyes that you need a vacation. What will you do now that you can't take the family to Black Rock?"

"I don't know." Zoe rubbed her forehead. "Everywhere else is either booked up or too expensive. We can't afford it on top of the boys' plane tickets."

"And of course JP hasn't clued in that this whole situation has ruined your holiday." Arliss glared at a collection of family photos on the wall. "You need good family times to keep everyone anchored. I'll talk to JP." She cut short Zoe's thanks. "Is there anyone at the office who'll come to Eric's funeral? I suppose it's too much to expect of them if JP won't."

"I get the impression the younger staff liked Eric, but Marcia, the acting head of Accounting, told me she'd wanted his internship terminated."

"I heard something about that when I was in last month. Apparently, she'd objected to him visiting the office over the Thanksgiving weekend. Interns shouldn't have an access card, and absolutely shouldn't go unsupervised — according to her, anyway. JP ignored her. Eric had the run of our house since he was four years old. Of course he wouldn't do anything to jeopardize our business. But Marcia always was a stickler for rules."

"You knew her before she joined TFB?"

Arliss shrugged. "Not as well as Phyl, obviously, since Phyl got her hired. But enough about that woman. How'd you get on with the Anders family last night?"

"We went to the Blue Christmas service, but I don't think it helped. His mother cried and his father stared off into space like he wasn't even there."

"I'm sure the kids were glad to get out of the house, though. It's been grim. Leslie was a stay-at-home mom for twenty-five years. Eric had leukemia as a preschooler, and she pretty much lived at the hospital with him for months on end. When he vanished, she fell apart completely. The other kids are more self-reliant. They had to learn early, with their dad gone so much for work and their mom at the hospital or fussing over Eric."

Zoe looked out at the fence dividing the two backyards, where snow clung to bare aspen branches, white against the brownish haze of downtown. The scene was starkly cold, like a faded Dutch winter painting. All that was missing was a canal with skaters. "Aidan handled Eric's friend pretty well."

"Calvin? Oh, he's lost without Eric. He's living in their basement now."

"Doesn't he have his own family?"

Arliss shook her head. "He's from Hong Kong. His mother was here the first year. When he started high school, she boarded him with another family and went home. I'm not sure she realizes how messed up he is."

"So Calvin had nobody except Eric, and now Eric's gone? It must be horrible for him."

"I doubt either Leslie or Brian has a clue what to do about him now. They don't know what to do with their own kids."

"I was thinking," said Zoe, "about inviting them to go cross-country skiing or something with my gang. The kids, not the parents."

"That's a wonderful idea. You should ask them right away."

"I don't want to intrude."

"I'll go over with you." Arliss stood up, pulling Zoe's mug from her lax fingers. "It'll be my excuse to muscle in and get them sorted out."

Excitement and terror buffeted Zoe. What if she was wrong about this ghost thing? What if she had a psychotic break? "Aidan isn't home. Shouldn't we wait?"

"He'll be back any minute, I'm sure. It's the weekend, so he's probably just gone to the grocery store."

All too soon, Zoe found herself inside the brown-brick house, shivering not from the cold, but from the shock of seeing how very close it was to her vision, down to the quirky blue vase full of fake sunflowers sitting on the hall table. She stammered out her invitation over the pounding of her heart, and held her breath while Clemmie accepted for all three kids in a hushed tone. Her parents never appeared.

CHAPTER FIFTEEN

"No, it really went okay," Lacey heard Dee say as she came down from delivering Loreena's breakfast tray. "I counted out all her pills just like you showed us." Dee hung up as Lacey entered the kitchen. "I'm liking it without Sandy around. I'm sure she's used to keeping secrets, but every time I say something about legal work or real estate, I'm aware she could violate my client's confidence without realizing. It ties my tongue."

"She's pretty sharp." Lacey reached for her favourite mug. "I bet she knows that we need the chalet sold. Has your mom asked you about the money situation?"

Dee shook her head. "I can't hide it much longer. I paid the power bill on my credit card, but I don't dare turn down the heat when Mom's so easily chilled."

"I'll get her an electric blanket for Christmas. You and I can wear sweaters."

Dee leaned her face on her palms. "I can't believe," she said, her voice slightly muffled, "the dead guy's now a Major Crimes case. My Christmas photos will be outdated before I can pitch the place to buyers. If I'd thought ahead, we could've done generic winter photos at the same time."

Lacey pulled up a stool. Dee's varnished log walls and black granite countertops had long ceased to impress, but she never tired of the view: white hillside, dark spruces, and clear, cloudless sky. "There wasn't anything to suggest that Eric went into the chalet, so maybe Major Crimes hasn't taped it off. You can never tell with those guys, though. I'll ask Bull if we can still —" She was interrupted by the chime of her phone. "Oh, speak of the devil." She thumbed the screen. "Yeah, Bull. What can you tell me about the backpack?"

"Someday, McCrae, you'll learn to say good morning like a normal person. No backpack."

"What do you mean?"

"What I said. Not on the body, not in the shed."

"Nobody abandons their car in a blizzard without taking their gear." Lacey swapped the phone to her other ear. "Maybe carbon monoxide was leaking in and he was disoriented, or his heater stopped working and he was halfway to hypothermia before he started walking. Like that guy in the Yukon Arctic Ultra race who took off his shoes and walked away from his sled into the bush. He'd been going hypothermic for twenty-four hours by then. Could this kid have wandered for a whole day without seeing a single other building? And why go into the shed instead of the chalet?"

"There's a snowmobile and ski trail running behind all those properties — access is behind the woodshed. If he came that way, the shed would be the first shelter he'd come to. The poppy was his, by the way. Fingerprints on the back. Must have been under his coat if he was wandering for long. The trail's being searched for the backpack, which will tell us which direction to look for the car in, but we haven't found either of them. And we still don't know who barred the door." Lacey heard the sound of shuffling papers. "McCrae, what about the sleeping pills? Have you learned anything from that woman?"

"The daughter only uses herbal tea for sleep. Zoe was complaining about not sleeping, and she looked like hell. In my opinion, if she had access to sleeping pills, she'd have taken them."

"Will you be talking to her again?"

"Unlikely. Unless you call her in and she asks for support. In which case I'll recommend she call a lawyer."

Dee pounced as soon as Lacey hung up. "Still no answers?"

"Negative. They don't know how Eric got to the woodshed, or whether he'd taken or been given sleeping pills, or who barred the door." Lacey swallowed a mouthful of coffee. "Now I have to phone Aidan Anders and tell him there's no backpack. No personal effects to comfort his grieving mother."

She was dialing when she remembered his request about business hours. Saturday midmorning was hardly that. She texted instead. *This is Lacey from last night at the church. Please call me today when it's convenient for you.* They ate toast in silence until Lacey's phone buzzed across the countertop. She snatched it up. "Lacey McCrae here."

"Hi Lacey, this is Aidan."

"Yes, I wanted to let you know about that backpack. The police say it wasn't found with him. It must still be in his car." She waited a few beats. "There wasn't anything wrong with his car, was there? Faulty heater or carbon monoxide seepage that might have made him disoriented?"

"No. He had it winterized only a couple of weeks before, when the snow tires were put on." Aidan muttered something under his breath. "What I don't understand is why he left it at all. We know the drill. We all have emergency kits — candles, food, space blankets. Our mom's a freak about stuff like that. It's like he ignored everything she's ever taught us about winter safety. It's not like him."

"Was he taking any medication that might have clouded his thinking?"

"Hell, no. Eric hated pills. He was really sick as a kid. For years he had to swallow more pills than food. Now he doesn't even take aspirin if he can help it."

"I understand he was driving out to see JP Thompson?"

"Yeah. He's a family friend. He gave me a work placement semester at his company's accounting department a few years ago, and when Eric needed an IT internship, JP offered it to him right off." He paused. "I guess those papers are still in the backpack. I didn't think to ask if Eric had left a copy at work."

"What papers were those?"

"Eric found something weird in the accounting software. That's what he wanted to talk to JP about."

If Lacey had been a police dog, her ears would have perked straight up. Was this perhaps a motive? "Can you tell me what he found?"

"It seemed at first to be a simple glitch in a computer program. I looked over a printout for him and told him what supporting documents to look for before he reported it."

"Did you tell the police about it when he went missing?"

"I forgot all about it. My mom was, well, a wreck, and none of us was thinking straight. I hope the IT guys caught the problem, or JP will be furious that I didn't tell him right away." His voice shook. "God, I don't need responsibility for this, too."

It's not your fault, Lacey wanted to say, but truthfully she had no idea how serious the accounting issue was. Or if it had anything to do with Eric's not surviving the attempt to tell his boss about it. Had anyone verified exactly what time JP returned to Calgary that day?

"Calvin knows more about it than I do," Aidan said. "He helped Eric sort it out."

The jittery guy from the Blue Christmas service. Oh, great.

"Can you ask Calvin if he'd be willing to explain it to me?" It might have no bearing on Eric's death, but if it looked like a possible motive, she could give Bull everything to pass on to Major Crimes.

"I can ask." Aidan sounded dubious. "Cal is not the most sociable even at his best. And right now, he's really not at his best."

"Dee," Lacey said, once she was off the phone. "Do you think your friend Marcia would be willing to tell me whether her company was having accounting trouble?"

It was near lunchtime and Zoe was looking gloomily at shelves full of old computers, monitors, keyboards, and printers. "You're sure they're all on this inventory?"

The IT tech twisted his pen and clicked the end a couple of times. "I checked it in September, but things do get moved around. We had an intern for a while who was supposed to sort them for disposal."

Zoe tensed. "Are you referring to Eric Anders?"

He clicked the pen again. "Yup. The guy who was lost in that blizzard. They found his body recently." He shook his head. "Shoulda stayed with his car."

"He'd probably be just as dead if he had," Zoe said through clenched teeth. "They haven't found his car yet." She eased her jaw. "Was he reliable? Anders, I mean. Would he have moved equipment without accounting for it?"

"Nah. Like I said, these are all surplus. We got them when we bought that last little gas company, and they weren't as good as what we had. Maybe we'll get another intern after Christmas to sort them out. If I'm here that long."

"Why wouldn't you be?"

"You hear rumours. I could look for another job, but if we're sold, there'll be a buyout of my stock from the employee ownership program. Higher than list price, I mean. Those paydays don't come along often anymore."

An employee retention plan — another thing Zoe had to talk to JP about. "I wouldn't worry about being sold just yet. No companies like making changes before the holidays."

"Did they have the employee share program when you worked here before? Because you might think differently if your retirement savings were on the line."

Zoe wasn't about to tell him so, but her savings *were* on the line. Her annual bonus had come in the form of shares those first few years. She pointed to the next shelf. "Are these all the surplus printers?"

"That's your second page. These, plus there are printers in each executive office, and in the copy rooms on each floor." He ran his finger down the page. "And the dedicated cheque-printing machine. I'm not sure what category it goes in for accounting or depreciation purposes, but it's probably not worth a buck. It's an antique, frankly."

"What makes it different from an ordinary printer?" She knew full well, having been there when it was installed, but the voice in her head seemed very excited about the cheque printer.

He coiled up a loose cable and wrapped a twist-tie around it. "It's a specialized combination of computer and printer, with controlled access."

"Show me."

The dedicated cheque printer was in the same supply room as it had always been. How could JP not have upgraded his cheque-writing operation? In her day, she would never have allowed the office to fall so far behind technologically. But then, her replacement had been more interested in marrying the boss than in keeping the company operating at peak efficiency.

"If I understand correctly, nothing gets plugged into this printer except during the twice-monthly payment run?"

He clicked his pen, which she had come to realize was his way of nodding. "It only accepts commands from the Accounting boss. No remote access, either. Like, you can't log in from home for that. You have to be logged in right here."

"Thanks," said Zoe. Cheque security remained exactly the same as when Arliss had set it up, way back when she still handled all the books. "I'll count the other printers myself." She took three steps and turned back. "Did that intern ever babysit this printer, or was that too important a task for him?"

Pen click. "He knew his stuff well enough for this, and most routine jobs. We'd probably have hired him as a summer student, except he wasn't committed to IT."

"What do you mean?"

"He hung with the Land guys, asking about well cleanup and environmental stuff. Wanted to switch his major. Say, Land has a printer, a giant plotter one. It's our single most expensive machine. It prints those wide sheets hanging off the walls, to show where the wells are. It probably has a separate accounting line, too."

Zoe thanked him again and moved along the beige-walled hallway to the land department. The common area, hung with plotter maps, was full of people donning coats or taking plastic containers out of a bar fridge. Under questioning, they didn't indicate that Eric had been a disruption in any way. Joanne, a middle-aged woman with harsh auburn hair, sniffed and blew her nose. She lifted a package of red licorice off a window-sill. "There are all these jokes about computer nerds eating licorice. Like if you feed them that, they'll never leave." She sniffed again. "I brought this in special for him, but he never came back."

Another man said, "You hear a lot about these kids not being good workers, but he was genuinely interested. Good attitude."

Joanne dropped her tissue into the wastebasket. "If there ends up being a memorial service, I hope they give us time off to go."

Zoe nodded and changed the subject. "Who do I ask about recent land swaps?"

"You're being really thorough," Joanne observed. "Is it true the company's going on the market?"

As per JP's orders, Zoe said, "I'm assessing so I can make a recommendation. Think about who wants to stay on during a sales process. It can be stressful wait-ing around for months, wondering if the buyers will hire you."

Joanne gave a wry grin. "Honey, I've been around four different companies under sale. If the retention package is good enough, I'll stick. Most of us will."

Marcia passed the common room door and came back to look in. "Zoe, I'm off for lunch. Want to come along?"

"No, thanks. I have to get home to check on my step-sons." But she followed Marcia out. "I meant to ask you again about teaching them to cross-country ski."

"When did you have in mind?" Marcia unhooked her winter coat from her office door.

"Boxing Day, late morning or early afternoon?"

"Let me check my schedule and get back to you."

Zoe intended to go back to her office and sort out the morning's data. Her feet, though, carried her to the cheque-writing printer. She stood looking at the clunky machine. Her hand stretched toward the back right corner and the connection panel: power cord, power button, empty pins for a network cable, empty USB slot. Her fingertips slid over the connectors, feeling for ... what?

"Something wrong there?"

She whirled around. It was Pen Guy from IT.

"Uh, no. I was just wondering how you've kept this old machine running all these years."

He scratched his ear with the pen. "It's a pain. Jams a lot. Like you said before, one of us has to babysit it during runs. We hand deliver any mangled cheques back to Accounting for them to verify and rerun. Most places outsource their cheque printing now, what's left of it, to a dedicated service. Email them the file and they send you back the cheques and reports, all ready for mailing and filing." He sneezed. "Sorry, something in the air in here is getting to me. Anyway, if you've got the boss's ear, maybe suggest to him that e-transfers are better for the bottom line ... and the environment." He collected a box of staples and left.

The instant he was out of sight, Zoe's fingers fumbled with the empty connectors again. She snatched her hand back and hurried out, feeling as though, for every step forward she took, she was being dragged slowly back. *What was it with that printer room?*

By lunchtime, Dee's borrowed Christmas trees were nearly decorated. The green one stood before the French doors in the dining room, decked with red bows and multicoloured lights, ready to shine for the skiers on the trail out back. The taller white one rose before the great-room windows, gleaming with silver and blue balls, and garnished with the same silver ribbon they'd used at the chalet. The fireplace and stair rails were draped with white lace garland and accented with more ribbon. It all looked quite festive in a frosty, wintry way. Lacey and Dee wouldn't have bothered if it were just them, but for Loreena's last Christmas, nothing was too much trouble.

Sandy arrived in time to hold the kitchen stool steady while Lacey finished trimming the upper branches of the white tree. Then Dee handed her the silver-and-crystal tree topper to set into place. It was done.

"Looks good," Sandy said as Lacey climbed down. "Here, take a picture of me in front of it to send to my grandkids." She hurried to the front hall and came back carrying a small yellow purse with purple and pink sequins in the shape of a unicorn head. "My grand-daughter gave me this to use while shopping for her presents. She'll get a kick out of seeing me with it."

The purse flared bright when the flash caught it. Lacey blinked away spots and checked the photo to make sure the unicorn had not been dazzled out of existence. "Is that all sequins?"

"Yup. And watch this." Sandy smoothed her hand over the unicorn and it vanished, leaving the bag plain yellow. She ran her hand up the other way and the unicorn reappeared. "Flip sequins: like magic to a seven-year-old."

After cleaning up the decoration boxes, Lacey hung a pair of battery-operated wreaths from the lights bracketing the front door. She'd have to come out each night to turn them off, but they'd welcome any visitors coming up the drive. "Look at me, thinking about holiday visitors," she told Dee when she came back indoors. "I'm getting soft."

"You're starting to thaw."

Dee plugged in the white tree and sat back to admire the show. "The house will look great after dark. Sandy, can you start lunch while we tidy up? Tell Mom I'll eat up there with her, if she wants me to."

But Loreena didn't want company. Over their soup, Lacey wondered aloud why every other house listed in the Lower Mainland seemed to sell in a day except for hers. Dee curled her lip. "You know damn well Dan won't sell if he can help it. As long as you're responsible for half the mortgage, he can stop you putting a down payment on a new place."

Sandy nodded knowingly. "My ex was an asshole, too. Dragged the divorce out for years. It took me twenty years to get back in the housing market."

"Great," said Lacey. "I'll be fifty before I can own a home again."

Dee ate the last of her soup. "No, you won't. I'll find you a starter property and an understanding mortgage broker. Even with the tougher mortgage rules, we'll work something out. But not for a while yet. I still need you here."

"Houses in Alberta are so expensive," said Sandy. "My son's place in Airdrie cost twice what mine did in Waterloo. If I move there, he'll build me a separate suite in the basement, but he can't afford to start it yet. He hasn't had much work lately. In this life, you always have the time when the money's not there, or the other way around."

Dee frowned. "I hope you aren't counting on working full-time for us. If my mom stays here, she'll go into a nursing home."

"I know that." Sandy smiled grimly. "My Alberta nursing registration's still active, so I can get a temp job pretty quick. Plus I ran into someone who owes me some cash from years ago. If I get that back, my son's arrears will be history by New Year's. We'll have a lot more flexibility then."

After lunch, Sandy went up to help Loreena prepare for their outing to the post office. Dee hit the couch with a stack of real-estate-related reading material. And Lacey used the office computer to search the help-wanted ads, looking for something that A) started after the holidays, B) paid well, and C) was flexible enough to allow for Dee's various medical appointments and rehab treatments.

Christmas was the season of miracles, right?

CHAPTER SIXTEEN

Zoe tore herself away from the cheque printer and decided to head home. She took Elbow Drive and soon realized she was coming up to the church where they'd gone for the Blue Christmas service a few days earlier. It was not her church — not even her religion — but maybe she could leave the ghost of young Eric there, where he had first seen his family through her eyes. On impulse, she veered into the parking lot.

The old building's central doors were open, and an older woman stood in the chilly entryway sorting hymnbooks. "Merry Christmas," she said.

"Merry Christmas to you, too. Would it be all right if I sat in the church for a few minutes?"

The woman nodded. "Of course, dear. But I'll be locking these doors when I'm done, so you'll have to exit through the side door."

Two paces into the sanctuary, a calm settled over Zoe. What felt like her first deep breath in a week filled her chest. She rolled her head, easing the tension from her neck, and gazed up at the high, hushed space. Winter sunlight scattered gems of colour from the stained glass.

She walked up the centre aisle, her footsteps muffled by the carpeting. The same Christmas bouquets flanked the chancel: evergreen boughs and tall sprigs with red berries, all tied up with red ribbons. Tall white candles had been lit on the altar. In the second pew from the front, she folded down the knee rest and slid into the remembered prayer position. The space was alive with the creaks and pings of the old building, the faint echoes of all the hymns that had risen to the dark beams over the past century.

How long she knelt, wordlessly wishing that God would clear Eric from her mind, Zoe couldn't say. But eventually a door opened, stirring the candle flames. She slid back onto the pew. The woman from the foyer approached the altar and trimmed a candle wick.

She looked over her shoulder as Zoe's pew creaked. "Sorry if I disturbed you."

"I should go, anyway," Zoe said, but she didn't move. Maybe Eric was Anglican and his ghost was comfortable here. Did Anglican churches have the same views on ghosts as the Greek Orthodox Church did? Nobody here knew her. Whatever she might say, however possessed or evil they might think she was, they couldn't stop her walking out the door and vanishing. Anonymity was at her fingertips. "I have a question about your faith. Is there someone here I can talk to? A priest or a reverend?"

"I'm Reverend Kartar," the woman said, smiling. "And from that look, I know you aren't Anglican. Does your religion not permit women to lead?"

Zoe shook her head.

The reverend sat sideways in the front pew, leaning her arm on the back. "Ask me your question."

"Well, I grew up Greek Orthodox, but I haven't been to church for a few years. We were here last week for the Blue Christmas service, and ..." Zoe stopped, not sure where to go from there.

"You lost someone recently?"

"Not me personally, no ..." Zoe bit her lip. Then she took a deep breath and began telling the reverend the story of how she and her daughter had found the frozen body of a young man and how, ever since, his spirit seemed to be following her around. "I know it sounds crazy, and I was medicated for a similar experience when I was younger, so I could be completely out to lunch here. But the ghost, if that's what it is, wants me to do things. Not I-want-you-to-kill-people kinds of things. More like he can't find some paperwork from his job and wants me to help him fix a printer. My church would say the devil was working inside me, but this doesn't feel evil. More sad ... and lonely. Are ghosts even possible in your religion?"

Reverend Kartar didn't shy away in horror or make the sign of the cross. "God loves all his children equally, dead or alive, but I'm afraid I don't have specific guidance for you on how to deal with a non-evil spirit that followed you home. Tibetan Buddhists have a belief that the spirit lingers near its body and can be spoken to, guided to let go of earthly things. I'm not sure how that works, but if you want more information, a member of our congregation often speaks to the departed. She might be of help."

What did Zoe have to lose? She was already sleep deprived and short of concentration. If the ghost whisperer didn't help or seemed like a flake, there was still the medication option. "I'd like her name, please. And thanks for not saying I'm crazy. I sure feel crazy these days."

"Partly it's the time of year. Christmas raises hopes and expectations, and with them comes so much work, especially for any woman who has to pull double duty between family and work."

"That's me." Zoe gathered up her purse and gloves. "No rest for —" She stopped. "I mean …"

Reverend Kartar grinned. "We're all a teeny bit wicked, one way or another. If not, I'd be out of a job. Come through to my office. I'll give you Bethanne's phone number and let her know I've referred you. You decide when or if you want to follow up. No expectations, no pressure."

Zoe blinked hard. When was the last time someone had told her there was no pressure? She followed the reverend to an office, received a scribbled note, and left with a warm glow in her chest. Whether she contacted this ghost whisperer or not, she felt less alone. Freed of the fear that she was under demonic influence, too. She could help Eric without worrying about being sucked down to hell.

Back in the van, humming a tune she didn't recognize, she checked the time in England and texted JP. *I want to take Eric's family and mine cross-country skiing. Can I raid the equipment room at the chalet to outfit everyone?* By the time she reached her driveway, his answer had come. *Take whatever you like.* A few minutes later, a second text followed: *Arliss has been at me about your vacation being spoiled. Book somewhere and the company will pay.*

Zoe stepped out of her van into the driveway, looked up at the weak afternoon sun, spread her arms wide, and yelled, "Thank you!" to the pale winter sky.

CHAPTER SEVENTEEN

Dee dragged Lacey into the office and shut the door behind them. "You'll never guess. JP just texted me to ask if I'd sell his Calgary house, too! A five-million-dollar Mount Royal property! And no dead bodies. I'm saved."

"Lord Tunderin' Jesus. What's the commission on five million?"

"Next year's income! Enough that I'd be dancing if I could." Dee took a breath. "This one I can pitch to select clients right away. I have to Skype JP back. Before we get down to business, I want you to give him an update on the police investigation. As much as you can freely say."

"In the old days I wouldn't have told you guys anything."

Dee pointed a finger. "But you aren't in the RCMP anymore." She started up Skype on her computer.

"Victim Services isn't that different. I can only tell him what isn't confidential. And don't mention his company's accounting problem. I'll bring it up myself, so I can see how he reacts. I'd have preferred to get more information first, but that's moot now. I thought you knew Marcia's last name, at least."

A bubbling ringtone sounded for a moment, then video filled the screen.

JP Thompson wasn't what Lacey expected. Not a smooth tycoon with a silk tie, polished smile, and perfect hair, but a balding middle-aged fellow, his sloping shoulders hunched under a mint-green polo shirt that clashed with his winter-pale face. Wire-rimmed glasses faded into sandy eyebrows below a creased forehead. His smile displayed the gleaming teeth of any man who could afford an excellent dentist, but otherwise, he was unremarkable. He cast a glance over his shoulder at the dark-panelled door behind him.

"What can you tell me about my chalet, Miss McCrae?"

Straight to the point, huh? "The police released the chalet, but the woodshed is still off limits."

JP's left eye twitched. "Does that mean they're not satisfied that Eric's death was an accident?"

Lacey examined JP's face. Who was he as a boss? As a family friend? Kind or ruthless? Rational or raging? "Eric wasn't moved after he died. That's all they'll confirm."

The lines above his eyes deepened. "Do we have to tell potential buyers that someone died there?"

Dee leaned forward. "Ethically, I absolutely must reveal that. It's honestly better to wait until the cause of death is cleared up. Buyers won't fall in love with the dream of carefree ski vacations when they might stumble over uniformed officers outside their new back door. If it's in the past, that's a different vision."

Lacey motioned her to back off. "I understand Eric was coming to see you that day about an accounting issue. Can you —" She rephrased. "Could that have had any bearing on his death?"

"Who told you that? I can't have rumours like that floating around."

Dee slid forward again. "There are no rumours yet. But a potential buyer might ask me why the young man was there at all, and it's better to have an answer handy than to grope for one in the moment. If you tell us everything, we can spin it appropriately."

"All right then." JP's eye twitched again and he glanced over his shoulder. "Eric got the wrong end of an accounting issue. We looked into the matter when he first raised it, and it was nothing. He was trying to impress me, I suppose, but what it amounted to was a simple misunderstanding of basic accounting procedures. When he called that day, he wanted to talk to me before work on Tuesday. I thought it was about his letter of recommendation. My sons were at the chalet, and since they all used to be friends, I told him to come on up." He rubbed a hand over his bald spot. "But when we heard the weather warning, we decided to head straight back to town. I assumed he wouldn't get on the highway after the warning, but I guess I should have called to let him know ..."

Yeah, he should have. Clearly JP didn't waste a lot of thought on other people's inconvenience. "So, you looked into the accounting problem?"

"That's right. It was nothing. It's such a shame. Eric had his whole life ahead of him. You know, I wrote him a recommendation letter for Simon Fraser University. He wanted to get in to their Environmental Sciences program in the new year. I still have the letter ..."

Lacey thanked JP for his time and excused herself, leaving Dee to their real-estate discussion. His move to England might have been in the works before Eric died, and if he'd really written a letter of recommendation, he was either innocent or far more calculating than he appeared. But his statements needed verification. If she asked him for Marcia's name and contact information, he'd guess that she wasn't satisfied with his answers. How could she verify anything about his company when she knew nobody in the Calgary oil patch except Terry Brennan, who was off cruising the Caribbean with Jan? Maybe Tom and his Commercial Crimes co-workers could shed some light. She'd meant to ask him about TFB Energy when she'd first learned JP Thompson had left the country. She pulled out her phone and texted. *Favour: heard anything about JP Thompson, TFB Energy, and potential accounting irregularities?*

Lacey was washing up the breakfast dishes when Dee came out of the office. "I hope I wasn't too forward with your client."

"Not at all," Dee said. "He's as concerned as anyone about Eric's death." She poured some coffee, tasted it, and dumped it down the vegetable sink. "Yuck. Sandy coffee. Anyway, he's determined to sell everything. With non-seasonal ski photos, I might unload the chalet before spring break."

"Do you know when he decided to up and leave?"

"Let's see. He first asked me about selling in late November, at that cocktail party in the Glencoe Club. He said he'd be in England for Christmas. It didn't sound like a permanent move back then. Why?"

"The timing is a bit suspicious, don't you think? His intern reports accounting problems, then dies on his property, and the next week he decides to sell up and leave the country?"

"You are still such a cop." Dee looked up as Sandy passed the doorway with her aged blue suitcase in tow. "All set for Christmas with the grandkids?"

Sandy paused. "Thanks again, Lacey, for lending me your car. It's going to be a wonderful Christmas." She wrapped a scarf around her throat. "You can phone me anytime if you're worried about Loreena."

"We will." Lacey tossed her car keys onto the counter. Her Canucks bottle opener clanked against the fire extinguisher. She really ought to swap it now that she lived in Flames territory. "The Civic's gassed up and I checked the tire pressure and stuff last week. Which way will you go?"

Sandy shoved her arms into her puffy white coat. "Same as last time: north past Cochrane and across country into Airdrie."

"I checked the road report for you — good winter driving all the way. If it's snowing when you come back, take Highway 2 toward Calgary, and then Stoney Trail west to the Trans-Canada. There's more traffic, so if you slide off the road you'll get immediate assistance."

Sandy pulled on her white toque with its pink sparkles. "I have decades more winter driving experience than you do, young lady. I'll be fine, and your car will be fine, too. Merry Christmas."

After she left, Lacey finished the cleanup, made a grocery list, and went up to ask Loreena if she had any last-minute requests.

"British Flake bars. I forget the company, but they have yellow wrappers. Dee adored them when she was little. I don't think she still cherishes them that way, but nostalgia adds to the flavour."

"Call my cell if you think of anything else. Meanwhile, stay in bed. We need you rested for Christmas." Lacey kissed Loreena's sparse white curls.

Downstairs, she counted out cloth grocery bags. "Dee, are you sure you'll be okay with your mom?"

"We'll be fine." Dee started a fresh pot of coffee. "And we'll have two days with decent coffee, now that Sandy isn't making it strong enough to strip varnish off the stairs. Anyway, I want Mom to myself for a bit. This whole assisted dying thing … I need to know she's not planning to die sooner so she can leave more of her savings to bail me out."

Lacey put a hand on her shoulder. "Just go easy. No pressuring her to move here or trying to talk her out of it."

"I wouldn't move her here, now I've done some research." Dee shuddered. "She was right about the religious roadblocks. Whole interconnected hospital/care-home networks are obstructing terminal patients not only from assistance in dying, but even from talking to someone about applying for it. That bus-shelter guy was the tip of the iceberg. I'd never put her through that."

"Glad to hear it. Make sure you tell her you'll support her, whatever her decision." Lacey gathered up the shopping bags and left.

Lacey didn't even get out of Bragg Creek before her phone rang. It was Eric's brother. She pulled the Lexus over by the grocery store. "Aidan? Hi."

"Hi. I know it's short notice, Lacey, but are you busy this afternoon?"

"I'll make time if your family needs something."

"I convinced Calvin to talk to you about that issue at TFB Energy. It's more complicated than I realized."

"I asked JP about it earlier today, actually, and he assured me it had been looked into. So you're not wearing that."

"I hope you're right. Do you still want the details?"

"Absolutely. Should I come to your house?"

"Could you meet us at the Timmies on 16th Ave near SAIT? Maybe about one o'clock?"

Lacey checked the time. "If I put off my errands until after. Hey, do you know a place I'd be able to get imported British candy, specifically Flake bars? I need a few for stocking stuffers."

"I know a place that sells those. I'll pick up some for you on the way."

When Lacey got to the Tims, Aidan pushed a half-dozen Flake bars at her and waved away the twenty she offered. Calvin grabbed a bar, peeled off its yellow wrapper, and bit halfway down the length. Curls of milk chocolate scattered over the table. He finished the whole thing before she got the rest stowed in her jacket.

It took some coaxing from Aidan before Calvin started to tell his story, and then it took serious concentration for Lacey to follow his rapid-fire speech.

"It was back in September," he said, "second week of Eric's internship, when he spotted Cylon Six."

Lacey made a mental note: two months before Eric went to Black Rock. "What's a silo six?"

"*Cylon* Six. It's a company name. Eric saw it on some consulting cheque when he was changing a printer cartridge. Of course he got curious. It's the name of a character on *Battlestar Galactica*. The sexy blond one, you know?"

Lacey decided "the sexy blond" was irrelevant. "So a cheque made out to that company name caught his eye and ..."

Calvin yanked the straw from his glass and waved it at her. "Cylon Six Inc. has no internet presence. No website, no business profile, no provincial registration that I could find. Not even picked up by those amalgamating websites. Just a post box."

"Why were you and Eric trying to trace this company?"

Calvin stared. "*Cylon Six*? It could have been a great source of *BSG* stuff. We had to find out and —"

Aidan interrupted. "Never mind about the freakin' TV show. See, Lacey, Eric found a monthly report during the end-of-September print run that showed several cheques made out to Cylon Six Inc. Nobody should have been buying TV-show crap through a company account, but that was the lesser problem, since the company apparently didn't exist. He came to ask me what I thought might be going on." He rubbed the back of his neck. "From an accounting perspective, I figured it was a verifier line in the program. You give it a placeholder name, and the cheques printed are dummies. They don't get added into the total expenditures, and they sure don't get cashed."

"I'm following you so far. What did you recommend?"

"I told him to add up the numbers manually, with and without the dummy entries. He came back a few days later and said the amounts were included in the total. So I said invoices must exist, and told him where they used to be filed when I did my work placement at TFB." He glared at Calvin. "I told him to *ask someone in Accounting* to show him one."

Calvin fiddled with his straw. "We went in on Thanksgiving weekend and hunted down every single invoice for September. And they were there. All of them." He flattened the straw and folded its tail over. "That should have been the end of it, but the wicked witch got on our trail."

Aidan sighed. "The current head of Accounting, he means. She also supervises the IT department. When she found out Eric brought his friend to the office unsupervised, she blew up. They shouldn't have been there, and they sure as hell shouldn't have poked around another department's files. The shit hit the fan."

"She wanted to get him fired. Fired!" Calvin repeated the word with an urgency usually applied to hurricanes, earthquakes, and other life-threatening events. "Losing your internship is harsh. Every job interview you have after that, employers figure you screwed up and turf your application. So we had to, like, prove he didn't deserve it." The whole straw was now folded like an accordion. "I was protecting him. I didn't do it for giggles."

Calvin — not Eric — had done something illegal? "What did you do?"

Aidan rubbed his neck again. "They snuck back into the office — after hours *again* — and Calvin hacked the freakin' cheque-writing printer."

"Ah." That sounded both foolish and illegal. And what the heck was a cheque-writing printer? "How exactly was that supposed to protect Eric?"

Calvin pushed his chair back. "If you're going to be an asshole about it —"

"I'm not. I'm just trying to understand. So, tell me what you found when you hacked the cheque-writing printer."

Calvin's lower lip pouted. "I found a script."

Aidan nudged him with an elbow. "She's not a geek. You have to explain what a script is." Calvin's eyes rolled so far they could have orbited a space station. Aidan shrugged. "A script is a short computer program with a specific purpose," he said. "Malware sites have hundreds of them, code that script kiddies download to try to hack into other people's computers. Send an email, lure the recipient into clicking a link. The script loads onto their computer, and every time they access their bank account, it transfers ten bucks to a website in Russia. For example."

Scripts, script kiddies, malware, Russia. Lacey's brain ached.

"You're saying someone loaded a script into the cheque-writing printer?"

Calvin stretched his accordioned straw across the table. "This script is called 33 because it does its thing every thirty-third iteration of the base program — in this case, printing a cheque. It's ancient in computing terms, ten years old at least. It only works on a limited set of business machines, and hardly anyone uses them anymore. Internet firewalls automatically block it, and even freebie antivirus software would catch it. It didn't appear on any of the workstations in the company. We scanned them all."

"At fucking midnight," said Aidan, "just begging to be busted."

Calvin's sideways eye roll said *whatever*. He continued, "The only place the script showed up was in the cheque printer itself."

"And that is significant because?" Lacey's brain caught up with her mouth. "Wait. Okay, if I've followed everything so far, this script told the printer to spit out a fake cheque every thirty-third time, one that could be cashed for real money. It was defrauding the company?"

"She wins the teddy bear."

Aidan pushed his mug away. "I can't believe you guys didn't tell me all this right away," he said to Calvin. "I'd have called Mr. Thompson myself. Eric never had to go out in that storm."

The anguish in his voice was mirrored in Calvin's face. The latter muttered, "He didn't believe Eric anyway."

"But you said there were invoices?"

"He asked the witch and she said it was nothing. I bet she didn't even look."

"Because it came from Eric, who was already seen as a troublemaker?"

He nodded.

"Somebody," said Aidan, "must have created and filed invoices after the fact, after the reports were printed. They had to cover the fake cheques, make them look legitimate if anyone followed up. The scheme was basically audit-proof except during a short window at the end of a print run — however long it took to print off half-a-dozen or so invoices to match the script-generated cheque amounts. They should have told me all of this."

"Was it all documented?"

Calvin nodded. "Eric made a copy of everything for JP, so they could go over it together. It was in his backpack."

The missing backpack. Was Eric killed for the contents of his backpack? If he'd told JP Thompson what he was bringing with him that November day, then JP had proven himself a highly competent liar. And possibly worse. At last, there was a motive for silencing Eric Anders.

"Calvin, how hard was the cheque printer to hack into? Did you need a password?"

He blinked. "Plugged in my USB cable and downloaded its memory. Easy."

"You had to be there to plug into it, though, right? It's not hooked up to the internet?"

"Absolutely not," said Aidan. "As I recall, it wasn't even hooked up to the company network, except twice a month for cheque runs."

"Somebody had to load the malware right onto the machine while standing there in the office?" That narrowed down the field of suspects to anyone who had access to a script website and to the cheque-printing machine.

Both men nodded.

"Any idea how long the script had been on the machine?"

Calvin shook his head. "We only needed to prove it was happening. Then we thought Mr. Thompson would order a proper investigation."

Calvin's watch pinged. He pulled three prescription bottles out of his jacket pocket, lined them up on the table, and got to his feet. "I need water."

Aidan spotted Lacey's attempt to read the labels. "Anxiety, muscle pain, and one that boosts the effects of the others. These are recent. He's also got sleeping pills for his chronic insomnia. I don't know how he can code with all that mucking around in his brain." He turned the bottles around and Lacey made a mental note of each name to pass along to Bull. The Medical Examiner's office would know what drug metabolites to test Eric's liver for. Considering JP Thompson had leaped to the top of the motive list, the RCMP could get a warrant to check his prescriptions, too.

Calvin came back and set about selecting his pills. She watched him swallow each one, taking precisely two sips of water in between.

"Why didn't you go with Eric that day? Wouldn't having you as backup have been a good thing?"

Glaring, Calvin grabbed his pill bottles, shoved them into his pocket, and walked off, jostling an old man in the doorway in his hurry to leave.

Aidan watched him go. "I should have warned you. He feels really guilty for not going along. They'd had a huge fight the night before. It was the last time they spoke."

"What did they fight about?"

"Eric got accepted to university in Vancouver. Cal said my brother was abandoning him."

"Where was he that weekend? Did he help with the search for Eric?"

Aidan looked blank. "I'm not sure. I don't remember hearing from him until maybe Tuesday."

Calvin had sleeping pills. Calvin had been angry. Calvin had known where Eric was going. What if he had gone along, or had met Eric there, lost his temper, and drugged his friend? Or simply driven away in Eric's car, leaving Eric locked in the shed to teach him a lesson about being abandoned? Calvin was clearly prone to mood swings, and he might not have been thinking about consequences.

Lacey didn't want Aidan to guess the trend of her thoughts, so she asked a different question. "Why was Eric switching majors and universities halfway through the year?"

"He didn't really discuss it with me, but I know he was getting more interested in oil spills and pipeline breaks." Aidan pulled his jacket on. "Oil spill remediation is a growth industry. More so than IT, where he was just another young geek on the lowest rung of an overcrowded ladder. Look, I don't know if any of this stuff about the script will be of any use, but the sooner you and the police figure out why Eric left his car and ignored all his winter safety training, the sooner my family can start to get their shit together. I hope."

Lacey thanked him and passed on her thanks to Calvin. Before Aidan had left the parking lot, she was calling Bulldog Drummond. The call went to voice mail.

"Bull," she said, "When you find that backpack, check for a bunch of computer printouts in it. There might be a motive there." If the printout was gone, that could mean Eric had already given it to JP. For an insane moment, she contemplated driving straight to Black Rock Bowl and walking the ski trail to hunt for the backpack herself. "Also, Eric's friend, Calvin Chan, has a pile of prescriptions, including some kind of sleeping pills, and he was apparently furious at Eric right before he vanished. No account of Calvin's whereabouts that weekend, either."

As soon as she hung up, her phone buzzed. A voice mail from Zoe, inviting her to go cross-country skiing and to bring along, if she could, grief counselling information for Eric's brother and sister. Given that they had more shocks coming when the RCMP officially declared a homicide investigation, Lacey figured that last was a request she must honour, whether she went along skiing or not. She called her Victim Services supervisor to request the resources. Hopefully the woman wasn't on holiday straight through Boxing Day. With that message done, she swallowed the last of her cold, slightly stale coffee.

Now where to turn?

Tom. He might not know anything about accounting fraud in connection with TFB Energy, but he'd know who to ask. She punched in Tom's number. He answered over a cacophonous level of background noise.

"Hey, guy, did you get my text this morning?"

"Lacey? I can hardly hear you. No, put that back, I said."

"What?"

"I'm Christmas shopping with the kids. Can't talk now. Darren, I said no!"

His voice faded out amid indecipherable shuffling noises. When he came back on, he said, "Can you meet me at home in a couple of hours? Marie would be glad to see you."

Before she could answer, they were disconnected. Rather than call him back, she called his home number. "Hi, Marie. I was wondering what your boys would like for Christmas. I already know to pick something reasonably priced, multi-use, not too stereotypically male, with no batteries, no noise, and definitely no guns …"

An hour later, Lacey pulled up in front of Marie and Tom's house and checked for Tom's truck. Not back yet. She grabbed the toy-store bag.

Soon she was settled in the warm kitchen, wrapping not only the gifts she'd brought but also part of the stack of gifts for Tom and Marie's extended families. As the two of them struggled to disguise the shape of a baseball bat and glove, she told Marie about coping with Dee's mother.

"She's terminal, with maybe three months left, and Dee was trying to get her to stay here to the end. But apparently she might not get approved for assisted dying in Alberta." The paper tore under her fingernail. "And I don't really understand how sick she is, or if she might be thinking of killing herself sooner if the pain gets to be too much. I wonder each night if she'll be dead the next time we open her bedroom door."

Marie taped down the tear. "The simplest way to ease your fears is to ask. Loreena wants to talk about dying. This is the biggest thing in her life right now."

Lacey shifted her hands to let Marie tape up the paper seam. "I don't want to give her the idea of suicide."

"Trust me, if she's talking assisted dying, she's already had it." Marie tied the bat's handle with ribbon. "As a dedicated health-care worker, I should be biased against medical assistance in dying. Especially since I'm also a Catholic. But there's Catholic and then there's Catholic, and I'm the kind who values birth control and medically necessary abortions. I wouldn't want to personally help a patient die, but in ten years of nursing, I've seen enough suffering to know that sometimes choosing it for themselves is their best possible option."

"Loreena says she might not get approved in Alberta because everyone's too religious here." Lacey pulled a talcum-powder box toward her, the kind that drugstores stack on their rack-ends for Christmas and Mother's Day. Wrapping for Tom's family was the closest she ever got to Christmas spirit, and here she was obsessing about dying people. She slid a piece of leftover holly paper under the talc box. "Do you know if there would be a problem applying here?"

"She would have to get her medical records transferred to a doctor here, apply through Alberta's process, and then go through the interviews again. If she's already got a supportive doctor in Ontario and she's well enough to travel home with her nurse, that's what

I would suggest." Marie rolled up a hockey toque and scarf in striped silver paper. "Not necessarily because we're all too religious out here, but because asking a doctor to help you die is a very personal conversation. It's a huge responsibility for the doctor, too. Nobody wants to spend the rest of their life worrying that a person they helped die might have changed their mind at the last minute. The better the doctor knows the patient, the more comfortable they'll feel about asking the questions and accepting the answers."

"Dee's talking to her mom about it this afternoon. I'm really out of my depth with emotional situations." Lacey carefully folded a corner. "Give me a mugging or robbery and I'll deal with it, show me a victim of a crime and I'll assist them. But this is like learning a foreign language."

"Well, the first thing about learning this language is that you have to give people time and space. Intensely emotional decisions shouldn't be rushed." Marie reached for the ribbon again. "Do you want to stay for supper, give them more time to thrash things out?"

"No, I'd better head back. Dee isn't quite stable enough on her feet to help her mom at bedtime."

"Well, call me if you need help while that nurse is away."

They'd barely moved the gifts to the tree when Tom returned, accompanied by a blast of cold air and two overexcited youngsters. Darren and Sam hugged Lacey and swarmed their mother, who ordered them back to the porch to remove their snow boots.

Tom swapped his car coat for an old parka split down one side and stained with indeterminate substances.

"McCrae, come out to the garage and see my Christmas present to myself."

"Some present." Marie's mouth twisted in a resigned half smile. "See you, Lacey. Call if you need me."

Lacey ruffled each boy's hair as she followed Tom out the door. He flipped on the garage lights and flung back a cover. "Voila!"

"You bought yourself a snowmobile?" Lacey looked over the shining Arctic Cat with a skeptical eye. "How much?"

"Enough." He crossed his arms. "It'll be sweet. Remember when you and Dan and Marie and I went sledding out at Revelstoke that weekend?"

"Yeah, I remember." She and Dan had rented separate machines, while Marie rode behind Tom. After a long fast run out to a steep, snow-filled mountain valley, Marie and Lacey tended the fire while Tom and Dan went high-marking, roaring up the slope and risking an avalanche to compete for bragging rights. Dan's rented machine had tumbled backward on him, triggering a mini snowslide that buried him up to his chest. She shook off the memory of his anger afterward before it could veer into the part where her wrenched arm had hurt for a week. He'd apologized. Heat of the moment and all that, he'd said. She realized she was rubbing the long-faded bruise and dropped her hand. "Tell me you bought Marie something equally nice."

"Three nights at a spa for her and her sister." He grinned. "Her mom's idea. Marie deserves a break. She's had the boys day and night all month."

"Big deal at work?"

She listened with half an ear while he expounded on a tricky case involving suspected money-laundering and an overseas entity on the terrorist watch list. "Of course, that means CSIS was involved," he finished. "You know how I love those guys."

"Like that asshole who warned me off the kidnapping case in North Van. Dave Whatsit. Bowling pin with dark glasses."

Tom wiped a sleeve lovingly over his gleaming new toy. "I ran across him recently. He was in town to interview at the universities. That's what he said, anyway."

"With him, that's as apt to be bullshit as not."

"Uh-huh. So what are you up to that needs input on oil company accounting practices?"

Lacey filled him in on her week, starting with Bull dragging her onto a crime scene in the wilderness. "Eric's best friend explained how they'd uncovered malware at this oil company that was siphoning money during the cheque-printing process. Eric was carrying evidence of the scam to show the owner of the company when he disappeared. He later turned up dead in the owner's woodshed."

"The owner didn't see him, then? Or did he?"

"Says he left for Calgary before Eric arrived, to avoid the approaching blizzard. Now he's left the country and isn't coming back. His company and his homes here are on the market."

Tom threw the cover back over his new Cat. "I haven't been working Calgary long enough to grasp all the nuances of oil companies, but basic corporate operations, sure. A malware siphon would alter the operating expenses reports. If the owner knew about it and stayed silent, he'd be party to fraud against any shareholders or future buyers, who base their decisions partly on the reported expenses. I don't remember hearing TFB Energy mentioned, but then, I haven't been listening for it."

He led her out to the drive and pulled the garage door down. A chilly breeze blew lines of stinging snow over the driveway. Across the street, a jolly fat man made of red and white plastic lit up the deepening dusk. Kids dragged a hockey net out of the road as a car came along, then dragged it back. Their game continued. The mix of players' ethnicities triggered in Lacey a wave of homesickness for the Lower Mainland, where people of varied ancestries mingled far more than they did in the parts of Calgary she'd seen. Or Bragg Creek, for that matter. She pulled on her gloves and fished the Lexus's fob from her pocket as she turned back to Tom. "Would the penalties for that kind of fraud be high enough to kill someone over?"

Tom picked up a child's sled and propped it up by the front steps. "When we were patrolling the streets of Surrey, we saw kids killed for twenty bucks worth of drugs."

"True enough. If you hear anything — like maybe that JP Thompson has already sought a fraud investigation — I'd like to know. If you can, that is." She wished him a merry Christmas and left him to his happy family.

When she reached Bragg Creek, she was struck anew by its Christmas-postcard appearance: rustic signs and log rails capped with fresh powder, evergreen boughs drooping under a pristine burden of new white. Home fit the image, too, with wreaths winking either side of the door and Jan Brenner's white tree shimmering in the living room window. She opened the mudroom door to the heavenly aroma of freshly baked cookies.

"Who's been baking?"

"Both of us," Loreena called back.

Dee grinned. "Mom gave the orders and I did the beating. She and Sandy smuggled in cookie cutters, plus a whole bunch of icing tubes and sparkly stuff last week. We're still decorating if you want to join."

Lacey washed her hands and slid onto a stool, salivating over the racks of cooling cookies. She'd expected to come home to a sombre mood, yet here they were, festive as anything, squeezing red and green and glittery gold icing onto bells and snowmen and other shapes. For now at least, questions about dying were set aside for the joyful business of living.

CHAPTER EIGHTEEN

At 9:00 a.m. on Christmas Eve, Lacey got a call from Cochrane RCMP's Volunteer Coordinator. Coughing like a sea lion, she said she'd assembled the grief counselling material. "All this should have been done by their assigned volunteer already."

"Maybe it was, and they forgot. That family's not taking everything on board right now." Lacey checked the time. "I can be there in half an hour, longer if I bring you all coffee."

"That's very Christmas-spirited of you, but I doubt the sergeant will be done with his interrogation any time soon. And he should be treating you, since you tipped him off about that young man's prescriptions."

"Calvin Chan, you mean?"

"That's the one. I like Tims Double Double if you're buying. And the receptionist drinks peppermint tea only. Pregnant."

By the time Lacey reached the detachment with a tray of takeout cups and a box of homemade Christmas cookies, Calvin had gone. The two civilian women fell on the treats with glad cries. A patrol constable helped himself to a handful on the way out the door. When Bull appeared, Lacey asked, "Did you pull in Calvin Chan on my say-so?"

Bull reached for the box. "What's it to you, McCrae?"

"Curiosity. Did he have the same kind of sleeping pills?" She lifted the lid, showing the iced and sprinkled cookies.

"Are you bribing a federal officer?"

Lacey grinned.

With a frosted reindeer in hand, Bull continued. "It's his prescription all right. He claims the jacket Eric was wearing in the woodshed was one of his, and the pill could have fallen loose in the pocket at any time." He bit off a leg.

"He does carry pill bottles in his pockets. I've seen them. Are you buying that it's his coat?"

He chewed thoughtfully. "Not on a money-back guarantee. It might be a pre-emptive strike against hair or skin samples that link him to the body."

"Calvin isn't exactly stable, but from what I've been told, he is intelligent. It's possible he went out there with Eric and disguised his involvement. Doesn't explain where he ditched the car, though. If it were anywhere in the city or on the plains, it would have been spotted by now. Plus, how would he have gotten back home?" She took the smallest cookie from the box and nibbled a corner. "Did he account for his whereabouts that weekend?"

Bull led the way to his office. "Firm silence on the subject. Tell me everything he said yesterday."

The report didn't take long. Giving it felt almost like being back on the Force, although Lacey had never reported to a sergeant as relaxed as Bull. If she'd passed the undercover course, maybe she'd have found the culture different over there. Less militaristic than the patrol unit, and maybe less resentful over women getting promotions, too. Or was that a pipe dream? The whole Force was rotten with misogyny. At every rank, in every detachment, she'd encountered crude jokes and unwanted attention, sulks and sneers, until she'd gotten married, basically pinning a *taken* label on her collar.

When Lacey arrived home she found Dee and Loreena still in their pajamas, mellowing in the living room as a fire sparked and popped in the big fireplace. They had every photo album in the house stacked up on the coffee table and were reminiscing. Lacey went to Dee's office and skimmed social media sites, dropped basic holiday greetings in a few people's feeds, killed off a phishing email, and read one from Jan Brenner filled with sunshine, good cheer, and complaints about the price of internet access on cruise ships:

> Thankfully we're sitting at this port for two days. The sea's like glass, but the constant vibration of those huge engines during a twelve-hour run between islands jangled me to the point of barfing. In port the engines are down to a dull rumble. Not as wonderful a trip as I'd expected, but it's way better than being rolled up in blankets on

the couch at home while Terry goes to all the holiday parties by himself. I'm able to walk around much more than expected, wearing that heart monitor to warn me when I hit the red zone, and Terry carries my folding chair slung over his shoulder for when I have to rest.

Jan sent greetings to Dee and hopes for her mother to have a peaceful visit. Lacey hit Reply and started typing. If anyone could explain whether a young man's interest in oil-well remediation and pipeline spills might become a motive for murder, it would be Jan's oil-patch husband, Terry.

When Zoe woke up on the morning of the twenty-fourth, the whole king-sized bed was hers. She rolled to Nik's side and nuzzled his pillow for a hint of his familiar scent. He'd crept out without waking her. He'd be downtown, waiting for his well to come in, missing dinner and possibly tomorrow's breakfast as well. There'd be three or four other reservoir engineers doing the same. The whole northern half of Alberta was only open for drilling when the ground was frozen solid, so most of the patch worked over Christmas. If the well came in today, Nik would take Christmas and Boxing Day to evaluate the initial reports, monitor the pressure testing, and then learn if he had a well or another dry hole. Not that the oil was worth as much as it had been two years ago, but it kept them afloat. Just as long as it was all done before the twenty-seventh, so the kids could have their ski holiday.

No message from Nik on her phone. There was, however, a voice mail from Marcia. "Any chance we can make that ski lesson this afternoon instead of the twenty-sixth? I have a booking for a group trek that day."

Traipsing downstairs a few minutes later, her old Garfield pajama pants flapping around her ankles, Zoe headed for the kitchen. The light on the coffee maker was on. There was a note beside the machine. *They're in the zone this morning. Could be a long day. Cross your fingers for a gusher.* He'd signed it with an *XOX*. She tucked the note into her pocket before texting Marcia: *This aft works. Black Rock Bowl at 1?* Then she made herself a toasted bagel and settled at the table to eat while the sky brightened and the pale winter sunlight crept down the wall to kiss her face. The tension of the last week was gone. She felt like herself again. The sheer relief of talking about the ghost, of learning she wasn't entirely alone in the experience, had given her nightmare-free sleep for the first time all week. She didn't need to call the ghost-whisperer woman. She'd handled an oil company staff of sixty; she could handle one dead intern.

Now to get the ski equipment organized. Taking her second coffee to her office, she dialed Arliss's number, put the phone on speaker, and leaned back in her chair.

"I'm calling to thank you for arm-twisting JP into paying for our ski holiday."

"You deserve it," said Arliss with her usual brusqueness. "Did you find somewhere decent?"

"Yep. Six nights at Marmot Basin starting on the twenty-seventh. Nik might not be able to go right away. He's waiting on a well."

Arliss groaned. "The oil-patch family in a nutshell. Drillers, riggers, geologists, engineers, all working when there's work and to hell with the calendar. How many Christmases with his boys has he missed because of drilling?"

"Not quite half the ones they've spent here." Zoe took another sip of coffee. "Speaking of the boys, I need to outfit them for cross-country skiing. JP says we can take whatever we want from the chalet, and we did use the snowboards the other day, but there might be things you want for when your kids are with you."

"My children all have new stuff now. Phyl outfitted everyone for skiing in Switzerland over New Year's. You take what you want."

"That's pretty much what JP said. But thank you. You've made a tremendous difference to our family vacation."

After a brief silence, Arliss asked, "Can you get some equipment for Eric's sister and brother, too? They haven't told their parents they're going skiing on Boxing Day. It must feel a bit like disloyalty, I expect. Smuggling their ski stuff out won't be easy."

"Their mother isn't any better?"

Arliss's sigh slithered through the receiver. "She might, in time, learn to disguise it, but no mother ever gets over losing a child."

"I'm pretty sure I wouldn't. But I'd try not to let the rest of my children suffer while I grieved."

"That's why you're taking those children skiing."

"Would you like to come along? You know them, and they've barely met me."

"Not a chance. I have to run interference at their house. There are funeral arrangements to be made, not to mention withdrawing Eric from his university and cancelling his loans. His dad is, as usual, hiding in his den, leaving everything to Leslie, who isn't capable of coping alone."

"I'm glad they have you. At the Blue Christmas service they seemed so lost."

Arliss's voice trembled. "If I had been a good neighbour, I wouldn't have recommended Eric for that internship. I feel like I contributed to his death."

"You? Why?"

"I told JP to give the position to him, like I did when Aidan needed an accounting placement. I even went into the office with him and introduced him around. When Marcia wanted Eric fired at Thanksgiving, I insisted he be kept on." She paused. "But JP agreed with me. Marcia has always been overzealous with the rules, and she never trusted my boys, either."

"You've known her a while, then?" Zoe vaguely remembered Arliss saying something about that before, but not the specifics. "Since before she started working at the company?"

"I saw her on our annual visits to JP's mother in Ontario. She was the accountant at Old Fran's nursing home. I didn't think that qualified her to leap straight into oil-patch accounting, but you may have noticed that Phyl always gets what she wants. That time, she wanted her pal to have a job in Calgary."

"I can't see snotty Phyl being best friends with no-nonsense Marcia. They must be twenty years apart in age, too."

"When Phyl took up with JP, she inherited those annual holidays at the nursing home. The kids said she got Marcia to show her around the region while JP was sitting with his mom." Arliss huffed. "After Old Fran died, Phyl got Marcia the job at TFB, and Marcia bought a cabin across the Bowl so they could ski together. On trails I bushwhacked thirty years ago." She paused. "Sorry. I'm trying not to be bitter that she's living the life I worked my ass off for."

Zoe signed off as soon as she decently could and wandered back to the kitchen, where Lizi was now up and whizzing a smoothie together. "You want half, Mom? Wheatgrass and bone broth."

"That looks utterly disgusting."

"The broth is almost flavourless and full of protein."

"I'll take your word for that."

Zoe's phone dinged. A text from Arliss. *I'll send you boot sizes and such for those three. Hopefully before you leave for Black Rock. The one cell tower up there gets overloaded during the holidays and flakes out during high winds.*

"Lizi, can you round up clothing layers to lend to that girl we're taking skiing on the twenty-sixth?"

Lizi nodded on her way out, her smoothie in one hand and her phone in front of her face, leaving Zoe to hope that she had actually registered the request. Honestly, nowadays you had to tell kids everything five or six times to make it past their preoccupations.

Probably it would be less aggravating to text her than to verbally remind her four more times. In the living room, in solitude, Zoe plugged in the Christmas tree. Then, snuggling under a fleecy blanket, she pulled a novel off the end table and settled in for a long, lazy morning. When Kai and Ari finally emerged from the basement, grumbling about time zones, she took her mug back to the kitchen.

"Change of plans, guys. Your cross-country ski lesson is this afternoon. Can you be ready to go in an hour?"

They got on the road with minimal fuss and an album from Ari's phone playing through the speakers — a fusion of Maori tribal music and modern folk rock. A few of the instruments sounded strange, and some lyrics made Zoe's ears twitch trying to understand them, but all in all the hour's drive passed pleasantly under sunny skies.

JP's yard had been plowed again. A path was shovelled to the ski room off the garage. As Zoe parked by the porch, she couldn't help but notice the woodshed with its last fluttering strands of yellow tape sitting amid drifts of undisturbed white. She shivered and shifted her eyes to the rear-view mirror, terrified lest the dead boy's eyes look back at her. But only Kai was there, gathering up his gloves.

"You remember where the ski room is," she said. "We have to get stuff for you two and Lizi, plus another girl named Clemmie who's a bit shorter than her, but about the same weight; Clemmie's brother Aidan, who's about your size, Ari; and another guy, Calvin, who's smaller than either of you."

The multi-year accumulation of winter sporting gear provided all they needed. They loaded up the van, and she drove them around Black Rock's upper road, arriving a few minutes past one at Marcia's small cabin on the north shoulder. As one of the few pre–ski hill buildings that hadn't yet been redeveloped, Marcia's place deserved its designation of "cabin." The original log building with its sagging front porch had grown to include a lean-to on one end and a two-storey extension on the other. The old sash windows looked like they'd been scavenged from even older buildings, and the upper floor's tiny windows had probably been repurposed from a 1940s basement. The vertical plank siding on the addition was painted brown, almost blending with the age-darkened logs. A rickety wooden shed backed on to the surrounding trees.

"This is more what I expected from a mountain ski shack," said Kai.

Marcia came out to greet them, her stocky figure dressed in trim black-and-white ski gear. "Zoe, are you skiing with us?"

"I'll be working over at JP's."

Marcia turned to the young men. "I'll teach you the basics here, and then we'll ski the trail around the upper Bowl to the chalet."

Zoe waved goodbye and backed out. The road that led down to the little town square was thoroughly clogged with traffic and pedestrians. She turned uphill, crawling along with the traffic, sparing glances out across the snowy ski runs demarcated by long copses of dark-green conifers. Skiers in neon floated up the lift lines, and snowboarders carved their way down the slopes. In the short tunnel that ran under the midway lift platform, all sound was cut off as abruptly as the sunlight. As she exited on the other side, three snowboarders shot over her van in quick succession. Idiots.

In the shade of the south shoulder, she began the winding descent, passing outcrops of boulders and a frozen creek, its miniature waterfalls gleaming icy blue amid the crevasses. The drop-off into the Bowl seemed steeper on this side, more dangerous. She gripped the wheel tighter. Out of nowhere, snow scrolled across the windshield. The wind wailed, dusk crept over the mountain. She blinked. There was no snow. No dusk. Only a light breeze like before. Out her windows was the same sunny afternoon across the Bowl, with brightly clad skiers chasing their flickering shadows down the hill.

Steering around another bend, she was enveloped by lethargy. She'd slept so well for a change. Why was she having trouble staying awake? Slowing down, she cranked the van around a sharper curve, hugging the steep hillside as a station wagon crept up the other way. More hard snow scoured the windshield. It must be blowing off the trees. But then it was gone, and there was no sense of its having been there at all. There were no melting droplets on the windshield. She yawned and rubbed her eyes, then fumbled in her pocket for some red licorice to chew, to fight the drowsiness.

Red licorice?

A horn sounded behind her. She slammed on the brakes and the van skidded to a stop, its hood just a blink from the ridge that marked the lip of the Bowl.

She could have slid right down the hillside into the trees below. What on earth was wrong with her?

So tired. That hot chocolate …

Wait, what hot chocolate? She slapped herself sharply on the cheek. Then she backed into her own lane again and pulled into the next driveway to let the vehicle behind her pass. It pulled up beside her instead, and the woman in the passenger seat rolled down her window. Zoe rolled down hers, too.

"Are you all right? That was a close shave."

"Yeah, sorry. I don't know what happened. I just slid toward the edge."

"I hope you don't have far to go."

"Just a few more driveways down."

"Do you want to follow us? We'll take it slow for you."

"Oh no, I'll be fine now."

"You're sure?"

Zoe nodded.

The good Samaritans went on their way, and Zoe put the van back into gear and cautiously edged out into the driving lane.

Red licorice.

Joanne in Lands had kept red licorice for Eric. Had he driven this way, half-asleep, while the snow was swirling over the mountain? If his car had slid off the road, it might be buried down amongst the trees. He could've climbed up to the road and trudged downhill, not realizing the relentless gale was stripping his body's heat with every step. Had the power line to the resort gone down by then? In the darkness, he could easily have missed the house and sought refuge in the shed, the first shelter he came to.

If Eric's influence was interfering with her driving now, she had to figure this out. She couldn't risk driving off the road when she had any of the kids with her. She pulled into JP's driveway and dug into her purse for the contact information the reverend had given her. She keyed in the number and, after introducing herself, said, "Please, Bethanne, can you help me?"

CHAPTER NINETEEN

The afternoon passed peaceably in leisurely three-way Scrabble games while old movies played on TV. Loreena won handily, as to be expected for a lifelong player against two novices, and claimed the best single-malt in the cabinet as her prize. Lacey checked on Dee's beef stew in the slow cooker, then took the drink to the living room. Dusk drew down beyond the cathedral windows, green spruces and white drifts both fading to wintry blues. They lit up the Christmas trees and the outside wreaths and ate the stew in the living room along with Lacey's baking powder biscuits, the only thing she could reliably bake on her own. The biscuits came out smelling divinely buttery and festive with the Craisins she'd added at the last minute.

The games, the wine, finally having an investigative direction for Eric Anders's death: all combined to unwind Lacey's semi-permanent shoulder knots. Her neck muscles seemed too loose, her head unsteady. How long was it since she'd stepped down from caretaking duty? Back on the Force, she could leave the work in the hands of others at shift's end, but ever since Dee had been seriously injured in that hit and run last June, Lacey'd had only random hours of respite from caregiving. Still, when Loreena asked Lacey what she wanted most for Christmas, she didn't say *a vacation*. Dee felt guilty enough about needing her help. But if Lacey could have any Christmas wish, it would be a few days entirely to herself in the next few weeks. Something to keep her in the game. She would have her life back properly in a few months, when Dee was stronger and Loreena was, well, gone. Meanwhile, there was tonight, and the two people she most cared about were warm, safe, and happy.

Once they'd eaten, Loreena said she was worn out, so Lacey helped her upstairs and waited until she was settled in bed. She gave the older woman a cautious hug. "I'm so glad you're here, missus. I've missed you."

Loreena's thin arms felt surprisingly strong around her. "I've missed you, too, Lacey. I know you were busy out there in B.C., but when you stopped calling and writing, I was worried." She hauled her crochet project out of its bag and twisted the blue yarn around her finger. "Light up that Christmas tree for me, would you?" she said, indicating an ornament on the bedside table.

Lacey turned it upside down to switch it on. Tiny gleams of coloured light danced from the branches, glowing from blue to green to gold to red and back to blue. "Where did this come from?"

"Early Christmas gift from Sandy. She decided I need a tree here for when I don't feel up to going downstairs."

"She thinks of everything."

"Yes." Loreena hooked her yarn and pulled it through in a steady rhythm, hardly glancing at her fingers. "She was a great nurse for all those seniors, a good support for me during my first chemo, and now she's a good friend, too. Not as close as you are with Dee, but good."

"I'm glad you had her, since Dee and I couldn't come to Ontario to help out. Can I get you anything else before I go down?"

Loreena patted the bed. "Put out the overhead light and sit here with me for a bit. We've hardly had a chance to visit, just the two of us."

Lacey scooched onto the mattress, careful not to jostle her. "Yes, it's been a long time."

"Since before you got married." The faded blue eyes watched her. "You haven't told me why you left B.C. Was it the strain of two Mounties in the same house?"

"I guess you could say so." Job strain was Lacey's standard excuse, usually delivered in a tone that discouraged further questions. Dee's mom wasn't a casual questioner, though. There'd been many conversations during university, when Lacey visited her little house in Waterloo — chats that had started with an innocuous question and ended with Lacey revealing her knottiest problems. But that was then. Her problems had been basic growing pains: which classes to take next semester, whether to keep lifeguarding in the summer or try a different job. They'd never discussed relationships. And anyway, how could she reveal the darker sides of her marriage or her job to a dying woman? "How about you? You've taken up crocheting since our last visit."

"Knitting, too. These are texture blankets." Loreena spread out her work, running one veined hand over an irregular blue patch with nubby bumps. "They're for dementia patients at the ward where I used to lead art activities. The residents find tactile stimulation soothing. We'll add charms, rings, and ribbons they can tie and untie."

"You don't do art activities anymore?"

Loreena wound up her finger with yarn and hooked a few more stitches. "My hands aren't steady enough any longer. Not for the detailed work I used to do."

"I'm sorry. You made amazing pictures. Crystal-clear reality in paint."

"I miss making new art, but there's still work to be done with the old stuff. Framing some for sale, gifting others to people who'll appreciate them. Gosh, if I didn't forget my new colouring book. The drawings are too simple for you and Dee, but maybe you know some kids who like dragons? It's on that long dresser, in the brown envelope."

Lacey found the colouring books. The dragons crept and stomped and coiled across the pages. "Tom's boys would love these. Are they all yours?"

"Yes, that's my third, and my favourite so far. The others had line drawings of my paintings for people to fill in however they wanted. A gallery in Waterloo sells them in its gift shop, and sometimes a friend takes a table at a craft fair."

"Will you do another?" Too late Lacey realized the unspoken implication. *If you live long enough.*

Loreena flipped the half blanket around and started working back the other way. "I might sketch some holiday decorations, and Dee can put out a book next fall for a stocking stuffer. How are you doing, really? Your life has changed a lot since this time last year."

"Yeah, it has." Lacey tucked her feet under her, flipping through the pages of the book. In one picture, a young girl in knight's armour was confronting a dragon tangled up in its own tail. "What's this one about?"

"Illustration for a children's story. She's a dragon-fighting princess. See the crown on her helmet?"

"You've shown her fighting spirit in just three lines of her face. How do you manage it?"

Loreena shrugged. "It's what I do. If I were capturing your face now, I'd try to reflect your avoidance. That's the second time. Tell me about last Christmas. You were working for the RCMP in Langley. Did you and Dan have a Christmas tree?"

The little tree ornament picked that moment to bathe the wall in red. Red for danger. Red for fear. Had Lacey already been afraid of Dan by Christmas? She hadn't ever identified that feeling, not that she remembered. His attack after Valentine's Day had seemed to come out of nowhere. But had it, really? Mid-January: her arm throbbed where he'd yanked it after the snowmobile trip, and she'd talked herself into accepting his excuse/apology. His surliness, though — that started in early December with news of her pending promotion. They hadn't put up any decorations, had no celebrations except their respective shift parties. Had they even bought each other presents? Why did she have no memories of that time? The little tree spread an icy-blue glow from its branches. She shivered.

"Christmas season we mostly worked, freeing up the officers with kids so they could go to school concerts and church things. You know, all the stuff families do in December. When we weren't working, we just tried to unwind and stay out of each other's way. The season is hell on all first responders." The glow on the wall cycled back to red again. Her stomach tightened. She put her hand up and rubbed her throat, trying to loosen a knot.

"What's wrong with your neck?"

Lacey froze. The room spun. She put her hand over her lips, suddenly terrified she'd vomit all over Loreena's texture blanket. Scrambling off the bed, she ran to the bathroom across the hall. Dropping before the toilet, she gagged so hard her ribs seemed to twist.

All that came up was a belch.

She slumped, resting her head on her arm, her face over the bowl in case the next heave brought up her supper, her wine, and her internal organs. The chill of the porcelain seeped under her skin. Surely her ribs hadn't re-cracked along last summer's fractures? She heaved again, holding her ribcage together with her other hand. Again, nothing rose but sour fumes. At least she was able to breathe. And shake. Her skin felt clammy all over. Did she have food poisoning? Norovirus from something she'd touched at the mall?

"Lacey?" The word came softly. A hand touched her shoulder.

When she was sure she wouldn't actually puke, Lacey huddled on the bed again, the nubby part of the crocheted blanket pressing against one cheek and Loreena dabbing a damp washcloth on her forehead.

"God, I hope I haven't given you my germs. If I ruin your last Christmas, I'll never forgive myself."

"You can't ruin anything for me, or for Dee. So put that right out of your mind." Loreena turned the wash-cloth and wiped it over Lacey's neck. "You don't have a fever. How's your stomach? Should I ask Dee to bring you a cup of my anti-nausea tea?"

"No." Lacey unwound from the half blanket and tilt-ed upright. "Don't bother her. I don't know what came over me there."

Loreena rescued the crochet project and draped Lacey's shoulders with the afghan from the foot of the bed. Then she crawled in among her pillows. "I asked you why you were grabbing your neck, Lacey. Your eyes bulged like you were being strangled."

Every muscle in Lacey's body seized up. She crashed onto the mattress, shattering like crystal dropped by some immense, invisible power. Loreena's hand held hers, a constant amid the chaos. She clung to it, sobbing as memory burst through her skin. Pain. Humiliation. Fear. Choking. Sensations, sounds, stabbing at her. Thoughts slicing like shards of ice. Eventually she lay shuddering and spent, sucking in great gobbets of air. Her face stung where tears seared it. Her throat burned where hands had grabbed it. Not her hands, and not on this night. It was another memory she'd overwritten, stuffed away, hidden from herself like that fear of the river she'd run smack into last summer. Only, unlike the river, this one had been frozen all year, and now that ice had smashed, reveal-ing the horror within.

"Dan," she whispered. "I was trying to remember whether I was already afraid of him by last Christmas."

Bit by bit, the shaming tale crept from her lips: how Dan had raged because his wife outranked him, how he escalated from sulking and criticizing to grabbing her arms hard enough to bruise. Then he started accusing her of an affair, which, not long after Valentine's Day, led to his attacking her in their own kitchen. Even as she'd leaped out of reach, she'd known a domestic violence report would be fatal to both their careers. She'd used every iota of cop control to stabilize the situation and get him to leave the house. He'd moved into a motel. But then came that incident on the river bank two weeks later, and she still wasn't sure if he'd overreacted in the moment or had deliberately tried to push her into the swollen Fraser River to drown.

"I gave up my career and moved away right after that, leaving him with the house. He's supposed to be selling it and splitting any gains with me." Lacey shuddered. "I've never admitted to a soul how terrified I was — I am — that he'd really kill me if I stayed where he could find me. I didn't tell anyone out there that I was in Alberta. Not while I was living with Tom and his wife, not for months after I moved in with Dee."

Loreena patted her tear-tracked cheek with the cool washcloth. "And last Christmas?"

The ice shard rose in Lacey's throat again. This time she recognized it for what it was: fear, and shame, and the flesh memory of Dan's hands at her neck. She swallowed, breathed deep, and sat up. No way would she take that memory lying down a third time. Pulling the afghan tighter, she squeezed Loreena's hand and let it go.

"At my shift party, everyone was congratulating me on my promotion, buying me drinks. I had a few too many and Dan drove us home. I was pretty much out of it between the booze and the heavy work week leading up to it, and didn't grasp what he wanted until he had half my clothes off on the living room floor." She'd never talked about sex with Loreena before. She had to force the words past the shame. "I told him to quit and go to bed. He didn't. He kept at me and at me until finally I gave in." She watched the lights on the wall shift from yellow to green. "Every woman's done that, right? Just let them have sex so they'll go to sleep and leave you alone?"

Loreena handed over the washcloth without comment. Lacey refolded it and pressed it over her singed eyelids.

"I let him do whatever and just tried to keep from puking up all the booze in my stomach. I remember concentrating on the ceiling light over his shoulder. The neighbour had one of those whirling-light decorations — it reflected onto our ceiling. Hypnotic. Somewhere in there Dan realized I wasn't paying attention, or maybe I did pass out for a minute...." Her breath soured with the memory; she willed the tainted air out of her. She draped the washcloth around her neck, temporarily soothing long-faded bruises that throbbed now with fresh life.

"He was yelling at me, and he had his hands on my shoulders, kind of pushing me into the floor. He grabbed my neck with one hand and I couldn't breathe. I grabbed it and he let go, but then he put his arm across my throat and held me there while he ... while he ... penetrated me. I fought but I wasn't strong enough and he just kept grinding …" Her throat burned the remaining words before they arrived. She hid her eyes, breathing to keep from screaming. *Don't fall over again. You're not a victim. You're a witness.* She rocked, and Loreena's hands on hers rocked with her.

"You're with me, Lacey. You're safe."

Sit up straight, open your eyes, and finish your testimony.

She straightened, lowering her hands from her face. "I couldn't push him off me. If he hadn't shot his load and walked away, I might be dead now."

The last words fell into the room as the fibre-optic tree bathed the wall in ice blue. She stared at the tracery of shadows as the world shifted around her, as the tree cycled to green, then amber. Amber for caution. How could she not have seen that attack for what it was: a brutal domination? She'd thought they were partners, their marriage a more equal one than those of the male RCMP officers with meek stay-at-home wives feeding their babies and washing their uniforms. Had Dan ever wanted the same marriage she did? Not when his way of dealing with his jealousy over her promotion was to subjugate her at home by any means necessary. Even …

Rape.

She shuddered with a sudden chill. That word. It was what victims said, what she wrote in reports. It wasn't *her*. Her stomach churned. Her fingers clenched the afghan's strands. She had been raped and had nearly died — nearly been murdered — while she was drunk and vulnerable. By her husband. She was a statistic.

Afterward …

She pulled in another calming breath and untangled her fingers. "I got up the next day and my whole body hurt. There were bruises on my neck, on my shoulders. Rug burns on my back. I asked what the hell he'd thought he was doing. He looked at me like I was crazy. He said I'd asked for it, I'd wanted a rough time. My memory was too patchy to be a hundred percent sure I hadn't said anything remotely like that, but I knew I'd tried to fight him off. So I told him to never do it again, then I showered and went to work." Went to work, kept her mouth shut, froze all the emotional fallout inside herself, and got on with the business of learning to be a corporal. Her fingers knotted in the afghan again.

"And you never told a soul."

"Of course not. A drunk woman agrees to a sex act and yells in the morning that she was violently raped? I'd be laughed out of the detachment. I was about to take charge of my first shift as a corporal. If I couldn't stand up to my own husband, how could I control all those other men who'd soon be under my command? Face them, knowing they knew I'd been raped? I squashed it all down and got on with training for my new job." Lacey watched the tree's tips glow through their colour cycle a couple of times. "I guess I understand now why I instantly believed he wanted to kill me that day at the river. He'd already come close once before."

"Not counting the day he attacked you in the kitchen."

"Yeah. That, too." Lacey looked down at her hands. The washcloth had fallen off her neck, and she'd unconsciously twisted it into a knotted blob. She untied it. "I'm sorry I dumped all this shit on you. I really tried not to. You've got enough on your plate."

Loreena reached out to hold her hand again. "You and Dee are my plate. As long as I live, right to my final breath, I'll be wishing and hoping for your happiness in whatever kind of lives you choose."

CHAPTER TWENTY

Zoe gave the gravy boat a final wipe with the dishtowel. From the dining room came Lizi's voice, bossing her brothers about setting a proper table. She heard Ari say, "Dad isn't here, anyway."

Lizi snapped at him. "'In this house, we keep standards, regardless of which parent is home.' That's a direct quote from Dad. He made supper lots of nights when Mom was at work. Now straighten out that silverware."

Zoe smiled as she decanted the gravy and surveyed the counter: Turkey on its platter. Mashed potatoes in their bowl. Veggies, both cooked and raw, pickles and pickled onions, stuffing. "It's ready," she called. "Everybody grab a serving dish." She watched her children weave around each other as if they'd eaten meals together all these years instead of being separated by half the world. Everything felt more normal today. No more intrusions from the ghost. Bethanne had been so reassuring. *You don't have to drop everything on his timetable*, she'd said. *Tell him you'll listen to him when the holiday's over.*

"I have time," Zoe repeated to herself. And yet, when they were all sitting around the table, plates loaded, talking and laughing, she wasn't surprised — not as surprised as Lizi, anyway — when a quote from that Australian sci-fi show fell out of her mouth. She even knew what that D'Argo character looked like: kind of orange, with squid-like tentacles on his face. It was like having fragments of someone else's memories mixed with hers.

As soon as she had that thought, a sense of Eric's desolation came over her, and she felt a shiver down her spine. This was a Christmas dinner Eric should have eaten with his siblings. *The dead grieve, too.* That's what Bethanne had said. Eric needed time to mourn his family and ease away from his life. When that was done, he'd drift away. Meanwhile, because this was his last Christmas, second-hand though it might be, she could let him share the jokes and laughter and food. The pickled onion she'd unthinkingly bitten into squirted its toxic juice all over her tastebuds. She blinked back tears. *Maybe not the food.*

Later, as she cuddled up to Nik, who slept hot and still, like a hibernating bear, she expected a deep and dreamless sleep. But what she got was a terrifying sensation of sliding toward unconsciousness, shivering to her bones, hugging herself to preserve warmth, and hitting the door with split firewood until the splinters drove through her glove. She woke to Nik holding her, murmuring, "It's okay, babe, I've got you." Instead of wood, she realized she was clutching his wrist.

"God, I'm so cold. I thought I was dying."

"If you've caught a chill, you shouldn't go skiing tomorrow. You need to rest."

She couldn't tell him that it wasn't she who was freezing, and that it wasn't her nightmare. It was Eric's. Suppressing a sob, she wiggled out of Nik's arms and got up. She tucked the duvet around him. "Go back to sleep. I'm getting some tea."

In the morning, finding Zoe had apparently slept off her chill, Nik decided he'd better go to work instead of taking over the ski trek out at West Bragg Creek. "Are you sure you're not coming down with something?" he said as he buttoned his sheepskin coat. "If you're sick in the hotel room while the rest of us are skiing, I'll feel too guilty to enjoy it."

She forced a smile. "If I feel like I'm getting worse later, I'll stay home and let you all go. I can join you in a few days, once I'm over it." She waved him out the door. Shutting it behind him, she leaned against it and closed her eyes. The guilt was all hers. She was setting him up to take the kids on the ski week without her.

They left the city on Highway 22, Zoe's SUV leading Aidan Anders's little blue car. Snow-covered paddocks and frosted fields gave way to evergreen forest. As they reached the Bragg Creek turnoff, Zoe passed her phone to Lizi.

"Text Lacey to let her know we'll be passing soon. Last name, McCrae."

"She doesn't want us to pick her up?"

"I offered, but she said she's bringing dogs and prefers her vehicle."

Clemmie squealed. "Dogs!"

"Is that bad?"

"I love dogs." She bounced upright. "I'm a dog walker at the Humane Society. I hope they aren't purse puppies. Imagine skiing with a teacup poodle under one arm."

Zoe's mouth burned with Eric's longing to talk to his sister. Ignoring the glitter of sunlight on the Elbow River, she crossed the bridge and followed the winding pavement into the hills. The vast West Bragg lot was nearly full, but she found a couple of empty slots far from the trailhead facilities. Aidan's car pulled in beside hers, and everyone piled out. While the kids unloaded the equipment, Zoe looked around for Lacey, wishing she'd thought to ask about the dogs' breed. Several varieties romped in the snow: everything from an English spaniel to a standard poodle and, yes, two tiny furballs in tartan parkas, their yips piercing the afternoon air. Neither of the dogs was attached to a woman tall enough to be Lacey. Meanwhile, Aidan was inspecting everyone's backpacks for survival equipment, adding extras he'd brought in a kit bag. Kai protested. "Avalanche shovels? I thought this was easy hills, not ruddy mountains."

"Their turf, bro, their rules," said Ari.

"First rule of the backcountry," said Zoe. "Always prepare to self-rescue. Second rule: plan to survive a whole night even when you're planning a short walk."

In a flat area near the snack shack, a woman with brown curls was coaching several novice skiers in short sprints: "Kick, glide, pole," she yelled. "Hips forward."

Kai's head turned. "Hey, that's Marcia, our cross-country instructor." He waved. Marcia's arm lifted, but her bellow didn't falter. "Herringbone. Sidestep. Herringbone." Kai shrugged and collected his skis. "Let's hit the trails."

When she turned off Dee's hill, Lacey reflexively checked on Beau and Boney in the rear-view. They were sitting upright in their compartment in the back, swaying with the turn, watching out the window with the happy concentration of dogs to whom any outing is an adventure. "I envy you," she told their unheeding russet heads. "If I hadn't promised to deliver this grief support stuff, I'd be happy looking out a window at home."

Happy. Not the right word, really. After last night's meltdown, she felt she might never be happy again.

A horn blared. She braked hard and steered back into her lane as a minivan shot past, its far wheels riding the plowed-up snow on the shoulder. *Jesus.* She'd driven half a million miles on patrol, yet here she was drifting into oncoming traffic over things that had happened a year ago. The dogs scrambled upright with no apparent ill effects from the sudden stop. She drove on. Would these issues she was dealing with have been resolved if Dee hadn't been injured mere days after her arrival? Would long summer evenings of wine and friendship have healed her? Maybe. But Dee had been attacked, and spent months in hospital and rehab, then undergoing long hours of physio. She'd had enough to worry about, and Lacey hadn't added to her burdens. She'd been happy to shelve the problem of Dan for later, hoping he'd sell the house, send her her share, and sign the divorce papers without further interaction. She'd been so naive.

She edged toward the snowbank as a caravan of ski-laden cars approached. No more taking chances.

She thought about Dee. While fetching Loreena's pills the night before, Lacey had found Dee at the kitchen island, her head on her arms, her sobs muffled. She had no room for Lacey's pain. "So," said Lacey, "you're not doing so well either? What with the cookies yesterday and all the laughing this afternoon, I thought you'd come to some resolution with your mom."

"More like overload. Or rebound. Take your pick. Between looking competent in front of Sandy and keeping it together for Mom, I'm way past faking sane when they're not around. It's been nearly a year since I first broke my ankle. No running off the stress, barely even a walk in the woods, and I don't know any other ways of coping." Dee's hand shook as she reached for her mug. "My go-to was always a workout, or sex, or wrapping a big commission. But I'm stuck for those, too. And I'm so freakin' broke."

Sex was the very last item on Lacey's priority list. She'd swallowed, reassuring herself that her throat still worked. "You might not be broke for long. I'm meeting Eric Anders's friend and his siblings tomorrow. If any one of them lacks an alibi for his death, the crime could be solved. Once an arrest is made and the first press reports die down, you could sell that place easily. Meanwhile, can't your mom give you an advance on your inheritance, enough to carry you until you're up to speed with work?"

Dee sighed. "I'm not taking her money. She might live longer than she thinks. What if she gives me the money now, and then needs it next year but I don't have it?"

Lacey fetched the half-empty can of evaporated milk from the fridge. She put a dollop in each cup. "That's a risk. But honestly, look at how frail she is, and how many meds she needs for pain and sleep. She's only here out of sheer stubbornness. She wanted to explain herself to you in person, so you won't feel abandoned when she chooses to die."

"I do feel abandoned," Dee said so sharply that Beau raised his head. She bent to smooth his neck. "You haven't lost a parent, Lacey, and you aren't close to yours, anyway. My dad died before I knew you, and that same dark void's been reaching for my mother since her first cancer. I'm not even thirty-five yet. People my age have parents and grandparents standing between them and oblivion. When my mother dies, whether by her choice or not, I'll be alone."

The last thing Lacey'd felt ready for was offering comfort while her whole body and spirit felt pummelled. But she'd reached for a box of tissues and shoved a handful into Dee's hand. Always looking out for the civilians.

The envelope of grief supports slid across the passenger seat as Lacey turned into the entrance to the West Bragg Recreation Area. Beyond this parking lot were forest, hills, and mountains. The first snow-capped peak rose above a strip of bare aspen trunks. Between the orderly rows of vehicles were disorderly clusters of people carrying skis or snowshoes. How could she find Zoe and her small group in this riot of colourful outfits? She'd been so distracted that she hadn't even made a plan for how to verify Calvin's alibi. She'd have to wing it.

A girl in a pink hat scrambled in front of the Lexus. Lizi? No, this girl had dark, curly hair. But Lizi's pink hat and blond, jagged hair gave Lacey something distinctive to look for. She cruised along the rows. There was the girl unloading skis from a minivan. Bingo! After pulling into a nearby spot, Lacey decanted the dogs and headed over. Boney and Beau sat at her command as she held out her hand to Zoe. "Thanks for inviting me along. The dogs love a run in the snow."

She shook hands and repeated names, making quick summaries for her mental notebook. The two stepsons had black, curly hair, their faces still tanned from the New Zealand summer. They both had large teeth and long limbs. Aidan stood eye to eye with them, but his skin was winter white, his cheeks concave. Behind him was Calvin, whose dark-rimmed glasses emphasized his sharp chin and jowls. His feet scuffed the packed snow. Clemmie, Eric's sister, seemed smaller than she had at the Blue Christmas service. Her wary brown eyes glanced over at Lacey before zeroing in on the dogs. She crouched down and held out a hand.

At a click of Lacey's fingers, Boney and Beau romped over to meet her. Clemmie mashed their ears and murmured nonsense while they leaned on her as if they had known her since puppyhood. Lacey left them there and went to unload her skis. She kicked the snow off her right boot and fitted the toe into its binding, then accepted her poles from Calvin, who had followed.

As Zoe led them toward the nearest trailhead, she waved to a woman leading a cross-country ski class. The woman lifted an arm.

Kai, who was skiing beside Lacey, said, "That's Marcia. She taught me and Ari to cross-country. Ten minutes on the basics, then she led us round the whole Bowl. There's a groomed trail that runs behind all those chalets and has its own traverse under the upper chairlift."

Zoe looked back. "We'll do the beginner trail first. At the halfway point we can choose between a longer, more challenging route or the easy way back. Who wants to lead?"

Aidan put on a burst, followed by his sister and Kai. Lacey let everyone but Calvin pass her. "How are you getting on back here?"

His eyes darted sideways. "Fine."

She tried a few more questions, got more one-word answers, and fell into line behind him. He wasn't the only one close to Eric who may have had a motive. Aidan or Clemmie could have hated their brother. Aidan, though ... if he had left Eric to die in an apparent misadventure, why raise the accounting error and offer a potential motive for murder? So far Clemmie, skiing along competently and talking to the dogs with no loss of breath, was an unknown. Maybe Eric had chopped off her doll's head a decade ago and she had waited until now for vengeance. But whoever had gone with Eric that day would have had to ditch his car and get home unquestioned, then sit tight through the weeks of the search. Could she hold up under that strain? The dogs adored her, which was a point in her favour, but utterly subjective. They kept returning to her after ranging down the line to check on Lacey.

Speaking of dogs, Lacey suddenly realized only one red plume was waving up ahead. "Boney!" she called out. The setter kept going. "Beau!" The dog stopped, looking over his shoulder. "Good boy." *Shit. Where was Boney?* "Clemmie," she yelled, "is Boney ahead of you?"

"I thought he was back with you." Atop the next ridge, Clemmie leaned far out over the rocky slope. "I can see his tail down in the creek. Looks like he's digging in the cliff."

Lacey leaned to look, too, but from her angle she couldn't see past the snow-heaped bushes. She kicked free of her bindings and squeezed through a gap, sending a mini avalanche down the bank. It wasn't as high here, and she easily scrambled down to the creek. Its waters had frozen and thawed and refrozen, forming fantastical structures of gleaming blue-white ice. A promising rusty patch was, on closer inspection, only a cluster of bare willow wands trembling amid the low-growing junipers. No Boney. The near bank was a jumble of snowy boulders at the foot of a rising rock wall. Someone whistled, and she looked up. Clemmie, clinging to a tree trunk and leaning out farther than was likely safe, pointed along the rocky cleft. Lacey trudged on, her cross-country boots slipping and sliding. If she didn't break an ankle down here, it would be a miracle. Blast that dog.

"Boney?"

She thought she heard a whine and pushed her hat back to listen. Water trickled nearby. Surely the creek was too shallow for him to have been swept under the ice. She edged around a bend and found his familiar traces: snow roiled up like only those long setter legs could do. The disruption ended at the cliff face.

"Boney!" she yelled. "Here, boy. Heel."

A bird sang. Snow sloughed off a spruce, landing with a *whump*. Across the creek a bare branch scraped on rock. Or was it a dog's claws? At last, she heard a whine, and followed the sound through the disturbed snow.

"Where are you, boy?"

A half whine, half bark answered her. At first all she saw was a glittering icefall rising four times her height up the cliff. Maybe it was all snowmelt, or perhaps in summer a smaller stream tumbled over there. Either way, it had built up into a majestic frozen waterfall. Its upper half glistened in the sun, meltwater trailing down to refreeze in the shadows, thickening the icicles that extended from an overhang like stalactites from a cave roof. They'd grown right around the trunks of nearby saplings.

Boney whined again, and she looked down. Near her knee was the tip of a red snout, barely visible be-tween a tree trunk thick as her thigh and an ice sheet compounded of many individual icicles woven through with slender willow branches. She crouched, stripping off her glove and sticking her hand up to the dog's nose.

A fraction of tongue attempted to lick it, but the canine mouth was well and truly wedged.

"You idiot. How did you get in there?" Lacey leaned back and looked along the curtain of ice. Beau stuck his head into a gap a few feet behind her. She yelled, "Stop!" Beau stopped. She stumbled over, took his collar, and guided him well away. "Sit," she told him. "Stay." He whined but didn't move. Boney whined, too. Suddenly, it was a whining competition. "Lord Jesus. I should have left you guys at home."

Clemmie appeared around the next bend. "Did you find him?"

Lacey pointed. "In there. Can you keep Beau out of the way?" She brushed away the ruffled snow and looked into the gap. The icicles at this end were thin, easily broken away, but where Boney's tail lay, barely visible in the overhang's shadow, they were thick as her thighs and interspersed with saplings. Kicking them in would not only hurt her, it would panic him. He'd damage himself struggling. Hell, claustrophobic as she was, going in there would be a test of her own resistance to panic. Still, a body length in, and she could pull him out backward. She'd be in there only thirty seconds. A minute, tops. "You freakin' idiot," she muttered, with feeling, and crawled into the roughly triangular tunnel formed by the rocky overhang and the icefall along its front. The light was dim and bluish. In places the ice was thin and pure, like window glass. She wasn't trapped. She was fine as long as she could see out. She tucked away her sunglasses and crawled on, her knees grated by gravel and chilled by frigid earth.

When she reached Boney, he tried to turn, but his snout remained wedged, like a toddler's head stuck halfway through crib bars. Beyond him the tunnel narrowed, but there was more light up there, where the saplings ended. She could go out that way if she had to. She wasn't trapped. A minute, maybe two, and she'd be out in the open air. She spoke to Boney before gripping his hips. If she could pull him gently backward, so that his neck was straighter …

He yelped.

"You're hurting him," Clemmie yelled unnecessarily.

Ya think? Lacey crawled in farther, conscious of the tree trunks blocking her view outside, and the ice-chilled air settling onto her sweat-dampened spine. *Get the dog and get out. A minute, two, tops.* She propped herself awkwardly on one ski boot and one knee. Leaning precariously forward to grab Boney's head, she eased it sideways. He thrashed, his back claws tearing at her thigh.

"Okay, easy now, boy," she said, stroking his ears and gritting her teeth against the sting in her leg. "One more try. Nose down, neck up, and …"

His head popped out. He flung it back, whacking himself against the back wall, then shook until his ears flapped. It was impossible to tell if he had cuts on his muzzle. As soon as they were out in the light, she'd check him over.

She was on her knees, crawling backward, dragging the fidgeting dog's hindquarters along with her, when Clemmie shrieked. A shower of cold white powder swirled into the tunnel.

Avalanche!

She threw her body forward and tried to protect her head while shielding Boney. Ice cracked and fell in on them. Snow billowed in and a cold heaviness pushed down on her, crushing her hips against the dog.

They were trapped.

CHAPTER TWENTY-ONE

A yell ripped through the peaceful wilderness. Zoe spun toward the sound. Kai lay sprawled in the bushes. Snow slid beneath him, exposing a frozen stream. The whole mass was tumbling over the ledge to the creek bed below. Branches broke as he grabbed at them. As his head neared the edge, Calvin flung himself down on the track and grabbed Kai's ankle. Momentum pulled them both another few feet before Calvin was able to dig the toes of his boots into the hard-packed track and stop them. Kai's head and shoulders dangled in mid-air. Aidan and Ari jumped in and pulled the pair back from the edge.

From a clearing farther down the ski track, Lizi waved. "Everyone okay up there?"

A second shriek came from below. "Help! Lacey's buried."

Lizi kicked off her skis and scrambled down to the creek bed. Zoe snaked past the guys and sped down the slope. Abandoning her skis in turn, she scrambled over the icy rocks and fell to her knees beside the girls, who were digging furiously at a tumbled bank of fresh snow. One red dog prowled at their backs, pushing between them to paw at the ice.

Zoe took a quick survey. The avalanche field extended barely two body lengths along the cliff and one outward. At the cliff wall, it couldn't be deeper than her waist. They ought to see something of Lacey by now. "Where exactly was she standing?"

"The snow didn't hit her." Clemmie wiped the back of one snow-covered mitten over her face. "She's behind the icefall with Boney. There's an overhang. Lacey, can you hear me? Boney? Speak, boy. Speak."

"Clemmie, take my shovel. You and Lizi sink a trench right along the icefall. Not wide, but as deep and fast as you can. We've got to make an air hole." Zoe tipped her head back. "Guys! We need all the shovels down here *now*!"

They quickly developed a rhythm, Lizi and Clemmie scooping snow out of the trench and Zoe pushing it clear. The dog prowled the length of the snowbank, whining. When the guys arrived, Zoe took one look at Aidan's shocked face and sent him off to get a fire going. He'd be having nightmares about his brother's fate. If Lacey didn't make it …

Clemmie pried up icy chunks and flung them backward without a glance. Calvin and Ari bracketed her, shovels digging in. The trench deepened, and through the built-up layers of ice, the dark rock of the cliff was revealed.

Zoe checked her watch. How many minutes now? How big was Lacey's air pocket? Ski rescue should be called, but she couldn't waste a digger to go hunting for a cellphone signal. The first priority was to get air wherever Lacey's face was. All her kids had CPR training. With five people, they could keep Lacey breathing for as long as it took help to arrive. They had to get her out alive, though. Everything else could wait.

Kai finally arrived, limping a bit, and Zoe turned him back. "Go help Aidan with the fire. She'll be freezing when we get her out … Keep digging, guys. We don't need a body-sized hole, just an air gap."

At last the ice showed blue and white across all four diggers. They were below the rock wall. She put her hand on Lizi's shoulder, stilling the frantic work. "Call the dog, Clemmie."

The girl did so, her voice tight and high. For a moment there was only the breeze and a trickle of moving water somewhere. Then a bark reached them, from a place near Clemmie's knees. "He's here!" she shouted. "Lacey, can you hear me?" A faint scraping came; a shadow pressed on the icefall in front of her. She tapped back with her shovel. "Cover your eyes. We're going to break through."

Ari flipped his shovel and pounded the ice with the handle. An icicle as big as his wrist fell inward. He smacked the one beside it, but it didn't budge. Still, they had an air hole. Was it in the right place? Zoe leaned over his shoulder.

"Lacey? Are you in there?"

Lacey's gloved hand emerged from the hole and waggled its fingers.

Alive! Zoe sank back on her heels.

Clemmie leaned down. "We see you. Can you breathe? Are you hurt? We're going to get you out."

CHAPTER TWENTY-TWO

Ten interminable minutes after that first icicle fell in on top of Lacey, Boney scrambled through the new hole in the icefall, sending a shower of icy snow down into the hole. She dragged herself in his wake. Her feet were back there somewhere, she knew, but she couldn't feel them any longer. Her neck muscles had also locked up, so tight that she couldn't lift her head to look for the sky she so desperately wanted to see. She awkwardly rolled onto her side and wriggled her body until her head and shoulders pushed through to the snow trench. Sunlight bathed her face and stung her eyes. Boney scrambled over and licked her cheek as the others crowded around.

"Pull her out," a man's voice said.

"No! Clear the way so she can come out level. Clemmie, take the dog." Zoe bent down. "Lacey, can you keep moving under your own power? We shouldn't yank you out in case your spine's damaged."

To get out of this death trap, Lacey would pull herself all the way to Calgary if she had to. Above her, Zoe's arms spread out, pushing everyone back, giving her room. Glorious room. Space to breathe. She thought she might be grinning like a fool.

Shovels scraped away the tight-packed snow beyond her head. "Try now."

She forced herself farther out on the snowbank. Her hips stuck in the opening for one panicky instant, but she got them past the tight spot, lined up her useless legs with the hole, then eased the rest of her body out of the icebound trap. She lifted her bare, freezing hand. "Hi."

Above her, voices muttered about "core body temperature" and "careful warming" and some other phrases that probably were important, but seemed less than vital in her current blissful freedom. Still, "911" meant something. She rolled onto her back, spreading her arms wide to reassure herself she really could stretch at last. "What's the emergency?"

One of Zoe's stepsons crouched at her side. "You are, luv. Up to your arse in icicles for half an hour. You're probably hypothermic."

"Oh." Lacey ran through her mental first-responder tool kit for hypothermia symptoms. "I was lying half on top of poor Boney, so I didn't lose much to the frozen ground. I'm not shivering, but I can't feel my feet. Is my speech clear?"

He nodded. "Like satellite radio. Can you roll up on one side? We need to get this thermal blanket under you."

Lacey rolled. Once the blanket was under her, she sat up and took stock. "Nothing broken, and the feeling's already starting to come back to my legs." With a vengeance. Probably they'd been asleep as much as frozen. She sucked in a pained breath.

"Your leg's bleeding."

"Boney did that. And now I can feel where his claws dug in. Anybody got a first aid kit?"

She heard crinkling as a second thermal blanket was wrapped around her shoulders. Zoe, almost in her ear, said, "What about your fingers? Frozen? One of your gloves is missing."

Lacey flexed her shrunken, white fingers, took off her other glove, and wrapped her warm hand around the cold one. It stung. "Ouch. Thawing already." With difficulty she dissuaded the anxious group from calling for an evacuation. Clemmie assured her Boney was fine except for a scrape on his nose, and insisted she shove a couple of clickable heat packs under her coat.

"Right into your armpits to reheat your core," she said, her brown eyes lined with worry. "You coulda lost five degrees of body heat in there. You have to put it back."

Lacey obeyed, shivering as she pulled her coat and sweater away from her skin. The damp inner layer had probably cost her another degree. She re-zipped her vest and pulled the foil blanket tighter around her. How many calories had she burned through in her barely-contained panic at being trapped? She'd need fuel to replace those. "Food?"

Zoe nodded. "Hopefully Aidan has hot drinks and snacks waiting at the fire. We'll load yours up with sugar. Ari and Calvin will chair-carry you. Girls, gather up the gear."

With no further effort on Lacey's part, she was soon huddling on a log by a campfire, swaddled in foil blankets and more heat packs. Her tingling fingers clutched a plastic mug of hot, very sweet tea. Aidan had cooled the first mug with a bit of snow and insisted she get it inside her at once. She'd been shuddering by then, colder almost than she had been half an hour ago. There was a scientific term for that — after-chill or something, when the cold already in the body worked its way deeper while the outside was warming up. The first infusion of heat and sugar had thawed her nerve endings. She held the second mug with steady hands and gulped down more tea. Heat up those insides; get the blood warmed up another degree. Melt the frozen flesh.

She sat up straighter and looked around. They were at a trail junction in a sunny aspen glade. A large signboard showed their location amid a maze of crossing trails. There was, she noted with relief, a short, straight one back to the parking lot. She'd had enough wilderness for today. She swallowed more tea and turned her head. Calvin rummaged in Aidan's backpack. On the far side of the clearing, Lizi threw sticks for the dogs. Kai knelt at her feet, unzipping a first aid kit with practiced hands.

"Let's see about that leg."

Clemmie leaped to her assistance, holding the space blanket up while she slid her pants down to her knees. She sat and was wrapped up again, leaving only her gouged thigh exposed.

While Kai was wiping the claw-marks with antiseptic, Zoe came over with a plastic tub of cookies, gnarly oatmeal ones studded with dates, cranberries, and some kind of seed. "Take two," she said. "And one for Kai when he's finished his medic stint."

The cookies further restored Lacey. Her shivering stopped and her head cleared. More than cleared, in fact. When she'd left home three hours ago, her whole being had felt shaky, like she wasn't quite touching the earth. After that close encounter with death, her feet, itchy as they were in the sweat-soaked socks, felt more firmly connected to the ground. She was alive. She slugged back the rest of her tea and held her mug out for a refill.

As Kai stowed the first aid supplies, having bandaged her to his satisfaction, Calvin approached. "Here's some dry socks," he said, "and a sweatshirt when you're ready."

Clemmie unlaced Lacey's boots and removed the right one. She towelled it gently and examined the toes. Lacey jerked her foot away. "Ouch."

"Sorry. I had to check. I don't see any blistering, so I guess they didn't freeze hard. The skin might crack later, though." The girl carefully rolled a fresh sock over the foot and eased the boot back on. Then she did the left.

What a relief to have warm, dry feet. Lacey sighed loudly, then looked up to find several sets of eyes on her. "I'm okay, really. It feels good, that's all. Sorry I spoiled the ski trip. The rest of you should go on, and I'll head back."

That suggestion set loose a chorus of objections, but in the end Clemmie and Calvin volunteered to accompany Lacey while the rest tackled the next section of trail. Kai insisted his ankle was fine now that he'd taped it, and he wasn't going to miss a minute of the skiing unless Lacey needed help reaching the parking lot. Aidan said he was done skiing for today and he'd help if Lacey needed it. With that settled, Zoe's family skied away.

Aidan sent Calvin and Clemmie to check for any equipment forgotten at the icefall. He shoved his folded shovel into his pack.

"We really ought to take you in for a medical evaluation."

"I'm okay. Honest. You guys were really well prepared and did what was needed." Even jittery Calvin had been calm under pressure.

"I didn't," Aidan said, looking pained. "I panicked. We've all had backcountry safety training, but when it counted, I couldn't use it. Is that what happened to my brother? Did he panic? Why else would he abandon his car and all his survival gear?"

Lacey summoned her old cop reserves and met his gaze firmly. "Whatever happened to Eric is not your fault. He was caught in a bad situation, and I'm sure he did the best he could to survive, just like you would. I see Clemmie's coming back. She doesn't need to be worried about you, too, does she?"

He glanced over his shoulder and made an effort to pull himself together. "No. You want a snowmobile sent back for you? They have one that pulls the trail-grooming machinery."

In the end, Lacey walked tamely back to the trail-head facilities with the happily tired dogs while Aidan, Calvin, and Clemmie formed a kind of honour guard, laden with her skis as well as their own. She changed her shirt in the washroom, shivering again as she replaced the heat packs with fresh ones from Aidan's seemingly inexhaustible supply. When she emerged, Clemmie was waiting with a cup of hot chocolate for her.

"Whipped cream, too." Aidan, she added, was making a report about the icy bend in the trail. Her eyes had a haunted look, and Lacey pulled herself up to deal with another onslaught of grief and guilt. It didn't come. Clemmie wasn't about to spill her woes to an adult she'd barely met. "I gave the dogs a drink."

"Thanks."

Leaving the Anders group in line for restorative snacks at the ski shack, Lacey put the dogs into their compartment before she crawled into the Lexus and cranked up the heated seat. It wasn't good environmental practice to idle a vehicle, but she wasn't yet mentally or physically fit to drive those fifteen minutes home. Nor could she drive away before the rest returned. She still had the pamphlets and forms to give to Zoe, and she had to repeat her thanks to all of them for digging her and Boney out. She leaned the seat back, pulled the car blanket over her body, and shut her eyes.

CHAPTER TWENTY-THREE

A tapping at her side window roused Lacey from her doze in the car. She tilted the seat upright. It was Calvin, holding yet another steaming cup. "Tea," he said, handing it in through the open window. "And here's a power bar. Hope you aren't allergic to nuts."

"Nope. Thanks."

The nap had cleared Lacey's head considerably, and the chill air pouring in the open window did the rest. She rolled the residual stiffness from her neck. "Where are the others?"

"Aidan and Clem are in his car. The rest aren't back yet."

"Climb in and talk to me for a bit, would you?"

He got into the passenger seat. "I saw you go into the Cochrane RCMP offices yesterday. You a cop?"

"Victim Services volunteer."

"I don't have to talk to you, then, right? And if I do, you don't have to report everything I say?"

"Correct. Talking to me is entirely up to you." She peeled the power-bar package open and took a bite. Salt and fat, crunch and delicious honey sweetness ...

She took another bite, leaving a silence she hoped he would fill.

"The police sergeant yesterday … I think he thinks I put Eric in that shed."

"Did you —" Lacey changed her question on the fly "— did you know he was going to Black Rock that day?"

"I knew it would be sometime that weekend."

"But you weren't with him."

"No. I was out of town."

"Then tell the sergeant where you were and you'll be clear."

He turned his cup in his hands. "I can't."

"Why not?"

"Because it's a secret." He pushed his glasses farther up his nose. "Like, an *official* secret."

That was unexpected. And likely not true, unless he'd hacked into some government network, in which case he would have been under surveillance, if not under arrest, by now. "If it's an official secret, you probably shouldn't tell me, either. Tell me this instead: was it your sleeping pill in Eric's pocket?"

"Yeah, probably." He seemed undisturbed by the question. "We swapped coats often enough. He hated pills, though."

"So, the only issue is proving where you were that weekend."

"Which I can't." Calvin opened his door and slid out. Lacey slowly followed, filing away his comments in her mental notebook.

Lizi's pink hat whizzed out of a trail beyond the snack shack. Zoe was behind her, with the stepsons presumably bringing up the rear. What about Zoe as a suspect, though? Did her current job for JP Thompson overlap with the accounting department, or the malware Eric had discovered? That could be checked. But really, would any mother send her teenage daughter to discover a body she'd left there? Shaking her head at her own thoughts, Lacey joined the others in greeting the returning skiers.

Zoe kicked off her skis when she cleared the last bare aspen trunks and eyed the sky while her breathing settled after that last sprint. The sun had disappeared behind boiling grey clouds with ominously billowing white bottoms. Snow in that lot for sure. The few remaining trekkers were stowing gear and kids into their vehicles. Marcia was collecting her students' equipment. Kai skied straight over to help. Lizi headed for the washrooms.

"Good run?" Lacey asked Ari and Zoe.

"Fast and hard," said Ari. "Great workout."

He excused himself to get a hot drink, leaving Zoe alone with Lacey.

"Are you really okay?" Zoe asked. "No lasting damage?"

"Better since I had a nap. They plied me with more hot drinks, and food, too."

Zoe shook snow off her toque and pulled it back on. "And the dog? Is he okay?"

"He's fine. Sacked out in the truck. It was a good run for them both."

"I'm glad everything worked out." Zoe started walking toward the cars, and Lacey followed. "I hope the Anders kids aren't too shaken up. When Arliss talked me into asking them along today, I never dreamed something like this would happen. A bit close to home, I'd say."

"Arliss?"

"Thompson. JP's first wife. She lives next door to the Anderses."

"Ah. She'd know them better than either of us, then."

Lacey's tone caught Zoe's fractured attention. "Why's that important?" she snapped. So much for keeping Eric's feelings at bay.

"Well, I just meant she'd know about the family relationships. For example, Aidan seems devoted to his siblings, but that could just be a cover for some deep-seated resentment. Maybe, as the eldest, he always had to look after them. You know, stuff like that."

Zoe corralled another surge of post-adolescent outrage before it hit her throat, but her voice still came out a bit sharper than she intended. "He didn't resent Eric enough to lock him in a freezing woodshed, if that's what you're thinking! He was a good brother." She sucked in cold air through her nose, keeping her mouth closed before anything more revealing could escape. When they reached her van, she propped the skis against it while she fumbled for her fob. Lacey silently helped her stow the equipment inside. With that done, Zoe forced herself to look up. "Have you got the grief counselling material for me?"

"In my car. I'll go grab it."

"I'll come with you." Zoe closed her tailgate. "I don't feel right about shoving pamphlets at them on top of this fiasco, but I'll give the stuff to Arliss and let her decide how to approach them. She can usually get people to do what she wants." She shivered, partly from the cooling of her sweaty undershirt and partly from fear that she would never be free of Eric's ghostly presence. Or his longing for the family she herself barely knew. She could feel so strongly that Eric wanted to go home with them. What kept him with her instead?

You can hear me.

Aidan's little blue car pulled up beside them, and he lowered his window. "We're heading into town. Thanks for asking us along."

"Yeah, thanks," said Clemmie. "Can you tell Lizi I'll text her when we're back in cell range?"

Their tail lights jiggled as they drove away, dragging a piece of Zoe with them. She didn't realize she was gritting her teeth until Lacey touched her shoulder.

"What?"

"I asked, are you okay?"

"What? Yes. Yes, fine. I just realized I'm freezing. I need to get my gang home. Looks like I'll have to drag Kai away from Marcia first, though."

Lacey fell into step beside her. "My legs could use a stretch, now that they've warmed up." They walked in silence until Lacey said, "You work in JP's office, right? Can I ask what Eric was like to work with?"

Eric again! Zoe flinched, but covered the movement with a sideways skid. "Ooh, icy bit here." She hollered up the empty slope to Ari and Lizi. "Come on, we're leaving."

Kai clipped the last set of skis onto the roof of Marcia's SUV. "Be right there."

"Nice young guys," said Lacey. "Helpful."

"Their mom did a decent job with them. Probably better than I would have in her shoes."

Marcia kept loading poles as the women approached. "Snowstorm coming in," she said over her shoulder. "I sent the class on ahead. Don't want to be responsible for them getting stranded."

Like Eric did?

Zoe's eyelid twitched. "Lacey, meet Marcia. She's a good instructor if you know anyone who needs ski lessons."

"We've met, I believe." Lacey held out her hand. "The Christmas market in Cochrane."

Marcia eyed her closely. "Oh. Okay. Yeah. You were with …"

"Dee Phillips. The real estate lawyer."

"Right. Right. Still in a wheelchair, huh? No skiing for her this winter." And with that, she turned to Kai. "Thanks for the help."

"No worries." He slung his skis and poles over his shoulder. "Keys, Zoe? I'll load these." He strode away, and his siblings followed.

Through a thickening fog of exhaustion and emotional turmoil, Zoe smiled at Marcia. "You'll bill me for that lesson, right?"

"Email okay?" Marcia pushed back her sleeve, exposing a bulky black wilderness watch, complete with a rim compass and what looked like GPS readout. "Gotta run. Nice meeting you again, Lacey. Happy holidays."

She leaped into her vehicle and was pulling away before Zoe could finish saying goodbye.

"Well, that was rude." Zoe rubbed a gloved hand over her throbbing forehead. It was exhausting trying to juggle the dead as well as the living.

Lacey took a few steps and waited for her to catch up. "So, Eric. Smart kid? Good at his job?"

Zoe's teeth clenched again. She opened them enough to mutter, "I didn't work there when he was interning."

"You'd have heard if he was causing any trouble, though?"

"That's not really your business, is it?"

"I'm just trying to get a handle on who would want him dead."

Zoe stopped. "What did you say?"

Lacey was staring at her. "Surely you know the RCMP is treating his death as suspicious."

"Yes, but ..." Zoe's head was spinning. She'd likely have fallen if Lacey hadn't grabbed her arm. "I guess ... I ... I didn't really think about what that meant. Somebody wanted him dead? As in, locked him in that woodshed on purpose?"

She was dimly aware of Lacey guiding her across the icy ground. Suddenly she was in the back seat of the van, with Lizi tucking a blanket around her. She closed her eyes, closed out the world, and abandoned herself to the storm inside.

CHAPTER TWENTY-FOUR

Lacey watched Kai shut the van's side door on his sister and stepmother. "Think she'll be okay?"

"Dunno. That's on me. Dad warned me she'd been having bad chills. I shouldn't have insisted we keep skiing. If she can't come to Marmot tomorrow, that'll be on me, too."

"She's an adult. She decided. And you all enjoyed it, right?"

"Too right. It was good sport and amazing country. Wild." Kai put his hand out. "Sorry for burying you. One lesson and I thought I knew it all. Marcia warned me about hot-dogging."

"I survived." She shook his big paw. "You only had the one lesson with her? I assumed it was more."

"She's a good teacher. You should see her cabin. Filled with trophies and news clippings about her wins; she was a biathlon champ twice. You know, skiing and shooting. Good pick for a zombie apocalypse team." He turned as Ari tooted the van's horn. "Gotta jet. Happy holidays, Lacey."

"You, too."

Lacey watched as they drove away, wondering why she felt so calm. For someone who had barely escaped death, she was not feeling terrible. All the care she'd received from Zoe and the others had warmed her soul. She was accustomed to being the caregiver, the one in control. In more than one sense, today had been just what she needed: a change of routine, a chance to set aside her caregiving duties, and a clear reminder that most people were helpful if given the chance.

She walked back to the Lexus and the sleeping dogs as fat snowflakes scudded across her path. Now she had to manage driving home in the growing gale. Snow spun across her headlights. Spruce branches slashed over rooftops. Coming down the final stretch toward the Bragg Creek Arts Centre, she passed a vehicle pulled hard against the snowbank. It looked like the ski instructor's big brown Suburban. It was still running, though the four-way flashers weren't on.

She'd stress all night that she'd left someone stranded in the storm if she didn't at least check to make sure they were okay. She backed up level with the driver's door and hit the power window. "Everything all right?"

It was Marcia. She lowered her phone from her ear and opened the window just enough to yell out, "Fine, thanks," then rolled it up again.

All right, then.

Lacey drove on. Beyond a screen of bare poplar branches and dark firs, the Elbow River swirled grey as the clouds above. At the intersection, an owl swooped across the road in front of her and into the Arts Centre parking lot, its white feathers blurring its outline against the snowy ground. Suddenly, the ski-laden SUV pulled up beside her, abruptly turned right, and sped across the bridge. Boney lifted his head and heaved a loud sigh.

"Almost home," Lacey told him.

As the snow thickened on the windshield, Lacey slowed, not because of the worsening visibility, but due to the weight of Dee's house looming ahead. She'd taken up the burden of Dee's recovery gladly. She'd accepted the temporary extra care of Loreena. She would enter the warm glow of holiday lights and not even mention being trapped today, because she didn't want to burden either of them with a moment's worry about her. When Sandy returned, she would take a few days to hang out at Tom's. The thought of just eating and sleeping, playing with the boys, and watching mindless action movies with Tom in the evenings was immensely appealing.

She took the dogs in through the mudroom, wiping off their damp feet and giving their coats a quick ruffle with a towel to loosen any shards of bark or other bits of wilderness. Eight gangly legs hurtled through the kitchen door. She followed, pausing to turn on the kettle for tea. "Hello! I'm back. Anybody want anything?"

Loreena's thin voice filtered into the kitchen, "If that's tea you're making, I'll take some." She added, clearly not to Lacey, "No, honey. You sit. You've been up and down a dozen times this afternoon and I'm sure your leg is sore."

"Shall I bring everyone some?"

"Thanks," said Dee.

Loreena, wrapped in blankets, smiled as Lacey entered. "Thank you, dear. Did you have a good afternoon?"

Dee looked up from fussing over the dogs. "Wasn't as grim as you expected?"

"It had its moments. Boney got stuck behind an ice-fall and had to be dug out."

"Idiot." Dee smooshed his ears. "And how was your sleuthing? Everybody's alibis check out?"

"Calvin — the computer nerd who helped Eric with the malware — he says he has one, but it's a secret. The brother and sister seem completely without motive, and their reactions are what you'd expect for people who recently lost a brother that way. Zoe has no motive, either, unless … could she run an accounting scam behind JP's back?"

"I doubt it. She wasn't even there during the past five years. She only came back last month to babysit the place while JP's in England."

"Would she cover for him if he did the scam himself, maybe to save money on alimony or cheat on his taxes or whatever?"

"Wow, paranoid much?" Dee eyed her sternly. "You're a civilian now, remember."

Loreena's blue eyes flicked between the two younger women. "Is it paranoia, Lacey, or do you have grounds for suspicion?"

Lacey leaned back in an overstuffed armchair. Outside the window, the snow kept falling. "Honestly, I'm groping in the dark for some angle Bull Drummond can follow up on. The longer Eric Anders's death is hanging over that chalet, the longer it is until Dee can sell it. Zoe, though … she was very evasive whenever I asked her about Eric. Could be a sign of a guilty conscience."

"You flinch whenever Dan is mentioned," said Dee.

Lacey's breath cut off like she'd been punched in the throat.

Loreena said sharply, "Dee! That's cruel. Honey, I'm sorry. She's only trying to show that Zoe's reaction could have lots of causes."

Lacey's face stung like she'd been slapped. She had to escape from these well-meaning people. Fingernails digging into her palms, she said with false calm, "Shall I start supper?"

"You go ahead," Loreena said. "I'm not hungry."

Later that evening, when Lacey brought up Loreena's tea and pills, the older woman was frowning.

"What is it, Loreena?"

"I hate to bother Sandy at her son's house, but with this snowstorm, I'm worried. I just want to make sure she's okay."

"Have you tried calling her cell?"

"I texted her twice on Dee's phone, but she hasn't replied."

"She could be driving with her phone off to save the battery. If she's not here in an hour, I'll follow up. You get some sleep."

Downstairs, Lacey picked up a novel and read until she realized she hadn't taken in a word in half an hour. Sandy still hadn't arrived, and she wanted to go to bed. Surely the nurse had stayed in Airdrie because of the storm. She should have called, though, so they wouldn't worry. It was after ten now. Was it too late to phone a house with little kids? Sandy would be back by breakfast time, and then Lacey could arrange a getaway for herself. Maybe Tom knew someone who wanted a house-sitter over New Year's. Total solitude would be heaven on earth.

In the dazzling morning that followed the night of freshly fallen snow, Lacey assembled a tray for Loreena. "Tea, boiled egg, toast, jam, and pills. Where are the Christmas napkins?"

Dee tugged one from a drawer and passed it over. "Your car's not back yet. I'd better phone Sandy's son. Mom's already asked for her."

"It was a rough night for driving."

Dee propped her hip against the kitchen island and scrolled through the contacts on her phone. "She doesn't strike me as the type not to call, though. Is it too early for me to?"

"Just call already. I'll need a report for your mom when I take this up." Lacey filled the teapot while Dee placed the call.

Dee had barely introduced herself when she gasped so loudly Lacey dropped the teapot lid. "What's wrong?"

Dee put a hand over the mouthpiece. "Sandy isn't there, either. She left yesterday, right on schedule."

CHAPTER TWENTY-FIVE

Lacey reached for the phone. "Is this Sandy's son? Hi, my name's Lacey. When exactly did your mother leave?"

"Yesterday at suppertime. About five."

"In the middle of the blizzard?"

"It hadn't started here yet. I figured she'd reach you before it really whited out."

"By then it was already heavy over here. You're sure she intended to come straight back?"

"That's what she told me." He sounded more irritated than worried. "She said she might stop by Big Hill Springs — that provincial park in the gully. We used to picnic there when I was a kid. She wanted to see what it looks like now."

"I can check on that."

If it was the same one that Lacey remembered, Big Hill Springs was a small park off the range road that ran straight west from Airdrie. She and Jan had taken the dogs there last summer, on the way to pick up some donated art for the museum. Maybe the car was sitting in a snowbank, and Sandy with it. "Is there anyone she'd stop to visit? A friend from the old days, maybe?"

She ran through the other questions any police officer would ask: Sandy's age, the clothes she was wearing, whether her cellphone was charged up, any medication or any illness that might affect her driving? How about her mood: any depression or emotional strain?

Dennis answered everything, ending with, "My mom is never depressed. After all the shit she's put up with in life, things are finally going right for her now."

After he promised to contact his mother's best friend back in Ontario in case she knew of other friends nearby, Lacey disconnected.

"Sandy seems far too conscientious to wander off when she knows we're expecting her. She could be stuck at Big Hill Springs. No cell coverage down there, as I recall."

Dee busied herself with the coffee. "Didn't she mention someone owed her money? Maybe she went to see them on the way and decided to stay when the weather turned."

"Could be. If only we knew who, and where. I'll check with the RCMP to see if any red Civics hit the ditch last night. If not, I'll drive the route in the Lexus. It'll take me a couple of hours there and back. What else did you have on today?"

"I wanted to reshoot the chalet pics this afternoon, minus the decorations. The outside ones were a bit dim, too. With the sun on all this fresh powder, though, it'll be awesome. But I don't like to leave Mom here by herself."

"I'll call Tom's wife to see if she can stay with Loreena. I bet she'd like an excuse to escape her post-Christmas children." And Lacey wanted solitude. Why hadn't Sandy phoned from wherever she was stuck? There were acreages all along her route if her phone wasn't working, and this morning's temperature and visibility were fine for walking.

"Happy holidays," she said when Tom answered. "Can I talk to Marie?"

Once the situation was explained, Marie said she'd come after lunch. If the nurse arrived meanwhile, she'd take herself and her book to the nearest coffee shop and sit blissfully reading for an uninterrupted hour.

Ten minutes later, Lacey was in the Lexus with a fresh mug of coffee. She headed north toward Cochrane. Everything was pure and clean this morning, blanketed in new powder. Off to the west, white peaks soared, brilliant in the morning sunlight. Highway 1 was heavy with ski buses bound for the Rockies' famous winter playgrounds: Sunshine Village, Nakiska, Mount Norquay, Lake Louise. Next to them, Black Rock Bowl was little more than a backyard bunny hill.

No sign of any small red cars in the ditches so far. At the intersection of the range road, she slowed. A Taurus with snowboards strapped to its rack sped away from the gas station, its tail sliding into her lane. She veered automatically, felt the SUV's tires bite the softer snow of the shoulder. The Taurus zipped across Highway 22, far too close to a farm truck's grille, and kept going. Powder hounds, risking it all for a few extra minutes on the slopes.

The lone road into Big Hill Springs wasn't plowed, but mounds along the sides showed it had been at one time. Now it was drifted over, higher in some places than the Civic's front bumper. If Sandy was down in the park, she'd had a cold night. Lacey's car had an emergency kit in it with all the necessities: candles, space blankets, protein and chocolate bars, drinking water. What it didn't have was traction enough for snow this deep. They'd have to send a tow truck. If Sandy was there.

As Lacey rounded the next bend, the bare valley spread out ahead, with the Calgary skyline visible in the distance. Her phone made that peculiar ping telling her she'd lost signal. Trees flanked the spring that gave the park its name, the pines laden with snow and the aspens stark against the sky. The park's car lot was a flat white field snowed up to the guardrails. No Civic there, and no Sandy, either.

Sunlight glinted off two older-model SUVs parked by the narrow concrete bridge. She turned around on the road and stopped beside them. When she stepped out, a hawk called overhead. Its shadow floated over the snow toward a group of picnic tables. A cluster of adults had cleaned the snow off one and set up a propane ring, with a battered black kettle just beginning to send out puffs of steam. Kids of various sizes scuttled around on neon plastic snowshoes, pushing each other into the drifts.

Lacey headed for the picnic table. "Have you guys been here a while? I'm looking for a friend of mine who might have been here earlier. An older woman driving a red Civic."

A man with a walrus moustache shook his head. "No tire tracks when we came out. You'd never get a little car out that road, anyway. Too deep."

The woman by the kettle said, "There was a red car here yesterday, before the storm. Tara and I saw it when we came in from skiing the valley."

"What time was that?"

"It was just starting to snow, so ..." She shrugged. "Maybe five-thirty?"

"Was a woman driving?"

"Couldn't tell. It was over the bridge before we reached the parking lot."

The timing fit. "Did you see which way it turned at the highway?"

"No, sorry. It was out of sight when we got there." The kettle whistled. "If it was heading east, it would have had to be really moving to keep ahead of Tara. That woman drives like she's in Grand Theft Auto." Lacey thanked her and trudged back to the Lexus.

Getting out of the Springs was no worse than getting in. She pulled over at the first gas station on the outskirts of Airdrie and called Sandy's son. "Dennis," she said when he answered, "any news?"

"I left a message with Mom's friend in Ontario, but she hasn't called back. This really isn't like Mom. My dad used to say she was flaky, but I've never seen it."

"She mentioned last week that someone around here owed her money. Any idea who that could be?"

"No." Dennis sighed. "If I hear from her, I'll tell her to call you right away. You'll do the same for me?"

"You bet."

Lacey drove down Highway 2 with blinding winter sunshine flooding her windshield. A dozen vehicles still lined the ditches. Chewed-up snow in the median showed where many more had already been hauled away. She stopped to question a lone RM sheriff who was directing traffic.

"You guys pull a red Civic out of this mess?"

He sized her up from behind his aviator shades. "I'll check." While he leaned into his car, she watched the gawkers impede the speeders, laying mental bets on which was most likely to cause another pileup. The sheriff slid a finger down his clipboard. "No red Civic. You lost one?"

"It's overdue. Single female driver, fifties, stocky with dark-blond curly hair — she left Airdrie during the storm yesterday and hasn't turned up at her destination."

"No single female drivers in the accident reports I saw. Want to file a report?"

"Not yet."

"Your choice." He lifted an orange flag and a stop sign and stepped to the roadside to make space for an emerging tow truck.

Lacey drove off as soon as the lane was clear. The sheriff's question had given her ease for the first time since waking up that morning. However personally inconvenient it might be, Sandy's absence wasn't her problem alone. There was a whole state machinery to deal with a missing person, if she and Dennis chose to activate it.

She'd never met Sandy's son, and she wondered if he might be lying to her about not knowing his mother's plans. Could he have reasons of his own, to do with money or family secrets, for wanting to keep police out of it for a bit longer? People were funny about involving the police in their private affairs. They didn't realize the cops were only interested in whatever was relevant to the immediate investigation, and didn't care that you'd had a fight with your parent five years ago unless it gave you a motive for killing them now.

That last thought brought her back to Zoe's collapse yesterday. It might have been, as Kai said, that she was coming down with something and shouldn't have skied so far. Or it might have been a reaction to the news that JP Thompson's pet intern had been murdered. Was Zoe even now rethinking an earlier decision to protect her boss over something that seemed unrelated to Eric's death? Making a mental note to follow up with Zoe in case she could shake some new information loose, Lacey cruised down to the Stoney Trail exit and followed it over Calgary's far north side, where the disturbed snow indicated many more vehicles had hit the ditches. Some were still there, but no red Civic. She'd have to check with Calgary police, too. Some mess she'd be in if Sandy didn't come back at all: no car and no respite from care-giving. Surely, by the time she reached home, there would be word from or about Sandy.

Bragg Creek's snow-laden pines and spruces were postcard perfect in the late-morning sun, but they didn't warm Lacey's heart like the sight of her Civic would. But it wasn't there. She parked by the deck, kicked the snow off her boots, and stomped into the mudroom. "Any news?"

"Nothing," said Dee from the living room. "Mom's in bed. I was just about to call Dennis again."

"Ask if his mom has his contact information with her. If she was in an accident and only had her Ontario ID, the hospital might be looking for relatives out east."

A short time later, Marie arrived. Lacey introduced her to Loreena before hauling Dee's camera equipment out to the Lexus. As they hit the highway, Dee called Dennis back for the third time. When she disconnected, she met Lacey's sideways glance with a shake of her head. They drove on toward Black Rock Bowl in silence.

The chalet's vast living room was a dim cave overlooking the great white Bowl. Zoe leaned closer to the hearth, drawing illusory warmth from its feeble flames. The bundle of birch she'd bought at that gas station wouldn't last long, and she absolutely could not face going into the woodshed to get more. Not even to keep at bay the sick feeling of freezing to death that was surely Eric's, not hers. Did he understand he'd been murdered? Maybe that was what he'd been trying to tell her all along. Maybe he knew who killed him.

"You want to talk to me? I'm here now. I'm listening."

The house creaked around her. Eric's emotions, so intrusive at other times and places, were quiet except for a bone-deep chill that gripped her. Maybe if she went to the woodshed …

She heard a vehicle's engine rumbling outside and the sound of car doors slamming. She scrambled up as the front door opened. Dee Phillips hobbled in, her plastic walking boot smothered in a thick, fuzzy ankle warmer. She stopped in the act of unwinding her scarf.

"Oh … hi … sorry, I thought the place was empty."

"My van's in the garage." Zoe tried to keep the resentment from her voice. "To discourage anyone from stopping by expecting to see JP and Phyl."

"Sorry to disturb you, but with the sale delayed, I have to take some non-Christmas-themed photos of the place. Lacey's outside taking outdoor shots now. Do you mind if I sit in here and wait for her?"

Zoe nodded. Hopefully they'd be done quickly, and she could salvage some of the afternoon for her ghost-whispering attempt. She wouldn't dare do it after dark. Too creepy. "You want a cup of tea?"

"Sure." Dee followed Zoe into the kitchen. "Honestly, some of Lacey's original photos were so murky they looked like crime scene shots in a movie." She put a hand to her mouth. "Shit, I'm so sorry. I didn't mean to remind you."

"I can't really forget." *Especially after yesterday.* Learning that the police thought Eric had deliberately been left to die in that shed had changed things. This wasn't about her being crazy so much as it was about finding out who had put him there. If it was someone she knew, someone connected to the company or to his family, other people she knew might be in danger. That was why she needed to try talking to him, and she couldn't do that until Dee and Lacey were out of here. Could she ask Lacey outright who the police thought had done it? Exposing her interest directly felt too risky. Maybe Dee was in Lacey's confidence and would open up if Zoe established a rapport.

"You and Lacey have been friends a while, eh?"

Dee draped her coat over a chair. "Fifteen years."

"You know, I can't quite picture her as a cop. She doesn't seem hard enough."

"Believe me, she was plenty closed off when she first left the Force. If I hadn't gotten injured, she'd be off in her own apartment somewhere, still encased in that emotional armour. I don't know what I'd have done without her."

"I'm sorry to pry, but how did you break your leg?"

"I was hit by a car while I was out biking. Lacey looked after everything while I was in the hospital. Now she's helping look after my mother." Dee's polished smile slid away, and she looked down at her laced fingers. Zoe instinctively reached out a hand. Dee jumped at her touch.

"Sorry." Zoe jerked her hand back.

"No, I am. You startled me, that's all. It's just …" Dee twisted her fingers tighter. "Well, my mother has terminal cancer. She came here for Christmas with her nurse in tow. I wanted to make it a joyful time, but all she wants to talk about is applying for assisted dying." Her face disappeared behind trembling hands. "Do you know what it's like to live with someone who's more than halfway out of this world?"

"More death." Zoe closed her eyes. "I don't know if I can take any more."

"I'm so sorry. Everything I say reminds you of that."

"I never forget. In fact …" Zoe hesitated. "I feel like he's around me all the time." Saying it felt like giving up a state secret. She held her breath waiting for Dee to recoil or, hopefully, to volunteer that the police were closing in on the killer. Then she could reassure Eric and herself that it would all be over soon.

Dee did neither. "That's how I felt when my father died. He had a stroke, and although he lived for a few more months, I never had an actual conversation with him again after that night. In my mind, though, it was like we were having a silent conversation every time I sat by his bed. Doesn't that sound crazy? But it was actually very comforting."

What a strange turn for the conversation. Zoe sat back. She'd already told two strangers about Eric, and here was Dee, all but issuing a personal invitation to confide in her, too. But she couldn't help thinking that Dee might tell JP about it, and JP needed to trust her right now. But what if JP was involved in Eric's death somehow? Maybe she was foolish to trust him. That thought shook her. Suddenly, talking about seeing a ghost seemed less risky than letting slip anything about JP's business to Dee, who might report it to Lacey, who would then report it to the police. Zoe busied herself making tea.

"If you think that's crazy," she said over her shoulder, "I can top you. Some of my relatives talked to ghosts." She told the safely distant story of her grandmother's cousin and the dead villager's adulterous love affair.

Dee laughed.

As Zoe reached for the sugar bowl on the window-sill, she caught a glimpse of the woodshed, and suddenly there was Eric at her shoulder. She could sense him, almost see his arm pointing at the little shed. *Why was it locked? Why was I in there?* The panic from her dream swept over her again. She clutched at the counter to steady herself. Eric didn't know he'd been murdered. She'd have to tell him. Roaring filled her ears.

Dee's voice came to her as if from a great distance. "Are you all right? Come and sit down." She put an arm around Zoe's shoulders and guided her to a stool. "Lord, you're freezing. Lacey said you conked out after skiing yesterday. You might have pneumonia."

"I'll be fine."

"You don't look fine." Dee grabbed her coat off the chair and wrapped it around Zoe's shoulders. "You look like you've seen a ghost."

"You've hit it in one go." Dee might think she was genuinely nutty, but what trouble could she cause beyond hinting to JP that Zoe wasn't all there? That wouldn't even be a lie. "I have seen one. And talked to him. This isn't my own cold. It's kind of … I've acquired a memory of Eric freezing to death — his last memory." Zoe scrunched up her eyes, afraid to open them in case Eric was standing right there, staring at her, his eyelashes rimmed with ice crystals. "I dreamed it the other night, and when I saw the woodshed just now, it all came crashing over me again."

"You're being haunted by the ghost of the dead intern?"

"Don't tell anybody," Zoe pleaded. "It sounds even crazier when you say it. But I'm telling you, I know what TV shows he liked. I know he called his little sister 'the Clemster' because she used to have cheeks like his hamster. Seeing his family at the church tore my guts out. I talked to the reverend there about it, and to a woman who routinely talks to people who have passed on. I didn't know then … I didn't understand that the police investigation was going on too long for this to have been an accident. Lacey told me yesterday it was a murder investigation, and I just couldn't deal with it. I needed time to process it. Do you know if the police have any leads?"

There. It was out. Zoe held her breath.

Dee shrugged. "If they have, they haven't told us. They're still plodding through the usual investigation, is what I gathered from Lacey." She looked up. "Why? Is there something you think they should know?"

"I'm not sure," said Zoe with complete sincerity. "I'm still struggling to believe anyone would kill him. I mean, Eric could have been one of my kids. It's unthinkable that this should happen to someone I know. Knew. I think I need that tea now. You?"

After she'd poured for both of them, careful not to look out the window this time, Zoe wrapped her hands around her mug. "It doesn't seem like Eric realizes he was deliberately locked in and left to … to die. So there's nothing I can do about that, even if I knew how to start investigating. I just want him to be at peace and move on."

"In university," Dee said, "I saw a film about a Tibetan death ritual. The monk went every day to this dying woman's house and read her a few pages from his book. It was instructions on how to let go of the things of this world and move on toward the place of reincarnation. He kept going and reading for thirty days, even though the woman died before the book was finished."

"Then you get where I'm going with this Eric thing. I didn't even believe in ghosts until last week, and I don't believe in reincarnation, but that woman I was referred to, she suggested I ask the ghost if there's any way I can help him let go of this world. That's what you were doing with your dad, maybe. It was like a Tibetan monk reading a book to someone who wasn't dead yet. Only you, yourself, were your dad's unfinished business. Did you ever ask your mom if she talked to him, too?"

"She was too busy trying to keep her own shit together. I guess now she's dying too, we should talk about what she has to let go of. Another death discussion for our final holiday together. So, that's what you're here trying to do? Talk to Eric?"

"Yes. I thought he might come into focus better out here."

"And did he?"

"He shows up in unpredictable flashes. Like just now when I saw the woodshed and suddenly it was like he was standing right behind me. He was really upset that that door was shut. The other night when I dreamed about him, he was trapped in the woodshed, beating on that door, trying to get out. And feeling so cold."

"You think he knew he was trapped in there? How horrible."

"Uh-huh. Except he can't tell me why he was there at all." That, too, was the truth. She sketched a bare outline of the things she'd felt were coming from Eric, and she was grateful Dee didn't gape or press for details. She heard the front door open, and a draught crept around her ankles. Boots stamped in the foyer. "Can we change the subject? Lacey doesn't seem like a woo-woo kind of person."

"No. She's definitely not," Dee said. "In the kitchen, Lacey!"

"You want to see these photos before I take my boots off? In case I have to reshoot?"

"You stay here," Zoe told Dee. "I'll bring the camera to you." As she walked out of the room, she felt Eric standing at the kitchen window, staring at the woodshed.

Dee pronounced herself satisfied with the exteriors, and they got to work photographing the interior spaces. After a couple of hours, Dee and Lacey finally packed up their gear and left.

Zoe let out a sigh and prepared to commune with Eric.

CHAPTER TWENTY-SIX

Lacey and Dee were driving past Waiparous Village when Dee looked up from the camera and said, "Chatting to Zoe today was quite interesting."

"Did she let anything slip about who might want Eric dead?"

"The exact opposite, actually. She's still shocked that anyone would kill him. And something else. Remember, years ago, I told you about talking to my dad while he was dying?"

"Vaguely, yeah."

"Well, Zoe thinks she's talking to Eric. She says he's upset about that shed door being barred."

"More like her subconscious sending her a message. That door being barred was all that kept the death from being ruled accidental."

"Zoe got the impression that Eric was very sleepy at the time, but also that he was panicking. Could she know about the sleeping pills in his pocket?"

"The police haven't released that information to the public, and they don't know yet if he actually took any." Lacey slowed for a farm truck to squeeze past. "She really thinks she's getting information from his ghost? Come to think of it, last week she asked Bull if they ever took tips from psychics. He figured she planned to call in an anonymous tip or something. She might not want to rat out JP, for example, but indirectly nudging the investigation might be a way around it. I should ask Bull if they got any so-called psychic tips."

"I don't think Zoe's that sneaky. And I get the feeling she's in over her head emotionally. Remember what a basket case I was last spring? Like that. She hardly sleeps, and she's been having horrible nightmares. Working for JP must be über-stressful for her right now, too."

"No doubt. I'm not too sure about JP either, by the way. I mean, he did leave the country abruptly. But my priority right now is finding Sandy. If she's not back with my car when we get home, I'm going to report it as stolen. I can always withdraw the charge if she's found with it, but reporting it will at least get the police looking for it. And it covers my ass with my insurance if it turns out she's totalled it."

"She must be back by now. She's too conscientious to just disappear without a word." Dee angled her phone toward the fading blue-green light of the western sky. "Hey, I have a signal again. Should I call home and find out?"

"We'll be there in twenty minutes. No sense getting your mom in a panic if the news isn't good."

But there was no Civic in the driveway, only Marie's van. All the main-floor windows were lit up, and when they came inside, they found Marie and Loreena sitting at the kitchen island clutching mugs. Loreena looked exhausted.

Lacey hurried over. "Bad news?"

Loreena shook her head. "No word at all. The only thing I can think of is that she's visiting that woman we met the day we went to the post office. I wish I could remember her name."

Lacey pulled up a stool. "She knew somebody in Bragg Creek?"

"We were at that little coffee shop by the grocery store, and there were three women sitting at the next table. One of them looked over a few times, and eventually Sandy said, 'I think I know her.' A few moments later, the woman came over and said hello."

"And you can't recall her name?" Dee asked.

"I'm sorry, I don't remember. It was something like Darla, or Alma, or Marlice?"

Lacey suppressed her impatience. With all the medications Loreena was on, she couldn't be expected to have perfect recall. "Did they act like old friends?"

Loreena sighed. "I think they mentioned Ontario. The woman had kind of a squarish face. She was quite stocky, with brown hair. They only chatted for a few minutes, and I was getting tired by then, so not really paying attention."

Dee patted her hand. "And you're tired now, I can tell. Maybe this description will jog Dennis's memory about people his mother used to know. I'll call him."

Lacey slipped her boots back on and walked Marie out to her car. "How's Loreena doing, really?"

"Well enough physically, but this worry isn't helping. You keep her calm and resting, keep an eye on her medications, and call me if you need anything." Marie hugged her. "If this nurse isn't back and you have to go out again tomorrow, I can come by again. My parents are dying for an excuse to have the boys to themselves."

Back inside, Dee had Dennis on speakerphone. The mention of the coffee-shop woman rang no bells for him. Lacey leaned over the phone. "Dennis, it's time you call the police to report your mother missing."

"It's only been twenty-four hours. I thought for adults you had to wait forty-eight."

"That's not set in stone. She's out of contact and that's unusual for her. Does she have voice mail that you could check from where you are?"

"Old-style answering machine. If her neighbour gets back to me, I'll ask her to check for messages. She has a key to Mom's place, to water the plants and stuff."

"This is the friend you mentioned earlier?"

"Yeah, her name's Pat. I'll give you her number, but she might have gone to bed already. She's older."

"I'll try her in the morning." Lacey jotted down the name and number. "Meanwhile, please, call the police."

"Which ones? Airdrie or Bragg Creek? Will they be open this late?"

"Cochrane detachment covers most of her route back. I can ask the duty sergeant if you can file tonight by phone. Have you called all the hospitals?"

"I've driven around to them all." His voice dropped. "Um, did my mom happen to leave any money there? I can't squeeze any more gas money from the grocery budget, and I have to keep looking for her."

Dee leaned over the phone. "We haven't felt right about snooping through your mother's stuff yet, but I guess we'd better. We'll call you back if we find anything."

While Lacey heated up soup and made grilled cheese sandwiches, Dee distracted her mother by relating Zoe's story of being haunted. She added a few details Lacey hadn't heard the first time through, such as Zoe having older relatives who'd also talked to ghosts.

This got Loreena's full attention. "I talked to your dad off and on for months after he died, forgetting he wasn't there to answer, you know. But then again, he didn't answer half the time when he was alive, either. Would this Zoe come and talk to me? If I can communicate after I'm dead, I'll be able to quit worrying about remembering everything I mean to say before I'm gone." She fidgeted with her empty mug. "Oh, before I forget, I think I should give Dennis some money to help him look for his mother."

Dee's voice was sharp. "You don't owe him that."

"I want Sandy found," said Loreena with equal bite. "I brought her here. That makes me partly responsible. Maybe that ghost woman could find her if she's dead in a snowdrift somewhere."

Lacey shook a finger at her. "Don't go there, missus. There's no reason yet to think Sandy's hurt, much less dead."

That evening, Lacey called Bull at home and brought him up to speed on Sandy, the missing Civic, and the tenuous lead of the coffee-shop woman. He recommended she give Sandy the night to reappear before officially reporting the Civic stolen. "She's an adult. For all you know she could be with a lover she didn't tell her son about. People in their fifties still have sex, you know."

After she hung up, Dee said quietly, "I wish I'd never brought up the ghost thing."

"As a distraction, it was definitely a success."

"Yeah, too much of one, maybe. Bad enough Mom thinks she can find Sandy that way. If she thinks she can talk to me after she's dead, why try while she's alive?"

Lacey had no answer for that. She headed into the office to check her email. She deleted a handful of spam, forwarded a phishing attempt to PayPal, and stared at a new email that had popped up from Dan. The subject line was "Merry Christmas," but beyond that opening, it could be anything from a forwarded holiday meme to another sneak attack on her shaky confidence. Or maybe he finally had an offer on the house.

Open, or delete? Her cursor hovered. To anyone else, his exact words might appear innocuous, but each subtle sneer would stick under her skin, worm its way in like foxtail grass to drain whatever strength she'd built up. When would she be free of him?

She'd read it tomorrow when she was rested and more resilient. She clicked instead on one from Jan Brenner:

> The motion sickness is getting better. I stayed on our stateroom veranda for the whole passage between islands this morning, since we were on the shady side. Glorious to watch the smaller boats whiz by, and the turquoise sea! It looks just like

in the brochures. We're in another beach bar with Wi-Fi, but off on a plantation tour soon. Rum this time, not that I can drink any, but Terry will enjoy it more than the banana one.

He wants me to pass along that TFB Energy, JP Thompson's company, has a good environmental record. They've even cleaned up poisoned assets they bought accidental-ly, although they could have dumped them on the province through a subsidiary like so many companies do. Won some kind of industry award for stewardship a couple of years ago, and created a bursary for grad students working on well-site remediation. So whatever made Eric decide to go into Environmental Studies, it wasn't suspicions of TFB hiding a toxic time bomb.

I half wish I was there to help with the sleuthing, but this sunshine and warmth is heaven. I've seen eight Santa Clauses so far today — more than the past five years com-bined — and they're really hot! Literally. Half-naked sweaty guys in red pants, sus-penders, and hats. It takes forever to upload photos, so I'll show you when I'm back. Hugs to you and Dee and the dogs.

Lacey hit Reply and started typing, filling Jan in on the missing nurse, the cross-country skiing, and Calvin's claim that his whereabouts were an official secret. She ended by reporting Zoe's story of being haunted by Eric.

The skeptic in me thinks she's looking for a way to feed information to the police without directly betraying her boss. If he's not hiding environmental disasters, the only angle left that I can see is the computer malware. I should have asked how much money got mailed out in those bogus cheques. Was it enough to cause problems with the sale, just like a polluted well site would? Unremediated well site = poisoned asset, right? See, I'm starting to pick up the oil-patch jargon.

It felt good to lay everything out where she could see it. She signed off and went up to bed with her book, but soon the worries crowded in again. Another night with no Sandy, another day with Eric's death hanging over the chalet sale. Her uneasy stalemate with her own status as victim — or survivor. And now Dan's unread email lurking like an unexploded bomb. The end of this year wasn't shaping up to be any better than the rest had been. Turning off the light felt more like defeat than a reprieve.

CHAPTER TWENTY-SEVEN

Early the next morning, Lacey settled in the office with her coffee and her phone. She dialed the Ontario number for Sandy's friend Pat. It rang eight times before clicking over to voice mail. She left a message, introducing herself and referencing Dennis. "I don't want to alarm you, but Sandy hasn't been heard from for a couple of days. If you know of anyone in Alberta she might have gone to see, please let us know." She ended with the numbers for her cell and Dee's landline.

She was on her third game of Solitaire when her phone buzzed.

"Lacey speaking."

"Hello?"

She categorized the voice: female, wavering, high-pitched, probably older. "Is this Pat?"

"Yes. Are you the lady Sandy is staying with?"

"One of them, yes. You got my message?"

"Well, yes. I got Dennis's message from yesterday, too, but he didn't say she was missing. Oh, dear."

"You haven't heard from her since she came out to Alberta?"

"She hasn't phoned, if that's what you mean. I haven't been home to check my email. I always stay at my daughter's over the holidays."

"Can you check your email from there?"

"Oh, no, dear. I have no idea how to do that. I barely remember how to pick up my phone messages."

"Perhaps your daughter or someone there could help you?"

"They wouldn't know what my password is."

"You don't know your email password?"

"No, dear. It's on a piece of paper stuck to my computer desk. Right where my grandson put it when he set me up." Pat seemed to realize this was an unhelpful response. "I'll see if my daughter can drive me home tomorrow to check."

"Would you know of anyone Sandy might have gone to visit out here? Maybe someone she used to work with?"

"I used to work there, too, if you mean at the nursing home. Ten years we carpooled. We live on the same block."

"Then maybe you'd know the woman Sandy talked to out here. Brown hair, squarish face, about Sandy's age. First name might be Darla or Alma or Marlice."

"It doesn't ring a bell, but I retired a few years before Sandy. She held on for three years more before she left. But the less said about that the better."

Lacey's ear twitched, like Boney's when he heard a treat bag. "Did she not leave the nursing home on good terms?"

"Now that's none of your business, young lady. She did nothing wrong, no matter what she was accused of."

Lacey asked again, but Pat was adamant. "I'll check my email tomorrow, and if there's one from her, I'll call you. I hope you find her real soon. You tell her to call me when you do."

She hung up, leaving Lacey to wonder what accusations had caused Sandy to leave the nursing home. Google told her the only significant Ontario nursing home scandal had involved a nurse who had killed off elderly residents. Sandy's name didn't appear in any news about the case, but if she were similarly suspected, might she have escorted Loreena west as a way to quietly flee Ontario? If so, Lacey's car might be in Montana by now.

The only useful result of her searches was the profile photo — posted last summer — on Sandy's otherwise inactive Facebook page. Lacey saved a copy and emailed it over to Bull. Then she phoned him.

"No hospitals or police reports on a subject matching that description," he told her. "Send over a photo of your car and have this woman's son come in to file a missing person report. I want to size him up in case he whacked mom with a wrench and dumped her body."

"And people think I'm cynical."

She sent Dennis the Cochrane detachment information and sought out breakfast. In the kitchen she found Loreena struggling to lift the kettle off its base. "Go sit down. I'll make breakfast."

Loreena shuffled to a stool. "I don't have much of an appetite. I'm worried about Sandy. And about her son. Can you show me how to email him money after breakfast? I'll give you some gas money at the same time, to cover all the extra driving you're doing. Maybe don't tell Dee, though."

"Tell Dee what?" Dee said from the doorway.

"No walking cast today, dear? That's an improvement."

"I'll put it on later, when we go out. What can we do about you today? I don't want to drag you around in Calgary. And somebody should be here if Sandy phones."

"Where are we going?" Lacey pulled eggs out of the fridge.

"To photograph JP's house in Mount Royal. Then to my physio appointment this afternoon. I thought I told you all that last night."

"If you had, I'd have invited Marie back."

"Maybe we should hire a home care service."

Loreena snapped, "I don't need a keeper."

Dee squinted at her. "Didn't you like Marie?"

"She was quite nice and certainly competent. But I'm fine on my own."

Lacey intervened diplomatically. "She asked to come back. She'd like to leave her sons with her parents for a day and not be stuck hanging around there herself."

Loreena's thin lips relaxed. "So, I'd be her excuse for an escape? In that case, I'd be delighted with her company."

Dee rolled her eyes.

Zoe greeted the first rays of sunlight with a cup of coffee in one hand and a pen in the other. An open notepad lay beside her laptop. JP's face peered at her from the screen. "That's the full list of essential personnel," he concluded. "The top five get fifteen percent of their annual gross, the rest ten percent if they stay in their current jobs until the sale's done or June thirtieth, whichever comes first."

"Marcia from Accounts Payable is an essential?"

"She's a special case." He rubbed his ebb-tide hairline and cast the familiar glance over his shoulder to check for his wife.

"Because she's acting head of IT, too?" Ignoring Eric's voice in her head was easier on top of a full night's sleep, but he wasn't entirely quiet in there. "Do they really need her when there won't be any capital projects? Someone else could sign off on the time sheets." And someone else needed to take over the production accountant position, or that whole income stream would be compromised by Marcia's incompetence.

"Accounts Payable won't change much either, and we've got people who know it far better than her. But she's Phyl's friend, and if she gets wind of others getting a better bonus, she may make things ... unpleasant."

She doesn't know shit about IT. Zoe couldn't quite keep Eric's sarcasm out of her tone. "When the time for severance packages arrives, will she be a 'special case' then, too? Or does she have an evergreen contract that you'll be paying out?"

"She'll get what everyone else does: one month's salary per year of work." Only three months' salary? That wouldn't help the acerbic accountant much. This might very well be her last decent job. Middle-aged women weren't a hot hire in any industry. For all his insistence on Marcia's retention bonus, JP didn't seem to realize or care that he would be pulling the rug out from under her right after that. He glanced down at his desk. "Is that everything?"

"Yeah, I think the rest is pretty straightforward."

"The police haven't released any updates on Eric's death?"

"Not to me." Lacey's words from the end of the ski trip came to mind, but that wasn't an official update. If the police made a public statement calling the death suspicious, she would tell him. She'd never before felt the need to keep things from him, but if he was keeping things from her about Eric's trip to the chalet ...

"Can you keep your ear to the ground today at the funeral? See what people are saying. If they're blaming me in any way, I need to know. And —"

"Why would they blame you?"

"Oh, you know how people talk. I didn't ask him to come out there. He approached me. And the blizzard wasn't my fault, either."

Typical JP. Just covering his own ass. Zoe straightened up. "Wait a minute, the funeral is today? Nobody told me."

"Arliss emailed me. I forwarded it to you, I thought. Or maybe to Marcia. She'll have circulated it to the staff." He gave her that old pleading look over his glasses. "If nobody from the company is there, it'll look like we don't care. You have to go. Say all the right things for me."

"Why me?" Instinct said to get up and run. Or scream at him. Or smash the screen. She could not watch Eric be buried. Not when he was too real, too present, in her thoughts already.

No, no, no, not ready to die, not ready to be dead.

Through clenched teeth, she said, "I have other work that needs doing. That's why I'm not on holidays with my family."

"If a couple of hours today will deflect a lawsuit, you need to take those two hours, Zoe. Please. I'm sorry you're missing out on time with your family, but your shares will tank just like mine if we end up in court. Lawsuits can drag on for years, and I want to push the button on this sale as soon as possible." He shoved his glasses farther up his nose. "Just go, okay? Once we can hand off to an outside sales management team, I'll pay for you to have a proper vacation someplace warm."

Trust JP to think he could buy her loyalty. Did he even realize how many meals and school outings and weekends with her family she'd missed during all those years she'd worked directly for him? Probably not. He'd counted on her, and she'd always been there. Once the company was sold and her shares paid out, she was done.

Meanwhile, there was the funeral. She definitely couldn't tell him her real reason for wanting to avoid it. "Your secretary could represent you," she suggested.

"She's about as warm as a glacier. This needs a personal touch. Arliss won't do it. She calls it a conflict of interest, but it isn't one, legally. She's just protecting her friendship with Eric's mom."

And why was protecting a friendship a bad choice for a woman who was no longer involved directly with the company? What he was really complaining about was that his ex-wife dared to put her friendships ahead of his business interests. Centre of his own galaxy, he was.

Zoe sat back in her chair and looked out the window at the white lawn, the bumps that were bushes and the mounds that were flowerbeds. So much had been buried. She shivered. He was right: her shares would take a hit if the company had a lawsuit hanging over it, or, heaven forbid, if someone connected to it was directly involved in Eric's death. Could she afford to kiss off that value after she'd sacrificed years of family time to earn it? A buyout represented Lizi's university tuition, paying down their line of credit, and maybe even topping up her neglected RRSP. And since he'd suggested it, she *would* make JP pay for this bit of blatant coercion to feel Eric's pain for two hours as he watched himself being eulogized and buried.

"All right, I'll go. But I'll expect two weeks at an all-inclusive resort in the Caribbean in February, and I want a bonus for my work over the holidays." She looked him in the eyes, daring him to tell her he didn't need her. Nobody knew the insides of that company the way she did.

He looked over his shoulder again as a door shut in some distant room. "Oh, shit. She's back. Okay, you go to the service and the reception, and I'll give you whatever resort you choose plus an equivalent cash bonus. But ... damn it —" He vanished without even saying goodbye.

Zoe's heartbeat drummed in her ears. She could not have felt more wrung out if she had just completed a triathlon — and it was only nine in the morning. The majority of the day's emotional obstacle course still lay ahead.

Toomie came into the room and meowed sadly. "Lizi's not here," she said, reaching down a hand for the snub nose to rub against. He leaped onto her lap and head-butted her chin. She wrapped her arms around him, burying her face in his soft, silky fur. "Oh, kitty, I wish my life was as uncomplicated as yours."

Lacey tramped through a light dusting of fresh snow to the front door and rang the bell. Zoe's place was a smallish, older house — not what she'd expected for well-connected oil industry employees. Vinyl siding, two storeys, barely room enough in the driveway for two vehicles.

Zoe answered on the first ring, opening the door so fast the wind tossed her hair across her face. "Good morning, Lacey. Here's the master fob and the alarm code for the house."

"Should we drop them back here when we're done?"

Zoe's voice was brittle. "I'll be at Eric Anders's funeral and then at the family reception. Bring it there if you're done in time."

"They hardly know me," said Lacey.

Zoe's lip curled. "Call it professional courtesy from JP's realtor, then. Come for lunch. There'll be tons of food. The address is on the back of the alarm code." She shut the door abruptly. Lacey stared at it for a moment, then walked back to the Lexus.

"I should have sent you to the door," she told Dee, "you two being confidantes now."

Dee took the square of paper. "Let's get this over with in time to eat before my appointment."

"We're invited for lunch at the funeral reception. I didn't say we'd go."

"If it's free food, I vote for going."

Lacey shrugged, and they drove off. If they did go, she could see for herself how the family was coping, and maybe Calvin would reveal whatever paranoid imaginings he believed were official secrets. The afternoon wouldn't be wasted if she could help rule a couple of suspects in or out.

Twenty minutes later, they pulled up in front of a wrought-iron gate in Mount Royal. The fob got them inside. Following Dee's directions, Lacey drove around back, where the fob also let her into the multi-vehicle garage. Ignoring the luxurious BMWs and Mercedes already parked, she stopped as close as possible to the door that led into the house. It was locked. The keypad bore a label from Wayne's security company. Could he be another source of information about JP and his company? She keyed in the code Zoe had given her, and the steel door opened onto a small foyer. One door led into another section of basement, a second opened on a stairwell, and between them stood a small elevator. She crowded into it with Dee and the camera equipment.

On the main floor, an expanse of grey marble gleamed in the light that streamed through a two-and-a-half-storey wall of windows. Classical-looking statuary gazed out at them from niches around the curving stairwell. Every word and footstep echoed. Lacey gaped. "I had no idea Cowtown ran to marble palaces. How big is this place?"

"You'll see." Dee flung her coat onto a bench. She took wide-angle shots of a few of the rooms and close-ups of some of the architectural details, such as the acanthus-leaf half columns that bracketed the dining room fireplace. Not a cushion was out of place anywhere. The only room at all personalized was a small study tucked away behind the immense living room. There, the mahogany shelves held worn books and framed photos of children in various stages of life. The newest showed them as teens and young adults. Some included Aidan, Clemmie, and Eric Anders, the last recognizable from the missing-person poster in Cochrane detachment. Dee selected a few pictures to prop on the mahogany desk. "For the homey touch," she said, snapping photos.

As they rode up to the second floor, Lacey said, "Judging by the character of this house, one of the residents is an icicle."

"That would be Phyl," said Dee. "The second Mrs. Thompson. She takes British reserve to Arctic proportions. JP is a typical businessman, not exactly nurturing, but next to her he's Mr. Personality."

They worked their way through the six bedrooms, each with an ensuite bathroom and walk-in closet, then headed down to the basement, where a home theatre to one side of a giant games room was balanced by a work-out room with a swimming machine on the other side. A guest suite lurked down there, too. Back in the garage, Lacey loaded the camera gear into the Lexus and took a moment, while Dee dictated a final note to herself to text Wayne a query about JP Thompson.

"Lunch at the funeral?" Lacey asked as she backed up the car.

CHAPTER TWENTY-EIGHT

This isn't me. The thought whirled for the hundredth time through Zoe's mind. The auditorium-like chapel was quiet but for the shuffling of feet and rustle of clothing. The heavy odour of stargazer lilies drifted from a dozen bouquets. *I hate lilies.* As the coffin was rolled toward the open double doors and the waiting hearse, she backpedalled down the side aisle. Sixty-five minutes of Eric's dismay, his shocked recognition of friends and relations, his mounting anger at the unfairness of being dead — it was as much as she could stand today. She'd waved the company flag, but no matter what JP wanted of her, she was done.

In the front foyer, Arliss Thompson took her arm and pulled her aside. "You snuck in at the last minute."

"I only heard about it this morning from JP."

"I assumed JP would tell you. Should have known better." Arliss's face hardened. "Couldn't tear himself away from his happy English Christmas, of course. I suppose it's enough that my son was allowed to fly home for the funeral of his oldest friend."

"TJ's here?" Zoe looked past her for the boy — now young man — and couldn't quite separate Eric's flood of pleasure from her own giddy realization that the burden of representing the company wasn't on her shoulders alone. Terrance John Thompson, young though he was, made a more than adequate representative for TFB Energy.

"Landed this morning and called me from the airport." Arliss tugged a toque on over her loose brown curls and fished a key ring from her pocket. "I delegated him to keep Calvin under control. I'm driving them to the cemetery now. Can you head straight to the house and let the caterers in?"

"Me? No, I'm not — I've got work waiting."

"Don't argue today, of all days. I need you there until I can take over." Arliss slapped a set of house keys into Zoe's palm. "Park behind my place to keep the road clear."

I can go home!

Zoe looked at the keys and felt herself turning away, thrilled to get to that house before anyone else showed up.

My room. My stuff. My life.

Beyond the churning in her stomach, a corner of her was happy for Eric's joy. Another hour wouldn't kill her, and it might help Eric finally say goodbye.

She forced herself to turn back to Arliss. "Any special instructions?"

"Food goes in the dining room. I got the boys to take out the chairs and push the table against the wall last night. Make sure they put the bar in the living room, near where people are coming in. A drink in hand will ease everybody's tension."

A drink would ease Zoe's, too, but it might weaken her tongue's fragile defences against Eric's thoughts, fears, and memories. There was too much already that she absolutely could not reveal in front of his devastated family. If she left right away, though, she could be halfway there before the funeral procession started, with lots of time for Eric to look around and do his remembering in relative privacy.

Home.

The caterer's van was idling out front when she arrived. She led it around to the alley and unlocked the back door. Eric's excitement throbbed in her veins. The kitchen seemed familiar: tidy and slightly shabby, its dark-veneered cupboards and cream appliances pre-millennium. She passed along Arliss's instructions to the caterers, then, feeling a bit dizzy, let her feet carry her up the half flight of stairs to the bedrooms. She entered the first small room and knew immediately it had been Eric's. She *felt* it.

The bed was covered in serviceable navy twill, wrinkled where somebody had sat. Books leaned on the shelves amid robots, spaceships, and other geeky gadgets — some recognizable from those sci-fi shows Zoe had never seen. A laptop on the desk was open, but the screen was dark.

In there. It's all in there.

She turned the laptop on. Her fingers settled on the keyboard, but she couldn't quite figure out what Eric was trying to type. She left it and opened the bottom dresser drawer instead. There, jumbled in with hiking socks and crumpled T-shirts, were tattered stuffed animals: a dog with long, floppy ears and a creature so thoroughly loved its original shape was lost. She pulled them out, squeezed them lovingly, and set them on the pillow. As she stood up, tears in her eyes, the first black limousine pulled up outside.

Lacey approached the front door and rang the bell. A vaguely familiar young man opened it. She introduced herself. "I'm just here to drop off something for Zoe. Do you know her?"

"Sure. I'll find her for you. Come on in, so I can shut the door."

He slid away through the crowd, leaving Lacey prey to the enticing scents of fresh bread and spicy meatballs, and other equally appealing aromas. Her stomach gurgled. Zoe soon edged into view from the kitchen. She seemed to have lost weight overnight. She swayed as she walked and put a hand on the wall to steady herself.

"You look done in," said Lacey. "Let me take you home."

"I can't leave yet. Can you come in for a bit, be my wingman until I can escape?"

"Sorry, I'm double-parked. The nearest empty space is too far for Dee to walk."

Zoe pointed across the living room. "There's parking behind the neighbour's house. I'll show you, if you'll please, please just come in for a bit. You and Dee. Eric's childhood friends are here and I can't —" She stopped and hurried Lacey out to the front steps. "I know this sounds crazy, but I can't take Eric away right now, not when it might be the last time he ever sees the people he cared about. I'm trying to do my best by him, the way that ghost-talker woman told me."

Lacey searched the older woman's drawn face. She might be nuts, but she definitely believed what she was saying. And she was suffering. "If Dee is willing, we'll come in. Do you need your jacket?"

"I'm not sure where it is. I'll run." At the Lexus, Zoe scrambled into the back seat. She repeated what she'd told Lacey.

Dee reached back and clasped her hand. "Of course we'll come in."

Leaving the Lexus between Zoe's van and a grey Volvo wagon with a ski rack on top, the trio slipped in the kitchen door.

Aidan immediately appeared. "Lacey! Good to see you." He turned to a young man at his side, the one who had opened the front door earlier. "Teej, this is Lacey, who took us skiing the other day. Lacey, TJ Thompson, our next-door neighbour. Oh, that's the doorbell. I'll go." He hurried off, leaving Lacey to introduce Dee and to eye up TJ. This was Arliss Thompson's son, who lived part-time in the modest split-level next door and part-time at that marble mansion in Mount Royal. What did he make of the gulf between his mother's modest life and his father's wealthy one?

TJ led them into the dining room. "Let me get you all something to drink. Tea, coffee, wine, whiskey?" Clemmie and three other teenage girls were huddled in a corner of the room. Clemmie's red eyes and streaky cheeks told their own tale — no reserved wall to hide behind today. She pushed through the buffet line toward them. Lacey introduced Dee as the dogs' owner, and belatedly realized Dee might hear the whole story of her and Boney's misadventure under the icefall. That had been only two days ago, but it seemed like weeks.

Dee smiled at Clemmie. "Lacey said my dogs really like you. If you'd like to come and take them trail walking sometime, I'll gladly give you my phone number." Clemmie's eyes spilled over. She wiped them on a shredded Kleenex. By then TJ was back, balancing two wineglasses and a teacup.

"Milk and sugar are behind you," he told Lacey. "I can bring you plates. Anything you can't have or don't like? Zoe, do you want anything else?"

The woman shook her head. "Get a chair for Ms. Phillips first, please. She's got a bad leg."

"Yes, please," said Dee with a sigh. "We photographed a huge house this morning."

TJ eyed her with new awareness. "Phillips? You're the realtor. Were you at Dad's place? Monstrous, isn't it?" He hooked an arm around the kitchen doorway and dragged in a stool. "Can you manage this? Better than sitting down low and being surrounded by people's belt buckles." He eased into the buffet line as Lacey helped Dee onto the stool.

Zoe whispered in Clemmie's ear and the girl's brows wrinkled. "Nobody's looked yet? Well, I guess it's okay. If the password's not Worble17, Cal might know. Worble is —"

"His stuffed animal," Zoe finished. "Back in a bit," she said to Dee. "The boys will make sure you're fed." She angled through the kitchen door. Lacey frowned. First Zoe was making a big deal of their coming in, and now she was taking off on them?

Clemmie twisted her hands together. "I should go with her. She wants to check my brother's laptop to make sure there's no confidential work stuff left on it. I don't dare ask my parents about that right now. Do you think it's okay?"

Okay to let Zoe tamper with Eric's laptop? He wasn't officially a murder victim yet, but there might be useful information on there. Now that Zoe knew Eric's death was suspicious, she could be deleting files to cover her or JP's tracks.

"I'll come with you," Lacey told Clemmie. "Dee, don't eat all my meatballs."

Dee raised her wineglass high as a woman pushed past. "Marcia?"

The accountant turned. "Oh, sorry, I'm trying to find out where they put my coat." She edged closer, her big purse bumping heavily against the door frame.

"Down in the rec room," said Clemmie. "I can show you—"

"I'll find it," Marcia said, and hurried away.

As Clemmie led Lacey to the stairs, a few people were leaving, shaking Aidan's hand and murmuring the usual kind of condolences. The children's father stood by the fireplace, giving minimal nods to the guests who passed him. Their mother was nowhere to be seen. A young man Lacey didn't recognize came upstairs carrying an armful of coats. The front door opened again, sending a swirl of icy air into the hall. Clemmie darted up the half flight of stairs and stopped in front of the first door, so suddenly that Lacey almost ran into her. Inside the small room, Zoe sat cross-legged on a single bed, hugging a limp stuffed animal and weeping silently. Lacey sent Clemmie off to fetch some tissues. She shut the bedroom door and sat down beside Zoe. "It's time you got out of this place."

Zoe blotted her eyes on her sleeves. "I'm so sorry Clemmie saw that."

"I told her you were exhausted from working too much over the holidays."

"Thanks." Zoe stared at the room's small desk. "It was right there two hours ago."

"What was?"

"His laptop." She lifted the stuffed animal. "This is Mr. Worble. Eric had him for seventeen years." Her eyes filled again. "I should never have agreed to come here."

"Wait. You saw the laptop here earlier, and now it's gone? Maybe someone put it out of sight for safety's sake. Did you look in the desk drawers, or the closet?"

"I checked." As Clemmie returned, Zoe untucked her legs. She set Mr. Worble on the pillow. "Sorry to upset you, Clemmie. I'm really overtired. Do you know where the laptop went? I'd like to check it and then get off home."

The girl looked around, confused. "It's been right there on the desk since the day he left. Maybe Cal finally took it downstairs. He's been hoarding other stuff down there."

"I'll find out." Lacey's stomach rumbled at the thought of the spicy meatballs cooling on her plate. "Let's leave Zoe to rest a bit longer. Clemmie, can you go tell Dee I'll be back in a few minutes?"

Lacey headed to the basement. Several winter coats remained, piled on the couch with scarves trailing from their sleeves. She opened doors onto, respectively, a storage room lined with shelves, a tidy room with a futon made up as a bed, and a cramped, dark bedroom that oozed with the smell of stale sweat. There was no sign of Calvin. Down another short staircase, a washroom door stood open. She availed herself of the facilities, glad of the relative quiet. As she came out, Calvin grabbed her wrist. "I need to talk to you."

She yanked her arm free. "Do not touch me again."

"Okay, sorry," he said, and hurried into a laundry room. "Come in here, quick." Shutting the door behind her, he hoisted himself onto a chest freezer and sat hunched, his hands fidgeting. A furnace rumbled to life behind the wall.

Lacey leaned against the washing machine. The chemical smells of bleach and fabric softener filled her nostrils. "Is this about where you were the day Eric went up to the chalet?" she asked. "Your alibi?"

Calvin sighed and stared up at the ceiling.

She tried again. "Calvin, just tell me."

"Okay. I applied for an analyst job with CSIS, and I was at an evaluation that weekend. It's supposed to be a secret."

"You?" Lacey barely stifled her incredulity. Paranoia she'd expected, but if Calvin believed he was going to work for Canada's spy agency, maybe he was well over the edge.

As if reading her thoughts, he flushed. "It's true. I had to sign a non-disclosure agreement to be there. If I tell the RCMP, I'm violating the agreement. If CSIS finds out I'm being questioned in a suspicious death, they'll shred my application." He hopped down from the freezer. "Look, I don't want to lose my shot. Could you be, like, my intermediary? Tell the RCMP that's where I was?"

Lacey frowned. "I can't take your word for something this important."

"I could give you my recruiter's number. If you made up an excuse and called him, maybe he'd tell you I was there."

Lacey studied the young man. He seemed intense today, but focused, not as jittery as she'd expected, considering he'd just attended the funeral of his best friend. Maybe he was heavily medicated. How likely was it that CSIS would be interviewing a socially awkward computer whiz who wasn't even Canadian? Still, if he gave her a name to call, and that person could credibly account for his whereabouts, he'd have an alibi for that November weekend and could be ruled out as a suspect. Bull could then chase other leads, maybe wrap up the case sooner.

She had him recount the smaller details of his weekend a couple of times — the room he was tested in, where he slept, what he ate and drank, anything she could think of that wouldn't be covered by his supposed non-disclosure agreement — and concluded that his details were consistent and given without significant hesitation, and that each telling was similar, but not identical. In police interviews, those cues indicated both an unrehearsed story and one unlikely to be entirely confabulated on the spot. Could he possibly be telling the truth?

"All right, then, send me the recruiter's number. If they confirm you were with them, I'll tell the RCMP you're in the clear. But you have to do something for me."

"What?"

"Find any other instances where that cheque printer malware, 33 or whatever it's called, has been used in Canada." It was a long shot, but maybe somebody at TFB Energy had used it before and brought it with them from another company. She could cross-check employee resumes with those companies — for employees who had resumes online, anyway. What other leads did she have? Somebody had killed Eric Anders for some reason, and the only thing that remotely resembled a motive was the accounting malware he'd uncovered.

Her hand was on the doorknob when she remembered the original reason she'd come downstairs. "Did you bring Eric's laptop down here? It's not on his desk."

"I don't touch his computers, he doesn't touch mine."

Alone in Eric's bedroom, Zoe sat on the bed with Mr. Worble. The urge to weep had left her. Given tacit permission to be here, she slowly uncurled in spirit and in body. "Eric, this is your room," she whispered. "What would you look at and touch if you could?"

A kind of peace settled around her, muting the sounds beyond the room. Slowly she stood and moved around the space, the limp toy tucked under her arm, running her fingertips lightly over furnishings, books, clothes hanging in the closet. Bidding each thing farewell. She hovered by the shelves, touching each spaceship in turn. Their names floated through her mind: *Millennium Falcon, Serenity, Enterprise, Andromeda Ascendant, Moya*, and the one Eric was most interested in, *Galactica*. She closed her hand around it and searched for a pocket to hide it in. No pockets in dress pants. Her purse was down in the van, her keys in her jacket, wherever that was. She set the ship back on the shelf. "Sorry. I can't take this away. Say goodbye." Turning resolutely, she left the room, her soul aching more with every step. Time to get out of here forever.

On the staircase, she all but ran into Eric's father. Eyes vacant, he sidestepped around her. Dizziness washed over her. *He's never been here for us. Now's no different.* She started to silently tell Eric that all parents loved their children, even if they couldn't show it, but then she registered the complete absence of emotion coming from Brian. He was going through the expected motions, no more. She'd felt it faintly at the Blue Christmas service, too, his detachment from the suffering around him, and had assumed it was his defensive reaction to overwhelming grief. But no. Arliss had quite aptly described him as 'checked out'. She watched him vanish into a bedroom before she headed downstairs. Her foot missed the edge of a step, but luckily Aidan was there to block her fall.

"Are you okay?" he asked, settling her on her feet at the bottom.

"Uh, yeah. Just overtired." Beyond him the living room was empty except for several caterers collecting cups and glasses. "Is everyone gone?"

"Pretty much. Arliss and Clemmie are packing up the extra food. They could probably use a hand. If you can spare another few minutes, that is. You've done a lot for us already."

"Of course I'll help." Zoe headed toward the kitchen, one hand on the wall in case another wave of dizziness hit.

The other women had gathered around the breakfast table, which was now loaded with platters. Dee was transferring cubes of cheese into Ziploc bags. Zoe picked an empty plastic tub from a stack mid-table. "What should I put in here?"

Arliss surveyed the depleted platters. "Dessert squares look about that size. If there's room, you can add those cookies. Did you want to take some home for your gang?"

"Mine are all away."

"Oh, right. Skiing. Your house must seem very quiet." Arliss handed a lid across to Clemmie. "I'll have to get real groceries now that TJ's home for the week."

Her son ambled in and hung Zoe's jacket on an empty hook by the back door. "Last coat from downstairs," he said, and filched a brownie from the platter. "Don't clean everything up. Aidan hasn't eaten yet."

"Neither has Lacey," said Clemmie. "Or did she leave?"

"She's my driver," said Dee, "so she'd better be here."

"She's downstairs." TJ handed Dee another Ziploc. "So, you're selling all of Dad's property, eh? I'm gonna miss Black Rock. We had some sick times out there in the old cabin."

"I recall an awful lot of complaining about it, too," said Arliss.

He grinned. "You gotta admit, clearing trail for weeks on end, getting chewed on by bugs and buzzed by crows, was no picnic." He added with obvious pride, "Mom was a slave driver. You remember, Zoe? She got all the cabins involved, and we cleared the whole Bowl Loop trail in one summer, each family doing the bit behind their place. The next Christmas and every one since, we were all out on them skiing, skidooing, snowshoeing. You can go a lot farther nowadays, all the way to Waiparous Village if you want. Mom's on the Backcountry Safety Association board, and she leads ski and horseback treks out from Saddle Peak into the real wilderness."

"Not so much anymore," said Arliss. "Sleeping on the cold ground has lost its appeal. I still love that whole area, though. After I heard JP was selling the chalet, I went out for a ski, for old times' sake. Just around the Bowl, hardly enough to work up a sweat, but it brought back good memories." She gave her son a one-armed squeeze. "We had great times there."

He squeezed back. "We sure did. If it was still the old cabin, I'd make him an offer on it. But not this new place — there are no good memories in it. Or in Dad's house, for that matter. That place is an ice palace. Christmas there would have been an overdecorated hell. The chalet wasn't much better after it was 'renovated.'" He mimed air quotes. "This year, trapped in a London hotel with Phyl and all her upper-crust rituals, was like hell's tenth circle, complete with demons." While he regaled them with tales of an English hotel Christmas geared toward spoiled rich kids, Aidan and Lacey came in. Dee pointed out Lacey's plate, with its room-temperature meatballs and limp salad. Aidan pulled a plate from the cupboard for himself.

"I take it Phyl's no easier to swallow over there?" he said. As he stretched for cold cuts, Zoe noticed a slight tremor in his hand. He'd done really well handling the reception crowd, but clearly it was taking a toll on him. She lifted the platter closer for him.

TJ shrugged. "I stood her as long as I decently could, but Eric was my best friend for ten years. So I got on the plane yesterday, and I'm not going back. Fran can fly home with Ben before school starts." The doorbell rang. "I'll get that. You eat."

Arliss snapped a lid down tight. "I'll say one thing about that expensive private academy: it taught my crass sons a few social graces."

"Social skills are useful in most professions," said Dee. "Pass that cookie plate over, please."

A woman's voice came from the front hall. Aidan's shoulders slumped. "I thought we were done. What's Marcia doing back?"

Zoe suppressed a shiver, whether from the draught or something less tangible. As TJ's voice and Marcia's receded toward the basement, Clemmie half-whispered, "I don't like that woman. She was awful to my brother."

Zoe frowned. "She's the last person I thought would come."

Arliss snorted. "Me too. She's got no sense of good corporate culture. That nursing home she worked for, it made a good atmosphere for the residents. The nurses mostly got along with each other, too. Not her. She treated the floor staff like dirt because their hands got mucky." As the voices came back up the stairs, she fell silent. For a few minutes, the only sounds came from the shifting of foods into permanent containers and the clink of glassware as the caterers packed away their property.

"Lost a glove," TJ reported as he returned alone. "It was in a couch cushion downstairs. Either that or it was just an excuse to come back and grill me about dear Phyl's Christmas. She wants me to pass along her best wishes for New Year's. I didn't tell her I'm not going back."

"How was she awful to Eric?" Lacey asked.

She's a bitch popped into Zoe's head immediately. "As far as I can tell," she said diplomatically, "she was a bit insecure because he knew at least as much about computer networks as she did. At TFB, Accounting supervises IT. That task devolved to Marcia last summer when someone went on mat leave. It can't have been easy supervising a bunch of guys who knew their job far better than she did."

"She doesn't like young men, period," said Arliss. "Probably doesn't know any personally. She tried to get Eric's internship pulled, just because he and Calvin were in the office unsupervised one night. You'd think they'd held a drug-fuelled rave in there. She's in over her head, but Phyl wanted her to have that job, and we all know that what Phyl wants, JP provides."

TJ slung his arm around her shoulders. "Easy, Ma. You're sounding bitter again."

Arliss's face flushed. "Marcia isn't qualified for oil-patch accounting, let alone heading Accounts Payable. If she hadn't been kissing up to Phyl on those long visits to your Grandma Thompson, she'd still be doing bed-pan inventory and complaining about the cost of adult diapers."

TJ snagged a cookie from under Dee's fingers. "Man, those visits. You made them so much fun when we were little, I don't remember ever caring that Grandma didn't recognize us. We always rented that same cottage by the river with the tree fort in the yard, and apart from obligatory visits to Grandma at the beginning and end, it was our summer holiday. Dad would hang out there, showing her photos of the old days, and you would play pirates with us." Then his grin vanished. "Not after Phyl, though. She hated every minute, resented being stuck in small-town Ontario. Even though she only had to do it for a couple of years before Grandma died."

Lost in Eric's memories of life in these familiar sur-roundings, Zoe was vaguely aware of the conversation shifting back to the family's Black Rock holidays. Lacey asked if TJ had come home with his father on that bliz-zard weekend.

"Separate vehicles," TJ replied, then changed the subject. Zoe stared hard at him. That was the very day Eric had died. Had he lingered, waiting for his old pal to show up? Had he locked Eric in the woodshed? But why would he? No motive, as far as she knew, and he had never been obviously unstable, or at least no more so than most teenagers.

Dee stood up. "We've got to go. My physio's in twenty minutes."

Lacey set her plate in the sink. "Thanks for the lunch. Clemmie, you call us if you want to visit Boney and Beau. Zoe, did you want me to drop you at home?"

Zoe shook her head. "I'll be okay driving, thanks. This quiet half hour with all of you has been wo—" She'd started to say "wonderful," but that would sound heartless to the young people whose brother had been buried today. *Dead-not-dead.* She swallowed. "Peaceful. I'll go say goodbye to your dad, Aidan. If he won't see me, you be sure and tell him the company will help with anything he needs done."

She grabbed her jacket and ran upstairs. "Turn the Page" was sending a bass rumble through the door of Brian's room. Instead of knocking, she darted into Eric's bedroom, snatched the *Galactica* model, and stuffed it into her pocket.

CHAPTER TWENTY-NINE

After physio, Lacey helped Dee into the Lexus.

"How come massages feel good, but physio is torture?" Dee groaned.

Lacey concentrated on the late-afternoon traffic. "That reception today. You had more of a chance than me to observe the Anders family dynamic. Anything seem odd to you?"

"Apart from how they're all in shock and mourning?" Dee watched the crosswalk light count down the seconds. "The parents totally abdicated. Might as well not have been there at all. The neighbour seemed bossy, but the kids need someone to take charge."

"The father's attitude bugs me," said Lacey. "It's like he doesn't care that his son is dead. You don't suppose he was that pissed because Eric was going over to the enemy?"

Dee looked sideways. "The enemy?"

"Switching his major to Environmental Sciences. Isn't that like treason to an oilman?"

"People in Alberta don't kill their kids for having different points of view," Dee said. "And don't deny that's what you were wondering. Although with all the parents freaking out over gay-straight alliances in schools and screaming 'better dead than gay' all over social media, you're forgiven for thinking some parents would. Anyway, I don't think Eric becoming an environmentalist would cause his father not to care that he's dead. Brian's utterly withdrawn from his whole family, and from the kids' reactions today — or lack thereof — it seems like that's their normal. Arliss Thompson would have a better idea of how they usually are. Or Zoe."

"Did you ask her to come talk to your mom?"

"She doesn't think she knows enough. She suggested we call Bethanne, the woman she talked to." Dee gazed west as they left the last subdivision behind. "Look at that chinook arch over the mountains. It's gonna be a lot warmer by morning."

Sure enough, they soon drove into the first gusts of the weather front, and in the distance, spindrift stretched its ghostly fingers from the mountain peaks. The sun vanished behind the clouds. When they reached home, they could hear the dogs whining from their pen.

"Oh, poor boys," Dee cooed. "This wind is getting in your ears, isn't it? You want to come inside?"

Lacey unlatched the gate, and Boney and Beau followed Dee to the house. As they stepped inside, Marie scrambled up from a kitchen stool. She relaxed when she saw them.

"What happened?" Lacey asked.

"We've had an incident," Marie explained. "Somebody came to the door about an hour ago and asked to take Sandy's things. Loreena insisted on phoning her son to confirm. He told her he hadn't sent anyone. I'd asked the person to wait outside while we checked, but when I got back to the door, they were gone."

"Man or woman?"

"Woman, I think." Marie held up her hand. "I can't swear to that, though. They were stocky, a bit taller than me, and bundled to the eyebrows in a brown scarf and hat. Deepish voice, but that could have been put on."

Dee dropped her face into her hands. "I can't deal with another prowler on top of everything else."

"It's probably just a misunderstanding," said Lacey. "I'll go out and make sure they're not hanging around still."

"Take the dogs," Dee said.

Boney and Beau leaped up hopefully, but Lacey shook her head. "They'll trample any traces."

Long blue shadows stretched over the snow, but the outside lights illuminated a set of footprints leading up the backyard. Lacey followed them, walking to one side to preserve the evidence. They'd be obliterated by morning, what with the wind picking up. She pulled her phone out and snapped a few photos of the clearest prints with her boot beside them for scale. Farther up the yard, indentations in the snow revealed someone had leaned skis and poles against a tree. Fresh ski tracks climbed the short slope to the trail that ran behind the houses. Using her phone's flashlight, she followed them down the hill until they were so mixed with other tracks that she couldn't be sure which were which.

She climbed back up to the house's yard. Of course, the prowler would go that way. During last summer's horrors, she'd examined every inch of the trails around here. Not only was there a road one steep ski down the back side of the hill, but the trail on this side crossed a lane not far down where a vehicle could be parked temporarily. She went inside and asked for a more thorough description of the visitor, but Marie couldn't recall anything else of note.

"Sorry. I'll leave you to it," she said. "Good luck figuring this out."

"The trails again," Dee said after Marie left. "It has to be someone familiar with this neighbourhood."

"Or someone who looked up your house on Google Maps, or saw some drone footage on a tourism website. In summer you can't see the trails well from above, but a winter shot would show them clearly as white paths through the bare branches." Lacey paced the kitchen and dining room, stopping to peer out the French doors. She automatically started the kettle for tea in passing. "I wish I knew what they were after. As far as I can tell, Sandy didn't leave anything of value here."

"The fact that they came at all ..." Dee straightened. "Could it have been Sandy herself? Watching to see when we left, then sneaking up, hoping to get her stuff and just vanish?"

"Unless that cheap Santa Claus brooch she left has overwhelming sentimental value, there's nothing worth the risk of coming back — *if* she's trying to get away. I'll call Bull and report a possible sighting, then run those last few things over to Dennis."

Dee lurched. "Tonight?"

"The sooner the better, don't you think? We don't want to give anyone a reason to be sneaking around here again."

"And how will they know the stuff's gone?" Dee's voice shook. "Come on, Lace, you can't leave me here alone with Mom while someone is prowling around my house. It's too much like what happened last spring. I can't stay here alone. I just can't." The dogs circled her legs, whining.

"Lord Jesus, I forgot. Sorry. I won't leave tonight."

It wasn't yet fully light when Lacey woke to her phone's buzzing on the nightstand. She grabbed it, still half-asleep, fumbled it to the floor, and retrieved it, muttering, "This better be important." A dial tone answered her. She hung up, and the chime for a voice mail sounded. She hit the button and put the phone to her ear. Calvin's voice rattled off a phone number and a plea to not mention he was being investigated. Honestly, he had a snowball's chance in hell of getting chosen for any sensitive government job. She rolled over and was trying to slide back into sleep when Tom's voice came back to her. "He was in town to interview at the universities." Dave from CSIS. She should have asked exactly when Tom had seen Dave. Wouldn't that just frost the cookies if it turned out Calvin was not delusional? She rolled upright, listened to the message again, punched in the number, and waited.

"*You've reached this number; please leave your reason for calling and a callback number.*"

"My name is Lacey McCrae, and I need to confirm the whereabouts of a University of Calgary student named

Calvin Chan on the Remembrance Day weekend. He gave this number for confirmation. If there's anything you can tell me about Calvin, please phone me or call Sergeant Drummond of K Division, RCMP, Cochrane detachment." She left her number and hung up.

Meanwhile, there was Sandy to follow up on. Overnight, while she'd lain awake yearning for a break from her continuing responsibilities, she'd had the persistent thought that the nurse might have disappeared deliberately, intending to be declared dead in the blizzard. That way, not only could she dodge any impending legal proceedings in Ontario, but also, her life insurance would pay out fairly soon, allowing her son to take care of his mortgage problems and probably get her a ticket out of the country. Lacey dragged herself out of bed. It was already ten a.m. in Ontario, late enough to call old Pat back and demand answers.

Before the coffee was ready, one of the dogs yipped happily out in the yard. She opened the mudroom door to a blast of spring-like air. Water dripped from the icicles along the pergola, and a scruffy man waited on the deck.

"Miz Lacey, good morning." Eddie Beal's earflaps were folded up, a concession to the chinook.

"Eddie? What are you doing here?"

"Egg day."

"You were here last week."

"Miz Dee phoned for more. Said she'd been at the Christmas baking."

"Oh, that's right. Come on in."

"I can only spare a dozen. Lots of folks devil eggs for New Year's."

"I'm sure that will get us through to next week. There's only three of us."

"They ain't found your car yet?" He caught her frown. "Heard it on the scanner yesterday. That nurse gone off with your car."

"That she did." As Lacey shut out the chilly morning, a thought hit her. Eddie Beal had lived here all his life. Although he was better with dogs than with people, there was a chance he could put a name to a description. "There's a person she might have gone to see, but we don't have a name. They met in the coffee shop by the grocery store before Christmas, and they hadn't seen each other for years. Can you think of any woman around here about my height, maybe midfifties, stocky, with brown curly hair? Name of Darla or maybe Marlice."

Eddie slurped his tongue over his front teeth. "Can't say that any come to mind." He handed over the eggs and made her sign the relevant line in his notebook. When she followed him out with the dogs' kibble, he added, "You could ask that ski trekker woman. I seen her talking to the nurse one day in Cochrane."

"What woman?"

"The one in the Backcountry booth beside me at the Cochrane Christmas market."

"Yes, we were all at the market. We talked to quite a few people."

"Not that day. Was a couple days later, near suppertime. I was heading home for chores, been up to see about some grow lights. Me and Eben are gonna set up a medical marijuana operation. We figure if we use solar and drop a micro-generator into our creek, power costs won't—"

Lacey interrupted Eddie's disquisition on pot-growing. "You saw Sandy, the nurse, talking to Marcia, the Backcountry ski instructor, in Cochrane one evening? Was this before Christmas?"

"Heck, yeah. Maybe the twenty-third, or was it Christmas Eve? Now, where was I comin' from? Twenty-second was an egg day, exactly one week ago today, so not then…. Hmm."

Eddie couldn't narrow it down any further. After a bit, Lacey thanked him and sent him on his way. That day at the Christmas market, she and Dee had chatted with Eddie and then with Marcia. Had Sandy and Loreena been with them at that moment? It was possible Sandy had simply said hello to a familiar face in a strange town. But it had to be checked. She fed the dogs, topped up their heated water reservoir, scraped the slush away under the pergola, and schlepped back into the house.

The coffee was ready, and she poured a cup before dialling Zoe's number. Hopefully she was up and not sleeping off the emotional upheaval of the funeral.

Zoe answered on the third ring. After hearing Lacey's brief explanation of the missing nurse and the need to reach Marcia, she said, "I've got her email address if that's any help. Or, both her numbers will be in the office directory. I'll call you with them when I get to work. Half an hour or so? She might even be there when I arrive."

"Thanks." Lacey signed off and called Dennis. As soon as she was sure Dee felt okay being left alone, she'd take Sandy's stuff back to him.

But he threw her a curveball with his first words. "I found an email from my mom."

"Where is she? Is she all right?"

He huffed. "Not like that. She didn't email me. She emailed Pat from my Gmail account. While she was here, I mean. I musta left it open, and she just started typing without realizing. Pat's address is in my Gmail, too, so it woulda filled in."

"When did she send it? What does it say?"

"Uh, hang on." He shuffled around. "It was Boxing Day, before she left here. It just says 'She'll pay.'"

"That's it? A single line?"

"Uh-huh. Three exclamation marks. Maybe Pat knows what's going on."

"She wouldn't tell me why your mother left that nursing home where she used to work."

"What's that got to do with anything?"

"I don't know, but your mother was out with Loreena that one time when they met a woman she knew from that nursing home. It's the only lead we've got."

"Oh, yeah. I still don't know who that coulda been. I'll ask my wife when she gets home. Her and Mom natter on for hours about stuff like that." He paused. "You thank Loreena for that money she sent. It will help out a lot."

"She's worried about Sandy, too. We all are." No need to mention her half-formed suspicion that Sandy was escaping from pending legal troubles in Ontario. "Now about that nursing home. Why did your mom stop working there?"

"Pissed at the management is all I heard. She seemed happy doing visiting nurse stuff."

"Call me if you find anything else. Like your mom's Gmail password scribbled on a sticky note by your computer."

"Only old people do that."

One old person, for sure. "I'll try Pat. If she's checked her email by now, she may know what that message referred to." Lacey pulled up Pat's daughter's number in her contacts list and punched it into the wall phone. She went through a child, then her mother before finally reaching Pat. "Did you get any emails from Sandy?"

"I haven't been home to check yet." Pat had abandoned the creaky, uncertain tone today. "My idiot grandson ditched his mother's car half a mile from here and left it in water over the radiator all night, probably because he'd been drinking. Block's frozen solid. His dad's gonna have to tow it back here after work and thaw it out. He oughta be grounded for a year. Don't you worry, though. I'll go right home and look for emails as soon as that car's sorted out."

Lacey started to fortify herself with a swallow of coffee, but discovered her mug was down to the dregs. "Sandy sent you a message from her son's account, saying 'She'll pay.' Did she mean someone was willing to pay her for something, or was she going to make someone pay, as in get revenge on them?"

"Lord love you, young woman, I have no idea. She'll have emailed me another time or two with details. Someone can run me over soon to find out."

"This will be the third day she's been missing. That woman she knew from the nursing home is the only lead I have. Please, even if you don't think it could possibly be relevant, tell me what happened to make Sandy leave her job."

"Oh, dear," said Pat, lapsing into her little-old-lady voice. "I hoped that was all over and done with. What I remember is a bit shaky. I didn't understand all the ins and outs."

"Do the best you can."

"All right, then. The manager found some kind of computer virus thing that was stealing money from the home's expenses, and Sandy took the blame for it."

"She planted a virus that stole money?"

Pat clucked. "She could no more do that than I can check my email from a strange computer. Two lost lambs, that's us in this electronic age. No, she took the blame for it. That's a whole different thing. The real culprit was a summer student, but he was the nephew of the owner. Nothing was going to happen to him. The home couldn't get the money back from their insurance without assigning blame. So the manager offered Sandy severance and a reference if she'd take responsibility and go away quietly."

"That sounds nuts."

"She didn't like it as much there without me, and she got on at the home care place pretty quick. We were both really mad about that bad flu year, though. No excuse at all. And she had to repay some of the severance as pretend restitution."

"What had the bad flu to do with the virus?"

"Nothing, really. Sandy hated watching the old dears come down with the flu and not understand what was happening to them, dying in agony when a flu shot might have saved them." Pat clucked her tongue again. "People with dementia are still people. They deserve a good quality of life, and that includes flu shots and other protections. The home was getting a lot of questions because of a run of deaths — three times the provincial average in that one winter, if you can believe it — and a financial scandal on top of it could've put the place out of business. Sandy took the blame so the old folks wouldn't get even more confused by being moved out among strangers. And to save everyone else's jobs."

"That's very noble of her." Lacey hoped her skepticism wasn't creeping through. So, computers stealing money showed up in both Eric's life and Sandy's. Was there a connection between the two disappearances?

Sandy had no connection to TFB Energy, though. That malware had to have been planted by someone who could walk right up to the cheque printer and plug in a USB drive. It couldn't possibly be the same malware, either, four years and four provinces apart. Still, she had to check.

"Er, what kind of virus was it that Sandy took the blame for? Did it involve printing cheques?"

Pat's voice rose. "Now how did you know that? I barely remembered it myself."

"Lucky guess. Did you ever hear if it had a name? Or a number?"

"If I did hear, it's clean gone now. You won't go repeating this, will you? Sandy did nothing wrong, and I won't have her reputation sullied while she's not able to defend herself."

"I won't unless it's absolutely necessary. Thank you for trusting me with the truth. Call me or, better yet, forward me any emails she sent you. Write down my email address and give me yours."

With that out of the way, Lacey hung up. Breakfast time. She'd just cracked fresh eggs into a bowl when her phone rang. She flicked it to speaker and left it on the counter while she added cream and whisked the mixture with a fork. "Lacey speaking."

"Hi, this is Marcia. Zoe said you wanted to talk to me. I hope this won't take long. I'm heading out to Black Rock Bowl to teach a class."

"I'll be brief. You couldn't know, but our hired nurse is overdue after her holiday. A neighbour told me today he'd seen you talking to her in Cochrane a day or two before Christmas. I hoped she might have mentioned something to you, maybe about plans she had, or someone she intended to visit."

"Why would I know your nurse?"

"She was with us when we met you at the Christmas market. December nineteenth, I think it was. She was wearing a puffy white coat."

"I vaguely recall seeing some other people with Dee Phillips, but you're the only one I'd recognize again, and that's mainly because I've seen you a couple of other times. If this nurse came up to me on the street, it must have been to ask for directions or something equally forgettable."

"If you remember anything else, please call me back."

Lacey hung up, not at all hopeful, and poured the eggs into the hot pan.

Dee wandered in, wrapped in her dressing gown. "Who were you talking to?"

Lacey recapped her morning phone calls while Dee made her mother's tea. "I have no idea where to turn next. I'll take Sandy's stuff back to Dennis, then what? Wait until my car turns up in a frozen pond and file an insurance claim?"

CHAPTER THIRTY

The cheque printer lurked in the corner of Zoe's vision, pulling her focus from copying the Cardium well-share agreements. Twice she copied the same five-page document, and once she made three unneeded spares of a single-page summary. *Leave me alone while I'm working!* she thought fiercely. *I'll go back to the chalet later and you can tell me anything you want.* She checked off another item on the list Accounting had left in her basket. Six more share agreements to go, and she could close the book on that section of her assignment.

The blond from Accounting wandered in, twirling a lock of her silky hair around one manicured finger. She opened the supply cupboard and gazed into its depths. "Did you know Eric Anders's funeral was yesterday?"

"The notice should have been circulated." Whether JP had forgotten to send it to Marcia, too, or Marcia had suppressed it because of her dislike for Eric, it didn't matter now. "Would you have gone?"

"Uh-huh." Blondie sighed. "He was a nice guy. There aren't many of those around."

So jaded, and in her midtwenties, at the latest. "It was a nice service," Zoe said, "but mostly people who knew the family. There didn't seem to be many people who just knew Eric. I'm sure he'd have liked you to be there." Which was probably true.

"He had good energy," the woman said, plucking a box of staples from the shelf before leaving.

Zoe yanked the agreement from the copier, re-stapled it, and stapled the copies. Another item checked off. A thought hit her: had Eric's family collected whatever possessions he'd left at his desk in the IT department? She could clean out his desk. Returning his stuff would give her an excuse to visit the house again and maybe find his laptop. Whipping through the last four documents, she dropped everything off in her temporary office and gleefully squeezed the *Galactica* model in her sweater pocket as she sped toward the IT offices.

"All gone," said the IT guy, clicking his pen, unaware that he was crushing her — and Eric's — hopes. "Arliss Thompson came for it last week. We don't say no to that woman. Even if she's not the boss's wife anymore, she's still a board member."

"I didn't realize Arliss spent any time here."

"She's been in a bit this fall." *Click*. "Keeping an eye on where her alimony comes from, I guess."

"Well, thanks." Zoe slouched out of the room, weary to the bone. The funeral hadn't been Eric's farewell. Instead it had energized him, and raised more questions for her about who wanted him dead. *I don't know what you want from me*, she thought crossly, then found herself clutching the spaceship model again. She yanked her hand out of her pocket and strode off, muttering.

"Did you say something?"

Zoe blinked. She was back in Accounting, and Marcia was watching her curiously from a doorway. "Uh, just making mental lists. There's still a lot of files to go through. A bunch of those early wells will be at the bottom of their production curve by now. We could sell them off for stripping and clean up the asset sheet that much more."

"Shouldn't those decisions wait until JP gets back?"

"If he *was* coming back, sure."

Marcia clutched the door frame. "What do you mean? They'll be back in January. Phyl and I are having lunch."

Oh, shit. Phyl hadn't told her dear friend she was moving. But surely Marcia deserved a heads-up about the changes, especially since they affected her job. She'd need to plan her finances. Zoe chose her words carefully.

"The impression I get from JP is that the company's going on the market right after the holidays, basically as soon as I've got the prep work wrapped up."

Marcia's small brown eyes opened wide. "Sell the company, for real? I thought—" She caught herself. "The business is one thing — we all know JP's not as young as he likes to pretend — but Phyl wouldn't move away without telling me. She couldn't."

She already has.

"Well, I'd better be getting on. If I can wrap this up today, I'll be able to join my family up at Marmot Basin after all." Zoe hustled into her private office and leaned on the wall, dizzy from the backwash of the other woman's emotions. Bethanne had said something about seeing more than you wanted to, once you started seeing at all. That had happened at the funeral with Eric's dad; she'd had the same dizzy feeling as he passed her. Seeing inside people, feeling all their emotions, would make life intolerable very quickly. Poor Marcia, though. She'd given up her job in Ontario to move here, and now she'd been sandbagged by the news that her job could vanish and her beloved friend hadn't even warned her it was coming. Marcia was being abandoned in real life the way Zoe intended to abandon Eric this afternoon at the chalet. *Sorry, Eric*, she thought, and gave the spaceship a sympathetic squeeze. *"Abandon" isn't the right word. But today's your last chance to tell me what you need. I can't keep living this chaos forever.*

Lacey lifted the tenth sheet of paper from the printer. This would have to be the last copy. The colour cartridge was failing, washing out Sandy's pale hair to almost nothing. Six posters for her to put up around Bragg Creek and Cochrane, the other four for Dennis. It didn't seem like much for a half hour's work, but it felt like she was doing something, at least. She found Dee in the living room, once more poring over real estate papers.

"You sure you'll be all right alone today?"

"I guess." Dee peered down the drive to where the Bragg Creek Arts Centre's rooftop showed through the winter-bare branches. "If you're going to be a while, I'll invite Rob from the museum up for supper. Mom hasn't met him yet, and he'll be a good distraction."

"I'll be back by supper. It's not even lunchtime yet." Lacey picked up the grocery bag with Sandy's clothes in it and called goodbye to the dogs as she passed.

She cruised up the highway past Cochrane and out across the cold, white prairie. The chinook had left its mark: Bushes and guardrails showed through the snow. The road to Big Hill Springs had mostly melted off.

She met up with Sandy's son, Dennis, at his neighbourhood skating rink. He pointed out his children: the girl skating carefully around the edges, practicing her little bunny hops under the tutelage of a teen who didn't look old enough to be teaching anyone anything, and the boy scrambling around with other rowdy kids at the far end. Lacey handed over the sack.

"This is all she left — pants and a shirt and one little box with a brooch in it. I made these posters using the profile photo on her Facebook page. You can show them around. Somebody must have seen something."

He took the papers in one calloused hand. "Thanks. I dunno what else to do. The police said they'd call, but they didn't. I waited all day yesterday."

"The waiting around is really hard. You haven't thought of any other angle we could try? Her email password, or a record of the phone calls she made from your house?" As she said the latter, she realized she hadn't gone back through the caller list on Dee's landline, either. Sandy might have made calls from that to avoid cellphone fees.

Dennis's fingers crimped the pages. "I can get her cellphone records."

"Really? I thought we'd have to convince the police to do it."

"Didn't they already look when I reported her missing?"

"It's not illegal for adults to go quiet if they choose, and your mother could file a lawsuit against them if they invaded her privacy and then she turned up safe. Unless they suspect foul play, they won't do more than check if her phone is still being used. How can you do it?"

"It's a family plan. I set it up when I was working steady, and I put roaming on it so she could use it in Ontario. Since I pay for it, I can see the calls on all three phones."

And keep tabs on your wife's calls. Lacey squelched her cynicism. Not all men organized their lives around spying on their wives.

"Can you email me a list of recent calls?"

He waved at the rink. "I'll do it when I get home."

The new lead buoyed Lacey on the drive back to Cochrane. Warm, fresh breezes wafted through the vents. Slush sang under the tires. Mountain peaks bloomed white and gold against the stark sky. Between those phone calls and the posters she could show around, she'd soon have a good lead. She'd find Sandy and get her Civic back. She couldn't possibly leave the nurse in charge of Dee and Loreena in order to take a personal wellness break — not after Sandy had proven herself so unreliable. Still, Loreena would be happier knowing Sandy was safe, and that alone would ease some of the pressure.

But trudging around downtown Cochrane, where the Christmas market blocks remained closed off by hay-bale barricades, Lacey's newfound optimism eroded. The hoop dancer and storyteller by the teepee didn't recognize the photo. Nobody at the coffee shop, art store, tea shop, or any other business recollected the sandy-haired nurse or the ten-year-old Civic. After two hours, Lacey left her second-last poster at the post office and headed back to the Lexus. As she stared through the windshield at the beautiful mountains, the urge to keep driving toward them grew. Too bad she couldn't head off to Black Rock Bowl and go skiing like a normal person.

Marcia was out there teaching a class. The photo might jog her memory.

Lacey checked in with Dee. Rob would be there in an hour. No worries if she was late home. She gave Dee her destination and approximate return time — good practice when heading out to wilderness alone — and left Cochrane on Highway 1A, revelling in a brief sense of escape. Sure, this was part of the investigation, but it was a couple of precious hours in which she'd be responsible for nobody but herself. She hummed "Walking in a Winter Wonderland."

Half an hour later, she passed the isolated house with all the Christmas lights. Soon Black Rock Mountain rose jagged above the trees. At the resort, the square was bustling, the parking lots packed, and vehicles lined the roadsides. Truly a magnificent day to be out in a winter playground. Now, which chalet was Marcia's?

"The class is over," said the woman at the café nearest the ski lift. "That's some of them over in the corner.

Their instructor, she's the third place up the north shoulder. Small log cabin, one of the oldest in the Bowl."

Lacey headed up the mountain. She recognized Marcia's place at once by the brown Suburban with the multiple ski racks. She and Dee had spotted the shabby cabin on their first trip to the Bowl, when Eric's body was found in JP's woodshed. Blasted by full sunlight, Marcia's ancient cabin appeared on the verge of collapse, its roof sagging and its smoking chimney askew. A rough path was cleared to the front porch. Another ran from a side door to what looked like an incinerator that puffed out smoke and embers. As Lacey stepped from the Lexus, Marcia appeared at the side door carrying an armload of paper. She stopped halfway to the incinerator, squinting at her visitor.

"Hi, Marcia." Lacey waved. "Got a minute?"

"What are you doing up here?"

"Can you take a look at this poster of our missing nurse? See if it jogs your memory?"

"I guess." Marcia looked at the stack in her hands. "Go inside. I'll dump these and be right back."

Lacey stepped onto the sagging porch. The worn boards creaked under her weight. The warped front door stayed stuck in its frame until she ruthlessly hip-checked it. She stepped directly into the small main room. The walls were constructed of caulked logs, with a fieldstone fireplace along the inner one. The grate was choked with papers, a small flame browning their edges. Through a bead curtain ahead was a rudimentary countertop. A doorway on her left revealed a narrow flight of stairs so steep they were almost a ladder.

There was one table covered in papers, a printer, and a laptop. For seating, the options were a spindle-backed rocking chair and a pair of drooping armchairs, their upholstery so faded that the original pattern was barely a suggestion. A handful of books occupied a bankers box on the floor. A flat-pack of more boxes leaned on the wall. Along a shelf were trophies and framed photos of people in cross-country ski gear. One photo in a place of pride on the mantel showed a tall, lean redhead with her arm around Marcia's shoulders. It appeared to have been taken outside the Thompson chalet.

She turned as the bead curtain rattled. "Are you packing up? Moving back to the city after the holidays?"

"This place is too far for a daily commute," Marcia said, leaning against the fireplace. "Officially I live in Arbour Lake, less than an hour from downtown. Know anybody who wants to buy a cabin? The land's worth a lot."

"I can ask. My roommate's a realtor."

"Oh, yeah, Dee." Marcia pulled herself upright with what seemed like immense effort. "I didn't realize she was so badly injured she needed a live-in nurse."

"The nurse is actually for her mother, who's got cancer. The stress of Sandy's vanishing isn't helping any of us." The fireplace belched smoke into the room. Lacey coughed.

Marcia poked the papers in the fireplace. "Look, I'm sorry about the nurse and all the stress, but today's really not a good day. Can you just show me the photo and be on your way?"

"Okay." Lacey handed over her last poster. "Does she look familiar at all?" She coughed again, her eyes stinging. Marcia peered at the poster. After a moment she handed the page back. "Vaguely familiar, that's all I can say." She turned away to wrestle open an aged sash window. "Could you ask Dee to phone me at work after the holidays? If she's interested in selling this place for me."

The fresh breeze whirled more smoke from the fireplace, aggravating Lacey's throat further. "Could I get a glass of water before I go?"

"Sure. Kitchen's this way." Marcia picked up a stack of manila envelopes from the desk before leading her through the bead curtain. She pushed aside pill bottles and first aid stuff on an open shelf and handed down a glass. "Drinking water's in the jug." As she opened the side door, she said, as if the words were being forced from her, "Have you ever been betrayed by someone who said they loved you?"

Had Marcia been dumped? Lacey splashed a mouthful of water into the glass and rinsed her mouth. "Yeah. My ex-husband."

"Not like that. By a friend." Marcia stood by the door, clutching the frame with one hand as if Lacey's answer was the most important thing in the world.

"No chance to be. I didn't have any friends while I was married." The truth of those words boomeranged on Lacey. In the RCMP she had mostly associated with co-workers, men who shared a code of conduct with other men. Too often, they'd seen her as a woman first and a fellow officer second. Tom was the only one she'd trusted, the only one who'd always had her back. Only since leaving the Force had she reconnected with women — first Marie, then gradually Dee, and eventually Jan, a new friend. How would she feel if Dee stabbed her in the back, or Marie turned against her? "It must be really rough, being betrayed by a friend."

"I did everything she wanted," said Marcia. "I can't believe she'd just walk away."

"I'm sorry."

"You can show yourself out." And with that, Marcia walked outside and down the path to the incinerator. She heaved the manila envelopes through the hatch. Sparks soared out the top, curling to ash against the vivid blue sky.

Zoe leaned another split of pine against the burning pyramid in JP's fireplace. "I don't know where your backpack is," she said to the empty room. "It wasn't in the woodshed, or else the police would have it, and Aidan says they don't. You must have dropped it somewhere." The image of a small red car pounded the inside of her forehead. "Stop it. You're giving me a headache. I don't know where your car is. Can you try to show me where you left it?"

The pounding came again. After a moment of disorientation, she realized the pounding wasn't in her head. Someone was rapping at the front door. Now what?

"Lacey?" Zoe opened the door wide. "What brings you way out here?"

"I was over at Marcia's and saw the chimney smoking. Wondered if it might be you."

"Well, come on in. I'm not getting anywhere, anyway."

"Trying to commune with the spirits of the dead again?" Lacey kicked the snow off her boots. "Sorry. I didn't mean to sound facetious."

"Well, you're right. It's been frustrating." Zoe led the way to the kitchen and filled the kettle. "Were you hiring Marcia for ski lessons? You don't need them."

"No, I was showing her a photo of our missing nurse. Somebody said they'd seen her with a woman who looked like Marcia. She didn't remember when I phoned, but I hoped the photo might jog her memory."

"You'll have to start at the beginning. What missing nurse?" By the time Lacey had filled her in, starting with the Christmas market and ending with Eddie Beal's dubious identification, the kettle had popped. Zoe started tea. "I'd be surprised if Marcia recognized her own mother today."

"Yeah, she seemed upset."

"Yep." Zoe fiddled with her spoon. "I had to break it to her this morning that her dear friend Phyl, the second Mrs. JP Thompson, has moved to England without a backward glance. Phyl moved Marcia here from Ontario, got her the TFB job, and encouraged her to buy that rundown cabin across the way. Phyl treated her like a best friend right up until she left the country without telling her she wasn't coming back. Now Marcia will be losing her job as well as her friend. She'll only be entitled to a tiny severance package because she hasn't been there that long. Middle-aged women don't easily relocate unless they have strong connections in other oil companies, which she doesn't. I don't know how she'll keep up the payments on her cabin and her townhouse."

"She told me she's selling the cabin." Lacey accepted a cup. "She's already started packing up and burning the trash. What a shattering thing to do to someone you called a friend."

Zoe stirred her tea. "Rich people ... they don't get what it's like to live paycheque to paycheque. Us ordinary people could lose everything we've worked all our lives for while they live on investments and trust funds as if nothing's changed." She looked around the kitchen. "This place sure changed. It used to be a homey cabin not much bigger than Marcia's. The Thompsons spent all their holidays and long weekends out here, skiing and tobogganing and such. Arliss taught them all to ski, cross-country and downhill, and made them help with trail maintenance. She gave those kids a work ethic even though the family was getting richer by the year. Hey, could the person who thought it was Marcia with your nurse be mistaken?"

"How?"

"Arliss is the same general height, and she looks a bit like Marcia. She's a member of the Backcountry Safety Association, too. She might have worked the booth at that Christmas market."

Lacey stopped swirling her mug. "Does she have any connection to a nursing home in Ontario?"

"If it's in Waterloo, she did. JP's mother was in a dementia ward there for nearly twenty years. What's that got to do with this?"

"Sandy ran into someone she knew from the Waterloo nursing home where she used to work. Dee's mom couldn't remember that person's name, but thought it might have been Marlice. That's kinda close to Arliss. Anyway, we're trying to track that person down in case Sandy went to visit her. Or she might know if there's anyone else in Alberta who Sandy would visit."

"It can't hurt to ask." Zoe pulled out her phone and flicked it off airplane mode. Her call went to voice mail. "Arliss, I'm with Lacey McCrae — you met her at the funeral reception. She's the one who went skiing with us. She's looking for someone who's gone AWOL, and you or someone who looks like you were seen talking to her in Bragg Creek and in Cochrane before Christmas. If this rings any bells, could you please call Lacey?" She recited the number and clicked off. "I hope that helps. Do you have a replacement nurse for Dee's mom?"

"We've been managing between me and Dee and my friend Marie — she's a nurse who's not working right now. After the holidays, we'll have to figure out how to get Loreena back to Ontario. Sandy travelled with her, and she was supposed to see her safely home again."

"Sounds complicated." Zoe squeezed her forehead between thumb and index finger.

"Headache?"

"More like a pounding through my skull. Eric keeps showing me his backpack, and I haven't the faintest idea where it might be."

"Nobody does. Do you know why it's so important?"

"Not a clue."

"Calvin told me Eric was carrying papers for JP Thompson that day."

Zoe dropped her hand. "If it's company business, it could be confidential. Do you know what it's related to?"

She felt Eric's excitement soar like sparks up a chimney and held her breath for Lacey's answer.

"What I understand from Calvin and Aidan is that Eric discovered malware in the cheque-writing printer. It was automatically mailing fraudulent payments out every time the accountants did a payment run. Eric told JP about it, but he had no proof then. This time he was bringing proof."

Malware-Cylon-that's-it-that's-it. Fireworks exploded behind Zoe's forehead. She gripped the counter for support, barely able to process the implications. When her head stopped ringing, she asked, "How long was it going on for?"

"They only knew about September. They thought when they told JP, he would order an investigation into the rest."

"There will be one starting now." The explosions faded. This Zoe could deal with. "I'll go back to the office tonight and call up the cheque log for September."

"If we could find the backpack, you wouldn't have to. It's probably in his car. Except the RCMP have searched for it, both before and after ... well, after you and Lizi found his body. You don't have any insights about the car, do you?"

"I wish I did." Zoe sipped her tea and thought about everything she'd experienced since she'd touched Eric's frozen face. All the times she'd been dizzy with emotion, or had seen things that weren't there, or ... had fallen asleep at the wheel. "Do the police know how Eric got to the chalet yet?"

"No. Why?"

"What if he came over the upper loop instead of straight up from the square, and slid off the road out of fatigue? He'd been driving in the blizzard for a couple of hours by then. I almost drove off up there myself in broad daylight." She glanced out the window. Blue shadows were climbing over the woodshed. "We could take a quick drive up there now."

"It's too close to dusk to see much today. We could search tomorrow afternoon, though, earlier in the day. Since the chinook, the snow level is lower, and some parts of the car might be visible."

Yes-yes-find-my-car. "You'd do this on a ghostly tip?"

Lacey gave her a stern look. "I'm not doing this because of any psychic shit. I'm doing this because the snow was too deep then to show any traces, and the police may have skipped the uphill stretch."

"As long as we do it." *Do-it-do-it-find-my-car.* Zoe looked at her visitor. Lacey seemed so hard, so pragmatic, and yet inside she was thoughtful, concerned for her friends and ... frightened?

All those times Zoe had seen inside people had been accidental so far. She'd never tried on purpose to tap into whatever it was; she'd simply been bowled over in passing by Marcia's misery and Brian Anders's detachment. This time, she closed her eyes and envisioned Lacey sitting there, with her expressionless face and blondish curls, her hands cupped around her tea. Behind her, a black cloud thickened into the shape of a man with wide shoulders and small, mean eyes. He loomed over Lacey, his hands reaching for her throat.

CHAPTER THIRTY-ONE

Ignoring the dogs' welcoming yips, Lacey slammed into the house. "What did you tell that woman?"

Loreena dropped a wooden spoon into the sink. Dee, in the midst of raising a stack of plates to the cupboard, set them gently on the granite countertop instead. "What woman?"

"She knew." Lacey growled the words. "She knew I was afraid of Dan. What did you tell her? How dare you talk about my marriage to a stranger?"

"I don't know what you're talking about." Dee propped herself against the countertop. "I haven't talked about your marriage to anyone, except, well ..."

"Me," said Loreena. "And I haven't told anyone, either. I didn't even tell Dee about the other night. Sit yourself down, maid. Tell us what happened."

Faced with their confusion, Lacey backed away. She slipped off her snow boots and hung her coat on its hook. Her head was whirling. All the way home she'd been seething with rage and hurt, believing Dee must have spilled her deepest secrets. That was how psychic fraudsters operated: worming out secrets and then pretending to "discover" them by mystical means when it had the greatest impact. But even if Loreena had told Dee about Dan and the strangling, Dee would never gossip about it.

"I'm sorry I blew up," she said, re-entering the kitchen. "It was Zoe. She asked me today what man I'm so afraid of. What man wants to —" She stopped there, unable to say the words that would expose her most raw underbelly. "I jumped to the conclusion she was talking about Dan, and that you must have told her about him."

"I didn't," Dee assured her. "I've hardly seen her without you around, and even if I had, your private life isn't something I'd spill. I'd never do that to you."

"Get that tea down you," said Loreena.

Lacey took a mouthful of tea so loaded with condensed milk that it slid over her tongue without burning. She dropped onto a stool. "Now I have an inkling of how Marcia felt when she learned Phyl Thompson isn't coming back from England."

"Marcia didn't know? How could she have missed the signs?"

"She seems to have no friends except for Phyl, who didn't tell her. Zoe told me she'd let it slip this morning and Marcia was still in denial." Lacey explained about running into Zoe at the chalet, and the possibility that Arliss Thompson was the woman Eddie had seen talking to Sandy. "Zoe left her a message, but she hasn't called me yet."

"Arliss," Loreena mused. "That could be the name. You don't have a picture of her, do you?"

Lacey shook her head. "But JP's mother was in a dementia ward in Waterloo for decades. Enough time that they'd recognize the sight of each other even if they weren't well acquainted."

"Arliss's family went there for two weeks every summer," said Dee. "Her son mentioned it at the funeral. When she calls back, we can finally find out what she and Sandy talked about."

"If she calls back." Lacey swallowed more tea. "I didn't say anything before, but Sandy left that nursing home under a cloud, accused of planting a malware script in their accounting system that stole money. Her friend Pat swears she wasn't capable of that level of computer manipulation, but it's possible she did do the stealing and just made up a story for Pat when she got caught."

"We saved you some supper." Dee put a plate of tortellini in cream sauce into the microwave to reheat and pushed a dish of freshly grated parmesan over to Lacey. "Rob made the sauce. He said to wish you Happy New Year."

Lacey nodded absently, still thinking through the implications she'd been too angry to focus on earlier. "What if Arliss planted the nursing home malware? Later, when her marriage was on the rocks and she needed money for a lawyer, she could have loaded the same script at TFB Energy, topping up her post-divorce income without JP's knowledge. Sandy would be able to add two and two. She's almost the only person who could."

"That's a huge leap." Dee passed Lacey the plate. "You don't know yet if Sandy and Arliss did meet out here."

"Eat before it gets cold," Loreena instructed. "We'll know more when we know more."

Lacey ate, grateful for the warm food and the comfort of knowing Dee had not betrayed her trust. Zoe must have taken a shot in the dark. What had she hoped to gain? Bull had speculated early on that she was unwilling to openly point a finger at someone. She might have regretted mentioning Arliss and hoped the change of track would throw Lacey off. Did Arliss have an alibi for the weekend Eric died?

Lacey hadn't yet worked out how she could find out when her phone rang. "Hey, Bull, what's up?"

"We found your car."

Relief spread through her, warmer than the pasta. "Sandy, too?"

"No. We had to pop the trunk to be sure. Found her suitcase. No purse, no keys."

"Shit. Insurance won't cover that trunk." The words had barely left her mouth when the implications of Sandy's abandoned suitcase hit her: a woman running off to start a new life doesn't leave behind her suitcase unless she has no choice.

"It's totalled, anyway. Back half in a snowbank, front end torched. A Stoney band councillor found it and called in the VIN."

The cream sauce turned to vinegar in Lacey's stomach. Car torched and driver missing, suitcase still there. There was no way to pretty up that picture. She forced herself to focus. "Stoney Nakoda First Nation is a long way west of Cochrane. How could she have ended up there?"

"If she turned west on 1A instead of going on across the river, one more turn would have brought her up into the hills. In the whiteout, she wouldn't necessarily have seen any of the nearby houses."

"Where is that exactly? I'm coming over."

"Save it until morning. Search and Rescue will stage at daybreak. That storm might have buried her, but the chinook will have uncovered her remains." He paused. "I don't need to tell you to keep that under your hat, right?"

"I have to tell Dee and her mom. They're right here." After swearing she wouldn't let them inform Dennis before the RCMP did, she set the phone down and looked across the island at two anxious faces. "They haven't found Sandy, but they found my car way out in the boonies. The way it was buried, they think she wandered away from it sometime during the blizzard."

Loreena closed her crepe-thin eyelids. "Four days ago. That means ..."

Lacey laid her hand on the older woman's wrist. "I'm afraid it probably does."

CHAPTER THIRTY-TWO

Lacey woke at dawn from a dream in which she was begging Dan for money to replace her car. His mocking laugh followed her into consciousness. Shaking it off with difficulty, she came up against an unrelated but intense belief that Eric's death and Sandy's disappearance were connected. Overnight, her subconscious had neatly listed the parallels in her mental notebook:

1. Both victims knew about the computer malware.
2. Both inexplicably abandoned their vehicles in snowstorms.
3. Both were connected by the Thompson family — more specifically, by Arliss Thompson.

Lacey checked her phone. No messages, no texts, not from Arliss or anyone else. She threw on her clothes and headed downstairs, mentally listing questions whose answers would either strengthen or weaken her developing theory of the converging cases:

1. Where was Arliss on the November long weekend? *Check with Zoe. If she'll even speak to you after the abrupt exit yesterday.*

2. How would Arliss have known exactly when Eric was going to show JP evidence of the fraudulent cheques? *Eric's mother. Ask Aidan if his mother knew where Eric was going and why.*

3. Arliss designed the accounting system at TFB and could surely circumvent it. Did she ever have access to the accounting office at the nursing home? *Ask Pat if she remembers Arliss or can find out about her office privileges there.*

4. If Arliss had been in contact with Sandy, her number might appear on both Dee's landline and Sandy's cellphone. *How to find Arliss's home and cell numbers? Reverse search didn't turn up anything last night. Ask Zoe, if etc. ...*

5. Where was Arliss on Boxing Day while Sandy was heading for Bragg Creek? *Try TJ, or get Aidan to question Arliss? Caveat: TJ might lie for his mother, or he might have stayed behind at the chalet in November to dispose of Eric for his mother. Would a devoted son kill his childhood friend at his mother's command?*

6. Had Arliss and Sandy planned to meet along the route home to exchange a blackmail payment? *Ask Pat, and hope the answer is in those unread emails.*

Lacey reflexively logged in to her email. Nothing from Pat, but there was one from an address she didn't recognize, with the header Your Malware List. Calvin had come through.

The email contained a table organized by the date the malware was found, the company or organization it had infected, how long it had run undetected, and a Notes column with additional information about the computer system and the action taken after discovery. Most instances were employees or teenage sons of employees who had found the script online and deployed it either directly into the machine or over an unsecured network connection. If not caught by a virus scan, the malware was usually uncovered within a couple of months by accountants flagging the suspicious payments. In one instance, a youthful hacker had set the mailing address to the home he shared with his mother, who worked at the targeted company. Starting ten years ago, the dates of the malware attacks got markedly further apart. Calvin had told her before Christmas that the script was now routinely blocked by automated virus scans.

Lacey ran her finger down the column and found the Waterloo nursing home. Bingo! A three-month active period four years ago in which the money stolen amounted to Theft Under $5000, and an unnamed minor was identified as the perpetrator by security tracking sites after he bragged in an internet chat room. No record of legal proceedings. That part of Pat's story checked out. Sandy hadn't planted the malware, and the management had hushed up the theft.

But … if Arliss hadn't planted the malware at the nursing home, she had no motive to silence Sandy. Unless one of her sons had done it … Pat hadn't remembered the details clearly. Could the culprit be the grandson of a resident rather than the nephew of an owner?

When she heard Dee shuffling to the kitchen, Lacey went to get fresh coffee. "Any chance that JP gave you his first wife's phone number?" she asked.

"None. Why?"

"It would save me some hunting, that's all."

Dee dragged the kettle to the sink. "Mom's awake. Doesn't look like she slept much. Have you had any word about Sandy?"

Lacey glanced out at the blue shadows in the glade. "The SAR teams will just barely have been organized. I don't expect an update until noon, unless …"

"Unless they find her body sooner. Poor Dennis. He must be frantic." With the kettle started, Dee brought out her mother's medication box to sort the day's pills. "It's callous to say this out loud, but I'm glad she had one last good Christmas with her grandkids. I hope they can remember that part, not whatever follows."

Lacey chewed her lip. "Bull thinks Sandy took a wrong turn in the blizzard, but he doesn't know yet she was going after someone who owed her money. What if that person couldn't risk it coming out that they'd defrauded the nursing home with a computer script? That wouldn't be a simple debt collection, but more like blackmail, whether Sandy meant it that way or not. I have to find out how well Arliss Thompson knew Sandy back at that nursing home. Aidan Anders might know her phone numbers."

"Why not ask Zoe?"

"After I left in a huff yesterday?"

"Apologize."

"But she knew stuff about me, about my deepest secrets. She's been spying on me."

"Or she's very observant. Or psychic. You know, the ghost …"

"This ghost stuff is a deliberate distraction from something she knows or suspects about Eric's death. Although she did seem genuinely surprised about the malware. She's starting a company investigation today."

"I thought you two were going to hunt for Eric's car today."

"I'd have to apologize to her before that could happen."

"And what are you waiting for?"

Lacey heaved a sigh. It wasn't the first time she'd had to apologize for jumping to conclusions. She'd once assumed Dee was too high and mighty to want to be friends again. And there was her hurtful sneer about Jan and her mysterious illness only last summer. Now that Lacey knew more about the condition — myalgic encephalomyelitis, or chronic fatigue syndrome — and the current treatment options, her snap judgment back then was even less excusable. Now it was Zoe's turn. Whether Zoe was getting guidance from the Great Beyond or not, whether she was peering into Lacey's soul or not, Eric's car had to be found so that Lacey could see whether those accounting printouts pointed to Arliss. Apology coming up. Again.

"I'll call her right after breakfast." As if on cue, her phone buzzed. Again, not Arliss. "Wayne? Happy New Year's Eve."

"And to you, McCrae. Are you planning to go work for CSIS?"

Lacey coughed. "Of course not."

"Then they don't need me to confirm your current cellphone number."

"Oh, shit."

"Is this anything I need to know about?"

"Is it a guy named Dave? I assume he's verifying that my number really belongs to me before answering my question. You know how those spooks are."

"Right. Confirming now." Clicking sounds came through as he texted. "The other reason I was calling: you requested info about JP Thompson. Still need it?"

"I'm not sure. He seems to be a straight-up guy as far as the oil business goes, but he left the country in a hurry after his company's intern disappeared."

"Eric Anders. Found dead in Thompson's woodshed at Black Rock Bowl."

"How did you know?"

"Thompson called me two hours ago. He wants me to hire an investigator to clear it up."

Lacey sat back. That single act pretty much demolished JP Thompson as a suspect in Eric's death. If the CSIS contact cleared Calvin, that left only Arliss.

As she hung up the phone, a text arrived from a blocked number: *Calvin Chan in my eye Fri 4 pm through Tues 10 am. Dave.* Another dead end.

"Can you check for a search update now?" Dee asked. "Mom's sure to ask."

Bull had nothing to report save that search teams were moving out in a fan from the car. With no evidence to offer him about Sandy's possible meeting with a possible debtor who was possibly Arliss Thompson, she instead told him that Calvin had an ironclad alibi from the federal government. "As for Sandy, can I tell her best friend in Ontario about my car and the search? She already knows Sandy's missing."

"It'll be on the news soon enough," said Bull. "I'll text you the GPS coordinates if you want to join up with a SAR team." She thanked him and hung up without committing. Traipsing through unfamiliar terrain without proper search-and-rescue gear would make her a liability. She'd be of more use tracing Sandy's final movements, and that meant tracking down her debtor.

Back in the office with a second coffee, she opened her email again. Nothing lurking there except the email from Dan that she'd been avoiding. Maybe it was obvious to everyone that she was afraid — not of him directly, as letting go of the dangerous denial about his abuse meant she'd never again let down her guard near him — but of the chaotic emotions evoked by any contact with him. The years of small humiliations, the constant undermining of her confidence, the isolation from friends and co-workers — classic abuser behaviours. How had she not seen them sooner?

That was the real source of her shame: how long she'd stayed, rationalizing his behaviour, talking herself out of trusting the same gut instincts that kept her safe on patrol. She'd had all the advantages of education, physical strength, and law enforcement training, not to mention the financial independence to walk away any time, and still, she'd stayed. On almost every shift, she'd attended domestic violence calls and listened to her male co-workers grumble about women who wouldn't leave their abusers. She'd wondered herself why they stayed. She'd been so judgmental against women with far fewer resources than she'd had. How could a person live that down? She dragged herself back to the present moment and a task she could succeed at: following up with Pat.

When she sat down to scrambled eggs with Dee a few minutes later, she reported. "Pat still hasn't checked her emails. She told me pointedly that it's a four-hour round trip to her place from her daughter's farm, and they can't tie up the family's only car at the drop of a hat. After I told her Sandy is presumed dead, she said she'd make every effort to get those emails today. For all the good it will do now." She poked her eggs with her fork.

"To be fair," said Dee, "Pat could've forwarded those emails the very next morning, and it would already have been too late. Sandy was gone a whole night before we even knew she was missing. Call Zoe."

"I understand that you don't believe in ghostly guidance," Zoe said for what felt like the eighth time. "Not two weeks ago, I didn't believe in it, either. Stop apologizing and start walking." She left the upper parking lot for the road, crossing just ahead of a minivan that surged from beneath the lift platform. Lacey followed, skipping nimbly between vehicles.

"You're sure Arliss is up at Marmot Basin with your family and Clemmie Anders?"

"Yes." Zoe climbed the plowed ridge of snow and peered down the Bowl. On the last day of the year, a sunny winter morning barely below freezing, the slopes teemed with skiers and snowboarders. "From what Arliss told Nik over breakfast today, Clemmie and Lizi have been in constant contact all week. Since TJ and his mother hadn't any plans for New Year's Eve, he suggested they should take Clemmie up north to join the fun. They hit the highway about the same time we were having tea yesterday, and Clemmie's sharing Lizi's room until I get there. If I still get to go. That cheque-printer problem" — she hesitated — "it has to be nailed down before the office reopens next week." Maybe the whole Eric issue would be sorted out by then, and she could enjoy Kai and Ari's final week hanging around Calgary, eating and sleeping, and playing board games. "I told Nik to remind Arliss to call you when she comes off the slopes today."

"Arliss can afford to take three people to Marmot for New Year's?"

"TJ can. He's got a fat trust fund and apparently a soft spot for Clem. Or he's bored." Zoe stepped aside as a VW beetle scooted up the hill. Lacey had been asking about Arliss all through the drive from Cochrane. Not that Zoe knew where Arliss had been on that November weekend nearly two months ago. She hardly remembered where she'd been herself, although she knew life had been a lot more normal back then.

Behind her, Lacey said, "If he'd gone over up here, the car would have landed on the ski hill and been seen immediately. It must be in amongst the trees."

Zoe shaded her eyes from the bright morning sun. "Once the sun passes that outcrop, this road will be in shadow." For an instant, the bright sky darkened. Weariness swept over her. Her hands ached as if from clutching a steering wheel that wasn't there. Sadness and confusion seeped through her. *So tired. I don't remember driving.* "Let's get walking," she said.

They trudged to the next bend and peered down at the spruces. Nothing. Lacey halted at the next turn. "See anything?"

Zoe shook her head. The trees wavered. Dizziness swept over her.

"Zoe? Are you okay?"

"What?" Zoe pushed a hand at her forehead, jamming her dark glasses askew. "Ouch."

"You zoned right out there. I thought you'd go over the edge." Lacey was holding her by the upper arm, peering at her.

"Yeah. I was out of breath and —" She looked around. This was where she'd almost driven off the road. *I don't remember.* "Eric doesn't remember, but I'm almost sure he came this way. He was so sleepy."

"That sounds like he'd taken one of Calvin's pills."

"Are you admitting he might have communicated something to me?"

Lacey put up her gloved hands. "I'm just saying, if he was hypothetically sleepy, he might have taken one of Calvin's sleeping pills, maybe by accident. They were in the pocket of the jacket he was wearing."

No no no no. I hate pills. "He hates pills. He wouldn't knowingly have taken one." Panic squeezed Zoe's throat. "Was I — I mean, was he maybe drugged?"

"The police are waiting on the toxicology report. And I shouldn't be telling you that. Sergeant Drummond already thinks you might be protecting someone."

"The only person I'm trying to protect is Eric." A chill breeze shook the branches above the road, sending a flurry of ice crystals down. She strode to the next bend and looked back along that stretch while a shuttle bus rumbled past. Its exhaust hung among the trees, tainting the clear mountain air. Only two more bends in the road and they'd be at JP's place, with nothing gained but a long walk back up to the parking lot.

As they rounded the corner, the shadow of the cellphone tower tipped across their path. Soon there'd be no sun on this slope. *I don't remember driving here.* The feeling of Eric's misery prickled at Zoe's eyelids. *It's okay*, she thought, giving the spaceship in her pocket a squeeze. *We aren't giving up.*

On she went, stopping every few feet to look down the slope below the road. Spiky spruce shadows leaned across the plowed lanes. Cars crawled down the hill, their windshields dazzling in the sunlight. JP's chalet was now only three driveways away. If the Camry wasn't between here and there, she didn't know where else to look.

The next gully was almost a miniature bowl, the road circling deep into the mountainside and back out. The sun didn't penetrate its farthest recess, and the snow lay deep among the spruces. She removed her sunglasses and stared into the gloom. Behind her came the rumble of another shuttle bus. As it passed them, sunlight danced on its rows of windows and bounced back across the hillside, where it hit the spruce trees below the road. Light glanced back from among the boughs, then it was gone. She squinted.

Lacey leaned on the snow pile beside her. "Did you see something, too, over there, just to the left of that rocky outcrop?"

"Yeah." Zoe pointed. "Something gleamed, I thought. It vanished so quickly."

"Maybe quartz in the granite?"

"Nope. This is sedimentary rock." After twenty years in the oil patch, hearing daily about the geological formations of the Eastern Slopes, Zoe knew the strata of this mountain. "Bare limestone above the treeline, slate and sandstone below. No granite. That's farther south, along the river valley."

"There's something shiny down there, anyway. Fix your eyes on that spot and let's try to get a closer look."

Zoe couldn't have looked away if she'd wanted to. Eric's excited murmurs accompanied her as she sidled along the tumbled edge of the plow's path. Where was another shuttle bus when you needed one to light up the hillside? Soon she got her wish, sort of: a minivan. The flash of reflected sunlight sent a dazzling echo back. There really was something near the outcrop of rock.

"Anything?" Lacey called.

Zoe skidded along the narrow shoulder, her eyes fixed on the outcrop. She leaned over to peer into the mass of trees. There! Beneath the branches, where three trunks huddled together.

Lacey arrived at her shoulder, puffing from a fast jog. "I wish I had a flashlight stronger than my phone's to bounce off whatever that is."

Zoe yanked a chunk of compacted snow off the plow ridge and heaved it at the spot. Snow cascaded as the chunk fell through the branches.

"You're burying it!"

Zoe grabbed another chunk. "I'm trying to clear it off."

After a moment, Lacey picked up a slab and hurled it. More snow slid away between the trees. Beneath the spruce boughs they saw a flash of chrome, and beside it, an arc of black tire and the rim of a bright-red fender.

CHAPTER THIRTY-THREE

Lacey leaned out over the drop-off, eyeballing the distance to the car. "About four metres down an eighty-degree slope. Bushes above, trees below. I can climb down to check the plate if you want, but how many red cars are missing up here?"

Bull's voice echoed through her earbuds. "You stay put. I'll send a crew with ropes and a winch."

"How long will that take? We're in the shade and it's getting a bit chilly."

"Nearest SAR team is only twenty minutes away, on Richards Road."

Lacey looked at the chrome bumper below, and at Zoe huddled on the snowbank. Twenty minutes was a long time to stand around on a freezing mountainside with a woman who couldn't stop crying. "We're almost at the Thompson chalet. They can meet me there. Nobody's going to disturb a car that far off the road before then."

An SUV pulled alongside, drowning out Bull's reply. The driver's window came down. "Is she hurt? Do you need a ride?"

"We're fine, thanks." Lacey saw them on their way. "Repeat that, please, Bull."

"I've ordered out a constable. If the tow truck arrives first, I'd appreciate you staying with the car until he arrives."

"Yes, Sergeant. Tell them to look for a stick with a glove on it." As if she'd leave before getting a good look inside that car. She tucked the phone away, marked the spot, and held out her bare hand to Zoe. "Let's get you a hot cup of tea."

Zoe's weeping eased, but she walked like a zombie. Inside the chalet she trudged to the kitchen with her boots on. Lacey kicked the loose snow off her soles and followed to start the kettle. Once the tea was steeping, she set a mug in front of Zoe, placed the sugar bowl and a spoon beside it, and dropped onto a stool. "You want to tell me why you were crying so hard?"

Zoe sniffed. "Eric. He was so damned happy to see his car."

The ghost again. "What does he think we'll find in it?"

"His backpack. An envelope for JP."

Calvin's voice replayed in Lacey's head. *Eric made a copy of everything for JP, so they could go over it together. It was in his backpack.*

"Will you be okay here alone for a bit? I have to go back to the car."

"Can't I come back with you? Eric will want to go."

"They won't let you near the car. It's evidence — the contents, too. Stay here and get warm."

Zoe stared into her mug. "I forgot. I kind of forget, sometimes, that he's ... not really here."

Lacey was standing on the road with her travel mug of tea when the red Camry began its backward crawl up the steep slope. A police SUV, a SAR truck, and a tow truck were the only vehicles now; everything else had been diverted to the north shoulder. The winch on the tow truck whined and stopped. The operator scrambled down the hill a second time while a SAR guy paid out his safety line. The car was snagged on something.

Constable Markov spoke into the quiet. "In the meantime, you want to see the search area around your car? The survey map's on my dash."

"Thanks." She grabbed the creased sheet and spread it on the hood.

He tapped it with one finger. "There's your car here, beside that slough. There are no recent breaks in the ice, but the sergeant says they'll put divers in if the ground search fails."

Lacey suppressed a shudder. At one time she'd aspired to be an RCMP diver, but an hour trapped on a sunken fishing boat, her nigh-empty tanks fouled in the tackle and her vision stolen by silt and darkness, had ended that dream. Placing her finger beside Markov's, she traced a line along a gravel road down to Highway 1A. If that isolated location had been a meeting place, Sandy's debtor — that sounded better than "blackmail victim" — had had a reason for choosing it.

"Are there houses near my car?"

"Not many, and they're widely scattered." He sketched a line sideways. "That's the top end of Stoney Nakoda First Nation. Mostly bush and a bit of pastureland."

"Nobody to witness a possible meeting, then?"

He shrugged. "And no reason for visitors to go there in the middle of winter. Door-to-door turned up two witnesses who saw headlights going north on Boxing Day, sometime after the first snow stopped."

"It was a blizzard at Bragg Creek until close to midnight that day. Where's that from the car?"

He pointed. "South-by-southeast. We're about the same distance north-by-northwest. Snow stopped around eleven-thirty at the Husky station off-ramp, where I spent all night deterring idiots and truckers from heading toward the mountains. Bitch of a wind, too, but then it went still as a grave at midnight. Couldn't ask for a better night, with the full moon on all that fresh snow. The next squall came through at dawn and half-buried my truck."

If Sandy hadn't gone through the Stoney Nation until close to midnight, where had she been from suppertime onward? Where was she now?

"This dotted line. Is it a real road running north, or one of those hiking trails?"

"Neither, really. That part of Richards Road isn't maintained. A Quadrunner or snowmobile might get you through, but no road vehicle." He put his finger on a spot closer to the wavy blue line of the Ghost River. "SAR teams are going south from there to meet the ones coming north. I was their liaison until I got called up here. If she wandered into the bush before that second big snow dump, we might never find her."

How terrible that would be for Dennis and his family, and for Loreena.

"How long is that unmaintained bit of road?"

"Maybe two kilometres. It comes out about ten K south of the Ghost River crossing."

Lacey laid her finger flat, estimating distances. "We're less than twenty kilometres from Highway 1A? I had no idea this deep wilderness was so close to civilization."

"By road it's a lot longer. No connection west of Highway 40."

Nearly fifty kilometres back along the winding Black Rock road, and another fifteen south to the Ghost. It was a miracle Markov had reached her as soon as he had. Six months ago, it had seemed unreasonable for the RCMP to take an hour to respond to a prowler call in Bragg Creek, but now that she knew the Cochrane detachment's territory a bit better, she figured they were doing damn well for a small staff with all these square miles of prairie and forest to cover. Not to mention hundreds of kilometres of highway and probably thousands more of back roads.

The tow truck winch whined again. This time the little red car rose steadily, and soon its wheels touched the road. The tow truck pulled ahead, setting the vehicle flat. Markov unclipped his flashlight and yanked a pair of latex gloves from the box in his car. Lacey peered over his shoulder as he opened the passenger door. Shoes, gloves, a window scraper, and a DQ bag lay loose in the front footwells. A yellow case held candles, matches, chocolate bars, and a space blanket still in its wrapper. Markov opened the glove box to reveal a registration folder, a first aid kit, and a stash of power bars. He ran his hands under the seats and came up empty.

"I don't see a backpack." Lacey straightened up, giving him room. "In the trunk, maybe?"

But there was no backpack and no envelope for JP there, either. Against all training and common sense, Eric had abandoned his shelter, food, and survival gear. For what? And then there was the car's position. "Markov, do you see any way this car could have gone over in this spot if it was heading downhill, toward the chalet?"

"Nope. Almost guaranteed it was going uphill. You can see from the front bumper that it hit those trees down there nose first. If it had gone off on the downhill it would have to slide sideways, and hit side-on. Someone going uphill missed the turn in the whiteout, or dumped it over deliberately."

"That's what I thought." If Eric had gone over here, climbed back up through the underbrush from his wrecked car, and struggled on foot through a blizzard for twenty minutes down the road again, his poppy would almost surely have been lost. More likely he'd driven right down past here to JP's yard, met his killer there, and then, after he'd been locked in the woodshed, the killer drove his car up a few turns and pushed it over the edge, expecting everyone would assume Eric had gone off the road in the blizzard. Not, Lacey reminded herself, that she was putting any stock in the idea that Eric had shown Zoe his route to the chalet. That was just an odd coincidence.

Markov looked at his watch. "I'm stuck here with the evidence, but you don't need to stay."

Lacey hadn't gone three steps when he called after her.

"If you're heading toward town, can you take a message to the north SAR staging area, to say I won't be back? There's no cellphone coverage over there."

The other search. The SAR workers there would know if Sandy had been found. "Show me where exactly it is."

"Which way?" Lacey lifted her sunglasses to look around. A sign on the right, past Zoe's bent head, read *Richards Road*.

Zoe peered at the map on Lacey's phone. "I think this is that Y junction. We keep going south here."

They wound down into a valley and crossed a box girder bridge over the ice-rimmed Ghost River. Up the other side, they passed a large house on a windswept knoll guarded by barbed-wire fences and *No Trespassing* signs. Another sharp bend took them west and south again. Lacey's phone pinged. No more cell signal. A sign near a gate read *Saddle Peak Trail Rides*. Several vehicles lined the road, and beyond them stood a small travel trailer. Lacey pulled up behind the last truck and got out. Through the gate a road led toward the western mountains. To the south was an open stretch between scruffy trees, straight as a road and filled with hillocks of snow disturbed by parallel snowshoe tracks. This would be the dotted line on Markov's map: two kilometres straight south to the Civic. No way Sandy could have walked this far in the middle of the night, not through fresh drifts. She'd surely be found nearer the Civic.

A white-haired man in a scarlet SAR vest leaned out of the trailer. "Help you?"

"Constable Markov asked me to tell you he won't be back. Another constable will have to come out as liaison."

"Tell them not to bother. The teams are working back north now, and we'll pack up. No sign of anyone having passed through. We'll check up the road a ways to be sure, but she'd have gone to one of those houses if she'd made it that far."

Lacey thanked him. Returning to the Lexus, she shook her head at Zoe's questioning look. The phone pinged as the signal returned. No way would she phone home with this report. Some things had to be said in person. They cruised down toward the bridge.

"Can we stop so I can pee?" Zoe asked. "All that tea and this bumpy road ..."

Lacey pulled over. Leaving Zoe to tramp down into the bushes, she walked onto the bridge and looked along the valley. The dark water of the Ghost River bisected a wide, snow-topped swath of gravel. No houses were visible from here, not even the big one on the south ridge. Wild mountains stabbed the pale western sky. Much closer, a rocky outcrop covered in icicles glittered in the midday sun, not even half as high as that icefall she and Boney had been trapped behind. That had been five days ago. The day Sandy was supposed to return.

Downstream, the water reflected the sky, disturbed here and there by eddies around the snow-capped stones. Someone had built a rock berm out from the south bank. Every so often a wave washed over its tip, sending a froth of bubbles downstream. As she watched one little patch of foam whirl out to the main channel, her eye caught a flash of vivid yellow between two rocks. It shifted as the water flowed around it. A plastic bag? She couldn't leave it there to wash downstream in the spring melt and tangle some hapless wild creature. Leaving the bridge, she edged down the rocky slope to the shore.

"Where are you going?" Zoe called.

"Picking up some trash." At the water's edge, she stooped. It wasn't a plastic bag at all, but a child's yellow purse. As she looked closer, purple and pink sequins flipped back and forth in the current, erasing and re-forming a unicorn's head. Sandy had run her hand up and down her granddaughter's purse, demonstrating the flip sequins to Lacey and Dee beside the Christmas tree. It couldn't be the same one. Not this far from the Civic.

Lacey hunted along the shore for a stick and dragged the purse from the river. Ignoring the freezing drops falling on her pant legs, she fumbled the zipper open. A familiar face stared up from a driver's licence photo.

A cloud swept along the river, dimming the light and turning the water black.

Lacey stood clutching the purse to her chest and scanned the stony shores, looking for any snow-covered lump the size of a body. The water wasn't deep enough to float a dead weight, or even to roll it over. But maybe that rocky outcrop upstream, with all the icicles coating its face …

As the cloud moved off, the sun sparkled on the water once more, reflecting up under the bridge. It glanced off a fall of icicles and cast a translucent glow into the triangular wedge where the bridge met the abutment. There seemed to be a lot of snow in that wedge. Snow that looked suspiciously like a puffy, white winter coat. Scrambling toward the bridge, she pulled out her cellphone. Two bars was barely enough power to get a call out.

"Bull," she said, staring along the underside of the bridge deck, "I found Sandy's purse with her driver's licence still inside. It's at the bridge over the Ghost River, not far north of the SAR staging area at Saddle Peak road. I'm starting a search of the immediate area."

"Understood. I'll send help."

Lacey disconnected and yelled up to Zoe. "Stay in the car!"

CHAPTER THIRTY-FOUR

When the first SAR truck reached her, Lacey was crouched on the rocks by the bridge's north end. Breathing deeply to quell her nausea, she waved an arm. The two-man team arrived at a jog. She couldn't speak, so she pointed. One man pulled out a radio, but moved away as he spoke. The other yanked a space blanket from his pack and wrapped it around Lacey. "Come away now," he said. "You've done your bit."

Zoe was back in the TFB office, finishing a late takeout lunch of chili with garlic bread, when her phone pinged. She hit pause on the video she'd been streaming, freezing the screen on a shot of the dark-haired admiral from the *Pegasus* and her lover, the blond Cylon. There was so much truth about women's toxic relationships right there: manipulation and gaslighting while smiling and acting like a best friend. The inevitable betrayal would be hideous.

The text was from Lizi: *Can we Skype?* She opened the connection in a corner of her screen.

"Hi, Mom!" Lizi waved at the camera. "Are you okay there by yourself? Are you remembering to brush Toomie? You know he gets cranky if he swallows too much hair."

Zoe made a face. "I stepped on a hairball this morning, thanks. He thoughtfully left it on the bathroom tile instead of the hall carpet. Are you guys having fun?"

"It's a blast. Clem, say hi to my mom."

"Hi, Zoe. Thanks so much for letting me come up and stay with Lizi."

"I'm glad you're enjoying it. What have you girls been up to?"

The highlight of the trip for both girls was learning to snowboard. This very morning they had both successfully landed their first jump on the real course, although sadly there were no photos.

"No flips yet," Lizi added, "but we're gonna try some grabs tomorrow, like those girls in the Olympics."

"Don't get too adventurous too fast. You don't want to break anything." Zoe looked past their glowing, laughing faces and expanded the window for a better view. The girls were in a luxurious living room, all varnished wood and big beams, with a gas fireplace taking up half the opposite wall. "Where are you? That looks like a private home."

"TJ got a suite. A bedroom each for him and his mom, plus the living room."

Zoe inwardly cringed. *Please don't let Lizi get a taste for the lifestyle JP's kids enjoy.* "Nice that he can afford it. Where's Dad?"

"Downstairs, having a drink with Arliss and the boys. They won't let us in the bar."

"Well, I'm glad of that. I'll give him a call." She signed off without mentioning Eric's car. If Aidan wanted to break that news to Clemmie while she was up there, let him pick the time. Meanwhile, Lizi and Clem's budding friendship sounded healthy, centred on learning new skills and testing their physical limits, not fretting about clothes or competing for male attention. On her screen, the blond Cylon gazed at the admiral it had manipulated to the edge of insanity. The creature — or the actress — looked a bit like Phyl Thompson there, with red exit lights tinting her spun-gold hair. Phyl had come to Canada a mere secretary, risen to executive assistant, married the boss, and gone home to England a millionaire's wife in all of ten years. Nobody did that well out of the oil patch without a plan and a significant degree of ruthlessness. Phyl, like the blond Cylon, had been determined to win.

Resisting the pull of Eric's interest in the video screen, Zoe called Nik's phone. The bar noise overwhelmed his greeting. He moved away from wherever he had been sitting, and it diminished.

"Is that better?" he asked. "How are you doing there? Are you coming up in the morning?"

"God, I wish." Zoe blinked back sudden tears. "I miss you. I really want to be there, having an uncomplicated holiday with you and the kids."

"Hon, are you crying? What's wrong?"

Zoe sniffed. "What isn't wrong? I'm at work tracing possible accounting fraud at TFB, and this morning at Black Rock, I stumbled on Eric Anders's missing car." He started to speak, but she kept going. "And two hours ago, I was with that Victim Services woman when she found a dead body."

"Another body?" Nik's voice rose, and probably his blood pressure along with it.

"I didn't see it. Lacey made me wait in the car. I'm so glad she did, because it must have been bad. She looked a wreck when she came back, and she's an ex-cop, so she's seen plenty." She pulled in a calming breath, and another. "I wish you were here tonight, so I could lean on you and be warm. I need a big hug."

"I wish that, too. Don't worry. I'll look out for the kids and bring them all home safely on Tuesday. You take good care of yourself. When this is over, you deserve every minute of that holiday someplace warm. Don't go getting soft on JP and letting him talk you out of it."

"No worries. I won't."

She was about to say goodbye when Nik said, "Arliss is here and wants a word."

"Hi, Zoe. What's this about a body? Don't tell me you found another one at the chalet."

"No, miles away: a woman missing since Boxing Day. And it was Lacey who found her."

"That's grim." The distant background of voices and laughter filled Arliss's brief silence. "I guess today's not a good day to call her about whatever it was she wanted to know."

Zoe struggled for a moment to remember what Lacey had wanted to ask Arliss about, but her eyes still stung with tears that wanted to fall — for Eric's lost potential, for her shaky sanity, for missing the ski trip, and ... well, for everything. She just wanted to finish this call so she could have some space. "Tomorrow might be better," she said. "She was pretty rattled when she dropped me off. But there is something you could do for me."

"Oh?"

"Keep an eye on Clemmie. Aidan may tell her sometime today that Eric's car has been found, once the police tell him. Don't you bring it up. Just, if she looks upset, ask her what's wrong. I don't know if she'll tell you. Compared to Lizi, that child is a sphinx." Zoe breathed deeply. Was that the last of her responsibilities today? Could she go back to tracing the accounting problem, which was mercifully all immutable numbers on paper and not filled with messy emotions? She was on the verge of asking Arliss whether JP had mentioned the malware at the last board meeting, but Eric's voice bounced from corner to corner of her consciousness. *No, no, no! Keep it quiet. Who to trust?* She asked for Nik back, said goodbye, and rang off. Around her, the muted rumble of air conditioning and the other sounds of an empty office building amplified her isolation. Calling up her favourite Baroque radio station on her laptop, she let harpsichords and violins sooth away the morning's tumult.

Her spreadsheet of payments to Cylon Six Inc. kept growing through the afternoon. The mental image of the soulless blond from the TV show intruded each time that name appeared in the cheque registry. Whoever had written the code must have been a fan. There were no payments after mid-October, when Eric had first reported it to JP, so he'd scared off whoever did it. As she worked back through earlier payment runs, a pattern emerged: thirty-three legitimate expense payments between cheques to Cylon Six, with the count carrying forward to the next print run to maximize the appearance of randomness. Each faked cheque's amount was 33 percent of the payment immediately before it in the run, a figure unlikely to attract an accountant's eyeball scan for anomalies. The address on the invoice was a post box in Canmore.

When last April's scam payments were listed, she subtotalled the column. In oil company terms, it wasn't much more than petty cash, varying amounts averaging a thousand a month. She rolled her neck and shrugged her shoulders. Time to pack it in for today. She could start again in the morning, dragging files up from the basement archives to look back further. "Happy New Year to me," she said into the hush, and clicked on the Cylon's face. She'd finish that episode before heading home to a hungry, bored cat and a lonely New Year's Eve.

Lacey shifted the blanket from her shoulders and swung her legs off the couch. "The whole afternoon gone and I've done nothing."

"You're still shaking." Dee reached for the mug with its syrupy dregs. "I can get you a refill."

"I've had enough." And she meant it in more ways than one. Huddling under a blanket, sobbing so hard her ribs hurt, she certainly didn't feel like the tough ex-cop Tom or Wayne or anyone else would recognize. Hell, she didn't even recognize herself. She'd never wept over a dead body in her life. And yet, when she'd stumbled in the door, shaking and teary, Dee and Loreena had rallied round with everything they could muster. Loreena might have turned white on hearing Sandy's body had been found, but she'd dragged Lacey to the couch just the same and wrapped her in the heated blanket. Dee had plied her with hot, sweet tea and fresh tissues. They'd both murmured soothingly and stroked her hair. Then more tea and more sobbing. Now she was done, but done what? She couldn't explain to herself why finding Sandy had hit her so hard; how could she explain it to them?

She had to face it: she hadn't exactly been an emotional rock ever since falling apart on Loreena's bed on Christmas night. She should probably get some counselling before she stopped functioning for a lot longer than a single afternoon. But then, in Alberta, where public systems were overloaded, she'd have to pay for it out of pocket, and she didn't have the money to spare. All she could do at the moment was make a mental note to investigate self-help coping for sexual abuse trauma. But finding out what had happened to Sandy and to Eric had to come first, as things would only get worse if she and Dee had to sell this house and move, especially while Loreena was so ill. She set her feet flat on the floor and concentrated on breathing. *You'll get through this, McCrae. You're tough enough. Suck it up, stand up, move your feet.*

"You had a bad shock this morning," said Dee.

"I saw a few bodies when I was on the Force, but they didn't hit me like this one. It's just bad timing. I'm so sorry, Loreena."

The older woman shook her head. "I'll be all right. I've had since last night to come to terms with the idea that she won't be coming back. It's Dennis and his kids I'm worried about."

"It'll be hard for them," Lacey agreed. "But I'm glad you're coping."

"I'll be back," said Loreena as she crept from the room, her spine bowed with fatigue and grief. Who would look after her now? Who would walk her through those final months of life?

"I've really got some digging to do," Lacey told Dee. "If Arliss is Eric's killer, and maybe Sandy's, too, I need to find evidence against her before she learns that she's under suspicion. Zoe or JP will surely let slip soon that they're investigating this fraud at TFB, and then she'll cover her tracks. She set up the accounting system at that company; she'll know how to manipulate it."

"You still think she pulled the same scam at that nursing home?"

"Why go after Sandy if she didn't?" Lacey got to her feet. "If Pat finally sends me the missing emails, this might all be cleared up by suppertime."

"Pat?" Loreena returned, carrying Lacey's sweatshirt. "Sandy's friend Pat?"

Lacey hurried to take the shirt from her. "You know Pat?"

"She goes to the same Dying with Dignity sessions as me. She supported her sister through it." Loreena settled on Lacey's vacated cushions and pulled the heated blanket over her own legs. "Someone should tell her Sandy's been found."

"We ought to leave that to Dennis," said Dee.

"Bring me a phone. I'll do it."

"Not yet," said Lacey. "Not until Bull okays it. They have a formal process of identification, and Dennis is the next of kin."

"It's been hours," said Loreena. "Surely they've contacted him by now."

"Not until the body's back at the Medical Examiner's in Calgary and ready for viewing."

Loreena shuddered. "I can't believe anyone would hit Sandy over the head and shove her body under a bridge. It's like a horrid old fairy tale."

Dee frowned. "She shouldn't have told you that. Sandy could have stumbled and hit her head on a rock."

Behind Loreena, Lacey shook her head. That was a comforting lie, but the battered flesh and exposed bone told a darker tale. The weapon had been wood, not stone. Dark shards of bark were embedded in the torn skin. That much had been visible by the light of her cellphone flashlight. Likely the autopsy would show an initial blow had stunned Sandy, and a later one killed her. Despite that, she'd been easy to identify, as she'd been perfectly preserved: buried immediately by blowing snow, frozen solid before the scavengers found her.

No good purpose would be served by putting that idea into Loreena's head, either. It was enough that Lacey would carry Sandy's shattered face into her own nightmares. Murder victims on the job were one thing, but this was the first one Lacey had been friendly with, shared meals with, watched movies with. This was personal.

"I feel," she said, and stopped, groping for the words. "If I'd been more aggressive in investigating Eric's murder, Sandy could still be alive."

The truth of it rocked her. She'd wasted a week suspecting Calvin and JP. If she'd questioned them directly at the start, the accounting fraud would have come out, and JP would have hired investigators immediately. It could all have been over by Christmas. Sandy would still be alive, planning her New Year's with her grandkids and worrying about her son's mortgage.

Loreena looked up. "Now, maid. It's nobody's fault but the killer's."

"That's right." Dee hugged her. "It's barely two weeks since Eric's body was found, and you learned way more than the police did. You found his car, too. Don't quit on us now." She tugged Lacey gently toward the stairs. "Go take a hot shower. Come down when you're ready to face food. One coconut bar on the way home can't keep you stable all day."

Loreena nodded. "I'll make you grilled ham and cheese the way you like it, with plenty of mustard. That'll warm you up."

Lacey took her time in the shower, letting the hot spray course down her skin, washing away the sick, hopeless feeling she'd carried ever since she'd kicked away the layers of icicles hanging from the bridge. The killer had concealed Sandy before the snowstorm, and before abandoning her car a dozen kilometres away as the crow flies, in a location almost guaranteed to cast suspicion on the residents of the Stoney Nakoda Nation. If she'd been carjacked, she'd have been found south or east of the car, and all her belongings would have been gone. Instead, her purse was found near her body with identification, cash, and credit cards still in it, and her suitcase was still in the trunk. That all argued someone familiar with the territory.

Arliss had led ski and horseback treks around there for decades. How had she — if it was Arliss — abandoned the Civic, though? A second vehicle? That required an accomplice. Was TJ back in the country a day earlier than he'd implied at the funeral? Lacey added that question to her mental notebook, beside the reminder that he'd been vague about exactly when he left Black Rock on the weekend Eric died there. He could have lingered with the excuse of waiting for Eric, then lied and said he didn't arrive at all. But again, Eric's car had been found near the chalet. TJ, or even Arliss, could have driven the Camry up there, pushed it off the road, and walked back down to the chalet and their own vehicle. No accomplice needed for that one. But why not leave Eric in his car and push him off the cliff, too? Her head was starting to hurt from too much thinking. She rinsed off a final time, crawled out of the shower and into her warmest PJs and robe, and headed down to the kitchen.

After the sandwich, followed by tea and Christmas cookies, she felt a lot stronger. She took a fourth cookie into the office and logged into her email. Time to face down Dan's lurking missive, then find out if Pat had forwarded Sandy's emails yet:

> You're down another half month on your share of the household expenses. When will you admit you can't make it on your own?

> I'm tracking every dollar you're short, and if
> you go ahead with the divorce I'll break you
> with legal fees. Then I'll buy up your debt
> and sell it to a collection agency. They'll
> hound you forever.

Coming on top of the day's events, the threat of complete financial ruin should have broken Lacey. Yet she couldn't raise an ounce of stress over Dan's threat. Any judge seeing this email would immediately toss out a lawsuit so plainly malicious. Dan was a province away, and if he came here to hunt her down, she had nothing left to lose by going public and having him charged with sexual assault and attempted murder. She had no career or reputation left to protect, and only a fragile strand of loyalty left for the RCMP, where male officers backed each other up and female officers fit in, kept quiet, or got out. She took a screenshot before forwarding the email to Dee, along with a short note:

> We know I can't afford your divorce lawyer,
> but is there a cheaper one you can think of?
> I'm so fed up with being threatened by this
> bastard, and I won't wait twenty years to re-
> build my finances like Sandy. She barely got
> sorted out before she was killed.

With that on its way, Lacey clicked on the next email. More spam. Nothing from Pat. Then she had a thought. She checked the Spam folder and let out a breath she hadn't realized she was holding. Three forwarded emails from Pat's address.

CHAPTER THIRTY-FIVE

Lacey moved all three emails to her inbox and printed off copies for an evidence file. The one dated December 25, likely the last sent from Pat's account, started without any lead-in:

> I told her I know she did it at the nursing home and now she's done it again out here. She changed her tune right away and begged for a day to get the money. I've got her for sure this time! Stay tuned.

Yes! It didn't state Arliss's name, but it confirmed that the nursing home was connected to Sandy's disappearance.

Nine p.m. on December 24:

> I was right about that computer virus thing. Over supper last night Lacey told Dee about one just like it at Mr. Thompson's oil company. That guy they found dead in the woodshed had figured it out. So she did do it again. If she doesn't want to be exposed,

she'll cough up that last payment she promised four years back.

She's doing what again? Calvin's table said it wasn't
Arliss, but a minor who had planted the nursing home
malware. If her son was the culprit, had she paid for
the cover-up that cost Sandy her job? JP couldn't have
known, or he'd have suspected his son at once when Eric
mentioned malware at TFB. Now, though, Arliss was
increasingly short of money, judging by her bitter comments at the funeral. This would have been a terribly
inconvenient time for Sandy to demand payment. Lacey
read on:

> She was at the oil company office today
> after it closed for the holiday. Covering her
> tracks with nobody around to see, I bet.
> She can't pretend it's nothing, like she did
> last week. When she came out, I told her I
> want that ten thousand bucks for my lost
> job or I'm telling Mr. Thompson all about
> the nursing home.

What more was there to tell? Arliss must have covered up computer fraud for one of her sons.

> All I really have to do is tell Loreena's
> daughter. She talks to him online almost
> every day. Maybe he'll give me a reward for
> exposing that cow. Either way, I'll be able
> to save Dennis's house. Merry Christmas
> to us!

Ten p.m. on December 22 — this was obviously
Sandy's first email to Pat after arriving in Alberta. Several
paragraphs detailed Loreena's reaction to the travel, the
delay at the airport because Loreena's daughter was late,
and a description of Dee's house that included the word
huge three separate times. And then:

> You'll never guess who I came face to face
> with while I was out with Loreena: that
> bitch from the nursing home. I should have
> reported the whole thing to head office as
> soon as she asked me to do it. She made out
> like she didn't recognize me at first but later
> she came up and said hi. I didn't say any-
> thing about the money in front of Loreena,
> but I saw her on the street in Cochrane
> today and told her straight up that she owes
> me for that. If I get any money out of her,
> I'll put it toward Dennis's mortgage.

Everything fit: Loreena and Sandy met a woman in
the coffee shop who didn't talk to Sandy right away.
Eddie saw Sandy talking to the woman on the street in
Cochrane — surely the same woman who'd paid Sandy
to cover up a minor's theft from the nursing home.
But a rich family's buying their teenager out of a theft
charge didn't seem to be enough motive for murder-
ing two people, three provinces away, four years later.
Lacey opened a blank document, dated it, and started
typing. If the motive still didn't make sense after she'd
summarized all the evidence, she would at least know
what was missing.

Three pages later, she attached Calvin's table and finished with her list of questions about Arliss's alibis for both deaths and the possibility that TJ was an accomplice in ditching the Civic. This was enough detail to send to Bull to help him home in on whoever had driven the Civic last.

As she pulled her phone to warn him the email was coming, she glanced up from the screen for the first time in a while. Beyond the window, night had fallen. From the kitchen came sounds of supper preparation: voices and the clatter of dishes. Now that she had shaken off her intense concentration, she smelled spaghetti sauce and ... was that garlic bread? If it was suppertime here, Bull would be eating, too, likely at home with his family on New Year's Eve. Another hour to rethink her conclusions wouldn't make a difference. She followed the aromas to the kitchen.

Loreena handed her a wineglass. "Did you find the answers you needed, dear?"

"Yes, thanks." Lacey swirled the tart red, savouring the flavour. "I'm more convinced than ever that it was Arliss Thompson Sandy was meeting. The emails Pat forwarded imply that Arliss got Sandy fired from the nursing home. Did she ever mention to you why she left?"

Loreena shook her head. "I remember she and Pat were both quite attached to some of the residents. Whenever one of their dotty old dears up and died of something preventable, they'd go on forever about slack quarantine practices and how things had been different in their day. Four winters ago was the worst. That was when Sandy was first starting with the home care service and I was in my second round of chemo. She'd say, 'What is going on over there? Did they get a bad batch of flu vaccine? It's supposed to be over eighty percent effective this year.' And then she'd tell me stories about the person who had died. They all had dementia in some form or other, but this one was unfailingly polite and gentle, that one was reliving his altar boy years and could always be calmed by reciting psalms, and Old Mrs. Thompson thought everyone was someone she knew from parties in the 1950s — you only had to say 'Bing Crosby' for her to wander off humming 'White Christmas.'"

"Mrs. Thompson? That's JP Thompson's mother?"

"Uh-huh. Sandy told me about her when she heard Dee was selling JP's chalet. The old lady had lost some of her brain function in her sixties after a medication mix-up, but was strong as a horse, otherwise." Loreena sighed. "Pat and Sandy were so upset when she died. She'd always gotten the flu shot before, but that winter, when all the others were dying, another nurse told Pat that the family had refused permission for it. Sandy intended to give them a piece of her mind at the funeral, but instead they had her cremated and shipped the ashes out west. While we were waiting to get off the plane in Calgary, Sandy said she was going to find out where the ashes were and go leave a token, for old time's sake."

Lacey swirled another mouthful of wine in time with her thoughts. Had Arliss denied her demented old mother-in-law's flu shot, perhaps in hopes of getting an inheritance before her divorce was final? What a shock, then, to be confronted by a nurse threatening to tell her ex-husband how she'd contributed to his mother's premature death. That motive would fill the gap nicely. What a good thing that report hadn't already gone to Bull.

Dee shuffled in with the breadbasket.

Loreena raised her wineglass. "The year is ending on a sad note, but a new one begins tomorrow. Let it be one of joy, in both endings and beginnings."

Lacey woke on New Year's Day with a fresh determination to wrap the investigation up as soon as possible. Wayne, her boss, had told her that he would soon be briefing a private investigator about Eric's death. If Lacey succeeded in solving the murder and the malware case, she would tell him not to bother. Maybe he could submit a bill for her time to JP Thompson instead. She didn't have a PI license, but the end result was the same. Maybe she should just submit a bill without waiting for Wayne to suggest it. Her time, her work, and her investigative skills had a measurable value, and she could certainly use the money. But first she had to wrap up the loose ends.

Today's goal: pin down Arliss Thompson in at least one provable lie.

An hour and two cups of coffee later, Lacey was going over her report to Bull for the third time, brainstorming ways to fill the gaps in her knowledge, when her phone vibrated. It was a number she didn't recognize, but she'd put out a few queries lately. It could be anyone.

"Hi, Lacey, this is Arliss Thompson. Zoe asked me to call you. I would've called yesterday, but she said you'd had a bad day and I should leave it until morning. Happy New Year."

Stifling her surprise, Lacey scribbled down the incoming number to check against Sandy's phone records. A 580 code would be Arliss's cellphone. "Yes, Mrs. Thompson. Thanks for calling. We met at Eric Anders's funeral. I'm not sure what Zoe told you."

"I hardly remember myself. Something about a missing person."

In the pause that followed, Lacey yearned for a magic mirror or a Skype connection, some way to evaluate the woman's body language. When Zoe had set up the callback two days ago, Arliss had barely been on anyone's radar. Now she was Lacey's main suspect in two murders. If she realized she was being interrogated, she'd try to cover her tracks. Best to stay neutral and let her think she was leading the conversation.

"The person isn't missing any longer."

"Oh, you mean Eric? You must be the PI that JP hired." Before Lacey could clarify, Arliss charged ahead. "This investigation has dragged on long enough, and the police have gotten nowhere. My son is in the lift lineup already. Should I get him to call you when he comes in?"

"That's not necessary at this time."

"Well, he could tell you better than I, because he was around that weekend. Out at the chalet, I mean, until the blizzard warning."

"He came back in his own vehicle, if I remember correctly?" Lacey poised her pen over one of Dee's yellow legal pads.

"That's right. Following his stepmother's car in case she slid into the ditch. He was quite frustrated by her driving."

Lacey made a note to check the order of departures and the number of vehicles with someone else. Maybe Bull had the information in his initial case notes. "You weren't out there with the family?"

"Hell, no. Not with Phyl — that's my kids' stepmother, the 'lady of the manor.' I was at the West Bragg ski trails. We planned to do the first grooming of the season, try out our new machine. But we barely got started before the blizzard warning got upgraded. It would only have to be done again after the new snow, so we quit. I headed into Calgary barely ahead of the storm."

Bragg Creek to Black Rock was an hour's drive. Arliss could have been warned by her son as he was leaving the chalet, and headed straight there to intercept Eric. "How did you know Eric was going to the chalet that day?"

"I didn't. TJ came for lunch the next day, on his way back to university. He went next door to say hi and found out Eric hadn't come home. The main search had to wait for that road to be plowed. I don't know if you've been out there, but it's forty-odd kilometres past Waiparous and drifts over something crazy. A few people were snowed in at cabins along the road, and they had to send a chopper in to check on them. They didn't see any sign of life at JP's and figured Eric must have turned back."

"Did you know why Eric was going out there?"

"To talk to JP outside the office, as I understand it. He'd run afoul of his supervisor at work and maybe was worried about his internship. I could have told him he had nothing to fear. JP swore to me he wouldn't cut it short on Marcia's word."

So far, the woman had an answer for everything. "Eric's family members never mentioned anything more specific?"

"Nope. By the time I got there, everyone was frantic. It only got worse the longer he was missing." Arliss sighed. "I've been doing backcountry safety training for thirty years. I would have sworn Eric knew not to leave his vehicle. And why didn't he break into the chalet? He must have known JP wouldn't hold it against him, no matter what Phyl might say. It doesn't make sense."

So, she didn't know the RCMP investigation had moved on to suspected homicide. Or she was pretending she didn't know. Lacey scribbled a note to that effect. Now, time to change tactics. "There's a related matter I'd like to clear up. Zoe might have mentioned the nurse who went missing in the Boxing Day blizzard?"

"Oh, right. The one whose body you found yesterday? How horrid for you."

"Yes, well, that nurse came from Ontario. She used to work at the nursing home where your mother-in-law lived. I understand you chatted with her before Christmas." Now, more than ever, Lacey wished this was a face-to-face interview. Would Arliss admit to two meetings, or only the one at which Loreena had been present?

"Oh, my god. That was Sandy?" Arliss's voice rose. "I've been waiting for her to phone me back ever since."

A bubble of glee warmed Lacey's ribs. If Arliss's phone number turned up in Sandy's records, proving they'd been in contact after Sandy left Bragg Creek, she'd be nailed in a flat-out lie. One falsehood would fray the edges of more until the whole fabric unravelled. "Where did you see her?"

"In Bragg Creek, before Christmas. I ran into her at that coffee shop. Didn't recognize her right away. You know how it is when you see someone in a completely different context from where you know them. Out of uniform, too. And I hadn't been to that nursing home in five years or more, so I wasn't even sure it was her, at first. When she told me about my mother-in-law's death, I was incensed. I went home frothing at the mouth."

This was a new twist. "You didn't know your mother-in-law was dead?"

"No, no, of course I knew that. But I didn't know why." Arliss's breathing whistled in Lacey's ear. "Sandy told me my ex-mother-in-law had been denied her flu shot not two months earlier. Old Fran was strong as a horse. She could have been living happily still, crooning along to Bing and Frank and calling everyone sweetie because she had no idea what their names were. I asked Sandy who had cancelled the shot so I could give them what for, but she didn't know. She was going to phone her friend back east and find out. I gave her my number and waited to hear, but she never called me back."

If Arliss hadn't cancelled the flu shot herself, that severely limited her possible motive for silencing Sandy.

In fact, it left only covering up computer hacking done by one of her kids. That was no stronger a motive for murder now than it had been earlier. Lacey gave her head a shake and regrouped. So far she had only Arliss's word on this; it wasn't even backed up by body language she could observe.

"And that's the only time you spoke to her?"

"Yes," said Arliss, without even a hint of hesitation.

"You worked the Backcountry booth at the Cochrane Christmas market? She was there at least once."

"I did a few shifts, but I don't remember seeing her there."

Without confirmation from Eddie that it was Arliss he'd seen with Sandy, Lacey couldn't push harder, so she backtracked. "The day you spoke to her at the coffee shop, she didn't mention knowing anyone else around this area, did she? Someone she might have been in contact with?"

"Not that I recall. But, as I said, I was quite angry about JP's mother."

"You weren't consulted about the flu shot? Were you not married to JP when his mother died?"

"Divorced. He was already married to his second wife." Arliss was silent for a long moment. "You know, I bet it was Phyl. JP would never have agreed to move to England while his mother was alive."

"You haven't told JP yet?"

"No point. He's already in London, and anyway, it's in the past for him. He doesn't do the past. The only times I've spoken to him recently, he's been hell-bent on avoiding a lawsuit from Eric's parents." Indignation throbbed in Arliss's voice. "He's not thinking like a parent at all. Casting blame hasn't even crossed their minds. They're swamped by grief and shock, falling apart at the seams. Although, between you and me, there wasn't much family cohesion before this happened. That's why I'm so happy Clemmie's out of there for a few days. She's a different kid up here with Zoe's girl."

"I'm glad to hear that."

Now what? Arliss wasn't the least bit defensive. Far from watching her every word, she was veering off confidently on tangents as they occurred to her. She'd make a good impression in a jury box, whether as a witness or a suspect.

Arliss said, half to herself, "I bet TJ could request information on his grandmother's flu shot. He's of age now, and one of her heirs."

"Did she leave much?"

"Some investments in trust for her grandkids. The main financial benefit of her death is that JP's not paying fifty grand a year for her care anymore. In the early years, we had to scratch for it, but now that's pocket change for him. He spent more on Christmas in London. Nice for him. TJ's paying for my New Year's, otherwise I'd be home alone with a box of wine from Superstore. Anything else you need, Lacey?"

"Before you go, can you tell me where you and TJ were on Boxing Day? Just for my records."

"I was with my neighbour, Leslie, trying to get her organized for Eric's funeral. TJ was in London, hunting for a plane ticket home. Two hours later and he'd have missed the service."

Lacey thanked her and signed off. Then she opened Calvin's email, copied from his table the line of data about the nursing home malware incident, and hit Reply. She asked him to dig up everything he could on that entry, including the real name of the hacker, if possible. Then, conscious of the fact that she was asking him to do something not quite legal, she added:

> Please find out what flight from England TJ
> Thompson arrived on — December 25, 26,
> or 27.

She sent the message, then looked again at the report for Bull. That gaping hole in the middle of Arliss's motive had to be filled in before she could send it. Presumably, Pat had been the person Sandy intended to ask about that flu shot. Calling her on a family holiday probably wasn't a great idea, especially as she may not yet have been told about Sandy's death. Stymied, Lacey headed for the coffee pot.

Dee was setting up her mother's tray. "Can you take this up?" she asked.

Lacey nodded. "Just going to check in with Bull first." She poured while the call was connecting. Bull might be off shift, but he would be keeping tabs on the investigation. They were still within that crucial first twenty-four hours after finding the body, which meant constables would be going door to door near both crime scenes — where the car was found and where the body was found. Who knew where a witness might turn up who could place Sandy with her killer?

"Happy New Year," she said when Bull picked up. "Sorry to bother you at home, but —"

"Yeah, you want an update. Not much to tell. Pretty clear case of blunt force trauma, but the autopsy has to wait. The ME's backlogged." He didn't need to elucidate. The season of brotherly love invariably yielded more suspicious deaths than there was staff to process. "Your keys weren't found with the body. They might be any-where between the Civic and the bridge."

"You don't seriously think she walked all that way during the night, through knee-deep snow, carefully clutching her little yellow purse but somehow losing the keys, only to run into someone who conked her on the head?"

"Unlikely, of course, but we have no evidence to the contrary. Residents of a house above the bridge report-ed being woken by someone cutting through their yard around three a.m. Their property is posted and their dogs usually roam, but due to the heavy snowfall, they were kennelled. Any tracks were buried by the second wave of snow. SAR thinks the victim was under the bridge before the first wave, due to snow cover techni-calities and lack of predation. Anything identifiable on your key chain that would help the searchers?"

"A Vancouver Canucks bottle opener and a Honda tag." Lacey pictured her keys arching across the kitchen and landing on the counter, Sandy scooping them up and heading off with nothing more on her mind than having a wonderful Christmas with her grandchildren and paying off her son's mortgage. "That reminds me, can I tell Sandy's friend in Ontario that she's been found?

I have to call her about something else, and it would be weird not to mention it."

With permission obtained, she added the house phone to Loreena's breakfast tray and took it upstairs. It would soften the blow on Pat if she could hand the phone off to Loreena.

Nobody answered at Pat's daughter's house. Lacey left a message to call her back, then left the same message on Pat's home answering machine. She left the phone with Loreena, who promised to ask about old Mrs. Thompson's flu shot first thing when Pat returned the call.

"If she hasn't heard from Dennis yet, you can tell her Sandy's been found, and that she's not coming home. But nothing about how she was killed, okay?"

"What are you up to this morning?" Dee asked when she came downstairs.

"Looking for Arliss's cell number in yours and Sandy's call lists. If she did have contact with Sandy and I can catch her in a provable lie, it means I'm on the right track."

"And if she didn't?"

Lacey spread her hands wide, mutely admitting that she'd have no idea where to go next.

CHAPTER THIRTY-SIX

Groping on the nightstand for her phone, Zoe knocked over the wineglass. It landed softly on the carpet, spilling its few drops of flattened bubbly. The text was from JP: *Happy New Year. Don't contact me today unless the building is on fire.*

"Happy New Year to you, too." She snuggled under the duvet, hoping to be lulled back into blissful unconsciousness. Before she achieved that state, though, the bed dipped as Toomie landed on it with all the grace of a baby hippopotamus. He stomped up her body from hip to shoulder. His whiskers tickled her cheek before he announced in his half-Persian, half-banshee wail that he was starving. She cupped a hand over her ear. Why hadn't she shut the bedroom door? He'd have stayed asleep in Lizi's room until she went downstairs.

He wailed again, like a teething baby.

"Oh, shut up! I'm coming."

By the time she'd pushed him off her and rolled out of bed, her brain was awake, clearing away the fractured images of last night's sci-fi TV binge. Today she'd finish that malware report, and tomorrow she'd have the whole day to deal with Eric's ghost before her family returned. Jumping from mom to ghostbuster to wife to file wrangler and back again at random had left her frazzled. Two of those roles must go, and soon.

She was getting dressed when her phone rang. "Happy New Year."

"And to you." Lacey sounded tired, but determined. "How are you doing after the stress of yesterday? How did you sleep?"

"Not too bad. I numbed my brain binge-watching TV. What about you? Any nightmares?"

"No. I was too worn out." Lacey sighed. "I really want to clear up Eric's death, and Sandy's, and start the year off without the shadow of ..."

"Of what?"

"Death, I guess." Lacey's voice sounded neutral, but her vibe was distinctly uneasy. Was she being haunted by the ghost of the nurse? Wouldn't that be a strange twist of fate? Unlikely, but strange things happened when a person touched the body of someone they'd known in life.

To test that theory, Zoe said, "I'm hoping to get clear of Eric's ghost in the next twenty-four hours. Having another person inside your head interrupting and distracting you whenever you try to concentrate is exhausting. Are you any closer to figuring out how he ended up locked in that shed?" The vibe this time was harder to pin down. Secrecy mixed with ... what? Sorrow?

"I hope that for you, too," Lacey said, not answering the question. "What are your plans for New Year's Day?"

"Going into the office. If I can work back to exactly when the malware first infected the cheque printer, it'll narrow down who might have planted it."

"I'm working on that from my end, too. Swap our findings this afternoon?"

"Sure."

"You haven't told anyone what you're working on, have you? About the malware, I mean."

"Only JP." *I nearly asked Arliss about it, but the voice in my head said no.* "With the company sale looming, we can't let rumours get started before we know the extent of the damage."

"Be sure to keep it that way. Somebody could seize the chance to cover their tracks."

Trust nobody. With a shiver, Zoe passed on her greetings to Dee and hung up to finish getting dressed. Downstairs, Toomie sat beside his half-empty kibble bowl and yowled at her.

"You're fat enough," she told him. "But since I don't know when I'll be back, you can have another half cup. Don't tell Lizi." After he'd eaten, Toomie head-butted her calf and followed her to the front hall. He leaped up to the table with much more grace than when he'd landed on her bed, and promptly sat down on the sweater she'd tossed there the previous evening. She tugged it out from under him. "Get off that. Eric's spaceship is in there."

Eric arrived in her head so suddenly she staggered. When she recovered her balance, she put her hand in the pocket and pulled out *Galactica*. "It's safe, okay?" she told the empty hallway. "I'm taking it with me."

Pulling her arms through the sleeves, she tucked the plastic model back into the pocket and dragged her ski jacket over it all. January first, alone in the office with a ghost and a plastic spaceship. That had better not be an omen for the year ahead. "Happy New Year," she told Toomie, then locked the door behind her.

Three hours later, she closed another invoice file and stretched her arms behind her head. Twenty months back, the creepy little malware script had printed out five cheques to the unknown hacker in one month alone. In oil company terms, a thousand or fifteen hundred a month wasn't much more than petty cash, although if the fraud had continued into this past November, it could have hit a couple of significant drilling contracts and doubled the year's take. It had stopped in mid-October, one payment period before Eric died.

She stacked up the current batch of file boxes and headed for the elevator. She'd previously felt creeped out in the basement archives of this building. Now that she understood she had been sensing Eric, being alone down there wasn't as scary. She slid the boxes onto their shelf, collected another six months' worth, and pushed the elevator button with her elbow.

As the elevator carried her back up, she thought about Marcia, who had been working Accounts Payable for more than three years and had apparently never questioned the invoices that crossed her desk for authorization. Arliss had often declared the woman unqualified for the job, and this proved it. JP could probably sue Marcia for negligence, but of course he wouldn't.

Phyl's friendship, such as it was, would keep Marcia safe from the consequences of her ineptitude.

Zoe stepped out on the TFB floor and all but fell over Marcia, who was kneeling on the floor stuffing things into her handbag. The accountant reared up in surprise. Her massive key ring sailed from her hand to chink against the frosted-glass doors of the conference room. Propping the file boxes on a magazine stand, Zoe hurried to retrieve it. "I'm so sorry. I wasn't expecting anyone else to be here today." She passed back the heavy key ring, carefully detaching her pinky finger from the bottle opener. "Oh, are you a Canucks fan? Have you been to see them playing the Flames?"

Marcia shoved the keys into the pocket of her parka. "No. What are you doing here today?"

No no no no no, trust nobody.

A reflexive chill ran up Zoe's spine. "Still tracking down old accounts that we might have to explain to a buyer's auditor. I'll be glad when it's over. What brings you in?"

"Finishing up year-end while it's quiet." Marcia got to her feet. "Anybody else around? Drilling still watching their wells?"

"Nope." Zoe reached for the file boxes. "I guess we're the only ones without a life. Happy New Year, Marcia."

"Yeah, same to you." Marcia's small brown eyes slid up the stack and examined Zoe's face. "You look like you've been at it a while. I'm going on a coffee run. Want me to bring you back a latte or something?"

"I'd kill for a two-shot double-caramel made with soy milk."

"Want a dollop of cheer in that? I've got a bottle in my drawer. Gift from my team."

"Sounds like heaven." Zoe headed to her office as the elevator doors whooshed shut, carrying Marcia away.

Lacey grabbed her travel mug off the Tims counter and screwed the lid back on. She already knew where Calvin was sitting, having spotted him through the window on her way in. She dropped her portfolio onto the table and slid into the chair opposite.

"Hi, Calvin. Why did you want to meet instead of just emailing?"

Calvin looked around the restaurant and out to the parking lot. He leaned forward. "You asked me to hack into an airline booking system. Do you think I'm going to put a response to that on the record where someone could find it later?"

"I wondered about that when I asked."

"Well, send another message telling me you realize you shouldn't have."

"You're not going to do it?"

"It's already done, but nobody needs to know that." He slid a folded sheet across the table. "That's everything on the nursing home malware incident. As for the other question, TJ landed at eight forty-three a.m. on December twenty-seventh. Do you want the flight number, too? CCTV from the airport caught his mother's vehicle picking him up in the loading zone at nine fifty a.m. They were at the funeral home when we arrived at ten forty for the service, which started at eleven."

He picked up his glass of soda, and Lacey noticed the absence of any tremor. Last time she'd seen him pick up a glass, he'd been shaky and had avoided her eyes. Now he looked at her directly. His speech was calm and measured, although he was a bit annoyed. This was a Calvin she could see working for a security services agency.

"Thanks for this. Of course I'll send you that email if you think it's necessary."

"I do."

"If you don't mind me saying, you seem a lot more, well, calm than the last time we spoke."

He nodded. "I was pretty messed up when Eric was missing. My doctor prescribed a lot of medications to help me cope. Now that the funeral's over, I'm a lot less stressed. I've started tapering off, getting ready for university next week. I have a bunch of work to make up from last semester."

"Oh," Lacey said. "I was under the impression that you'd been medicated for some time."

"Let me guess: TJ's mom. She's a nice lady, but when she looks at me, she sees an Asian, a foreigner, someone she doesn't have a read on. The pills I got after Eric went missing are another sign of my strangeness. TJ's whole family is convinced that some fresh air and exercise will get you through anything."

"Does Eric's mom not feel the same?"

"Eric's mom wanted whatever he wanted. If he breathed funny, she was right there asking if he was getting a cold. My mother is equally obsessed with me.

One of the reasons I lobbied so hard to stay in Canada for school." He turned his glass in his hands, showing the first sign of nerves since Lacey walked in. "I've covered my tracks, but you can't ever tell anyone I did this for you. I can't be caught hacking while I'm being vetted for a federal agency."

"You got it." Lacey popped the spout on her travel mug. Steam seeped out, scalding her lip. She closed it up again. It would be drinkable on the drive back to Bragg Creek. "I don't suppose you have Arliss Thompson's landline number?"

He took out his phone. His fingers flickered quickly over the screen. A second later, her own phone pinged.

"Did you just look up her number online?"

He rolled his eyes. "She gave us all her numbers before the ski trip in case we needed anything. I just texted it to you. I also emailed you a contact sheet from my old TFB file. It's current up to November first." He turned his glass around again, staring into its depths. "Do you think finding that malware script had something to do with Eric's death?"

Lacey looked him over. Could this Calvin cope with the truth? More importantly, could he keep silent about it? "It might," she said. "I wish we had Eric's printouts, but they weren't in his car, and the police haven't found his backpack. If the killer didn't destroy it, it'll be buried in a snowbank somewhere."

"Will Mr. Thompson investigate properly this time?"

"He's already got someone looking into it. They have to go back and recheck all the records to figure out the same things that Eric had documented."

"Why don't they use his backup? It has everything on it." As Lacey gaped, he continued, "Oh, crap, I guess nobody knew where it was. It's on a USB stick. It should be in his room."

"Somebody took his laptop. If they knew there was a backup, wouldn't they have taken any USB sticks that were there, too?"

He shrugged. "Who'd look for storage in a *Battlestar Galactica* model sitting beside a bunch of other spaceship models?" When she raised an eyebrow, he grinned. "It's a thumb drive disguised as a spaceship. Supersecret, unless you're a *BSG* fan who saw it on ThinkGeek back when they had them in stock."

Lacey hadn't paid much attention to the spaceships on Eric's shelf. At the funeral, her attention had been on the laptop, and on keeping Zoe from falling apart too much in front of Clemmie. "Can we go get it now?"

"I'm not staying there anymore, but I can text Aidan."

"I'll do it." Lacey stood up and held out her hand. "Thank you, Calvin. You were a good friend to Eric, and you've helped me with this investigation. Good luck with CSIS."

She walked out to the Lexus with a new spring in her step. Eric's records could confirm that existence of September's fraudulent cheques, even if someone had tampered with the accounts afterward. The cheques must have been deposited somewhere. If she could find Arliss's bank account and compare deposits and dates ... but how? She looked back at Calvin, sitting over his empty glass. He could find out for her. Was it fair to ask him to do something even more illegal than hacking into airline manifests? If she found either of Arliss's phone numbers in Sandy's records, she wouldn't need to ask him. She'd have proven a clear lie, and the official investigation could unfold from there. The RCMP would be able to get a warrant for the information.

She got behind the wheel, but instead of starting the engine, she opened her portfolio. With Arliss's contact information displayed on her phone, she took out the list of cellphone calls Sandy's son had given to her and scanned the column of numbers. Nothing. She flipped to the printout of calls made from Dee's landline. Neither of Arliss's numbers appeared there, either. She propped the phone up in the dashboard holder and started again at the first sheet, using her finger to make sure she didn't skip a single number. Then she sat back, frowning. Neither Arliss's landline nor cellphone number showed up in Sandy's or Dee's phone records.

Could the arrangements all have been made by email? How illegal would it be to ask Calvin to hack into a Gmail account or two? She looked back at the Tims, but his chair by the window was vacant. Just as well. Evidence acquired by hacking wouldn't be admissible in a trial, anyway. There had to be another angle. Maybe Eric's backup would give her a fresh lead.

Fifteen minutes later, she stood staring at the bookshelf in Eric's bedroom. "You're sure it's not one of these?"

Aidan ran his hand along the shelf again. "*Enterprise* is a USB webcam, but all the rest are plain model spaceships. *Galactica* isn't here. You're sure Cal said it was that one? Maybe Clemmie took it. She's a *BSG* fan, too."

"I thought she was off skiing in Marmot Basin."

"Uh-huh. Let me text her."

"Will she answer right away?"

"Not likely. It's only urgent if the phone rings. I'll give her a call." He got his sister's voice mail and left a message. Then he keyed in another number. "I'm looking for Clemmie, Mrs. Thompson. Is she there?" He put the phone on speaker.

"She's halfway down the mountain right now, going like stink," said the older woman. "Is it urgent?"

"I've called and texted her, but I hope you can tell her to get back to me ASAP."

"When she reaches the bottom, I'll tell her. No more bad news, I hope. She's coping okay about Eric's car, but I don't want to upset her again."

Aidan told Arliss about the thumb drive. As Lacey waved frantically at him for silence, he blurted out that Eric had been looking into a malware script at TFB. Shit! Why hadn't she warned him to keep quiet? Arliss could learn of the drive's location from Clemmie and be back here to destroy it by midnight if they didn't find it first.

Arliss's voice rattled from the tiny speaker. "JP told us the malware issue was a false alarm. Marcia caught it before it did any damage."

She admitted to knowing about the malware? That didn't add up in any way with Lacey's theory. She leaned toward the phone. "When did he tell you that?"

"At the shareholder meeting, when he first floated the idea of selling the company. Last week of October, I think."

Just when Eric was assembling evidence of the very real damage being done by the malware script. As the wheels began to turn in Lacey's head, Aidan said, "Eric had proof it was real. That's what he was taking to the chalet that weekend."

"It was real? Does JP know this? Is he looking into it?"

Aidan looked questioningly at Lacey. She puffed out her cheeks, thinking hard. Once again, Arliss was not reacting like someone with a guilty conscience. Maybe, if she raced home to cover her tracks, Lacey could dog her every step until her own actions convicted her. If she was innocent, she'd stay where she was.

"Yes, JP knows," she said. "If we had Eric's thumb drive, we could save Zoe a lot of work."

Arliss gave a disgusted huff. "Of course, he'd make it Zoe's job, and on New Year's Day, too. She should be up here skiing with us. He should have made Marcia work the holiday, since she's the one who missed it the first time. Spotting accounting malware is supposedly her area of expertise. She even carries a souvenir one on her keychain. She brags about how she caught it at the nursing home."

Nursing home? The truth hit Lacey like a bolt of lightning. "Did Marcia work at the nursing home where your mother-in-law lived?"

"Sure. That's how she and Phyl got to be friends. She'd take Phyl out shopping to alleviate her unutterable boredom while JP was visiting with his mother. After his mom died, Phyl insisted Marcia be given a job here in Calgary. When JP sells the company, I don't know what she'll do. The new owners won't keep somebody around who doesn't know the oil business."

How Lacey got off the phone and out to her vehicle so fast, she couldn't quite be sure. She sat there clutching the steering wheel, staring straight ahead while her carefully constructed theory fragmented and reassembled itself, replacing Arliss with Marcia:

1. Marcia had worked at that nursing home when the hacker loaded the malware, and when old Mrs. Thompson died after not getting her flu shot.

2. Marcia was a friend of the new Mrs. Thompson, who wanted to live in England.

3. Marcia and Arliss were both stocky brown-haired women over fifty. They'd both worked the Backcountry Safety Association's booth at the Cochrane Christmas market.

4. Marcia carried around the nursing home malware script on a USB drive, which she could easily have stuck into the cheque-writing printer any time she wished.

Lacey angled the sheet of paper Calvin had given her to the light at her side window. Three paragraphs of small print provided information about the nursing home malware incident, including the name of the hacker — nobody she recognized — his Queen's University student email address, and, farther down, the name of the accountant who had uncovered the malware: Marcia.

After that, it was easy to look up Marcia's office, cell, and home numbers in the TFB staff directory and compare them against Sandy's phone record. One call from Sandy's cell to Marcia's office number, another to Marcia's cell, and the last one after five p.m. on Boxing Day from Marcia's cell to Sandy's. Lacey's memory flashed the brown SUV with its loaded ski racks pulled over near the Bragg Creek Arts Centre while Marcia talked on the phone. Her stomach turned over. Had Marcia been luring Sandy to her death at that very moment?

If Marcia learned her fraud was being investigated again, she'd immediately try to cover her tracks at TFB Energy. Zoe was working today. She must be warned before she ran into Marcia in the office. If she let slip what she was working on, or if Marcia guessed, she'd be in immediate danger. With two murders on her hands so far — she'd probably indirectly caused JP's mother's death, as well — Marcia would have no compunction about disposing of Zoe, too.

CHAPTER THIRTY-SEVEN

Lacey texted Zoe before starting up the SUV. There was no response by the time she got out of the neighbourhood, so she made a split-second decision to check Zoe's house first. It was much closer than the office. If Zoe was safe at home, there was no need for panic. But every minute she was in the office, she'd be at risk. While Lacey waited to turn onto Macleod Trail, she told her phone to dial Zoe's. The call went to voice mail. Calling the landline sent her to voice mail, too. She pulled in to Zoe's driveway, left the Lexus's door open, and ran to pound on the front door. No answer. She peered through the tiny garage window. No minivan. The downtown office, then. Before she left the driveway, she checked Calvin's staff directory. But Zoe had no office number listed. Damn! She hadn't started working there until after the first of November. The main company number was listed, but there'd be no receptionist on New Year's Day to route a call to Zoe. It looked like Lacey's only option was going there in person.

Come to that, how would she get into the building? Security guards didn't let random strangers in, especially not during holidays, when the regular staff were away. Wayne's company handled JP's home security; maybe he could get her into the office. She told her phone to call his number. Barely pausing to apologize for interrupting his New Year's Day, she made her request.

"Sure," he said. "I do the company's physical security audits every six months. I'll meet you there with my pass card."

Twenty minutes later, Lacey sat waiting in the Lexus outside the office building on a deserted Sixth Avenue. She anxiously called Zoe's cellphone again. When it kicked over to voice mail, she disconnected. There was no point in leaving another message.

She told herself she was overreacting, that Zoe had gone out for a holiday supper and turned off her phone. Maybe she'd changed her mind and gone north to join her family. But Lacey's old police instincts were twanging, and her gut was churning up that same sick feeling it had had last summer when she'd gone looking for Dee. Something was wrong. Out of desperation, she called Arliss Thompson back.

"Hi," she said, making a deliberate attempt to control the intensity in her tone. "I was wondering if Zoe's husband is around, or if you could give me his number."

Arliss put her hand loosely over the receiver and said, "Go get your father." Then she came back on the line. "He's on his way. What do you need?"

Lacey had a flash of sheer panic. Should her fresh interpretation of the facts be wrong, Arliss or TJ would have all the warning they needed to clear their trail. But Marcia as the murderer ticked all the same boxes as Arliss, starting way back in Ontario when she'd denied an old woman her flu shot. Whether that was done at Phyl's direct request, or in a self-motivated effort to rid Phyl of "that turbulent priest, like Henry II said of Thomas Becket," old Mrs. Thompson was surely dead before her time. Eric's murder had been another indirect one — sedate him and let the cold do the work — but Sandy's death had been a hands-on killing by a strong and determined murderer. Zoe would be blindsided by an attack. Lacey took a deep breath, silently expressed her great hope that Arliss wasn't involved at all, and spoke from her gut.

"Zoe isn't answering her phone. She might be in the TFB offices working on the malware investigation, and if so, I'm afraid she's in danger from the person who planted it. I'm really hoping Nik has heard from his wife that she's someplace else, someplace safe, and she's just turned off her phone for a while."

Arliss spoke to someone on her end again. "Get TJ." To Lacey, she said, "As far as I know, Zoe is at work today. Nik's boys were giving him a hard time about that. I'll get TJ to call building security and tell them to give you full co-operation. We can be there in two hours if we fly."

"Don't call a pilot just yet. As soon as I'm in the building, I'll know whether I'm overreacting."

"Here's Nik," said Arliss. Holding the phone away from her mouth, she filled him in with three terse sentences.

Nik came on the line. "Jesus. You think Zoe's in danger? As far as I know, she was spending today at the office. She used to practically live there. That's why I was glad when she quit at TFB. If she gets hurt, I'll sort JP proper."

"I'll let you know shortly whether she's all right. I apologize for disrupting your afternoon for what might turn out to be a false alarm." Lacey slid out of the Lexus as Wayne approached.

"Still no answer?" he asked, his breath a fog under the streetlamps. She shook her head. He swiped his pass card over the door pad, walked in, and addressed the security guard at the desk. "Hi, Jim. Anybody sign in to TFB today?"

The guard tapped his keyboard. "The owner's working in one of the little companies up on ten, but nobody from the bigger companies has signed in. If they went straight up from the parkade with a key card, though, I wouldn't see them."

"We're going up to search six and seven," said Wayne. "If we have to call for backup, let them in and direct them, please."

Wayne led the charge to the elevator. "The TFB layout covers two floors, each with a ring corridor. Personal offices on the outside, shared spaces in the core. Where is she likely to be?"

"Wherever the accounting files are stored."

"Six first." As the elevator rose, the tension made both of them step to the sides of the space; when the door opened, they had maximum field of view. But the elevator lobby was empty. "You go left, I go right."

Down the hall Lacey went, wishing she still carried a service weapon. She didn't call out, but glanced into each office as she passed, listening for footsteps or voices. The faint sound of violins floated from an office halfway along the hall. She paused beside the doorway and scanned the small room. It was empty, the desk bare except for a laptop whose speaker was providing the soundtrack. Wayne appeared at the far end of the corridor, spotted her, and shook his head.

"Somebody was here," Lacey said when he reached her. "Where's the cheque printer?"

Wayne guided her through the central core of interconnected spaces: open filing racks, long tables covered in maps, and small storage rooms. He pointed to a doorway. They approached one to each side like in the old days — but this room, too, was empty.

"Try phoning again," said Wayne.

Lacey dialed, and seconds later a trill sounded, briefly drowning out the violins. She ran back to the office where the music played. As the call went to voice mail, she hit Redial. Two seconds later, the trill came again. She followed the sound ... and there was Zoe's phone under the desk, its electronic ringtone amplified by the metal footwell.

Zoe came awake slowly, soothed by the familiar jiggling of the van and the rumble of the road. She opened her eyes to darkness save for the dashboard lights, and watched groggily as a yard filled with Christmas lights drifted past the window. The forest closed in. In the beam of the headlights was a snowy road. Where were they going again? Oh yes, skiing with the boys and Lizi.

"Aren't we there yet?" she asked, rolling her head to face Nik. It took her a few moments to realize that it wasn't Nik behind the wheel, nor was it one of the boys. She fought her way clear of the drowsiness and rubbed her eyes. "Marcia?"

"Oh, you're awake. Are you feeling a bit better?"

Zoe pushed herself upright. "Why are you driving me? Where?"

Marcia clenched her hands tighter on the wheel. "You don't remember? I found you absolutely dopey in your office, and when I offered to take you home or call your husband, you said no. You wanted to take a drive in the country to clear your head. You handed me your car keys and asked me to drive. I barely got you into your van and you conked out completely. You seemed to be sleeping okay, just muttering once in a while, and you didn't have a fever. I figured maybe you haven't been sleeping well and need a hard-core nap."

Zoe looked around at what little she could see outside. She didn't remember feeling particularly exhausted, mostly frustrated and angry at Marcia for not catching the malware, then for lying about it after Eric found it. Did she expect to cover up her incompetence indefinitely?

"Where are we?"

"Most of the way to Black Rock Bowl. I figured I should come out and check on my cabin, anyway. During the holidays there are always rowdies around, ready to break a window and steal stuff. We can have supper there and head back into town after."

Zoe leaned sideways against the window, then lifted her head. There was a sore spot above her ear. She'd obviously been bouncing her head off the door for quite a while. "I, um, didn't say anything weird while I was asleep, did I?"

"Something about a spaceship was all I could make out. You been watching the sci-fi channel?"

"A bit." Zoe folded a corner of her scarf up to protect the sore spot on her head and settled back, watching the road unfurl in the headlights. Black Rock Bowl. Wild lands and wilder animals. And Eric. She had been at the office, unwinding the malware trail, waiting for Lacey to call back. She'd gone down to bring up older file boxes from the archives, and when she came back, Marcia was there. Marcia brought her a soy caramel latte. She'd drunk it — the fuzz of sugar and milk still coated her teeth. Then, despite the flood of fresh caffeine, she had fallen deeply asleep.

Shifting her half-closed eyes, she watched Marcia. That massive key ring of hers lay on the dash, winking in the reflection of the console's lights on the windshield. A small USB drive hung between two linked rings of keys. Why was that important? Lacey's explanation of the malware: whoever installed it had to stick a USB or external drive right into the cheque printer. Marcia ran with Phyl and her friends, an expensive crowd. Was her salary adequate for that lifestyle?

The next time Zoe opened her eyes, they were rumbling over the little log bridge toward the lively, crowded shopping square at the base of Black Rock ski hill. Every one of the storefront candle lanterns was lit. The huge Christmas tree glittered in their midst, flickering lights dancing on the surface of every giant hanging ball. She watched it pass in a dreamy state that felt oddly familiar. Had the stress of juggling the ghost and the mess at TFB finally snapped her mental control? Her eyes fell on Marcia's keys again as they skidded across the dash toward her. She grabbed them as they slid off. Uphill now. Marcia was going to check on her cabin. Nothing odd about that.

Sure enough, the van pulled into the third clearing and stopped by the sagging porch. Marcia helped Zoe out as if she were an invalid, guided her indoors, and parked her in an old rocking chair.

"I'll get a fire started, and soon we'll be warm as toast. Don't take your coat off yet."

Zoe leaned back and shut her eyes, listening to the rustle of paper and the dull thud of logs, the scratch of a match, and finally the welcome crackling of flames. She heard dishes clattering in the next room, but moving seemed like too much work, so she stayed where she was. Next thing she knew, Marcia was tapping her shoulder.

"Here, have some hot chocolate, dear. I'd put brandy in, but I'm not sure you need any more sedating." She moved away again once Zoe had securely grasped the mug.

Zoe's fuzzy mouth recoiled from the very idea of hot, sweet milk. What she wouldn't give for a nice glass of cold water and a toothbrush. Mouthwash, too. There might be some in the bathroom, if this place had a bathroom. She looked around, noting the open bankers, boxes, and stacks of paper everywhere. She got to her feet cautiously and fixed her eyes on the mug as the liquid sloshed perilously close to the rim. Best to drink a bit so it didn't spill. She lifted the mug to her lips.

NO NO NO don't drink it!

Her head rang. Staggering, she grabbed at the table to stay upright. The mug slid through her fingers. It tilted in mid-air, spraying a brown stream across a nearby printer as it fell. She lurched over, snatching the stack of pages off the out-tray, watching in dismay as the liquid rolled down the plastic slope into the machine. Oh, God. She'd owe Marcia a new printer.

The last page in the stack was splattered with brown dots. She shook off the liquid before it could soak through more pages. Then she held it up, checking for bleed-through. It was an invoice for Cylon Six Inc., dated December twenty-ninth.

She stared at the company name, and the date, and back again. This invoice was payable as part of the year-end print run. The cheque would even now be sitting in the mail room, waiting to go out when the office re-opened. What was Marcia doing with a current fraudulent invoice when she hadn't noticed any of the previous two years' worth? Flipping back through the stack of papers, she found that all eleven of them were Cylon Six invoices, dated over the last two weeks. Was this a belated investigation?

She struggled to focus her fuzzy thinking. With the office closed for New Year's, the only person who would have seen the year-end payment printout was the accountant who authorized the printing of the cheques. Marcia. The person who'd planted the malware script had to get their hands on the printout and create fake invoices from their fake company quickly, to match the faked cheque amounts before the mailing went out.

The person printing out fake invoices was, therefore, the person who planted the script.

She looked up to see Marcia staring at her from the doorway, and she set the splattered page back down on its pile.

"It was you."

Marcia stepped into the room, filling it with a tsunami of conflicting emotions. "I'm sorry you saw that. But it won't make any difference now."

CHAPTER THIRTY-EIGHT

Lacey scooped the phone from the floor. "She wouldn't leave this behind."

Wayne hit his own phone. "Hey, Jim. Can you check video of the parking garage and tell us if there's a —" He paused, looking at Lacey. She supplied the vehicle makes: Marcia's brown Suburban and Zoe's dark-blue Dodge minivan. He passed the info along and waited. "Hi. Yeah, thanks." He looked up at her. "The van's gone. The SUV is still here."

"Working theory," said Lacey over the pounding of her heart. "Marcia discovered what Zoe was looking into and took her away to dispose of her. Taking Zoe's vehicle is part of her standard misdirection." Saying those words out loud crystallized all her fear. She must not let it freeze her. Zoe must be found alive.

After a bone-deep shiver, Lacey crushed the fear into the familiar hard sphere she'd developed while on the Force. Marcia lived in Arbour Lake, almost on the direct route to Cochrane.

"Call the city police," she told Wayne. "Tell them we have a hostage situation. Zoe is likely either injured or drugged and is being driven in her own vehicle. Tell them she's in immediate danger. Focus on northwest Calgary, around Arbour Lake." With luck they already had a chopper in the air and could quickly cover Crowchild Trail from above. "Next, Cochrane RCMP. They have to stop all blue minivans on Highway 1A from the city outskirts to the junction of Highway 40, and separately at Black Rock Bowl. I'll check Marcia's Calgary place first and head for the Bowl if I don't catch up to them there."

She was running as she left the building. She dropped her phone into the dashboard slot, started driving, and said loudly, "Call Arliss Thompson cellphone." She was crossing the 10th Street bridge when Arliss answered. "Bad news. It looks like Marcia took Zoe from the office. Can you text me her home address in Arbour Lake? I'm heading that way now."

"Yes," said Arliss, and issued crisp instructions away from the mouthpiece. "I'd bet on Black Rock Bowl, though. More isolated."

"RCMP is heading there now." That had better be true. If Wayne thought to call Bull directly instead of going through Dispatch, he'd bypass a lot of explanation. Lacey steered around a line of slower vehicles and put her foot down, wishing she had a bubble light and a siren. "I'm relying on you to keep everybody up there calm. I'll report in as soon as I know anything for sure." The address text came in — she sent it to Wayne for the city police and toggled the address to Google Maps. Not far now.

The backs of houses flashed past on Crowchild Trail, mocking her haste with their holiday lights. She peeled off into Arbour Lake, passing row houses hung with wreaths and other decor. Santas and reindeer glowed from pocket-sized lawns. Marcia's, though, was dark. No decorations, no lights. No vehicle in the drive.

No answer to her knock.

Between the blind slats she saw a barren living room faintly lit from the kitchen beyond. Abandoning the front door, she ran around the building and up the back steps. The dim light from the stove revealed another empty room, its counters bare save for a coffee maker, a water glass, and a couple of pill bottles. She texted that information to Wayne while she hurried to the Lexus. If Marcia doubled back here, the city police could grab her.

Back on Crowchild, Lacey headed northwest again. Almost an hour to Black Rock and no way to know how far ahead Marcia and Zoe were. As she cleared the last set of traffic lights, she sped up, peering at each minivan she overtook, looking closely at the driver of any dark-blue one. Why hadn't she noted Zoe's licence plate? Surely the police had it by now, but it didn't help her any.

Twenty minutes later, she was freewheeling down the hill into Cochrane when she saw a cruiser by the roadside ahead, lights flashing. As she slowed, she saw the officer standing by the driver's window of a dust-brown Acura. Nothing but a routine traffic stop. She sped up. At the stoplight she realized this was the same intersection where Sandy, coming down from the north, had turned right instead of going home to Bragg Creek. Crushing that sick recognition into the ball of "later" emotions, she called Bull.

"Alert went out twenty-seven minutes ago," he said. "I've got a patrol at the Black Rock turnoff and one heading in to check Marcia's cabin. If she's passed the one, the other will find her." With a clear mental map of the clogged loop of road around the mountain's shoulders, the hordes of holiday-makers crowding the square and the chalets, Lacey couldn't be so sanguine. Marcia knew that territory better than any of the RCMP. She'd evade them.

She swung the Lexus off the main highway onto the forestry road, out into the dark winter wilderness. After a twisting, skidding drive at unsafe speeds, punctuated by the near miss of a leaping deer, she passed the turnoff to the trestle bridge. GPS worked on this stretch, and as she slowed behind a horse-drawn hay wagon pulling a load of merrymakers, her phone map showed how Marcia must have gotten away with killing Sandy near the bridge. After dumping the Civic on Stoney lands, probably expecting it to be stripped or torched within twenty-four hours, she had only to ski straight up the abandoned stretch of road and cross the river to wherever she'd left her vehicle. Bull had said a house above the bridge reported someone passing by in the wee hours. Twelve kilometres was a mild ski trek for Marcia. She'd had full moonlight and fresh powder. Had she been troubled at all by passing the place where she'd left Sandy's body?

At the Black Rock turnoff, RCMP constables were checking vehicles going in and out. Lacey pulled up and showed her driver's licence to a woman she vaguely recognized from Cochrane detachment. "I'm the one who called this in. You haven't seen a blue minivan go through?"

"Not yet. We're telling the civilians it's a holiday checkstop. Constable Markov is at the Bowl."

Lacey thanked the constable and drove through, her fingers twitching on the wheel. Traffic was clumped up after the checkstop and it was too dangerous to speed. The forest crowded in. Through the trees came the roar of snowmobiles; their headlights bobbed and danced along unseen trails. The yard full of Christmas lights was a beacon of either good hope or false optimism; she welcomed it because it meant she was nearly there.

The square was as crowded as she'd expected, the road around it choked with vehicles. The ski hill glowed under spotlights on the lift pylons. The skiers coming down were hung with Glow Sticks, yellow and pink stars in an ever-changing constellation.

No sign of Markov's truck. She threaded through and up the north shoulder. One clearing, two clearings, three. Marcia's cabin: dark, sagging, seemingly deserted. No minivan. She slowed, scanning for signs of occupancy. Behind her someone honked. She pulled over and got out. When she'd been here before, this had all been deep snow. The chinook had melted it down to an icy crust. Tire tracks led around the cabin. The snow crunched underfoot as she followed them.

Away from the lighted Bowl, the darkness thickened. She stopped, waiting for her eyes to adjust. A few steps farther and the minivan's outline appeared deep in the cabin's shadow. The glade swept out in a white semicircle rimmed by dark firs. A ski track led up a narrow gap to the Loop Trail. Marcia wouldn't take Zoe skiing. Was she holed up indoors in the dark, waiting for Lacey to leave? Or had she left her hostage helpless in the van? With a wary eye on the black windows of the cabin, Lacey eased toward the vehicle. She didn't dare call out.

The acrid tang of incinerator smoke caught in her lungs. What a time to be burning trash. Or was that all Marcia had burned? Lacey sniffed cautiously, fearing the worst. No reek of human flesh, that sickening barbeque she'd twice inhaled while directing traffic around vehicle fires. She made a note to have someone search the incinerator for evidence. Maybe Eric's backpack or car keys were in it.

She heard a thud overhead and flattened her back against the van.

A painted dowel landed at her feet. One end was jagged, like it was broken off the leg of a chair or table. She looked up again. From a tiny window in the two-storey addition, a pale hand waved at her. She whispered, as loud as she could, "Hello? Zoe?"

"Lacey?" The voice caught on a sob.

Another waft of smoke took Lacey by surprise. She waved it away and looked over her shoulder. No sparks rose from the incinerator. She scanned the cabin's ground-floor windows, hoping her new fear was baseless. But it wasn't. Smoke was seeping out around the kitchen window. The pane was blackened not by darkness, but by soot. Sullen red and yellow moved within the house. If she opened the door or broke a window, the fresh air would fuel an immediate conflagration. And Zoe was trapped on the second floor.

CHAPTER THIRTY-NINE

More smoke curled out around the kitchen window. Lacey tipped her head back. "Can you get out that window and drop down? I'll catch you."

Zoe sobbed again. "It's too small. The door's locked. There's smoke coming under it. I stuffed a blanket against it, but it won't stop flames."

"Is there anything in the van we can use to pry out the window frame?"

"A jack handle, in the very back under the floor."

"Keys?"

"Marcia has them."

Lacey pulled her phone out and flicked the flashlight on. She tried the van's door handle. Locked. The light showed her the piece of table leg on the snow. She grabbed it and swung hard at the driver-side window. The glass spiderwebbed. She punched the dowel through and peeled away the crackle with her gloved hands until she could reach in and unlock the door. Scrambling over the driver's seat, she aimed her flashlight again and awkwardly lifted the tire-storage lid to retrieve the tire iron. A coil of lightweight nylon rope lay beside it. That wouldn't support Zoe's weight, but it might have another use.

Leaping out the back door, she tied the crossed iron securely to the rope. "Stand back," she yelled. She swung the heavy star on its rope and let it fly at the upper window. It clattered on the wall and fell to earth, vanishing into a snow drift. She hauled it in by the yellow rope, checked the knots, swung, and hurled again. This time it went through with a great crashing of glass. Zoe screeched.

The kitchen window cracked ominously. Flames licked at the glass. If the pane broke, the fire would billow up the outside wall. Overhead, Zoe's furious blows sent shards of glass and fragments of frame showering down.

Lacey jumped out of the debris zone. "I'll hunt for a ladder."

She frantically searched along the porch and sides of the smouldering cabin. No ladder. No Marcia, either, unless she was hiding in the dark forest, watching. She ran back. "How's it coming?"

"It's getting loose," Zoe yelled, "but it's hotter now. Smoke's coming through the floorboards."

"Keep hitting. I'll check the shed."

Lacey powered through the crusted drifts. The shed had settled so far sideways the door was warped. She kicked at it in desperation. When the rotted wood gave, she stumbled inside. There was a rickety wooden ladder missing a couple of rungs, with others dangling. The ladder caught in the shed door on her way out and she wrenched it free. As she ran across the yard, it snagged on bushes. She yanked it off them.

Smoke gusted from the window where she'd last seen Zoe. She slammed the ladder up against the wall.

"Zoe! Zoe! I'm coming up."

A pale arm appeared through the smoke. Zoe was desperately prying at the window hinges. Lacey got one hand on the window and hung her whole weight off it. One hinge broke free. She closed her eyes as powdery splinters skimmed her cheeks. Thicker smoke billowed up around her.

Zoe coughed. "I'm on the bed now, no leverage. The floor is too hot."

"Pass me the tire iron."

It was a tricky left-handed swing while Lacey's right hand clutched the ladder rail, but she managed to land a blow in the V between frame and hinge. She smacked it again, metal striking metal. Smoke curled up her body. Flames licked from a lower window. One more blow.

The hinge ripped free, taking the side frame with it. The little window fell past her. She hooked the tire iron on the windowsill, propped her knees against the rungs as best she could and got both hands on the lower frame. Yanking as hard as she could, with Zoe pushing from inside, they tore the board away, leaving a jagged hole.

"Can you make it through?" Lacey yelled.

Zoe's feet appeared, and she wriggled out backward. Lacey guided her over to the uppermost rung. She eased herself down, feeling for each rung below lest it give way under her boot.

The heat was intense. The night spiralled yellow and gold and black, smoke and ash and embers. Coughing, she dropped another step. The rung snapped beneath her.

Zoe's foot grazed her cheek. Flames swam up the wall. She jumped clear of the ladder and staggered backward, her shoulder slamming against the van.

"Broken rung," she yelled as Zoe's foot scrabbled for support.

Flames licked up the old logs, feasting on the fresh air and long-dead wood. Ignoring the throbbing in her arm, Lacey grabbed Zoe's hips and pulled her from the ladder. Together they stumbled away into the snowy field as another window crashed to the ground. Sparks soared into the starry night.

CHAPTER FORTY

Zoe watched the roof collapse. The fire roared, glazing the whole glade in gold. She shuddered, pulling her sweater up to her throat. Away from the flames, the chill bit through her clothing.

"Where's your coat?" Lacey asked.

"I had to take it off to get through the window."

Lacey stripped off her jacket and wrapped it around Zoe. Snuggling in, shoving her freezing arms into sleeves prewarmed by body heat, Zoe took a deep breath. Or tried to. Coughing wracked her chest.

"Let's get you away from here." Lacey led her wide around the flaming building. Onlookers had gathered on the road. An RCMP officer pushed through them. "Markov," she yelled, waving.

He ran toward them. "Fire truck from Ghost is inbound. Anybody else inside?"

"Zoe, where's Marcia?"

Through coughing fits, Zoe managed to get out, "She left ... on skis ... up the Loop Trail, I think."

"Why didn't she take the van?"

"I ... don't ... know."

"Saw your light bar, I bet," Lacey told Markov. "Move the checkpoint to the bridge just outside Black Rock. Stop everything leaving. She's desperate enough to steal a vehicle, and there's plenty to choose from around here."

"Search the Loop Trail," Zoe rasped, "and ... empty chalets." Her tongue tasted like day-old cigarettes dipped in pine tar. What she wanted was a warm bath and clean clothes. And privacy so she could fall apart.

Lacey must have sensed Zoe's discomfort. "I'll take Zoe over to the Thompson chalet. Send an EMT when they get here. If you trust me, I'll bag the clothing and photograph the injuries so we can make her comfortable more quickly."

Markov pulled out his phone and snapped a half-dozen photos of Zoe: hands, face, ripped clothing, blistered boots. She let herself be bundled into the Lexus, too exhausted to put on her seatbelt until Lacey reminded her. Heat rose from her seat when the engine started, easing into her frozen legs and creeping up her back as the vehicle backed away from the burning heap of the cabin.

"God," she said, "I'm exhausted."

"Adrenalin's wearing off." Lacey honked at the gawkers. "And she most likely drugged you. You'll be hellish sore soon. There must be first aid supplies at JP's place. We can clean your scrapes and pull your splinters there."

At the word *splinters*, Zoe stared at her stinging palms. Jagged spears of dark wood were visible in the dashboard's glow. "Holy shit. I didn't feel those going in."

"You had other things on your mind." Lacey honked at another group standing on the road. "Markov's gonna need someone on traffic ASAP."

"We could have waited so you could help. My splinters aren't going anywhere."

"I'm a Victim Services volunteer, not a cop. You're my priority." Lacey was matter-of-fact. The vibe that came with the words was calm and focused, showing no sign that she yearned to be back where the action was.

Zoe yawned, which set off another bout of coughing.

"It was Marcia all along," she finally managed to say. "With the malware, I mean. I think she drugged me in the office, because when I woke up we were already most of the way here. She tried to get me to drink some hot chocolate, but I didn't. That was probably drugged, too." She shuddered. "Actually, Eric's voice came to me so strongly that I dropped the mug on the printer. That's when I saw the Cylon invoices. She was stealing more money from the year-end payment run."

The enormity of her escape crashed over her. Eric had saved her life. "If I'd drunk that hot chocolate, I'd have fallen asleep again and been helpless once the fire started. I'd be dead right now." The horror of never waking, never seeing Nik or Lizi again, washed over her. She sobbed until they reached the chalet.

When they got to the front door, she had to pull herself together to punch in the entry code. Then she staggered in, trailing snow and soot across the living room floor as she headed for the farthest door beyond the stairs.

"What's in there?" Lacey asked.

"Master suite. Phyl's bathroom. First aid and a shower. I reek."

"Let me." Lacey entered the dark room first, fumbling for a light switch.

Zoe sat on the bed and eased the coat off over her seeping palms. She wanted to sink into the bed and stay there.

Lacey helped her undress, carefully photographing each item of clothing on and off Zoe's body. "Chain of evidence," she explained when Zoe asked why. "In case a jury needs to be convinced we didn't switch any items. I don't suppose there are any paper bags around? They're supposed to be used for any damp materials to avoid mould growth or spoilage of biological samples."

Zoe shook her head, feeling each muscle tug at the others. "There might be a dry-cleaning bag in Phyl's closet." Lacey went to look and came back with a sleek black-paper shopping bag handled and embossed in silver, a relic from some high-end clothing boutique. After giving it a good shake to get rid of miscellaneous fibres, she folded each item of clothing into it. Then she took photos of every scrape, burn, and splinter on Zoe's aching body. Zoe directed her to the first aid kit, and Lacey set to work with hydrogen peroxide and a pair of tweezers. When she was done, she dabbed antibiotic ointment on the wounds and wrapped them in gauze. She got to her feet with the first signs of weariness that Zoe had yet noticed.

"Stay there. I'll raid the closet for something you can wear."

Zoe groaned. She was so tired, but each time her eyelids drifted shut, a vision of flames and snow and shattered windows flared up behind them. As Lacey helped her into some of Phyl's workout gear, the silence was broken by the sound of breaking glass.

They both froze.

"Did you hear that?" Zoe whispered.

"Shh," said Lacey. "Wait here." She crept over, turned off the light, and slowly opened the door. Then she was gone, leaving Zoe in the dark bedroom.

Alone in the dark. Again.

Zoe crept to the door and peered out. The long, shadowy living room was slashed by a yellow light coming from the kitchen. Neither she nor Lacey had turned on that light. Someone had broken in.

CHAPTER FORTY-ONE

Pressed against the wall near the kitchen archway, Lacey clearly heard the sound of a drawer sliding open, then the muffled chink of keys. She tensed as footsteps sounded, and relaxed a bit as the back door closed, leaving the kitchen silent. She risked peeking into the room and saw a head moving on the porch outside. Boots tramped down the wooden steps. It was so quiet she heard the squeak of snow as they moved away.

"Did you see who it was?" Zoe whispered behind her.

Lacey jumped. "Jesus!" she hissed. "Don't do that!"

"Sorry. Did you see who it was?"

"All I saw was a head of brown hair and the collar of a white and black ski jacket."

"That's Marcia! Why is she here?"

"Are there keys in a drawer by the fridge?"

"Oh, shit. Yeah, for the snowmobiles."

Lacey spun around. "Where are they?"

"In the garage, filled with fuel and ready to go. The trails behind here run all the way past Waiparous."

"And across the river and down to Highway 1A ... Can you manage my phone?"

Zoe looked down at her dressings and nodded. "I think so."

Lacey handed her the phone. "Call Sergeant Drummond. Tell him what's happening. Under B for Bull." She darted across the living room. A moment later she eased the front door open and slipped out onto the porch.

Zoe retreated to the master suite, where the blackout curtains hid her from anyone in the yard. She turned on the bedside lamp, laid the phone beneath it face up, and clumsily scrolled through the contacts list until she found Bull's number. She hit Dial and put it on speaker-phone. Sergeant Drummond barked his hello, and Zoe whispered back. "It's not Lacey, it's Zoe. We're at the Thompson chalet. Marcia just broke in and took the snowmobile keys. The machines are in the garage. Lacey went out to try to stop her. Can you send someone?"

"On our way. Lock the doors and stay inside, away from the windows."

She disconnected. Stay inside? But Lacey was out there alone. She crept out of the master suite and stared across the dark living room at the ghostly glimmer of the front door. Out there was the woman who had killed Eric, who had tried to kill her. If Marcia made it to the trail, she'd be gone before the RCMP could get here. Lacey had no weapon, no backup. She might even be killed. This was no time for staying locked in the house!

Zoe ran to the foyer and grabbed the nearest ski jacket off the coat rack. A toque fell out of the sleeve as she pushed her hand through, and she tugged that over her hair. Then she shoved her feet into boots, opened the door, and crept outside.

When the lights in the garage came on, Lacey left the shelter of the Lexus and dashed across the yard. Flattening herself against the garage wall, she edged along to the first window. She peeked inside, but could only see the concrete floor and several snowmobile suits hanging on a rack. She crept along the wall, wincing each time the snow crunched beneath her boots. As she reached the side door, she found it ajar. She hesitated. Only an hour ago she'd told Zoe she was no longer a cop, and yet here she was, out of shape from months away from the gym, about to burst in on a possible triple murderer, unarmed, with no backup. But what was the alternative? Even if the RCMP were on their way, it would take ages for them to get here from the far side of the Bowl. She was on her own.

She slid past the door and peered in the next window. It showed her the whole back half of the garage, containing a large tool bench, a pair of well-used dirt bikes, and two gleaming snowmobiles whose noses pointed at a single-wide garage door in the rear wall. It was closed for the moment. Marcia was bending over the nearest snowmobile, strapping a fuel can to its cargo rack.

Lacey assessed the situation. Marcia had come via the ski trail, straight to the back door of the chalet. She'd left the same way, so it was possible she hadn't seen the Lexus parked in the drive and didn't realize anyone was in the building. She wouldn't have turned on the garage lights unless she'd thought she was alone. The element of surprise lay with Lacey. The yard was quiet, the only sounds coming from inside the garage: some shuffling and a clunk that was probably the fuel can. As long as she could hear Marcia in there, she had time to plan her attack.

Snow crunched behind her.

She whirled around. The yellow garage light faded from her vision, leaving the yard pale in the starlight. Nobody was there. Inside the garage, something clanked. She crept back along the wall, eased the ski-room door open wider, and slipped inside. It wasn't much darker than outside, and the light from the main garage outlined the inner door. She tiptoed across to it and put her eye up to the crack.

Marcia entered her narrow field of vision to drag a snowmobile suit off its hanger. She removed her ski boots and climbed into the suit. She grabbed snowmobile boots, gloves, and a helmet from a shelf and walked toward the back of the garage. Lacey heard a snow machine rumble to life. She cracked open the door to the garage and looked in. Marcia, now standing beside the machine, picked a backpack up off the floor and slid her arms through the straps. She trudged over to the wall and pushed a button. The single garage door began to rise, spilling yellow light out onto the snow. A pair of legs was visible — someone was standing out there.

Marcia gave a glad cry. "Phyl! What are you —"

Zoe ducked under the rising door, brandishing a chunk of firewood like an avenging angel. She ran straight at Marcia, swinging wildly.

As Marcia grabbed at Zoe's arm, Lacey bounded out from hiding. She leaped onto the seat of the idling machine and hurled herself through the air. Her shoulder rammed Marcia between the shoulder blades, slamming her face-first into the wall.

Lacey barely got her feet under her before Marcia pushed off from the wall, turned and lunged at her. Zoe stuck out a foot and tripped up the accountant. Marcia went sprawling across the hood of the snowmobile. As she struggled to stand up, Lacey grabbed her by the shoulder and shoved her down to the floor, planting a knee on her back in the best police tradition. For good measure, she wrenched one of Marcia's arms up and held it firmly between her shoulder blades.

"Zoe," she said, breathing hard, "Find something to tie her up with."

CHAPTER FORTY-TWO

Lacey dragged Marcia to her feet as the sound of sirens reverberated up the Bowl. Soon the flashing blue-and-whites danced through the trees. As she pulled her captive out to the yard, an RCMP SUV wheeled in, its headlights bathing her and Marcia in a bright white glare. Someone jumped from the driver's door and ran toward them.

"Stop right there!"

"It's me, Bull," said Lacey, squinting against his headlights. "We got her."

Lacey and Zoe sat on the living room couch across from Bull Drummond. Lacey had explained, from the beginning, everything that had transpired since she first found Zoe's phone on her office floor. After he'd grilled first Zoe and then Lacey about the events at Marcia's cabin and at the chalet, Lacey handed over her phone so he could examine the photos of Zoe's injuries. "Her clothes are bagged in the bedroom."

Bull thumbed through the photos and glanced at the tattered gauze on Zoe's hands. "That's solid coverage of the evidence handling. Thanks. It should be enough to anchor an attempted murder charge. What about the accounting fraud angle?"

"Zoe saw invoices for the fraudulent company in the cabin, but any material evidence of Marcia's ongoing theft probably went up in flames." Lacey rubbed her shoulder. "If you can find a money trail connecting the earlier cheques to her, we ... you can prove she had a motive for Eric's death. Apparently, she carried the malware script on a USB stick on her keychain. But she likely left that behind in the cabin, along with Eric's paper printouts and his backpack, hoping all the evidence would be destroyed in the fire. I think she also stole a thumb drive backup from his house the day she took his laptop." Lacey shook her head. "They must have been in her bag when she left the funeral reception. To think, she banged me in the hip with her bag of stolen evidence on her way out. But even if I'd searched her, I never would have suspected a plastic spaceship was the USB backup."

Zoe started to say something, then shook her head wearily.

Lacey looked at her. "What?"

"*Galactica.* Eric's backup." Zoe's shoulders slumped. "I took it from his room after the funeral."

"Where is it now?"

"In my pocket."

"Your coat?" Lacey asked. "That burned, remember?"

"No, it was in the pocket of my sweater." Zoe pointed toward the master suite. "It's in the bag with my other clothes."

"Stay right here, both of you." Bull marched off and came back a minute later with the black bag. He pulled a pair of latex gloves from the packet in his pocket and fished Zoe's sweater out. He lifted the grey plastic spaceship from the pocket and held it up. "This it?"

Zoe nodded.

"And are these your keys?"

"Marcia's." Zoe stared at the linked rings of keys. "They were on the dash in the van. I grabbed them. She has mine. Or had them, anyway."

Bull's thick fingers splayed the keys. "There's a USB stick on here. Also a Honda tag and a Canucks bottle opener. McCrae, can you identify those?"

The sound of a helicopter drowned out Lacey's answer. The doors rattled in their frames. A bright light poured in through the front windows, then vanished as the copter roared over the house.

Lacey ran to the kitchen and flung open the back door. Bull and Zoe followed.

They watched as the chopper set down between the back porch and the woodshed, sending up a blizzard of snow and twigs. A young man jumped down and turned to help a woman get out. A third man, taller, came out behind them, ducking as the blades whirled overhead.

Zoe screamed, "Nik!" and ran down into the snow in her socks.

Arliss Thompson stomped up the steps and glared at Lacey. "You said you'd call us right back."

EPILOGUE

Five days after the fire, Lacey sat with Loreena in the Lexus as the sunset painted the condo building's windows with pinks and tangerines. "Buying a single condo to rent out? Are you sure this is what you want to do with your life savings?"

Loreena nodded. "As partners, with my money paying for it and Dee managing the tenant, all the rent beyond the reserve is ours to split as long as I'm alive. I'll have what I need to cover my last months in a nursing home, and she'll have a top-up to cover her mortgage on the Bragg Creek place. When I'm gone, the property transfer will be seamless." She turned her pale-blue eyes toward Lacey. "I've worried so much about you two. When I was your age, my husband and I were ten years into a reasonable mortgage supported by two incomes. When Dee's dad died, the insurance paid it off. Now I see so many young women like you and Dee struggling to pay for a home and a vehicle, and everything else on a single salary. Women's financial lives are precarious. Look at Sandy. It took her twenty years to be able to afford her own home. She'd barely unpacked.

And Dee could have lost her home because of that hit and run last summer. This will give her security now and in the future."

Boney and Beau shifted in the back. Lacey checked the mirror. They were watching a standard poodle stroll past with its owner. It seemed like a good neighbourhood, at least in the daylight. Somewhere she could be at ease. As if she could ever afford to live here.

"It's true, Loreena, and the older we get the more is at stake. Marcia's a good example. If Phyl Thompson had left her alone to work her small-town job and pay her small-town mortgage, she would probably still be there, bored and lonely maybe, but not tempted to commit computer fraud, let alone murder. Not that I'm condoning her actions. Murder is inexcusable. But I can see how she got to the point of stealing money from a company that seemed to have plenty in order to afford her one-sided friendship with Phyl. And then she became even more desperate to cover up her theft when it looked like it would be exposed. She would have lost everything, Phyl included. If Phyl had told her their friendship was already over, would Marcia have killed Eric, or just sold up and gone sadly back to her old life in Ontario?"

"She made those choices, though. You can't know what she might have done." Loreena turned to the window again. "I don't want that desperation for my daughter. I don't want it for you, either. I want you free of Dan, for a start."

"I've already contacted a divorce lawyer."

"I know. You might not want to talk about it, but before I leave I'm going to give her an affidavit about our conversation on Christmas Day, that night you told me about." She didn't say "the night he raped you," but her meaning lingered in the air. Lacey's hand automatically went to her throat; the memory of those bruises still ached at moments like this. Loreena didn't seem to notice. "I want it all on record so it can be introduced in court if you need it, whether I'm capable of testifying then or not. And I think you should talk to a domestic violence counsellor, both for evidence purposes and for your own healing. The local women's shelter can point you in the right direction. If you need money, I'll pay."

Lacey lowered her hand. She felt on firmer ground here. "Wayne recommended me to his friend who runs a private investigations firm. He may have some work for me." Sitting surveillance for hours on end would be dull, but the pay was respectable. She would have to pass the Alberta PI course, but that surely wouldn't take long.

Both dogs got to their feet and whined.

"Here she comes."

A moment later, Dee chucked her cane into the back seat and eased herself in after it. She propped her tired ankle up on the armrest between the front seats. "That went very well. We can start the paperwork first thing Monday morning and be the official owners before you leave for home, Mom. I'm starving. I wonder who else is invited to the feast. What do people eat on Russian Orthodox Christmas Eve, anyway? Not turkey, I bet."

"Boiled wheat with honey," said Loreena, "but that's all I know."

"Sounds delicious," said Lacey, as she pulled away from the curb.

When they arrived at Zoe's house, Lacey parked in the driveway close to the front steps. Kai and Ari rushed out, boots on but coatless, to open the vehicle's doors for them. "No wheelchair ramp, sorry," Kai told Loreena. "Will you trust me to carry you in, Missus?"

She smiled. "I'd be delighted."

Ari gave Dee his arm and took the bag with the dogs' travel dishes in his other hand. Lacey got the leashes and opened the tailgate. Once they were clipped on, she let the leggy pair jump down. By then, Clemmie and Lizi were beside her, properly jacketed and wearing toques. Clemmie crouched down and gave the dogs a thorough greeting. Lizi ran her gloved hands over their heads.

"We're going to the store for more whipping cream. Can we take them with us?" Lizi asked.

"We'll be careful," Clemmie added.

Lacey saw them off before taking the wine from the back seat and locking the car. She paused on the sidewalk, admiring the traditional green Christmas tree in the picture window glowing with multicoloured lights. The whole holiday season had been shadowed by death and worry. This was a chance to set it all behind them and start the year afresh.

Zoe met her at the front door with a warm hug. The tantalizing aroma of roasting meat hung in the air. "I'm so glad you could be here. Come on in. Aidan and Nik will join us after work."

In the living room, a log fire crackled. Loreena was already tucked into an easy chair, her feet resting on an ottoman. Ari took orders and brought drinks out for everyone. As Lacey swallowed her first mouthful of wine, Kai started peppering her with questions. "While the kids are gone, what can you tell us about what's going on? What is Marcia being charged with? When is the trial?"

Lacey lowered her glass. "What I've pieced together, from Zoe and Arliss and the police, is that it all started four years ago in Ontario. There was a cyber attack on the nursing home, and Marcia caught it, like any halfway competent financial accountant. That's where the malware script came from. She hardly knew Phyl Thompson then, but Phyl made friends with her. Marcia confessed that she'd withheld old Mrs. Thompson's flu shot, hoping she'd die, and even steered sick volunteers toward the old lady. She said that Phyl had told her on the phone what to do. But there's no evidence beyond her word."

Zoe's lip curled. "Phyl won't admit to anything. She'll come out of this unscathed."

"Regardless of whose idea it was, it worked. Mrs. Thompson caught an upper respiratory virus and was dead two months later. When Sandy threatened to tell JP about the nursing home incident, that's what Marcia thought she meant. But Sandy almost certainly meant the malware; she'd heard me and Dee talking about it and jumped to the conclusion that Marcia had been covering up her own theft years ago when she got Sandy to accept the blame. But Marcia hadn't stolen from the nursing home; she just kept the script as a trophy. At

TFB, she only started using it in her second year, when she couldn't cover a payment on her cabin. In her mind, stealing was a crime she had to commit in order to stay friends with Phyl."

"She should have been charged with the murder of that old lady," Ari muttered. "They both should."

Lacey shook her head. "There's no evidence they caused her death. The old woman might have died that winter, anyway."

"Phyl Thompson, from all you say," said Loreena with a frown, "was young, glamorous, and rich. She could easily have manipulated a plain, friendless, middle-aged woman with implied promises of a more glamorous life."

Zoe nodded. "Just like the blond Cylon and the Battlestar admiral."

Lacey shook her head again. "Can't be proven. And it doesn't need to be to keep Marcia behind bars. She had a prescription of the same type of sedatives found in both Eric's and Zoe's systems. Plus, the RCMP found Eric's phone number in her incoming calls list from the same afternoon he vanished. They'd assumed at first that it was a work-related call, but what it means is that she knew he was out at Black Rock Bowl that day, and so was she. He called her when he realized JP had left. She admitted she told him to come to her place to wait until JP returned, knowing full well JP wasn't coming back. She claimed she only drugged him with laced hot chocolate to give herself time to think."

"Hah," said Dee.

Lacey shrugged. "I doubt she knows exactly when she decided he had to die. She panicked when he insisted on going back to JP's, even though she knew nobody would be there. So she followed him, and told him she'd take his backpack and stuff indoors while he got more firewood. But her dear friend Phyl had never given her the updated entry code, so she couldn't have gotten inside. She didn't tell Eric that. She just followed him to the shed and locked him in, then dumped his car."

"That's really cold," said Kai. "Premeditation makes it murder, right? It would back home."

"It's hard to prove premeditation," said Lacey. "Sergeant Drummond told me Marcia swore she didn't intend for him to die, just to be delayed until she could figure out what to do. Same with dumping the car — another delay. Then she drove back to her cabin, chucked his backpack into the incinerator, and settled in to wait out the storm. Oddly enough, if she'd left his car in JP's yard, she might be in the clear now. But she couldn't count on the area being snowed in for long, and it would have been a disaster for her if he'd been found alive. That one action she took to throw searchers off the scent is now the evidence that seals her fate."

Kai asked about the nurse's death. Mindful of Loreena's sad expression, Lacey shook her head. She wouldn't go into the brutal details that she had seen in that agreed statement of facts on Bull's desk: how Marcia had arranged to meet Sandy at the deserted summer camp near the Ghost River bridge, tried to talk her into waiting for her money, and bludgeoned her in a fit of rage at being refused. Major Crimes had decided to send that version to the prosecutor even though they suspected she had planned to kill Sandy regardless. An angry attack already confessed to was more certain of conviction than going to trial and trying to prove pre-meditation for a first-degree charge.

"Marcia confessed, that's the important thing," she told him.

When he asked again for details, Loreena changed the subject. "Is that pretty embroidered towel in the window part of your holiday tradition, Zoe?"

Zoe nodded. "It's hung on Christmas Eve to let the dead know that they're welcome."

"And you'll see a bowl of hay on the dining table," Ari added, "but I can't remember what that symbolizes."

Zoe grinned. "I'm not sure I remember myself. Religion hasn't been a big part of my life since I was a child. But the twelve dishes are for the twelve apostles. We're having roast pork in place of a suckling pig, plus a goose, smoked salmon, and a bunch of side dishes. Speaking of which, Lacey, can you give me a hand in the kitchen?"

Lacey left Ari telling Dee about their skiing adventures and Kai showing Loreena the tree decorations he'd made for his father years before.

Once in the kitchen, Zoe turned to Lacey. "I didn't want to say anything in front of the others, but I think you should send JP an invoice for your investigation."

"I'm not a licensed PI."

"No, but you're the one who solved it for him." Zoe rearranged a few carrot sticks on a plate. "I was with you for quite a bit of that time, and I know there were other times you were investigating when I was elsewhere. You could bill for dozens of hours, especially considering the amount of travel back and forth between Calgary and Black Rock." She looked up. "Lacey, don't sell your skills short. I've seen this all too often in the oil industry: highly competent women not getting our due because we're not as convinced of our value as barely average men are of theirs. At the very least, discuss it with Wayne. If you put in an invoice, or if he does it for you, I'll make sure it gets paid."

"You'd do that for me? Even though all I wanted was to clear up the mess so Dee could collect a commission off the chalet sale?"

"Women must watch out for women in any industry. Arliss taught me that." Zoe handed her a knife. "Can you slice the radishes for the salad?"

"As many as you like."

After a few minutes, Lacey asked, "How are you doing with the ... with Eric? Has he stopped haunting you?"

Zoe rested her hands on the counter and gazed out the window at the snowy backyard. "You know, now that everything has calmed down, I'm starting to wonder if it was ever him at all, or if my subconscious mind was just putting together clues, and it chose that bizarre route to bring them to my attention. Try as I might, I can't think of a single thing he told me that I couldn't have guessed from things I'd heard and seen over all the years I worked around the Thompsons, hearing about their kids and neighbours."

"Even the *Galactica* thumb drive?"

Zoe gave a half laugh. "Now, that I'm not so sure of. Nik watches a lot of sci-fi shows, and it's possible he once showed me that thumb drive as a hint for a stocking stuffer or something. Since I've seen half the series myself now, I have no idea what I knew before and what's fresh." She scooped steaming veggies into a bowl. "I have to stop myself from calling Clemmie 'Clemster,' and I have no idea where I might have heard that nickname. I'm also debating whether to tell Lizi about any of it. Considering it seems to run in the family, someday a ghost might try to talk to her, too. She'll probably think I'm nuts. I just don't want her questioning her own sanity, I guess, if it ever happens." She set an empty pot in the sink. "As for Eric, I still think of him all the time. I wish he'd been allowed to finish school and become an environmental scientist and help save the world. I feel like I know him now on a level nobody else did, or ever will. This might sound strange to you, but I might have a private ceremony to, you know, send him on his way."

Dee wandered into the kitchen. "I came to help, but it looks like you two have things in hand. Those young men, Zoe — what charmers! Mom's giggling like a teenager."

Zoe laughed. "They sure are. So, what will your mom do now that her nurse is gone? Stay with you?"

Dee shook her head. "No. Sandy's friend Pat is coming out for Sandy's funeral, and she'll fly home with Mom afterward. They knew each other a bit before, and now they talk almost every day. Pat's going to walk the assisted dying path with Mom, and she's going to be getting another visiting nurse to help at home."

Zoe handed Dee a washed cucumber and a cutting board. "You seem a bit calmer about the situation."

"Uh-huh. I've been thinking a lot about it. You both could have died last week, with no warning, no chance to say goodbye. My mom has given me that opportunity, and I'm going to take it gratefully. She promises to keep me in the loop about her health as it changes, so I can plan when to be there without it being an emergency. And I promised to hit my physiotherapy exercises hard so I'll be in shape to go when she needs me."

They heard boots stomping across the deck, and Lizi appeared at the window. Zoe opened it, dislodging a row of tiny icicles. The girl leaned in. "Ms. Phillips, do the dogs have a ball or something to play with? The Clemster says we should tire them out before supper."

"Meet me out front. There are some toys in the truck." Dee handed the cucumber to Lacey and shuffled out.

Zoe shut the window carefully and turned to Lacey. "'Clemster.' She must have heard that from me, right?"

ACKNOWLEDGEMENTS

As well as computer crimes and murder, I've touched other potent topics in this book, namely intimate-partner sexual assault and medical assistance in dying. For the first I've included a list of resources on pages 408–9. For the second, I am grateful to not only the people to whom this book is dedicated, but to other terminally ill patients, their family members, and the doctors and nurses who shared thoughts on the principle and act of helping people to die. If you want more information, please visit Dying With Dignity Canada at dyingwithdignity.ca or its appropriate provincial counterpart.

Since I'm an unabashed miner of my friends' areas of expertise, many other people also gave of their time, wisdom, and experience to help this story feel as real as possible. So thanks also go to: Darlene Wong, whose decades of experience with oil company financials underpinned Zoe's sales-preparation process for TFB Energy; Kevin Jepson, whose technical expertise in oil company computer systems and network security supported the purely fictional hacking of that old machine; Worship Pastor

Peter Justine, whose long experience directing church music wrought the Blue Christmas service; Rosemary Abram, rental properties investor and a great temporary landlady, who contributed the logical solution to Dee's money woes; Keith Cartmell, the series' location scout and tireless photographer of potential body-dumps in all weathers; Eric Arrata, for sharing his hiking adventures in the Ghost Wilderness, where I only planted my fictional ski resort on a real mountain and carved a road to reach it; and the held-nameless manager and police officer who shared their first-hand knowledge of the northern edge of Stoney Nakoda First Nation.

A land-and-people acknowledgment: This book takes place in lands covered by Treaty 7, signed in September 1877 between the Canadian government and five First Nations: the Siksika (Blackfoot), Kainai (Blood), Piikani (Peigan), Stoney-Nakoda, and Tsuut'ina (Sarcee), specifically between Bragg Creek and the Ghost Wilderness. Out of respect for the peoples of Tsuut'ina and Stoney-Nakoda First Nations, I've kept my characters outside the boundaries imposed upon them by the government of Canada. The women of those Nations could tell many stories — what obstacles they face, their deep connection to their ancestral lands, and their personal triumphs — that would bring welcome dimensions to my tales of modern women's lives in the Alberta foothills. But their stories are not mine to relate, and incorporating them into my books without significant consultation and explicit permission would constitute egregious cultural trespass.

I wish to thank Michelle Robinson, Red Thunder Woman, for answering my questions and for her podcast

Native Calgarian (nativecalgarian.podbean.com), which enhances my awareness of and respect for cultural boundaries, both physical and intangible. Where my text departs from referring to those Nations by their Indigenous names, I have done so to reflect the ways that the various characters name those lands in conversation, based on their own backgrounds and experiences.

On a lighter note, there's no snack shack at the West Bragg trailhead. But there should be.

If you have been impacted by sexual violence within or outside of intimate relationships, you are not alone. Across Canada, help is available.

VictimLink BC is a 24/7 toll-free, BC-wide telephone help line: **1-800-563-0808**.

Alberta has the new "One Line" service for phone, text, and chat. **1-866-403-8000** is staffed daily from 9 a.m. to 9 p.m. by trained responders.

Manitoba' 24/7 Sexual Assault Crisis Line is **1-888-292-7565**.

For the hearing-impaired TTY: **204-784-4097**.

In Ontario, call the Assaulted Women's Helpline **1-866-863-0511**.

TTY for hearing-impaired: **1-866-863-7868**.

In Quebec victims of sexual assault can call **1-888-933-9007**.

NFLD 24 Hour Crisis Support Line : **1-800-726-2743**.

Nova Scotia Sexual Assault & Harassment Line noon to midnight daily **902-425-1066**.

New Brunswick (Fredericton Sexual Assault Centre) 24/7 Help Line **506-454-0437**.

PEI Rape & Sexual Assault Centre (not a Crisis Line; also accessable via Facebook) **902-368-8055** or toll free **1-888-368-8055**.

Nunavut Kamatsiaqtut Helpline in English and Inuktitut: **1-800-265-3333**.

Book Credits

Developmental Editor: Allison Hirst
Project Editor: Jenny McWha
Copy Editor: Catharine Chen

Cover Designer: Laura Boyle
Interior Designer: Sophie Paas-Lang

Publicist: Saba Eitizaz

dundurn.com   dundurnpress
@dundurnpress   dundurnpress
dundurnpress   info@dundurn.com

FIND US ON NETGALLEY & GOODREADS TOO!

DUNDURN